SELECTED SHORT STORIES

Other Books by Cecilia Manguerra Brainard

Acapulco at Sunset and Other Stories
A La Carte: Food & Fiction (Co-editor)
Angelica's Daughters: A Dugtungan Novel (Co-author)
Behind the Walls: Life of Convent Girls (Co-editor)
Cecilia's Diary: 1962 - 1968
Contemporary Fiction by Filipinos in America (Editor)
Fiction by Filipinos in America (Editor)
Finding God: True Stories of Spiritual Encounters (Co-Editor)
Fundamentals of Creative Writing
Growing Up Filipino: Stories for Young Adults (Editor)
Growing Up Filipino II: More Stories for Young Adults (Editor)
Journey of 100 Years: Reflections on the
Centennial of Philippine Independence (Co-editor)
Magdalena (Novel)
Magical Years: Memories & Sketches
Magnificat: Mama Mary's Pilgrim Sites (Editor)
The Newspaper Widow (Novel)
Out of Cebu: Essays and Personal Prose
Philippine Woman in America
Please, San Antonio! & Melisande in Paris (Co-Author)
Selected Short Stories by Cecilia Manguerra Brainard
Vigan and Other Stories
When the Rainbow Goddess Wept (Novel)
Woman with Horns and Other Stories

Selected Short Stories

Cecilia Manguerra Brainard

Published by PALH
(Philippine American Literary House}
P.O. Box 5099
Santa Monica, CA 90409, USA
PALHBOOKS.com

Library of Congress Control Number: 2021906296

ISBN: 978-1-953716-01-9 (Paperback edition)
ISBN: 978-1-95371625-5 (Hardcover)
ISBN: 978-1-953716-02-6 (Ebook edition)

Selected Short Stories by Cecilia Manguerra Brainard is simultaneously published by the University of Santo Tomas Publishing House,

Cover art and design by Felix Mago Miguel

CONTENTS

INTRODUCTION

I like to say that my stories explore my Filipino and Filipino American experiences because I was born and raised in the Philippines and migrated to the United States in 1969.

I also like to advise younger people especially, that one needs to know where one came from in order to know where one is going.

Generally my writings—fiction and nonfiction alike—follow the above statements: they delve into my personal history as well as the broader Philippine and Philippine American histories.

Each of the thirty-nine stories in *Selected Short Stories by Cecilia Manguerra Brainard* was born from my obsession over a character, a time period, a situation, or a place. In other words some "*thing*" grabbed my interest and rooted in my imagination, prompting me to give the numinous "*thing*" form.

I have grouped these stories according to the setting of the stories: Part 1 in Ubec; Part 2 in other parts of the Philippines; and Part 3 in other parts of the world.

Many of the stories in Part 1 are early writings. I was born and raised in Cebu and while exploring the craft of fiction writing, images from my childhood bloomed in my imagination and became my subject matter. However I quickly discovered that my imaginings and retellings could not be limited by the reality of Cebu and thus I created Ubec (Cebu backwards). This mythical place allowed me to recreate as I please, even while drawing from the actual history, geography, culture, and people of Cebu. My three novels, for instance, which are not in this book, are set in Ubec and explore the history of Cebu. *When the Rainbow Goddess Wept* is a coming of age story of a young girl in Ubec during World War Two; *Magdalena* is about three-generations of women in Ubec whose lives have been affected by the Philippine-American War, World War Two, and the Vietnam War; and *The Newspaper Widow* is a literary mystery set in 1910 Ubec with a widow as protagonist—my widow character was inspired by the great-grandmother.

Likewise the short stories in this collection relate to specific historical times: Spanish, American, and Japanese occupations in Philippines, Marcos dictatorship, Vietnam War, immigration issues in the US, and more.

Part 2 includes stories that grew out of my fascination with Manila where my family kept a second home. Manila was where I went to high school and college; it was where I lived with my widowed mother. I have many poignant memories about Manila, which are reflected in some Manila-stories.

The stories set in Vigan grew out of my infatuation with this lovely Spanish colonial city in northern Philippines. In fact I was working on a novel set in Vigan when my mother died, and the novel was aborted. I was able to convert some of the chapters into short stories contained in this section.

Part 3 includes stories inspired by my life in the United States as well as my contact with other peoples of the world. After college I migrated to the United States where I experienced what many immigrants had—hardship as well as generosity from my adopted country.

All the stories in this book were previously published in journals and in my short story collections: *Woman With Horns and Other Stories, Acapulco at Sunset and Other Stories,* and *Vigan and Other Stories.* Many of these stories continue to be used in classrooms, such as "Woman with Horns", "Flip Gothic", and "Romeo". (It amuses me to find student theatrical skits about these stories posted on YouTube.)

I have always found it gratifying that teachers find my stories worthwhile education tools and hope this new edition will be more easily accessible to them, librarians, students, and readers of good literature.

Thanks to my husband Lauren R. Brainard and three sons (Christopher, Alexander, and Andrew) for their ardent support of my literary efforts.

~Cecilia Manguerra Brainard

Part 1

THE BLACK MAN IN THE FOREST

Philippines, 1901

By mid-day, the old general and his men stumbled into that part of the forest where they felt they could stop and make camp. The stronger men immediately searched for food; some dug for roots, others set traps for lizards and sparrows. The skin-and-bones ones collapsed in heaps under the bushes.

General Gregorio studied his men then did something he instructed them never to do—he left the scraggly group of soldiers and walked to the river. He drank some water and sat on a boulder to contemplate his situation. He had seven men, three guns, ten bullets, and eight rusty machetes. They had no food nor medicines. Even before this point of desperation, they had relied on saliva, herbs, and faith to heal their wounded who eventually died and were buried in unmarked graves as his army was driven back into the mountains by the Americans.

He stared at his gun with two bullets and the machete hanging from his belt, and he snorted at his fate. Their only hope was to find General Macario and his regiment. Otherwise they would all be killed by the snotty-nosed Americans—young enough to be his grandchildren—with their blue uniforms and Krag rifles.

General Gregorio was thinking this when a shot split through his reverie, knocking him over. He felt a sharp sting on his left thigh, then warm fluid oozing down his leg to the river bank. When he fell, his hand had been on the gun and he lay there not breathing, willing his heart to be still. The general heard the crunching of twigs, the rustling of bushes, and heavy footsteps. He felt a foot poke him in the back. When he heard the metallic sound of a rifle being cocked, General Gregorio swiftly rolled over and aimed his gun. He fired a bullet that entered the forehead of a black soldier. With a frozen look the black man cried, "Sara," then crumpled.

Although his left leg felt like burning coal, the general got up and fired the remaining bullet into the man's chest. Then he kicked the soldier's rifle away. Certain that the man was dead, the general went to the river and ripped his pants to tend his wound. He washed it and squeezed the flesh around the bullet hole to force tainted blood out. It was a clean wound; the bullet had gone straight through, and the general was relieved. He had seen too many wounds fester. He had watched men lose parts of themselves, first a hand, then an arm, until their brains went into delirium from the poison travelling through their arteries and finally they died.

All his men, even the frailest with death looking over his shoulders, rushed to the river. They were shouting, waving their guns and machetes. One of them thrust his knife into the black man's heart. The small dark one among them who had healing hands went to General Gregorio and inspected his leg. He tied a piece of cloth around the general's thigh to slow the bleeding and said they would have to use the juice of guava shoots to hasten cure. "The dampness of the forest," he said looking around, "is not good for this."

The general realized that his legs were wobbly and that his hands were shaking fiercely. Embarrassed at his weakness, he shooed away the little man who then joined the others around the corpse.

"If not for his uniform, I'd swear he was an agta or some other enchanted being," said the soldier whom they called Liver-eater. He was a big man from the north who liked to eat his enemies' livers for courage.

"He is big but he's not enchanted," another replied. "I have seen black men among the enemy."

Liver-eater spat on the ground next to the body. "I have seen only the ones like albinos with hair the color of corn kernels. Some have cat-eyes; scared the shit out of me. But the albino-types—their liver is filled with bile and tastes bitter.

The small dark one knelt down and put his hand against the soldier's hand. "Look, he's darker than me. He must have been under the sun for a long time. And his arm is twice as long as mine. He must have eaten well." The small man pinched the soldier's arm. "Damn, the man's got flesh! This man ate meat and all the rice he wanted. None of that fish and corn meal I grew up on. He had thick goat's milk, butter so rich it made you dizzy, and sticky wild honey."

The talk of food made them sigh, even General Gregorio. Their mouths watered at the thought of real food; their spirits longed for companionable meals with charming women and happy children. Their minds began fixing on memories: Christmas dinners with families where they gorged on roasted pig and pickled papaya; picnics where they feasted on enormous Lapu-lapu fish stuffed with tomatoes and herbs; May fiestas with hams, potatoes, and sweet gelatinous desserts. They had subsisted on roots and lizards, listened to children wailing, smelled the stench of blood for so long.

"Well, now," General Gregorio said to snap them out of their dreams, "there might be more Americans around." He ordered some men to patrol the area and told the rest to continue with their business. "I'll handle the dead man and I'll distribute his belongings tonight," spoke the general.

All but Liver-eater left. With feet planted apart, he stared evenly at the general, stubbornly refusing to budge. "We'll see," the general said in a loud voice, standing erect on his weak legs until Liver-eater walked away.

General Gregorio had been a soldier for enough time for a chico tree to grow from a seed to maturity. He had personally killed seventeen Spaniards, Americans, and even Filipinos. Once, he had hanged a handsome, big-bosomed woman who had betrayed them. He had done many things to survive, to make his beliefs reality, but he did not consider himself a barbaric man, and eating human flesh was abhorrent to him.

He began to feel dizzy so he sat on the ground and put his head between his legs. When his head cleared, he checked his leg once more, tightening the cloth, muttering merde because of the excruciating pain that radiated to the tip of his hair. He was an old soldier and he had been hurt before. He had two giant scars: a saber-mark on his right arm and a machete-gash on his back; but he had never been hit by a bullet until now. An anger welled in him. If the wound rots, he could lose his leg, he could die—the general glared at the dead man wishing there was still life in him so he could snuff it out again. But the black soldier was immobile like a beached whale, with flies buzzing over him, some sucking his blood. General Gregorio noticed that the man's eyes were open. The dead man still had the frozen expression of terror on his face. General Gregorio felt a sense of elation, of vengeance.

But soon his elation gave way to fear because the soldier seemed to be staring across the river. Afraid of an enemy attack, the general glanced that way but saw only huge rocks, thick vegetation, and monkeys swinging in the branches. Shafts of sunlight streamed into the forest. In the distance parrots screeched.

Calming himself, the general turned to the black man once more. He observed the neat little hole on his forehead and the blood crusting on his springy black hair. The dead man's mouth was slightly open, still saying the "a" of Sara. The general flicked the flies of the man's face, wondering who Sara was. Years ago, when the Spaniard had swung his saber at his face and his right hand had flown up to catch the sword, General Gregorio had shouted "Mama." When the traitorous Filipino threw the machete at his back, he had called out "Marta." Sara must be his wife or lover, thought the general. Instantly he had the mental image of a young woman with skin the color of narra wood, humming as she scattered sliced onions over a thick slab of meat.

Shivering at his vision, the general proceeded to gather the man's possessions: a rifle, thirty bullets, a pair of leather boots barely scuffed, a chewed-up bit of beef jerky, a gold pocket watch, a knife, some silver coins, but no pictures, no papers of identity whatsoever. In this forest, on this river bank, this black man was nameless. And yet, the general thought, surely he did have a name. He most certainly had a mother who had carried him in her womb, brought him into the world, and gave him a name. There was a woman Sara whom he remembered even as the bullet pierced his skull—and surely Sara called this man by name. The general became somber at these thoughts and he felt a longing to name his person. He called him John because it seemed that many Americans were named John.

John's eyes made the general uneasy so he closed the eyelids stretching the skin over the troubled eyes. Then the general forced the black man's jaws together. General Gregorio sat back and tried to imagine a hint of peace on that face. But the blood on the forehead and chest troubled him. Ignoring his pain, the general dragged the man near the water and washed the blood from his head and hair. He removed the bloody shirt which he washed in the river, then he cleaned the man's battered chest. As the general rubbed off the sticky blood and poured water over the dark oily skin, a strange feeling crept into the general's heart. He looked at John who was young, strong, and dead. If the black soldier had been a better shot, General Gregorio would have been in his place.

And if he were dead, who would mourn him? His parents had long been dead, his mother dying during childbirth and his father from cholera. Marta, whose memory he nurtured in his soul, was a grandmother to grandchildren who were not his. He had spent so many years being a warrior, a soldier so long that he had forgotten the silky feel of a woman's hair, her gentle laughter; so long that he had forgotten the hush and peace of an old stone church; so long that often he forgot what he was fighting for; so long that he was reduced to fighting for mere survival. He had no real ties, no family, no friends. No one would mourn his death.

This made him sad and this sorrow saturated his being. He waited for the sun and air to dry John's skin and shirt, and before his muscles became rigid, the general put John's shirt back on. It came to General Gregorio then to change John's name to Abraham because it was a more unique name, a name that went better with Sara.

General Gregorio buttoned up Abraham's shirt and covered the buttonhole with his hair. Now Abraham looked better; he appeared like a giant boy sleeping and dreaming troubled dreams.

Liver-eater appeared on the riverside with an insistent face and the general waved him away. When at last Liver-eater begrudgingly left, the general looked at Abraham who was now turning stiff, and he could not bear the idea of Liver-eater getting hold of him. His leg throbbing with pain, the general brought Abraham to the river where the current was strong. He released him and watched the body float downstream until it sank. Gathering his thoughts, General Gregorio decided to tell his men that the river had risen, taking Abraham away. He would lie to give the black man this bit of dignity. And tomorrow, they would have to start at dawn, before the fog lifted, before the sun's rays slanted into the forest, and they would have to find General Macario and his men, or perish.

WOMAN WITH HORNS

Dr. Gerald McAllister listened to the rattle of doors being locked and footsteps clattering on the marble floors. The doctors and nurses were hurrying home. It was almost noon and the people of Ubec always lunched in their dining rooms with high ceilings, where their servants served soup, fish, meat, rice, and rich syrupy flan for dessert. After, they retired to their spacious airy rooms for their midday siesta. At three, they resumed work or their studies.

His assistant, Dr. Jaime Laurel, had explained that the practice was due to the tropical heat and high humidity. Even the dogs, he had pointed out, retreated under houses and shade trees.

Gerald could not understand this local custom. An hour for lunch should be more than enough. He barely had that when he was a practicing physician in New York.

He reread his report about the cholera epidemic in the southern town of Carcar. Thanks to his vaccination program, the epidemic was now under control. The success was another feather in his cap, one of many he had accumulated during his stay in the Philippine Islands. No doubt Governor General Taft or perhaps even President Roosevelt would send him a letter of commendation. Politicians were like that; they appreciated information justifying America's hold on the archipelago.

He glanced at the calendar on his ornate desk. It was March 16, 1903, a year and a half since he arrived at the Port of Ubec aboard the huge steamship from San Francisco. Three years since Blanche died.

His head hurt and he removed his glasses to stroke his forehead. When the headache passed, he straightened the papers on his desk and left the office. The quiet of his wing of the Ubec General Hospital annoyed him as he walked past locked doors, potted palms, and sand-filled spittoons.

In front of Dr. Laurel's office, he saw a woman trying to open the door. She looked distraught and wrung her hands. She was a native Ubecan—Gerald had seen her at the Mayor's functions — a comely woman with bronze skin and long hair so dark it glinted blue. She wore a long blue satin skirt. An embroidered panuelo over her camisa was pinned to her bosom with a magnificent brooch of gold and pearls.

"It is lunchtime," he said in English. His Spanish was bad and his Ubecan dialect far worse.

Dark fiery eyes flashed at him.

"Comer," he said, gesturing with his right hand to his mouth.

"I know it's lunchtime. It wasn't, fifteen minutes ago." She tried the door once more and slapped her skirt in frustration. Tears started welling in her eyes. "My husband died over a year ago."

"I'm sorry."

"I'm not. He was in pain for years. Consumption. I have been coughing and last night, I dreamt of a funeral. I became afraid. I have a daughter, you see."

"Dr. Laurel will return at three."

"You are a doctor. American doctors are supposed to be the best. Can you help me?"

"I don't see patients."

"Ahh," she said, curved eyebrows rising. She picked up her fan with a gold chain pinned to her skirt. "Ahh, a doctor who doesn't see patients." She fanned herself slowly.

Her words irritated him and he brusquely said, "Come back in a few hours; Dr. Laurel will be back then." She stood there with eyes still moist, her neck tilted gracefully to one side and her hand languorously moving the fan back and forth.

***

"It was nothing," Jaime said. "I listened to her chest and back. There are no lesions, no T.B. I told her to return in a month. I think she is spectacular; she can come back for checkups forever." With mischief in his eyes, he added, "Agustina Macaraig has skin like velvet; if she were not my patient—"

"Jaime, your oath. You and your women. Doesn't your wife mind?" Gerald said.

"Eh, she's the mother of my children, is she not?" Shrugging his shoulders, he fixed the Panama hat on his head.

It was late Friday afternoon and they were promenading in the park, trying to catch the cool sea breeze. The park was in front of an old Spanish fort. There was a playground in the middle and benches were scattered under the surrounding acacia and mango trees. Children led by their yayas crowded the playground. Men and women walked or huddled together to talk about the day's events.

As he walked by the playground, Gerald was surprised to see Agustina pushing a girl of around five on the swing. When the child pleaded to do the pushing, Agustina got on the swing. He watched her kick her legs out and throw her head back, her blue-black hair flying about. She was laughing, oblivious to the scandal she was causing.

"The people don't approve of her," Gerald commented when he noticed women gossiping behind their fans, their eyes riveted on Agustina.

"There is a saying in Ubec, 'A mango tree cannot bear avocados,'" Jaime continued.

Gerald shrugged his shoulders.

"Look at her. Is she not delectable?" Jaime said. "People say she is wicked, like her mother. She has a very mysterious background."

They sat on a bench next to a blooming hibiscus bush where they could see her. The child pushed her hard and Agustina's infectious laughter rose above other sounds.

"I can see why the people would despise a widow who carries on the way she does," Gerald said.

"But, friend, you don't understand. We love her. She is one of us. It's just that Ubecans love to gossip, even when she patiently nursed her husband. They said she had lovers, but for five years, she took care of him. The people of Ubec like to talk. Over their meals, they talk; after eating, they talk; outside church after worshipping God, they talk; during afternoon walks, they talk. Just like we're talking, no?"

"I did not come here to gossip. I was perfectly content planning my bubonic plague campaign when you—"

"Friend, you don't know how to enjoy life. Look at that sun turning red, getting ready to set spectacularly. It is a wonderful afternoon, you walk with a friend, you talk about beautiful women, about life. Now, let me finish my story. People say her mother—a simple laundry woman—jumped over the seminary walls and behind those hallowed walls, under the arbol de fuego trees, she bedded with one of Christ's chosen."

"Ridiculous!"

"Ridiculous, nothing," Jaime replied as he pulled out a cigar from his pocket and offered it to Gerald. "Tabacalera, almost as good as Havanas."

Gerald shook his head. "Thank you, but I don't smoke."

"You don't smoke; you don't have women; you are a shell. Bringing you here was a chore. Are all American doctors like yourself? If they are, I wouldn't be caught dead in your rich and great country. You look like a god from Olympus—tall, blonde with gray eyes. You're not forty, yet you act like an old man."

"Jaime, skip your lecture and get on with your story." Gerald watched Agustina loll her head back. She was biting her lower lip, afraid of how high she was.

"If you were not my boss, I would shake you to your senses. Anyway, the story goes that Agustina was born with horns."

"Horns?"

"Like toro, yes." Jaime put his finger to his forehead. "At noon, her mother went to the enchanted river to do her wash. The spirits roam at that time, do you know that?"

Gerald shook his head at this nonsense. "I swim almost daily at your so-called enchanted river and I have seen nothing but fish and an occasional water buffalo. Filthy animals."

"Well, maybe there are or aren't spirits, no? Who are we to say there are none? The people say that her mother had—ah, how do you say—an encounter with an encantado, a river spirit. And Agustina is the product of that brief encounter."

Gerald watched her jump off the swing, her skirt swirling up, her shapely legs flashing before his eyes.

"She doesn't look much like a river spirit's daughter, Jaime," Gerald said with a snort.

"Beware, you can never be sure."

She took the girl's hand and they ran to a group of women. Agustina carried on an animated conversation then waved goodbye. Before she turned to leave the park, she looked briefly at Gerald. He caught her gaze but she quickly lowered her eyes and walked away as if she had not seen him.

***

On the way to the Mayor's house, Gerald thought that attending social functions was part of his job. He was not only Ubec's Public Health Director, he was also an ambassador-of-sorts for the United States. The truth was, he didn't really mind social affairs at all. They kept him occupied. When he was busy, he didn't have time to think about the past, to feel that shakiness, that pain that had possessed him after Blanche died.

During the day he was fine; he worked, lunched, swam, went on promenades, had rich frothy chocolate with the men. Later he dined, sipped after-dinner brandies and liqueurs, and chatted until way past midnight. It was when the servants locked the doors and the house was still, when the only sound was the lonely clatter of the night watchman, that he would feel his composure slip away. His heart would palpitate and an uneasiness would overcome him. He would try to cram his mind with thoughts—health education campaigns, sanitation programs, quarantine reports—but the disquiet would stay with him.

The Mayor of Ubec, a small round man, greeted Gerald warmly. He introduced him as the great American doctor who was wiping out cholera, smallpox, and bubonic plague from Ubec. The people knew him of course and they shook his hand heartily. They congratulated him on his recent success in Carcar and inquired about his current bubonic plague campaign. Rats, Gerald explained, transmit the disease; therefore getting rid of the pest by traps and arsenic poisoning would eliminate the problem.

When the food was served on the long dining table with tall silver candelabras, the Mayor teased Dr. McAllister for his squeamishness at the roasted pig. The women giggled demurely, covering their mouths with their hand painted fans or lace handkerchiefs, while the men laughed boisterously. The Mayor's mother, a fat old woman with a mustache, tore off the pig's ear and pressed it in Gerald's hand. "Taste it, my American son," she said. Laughing and clapping, the people urged him to take a bite until he finally did.

When he later went to the verandah to drink his rice wine, he saw Agustina standing there, gazing at the stars. She looked different, not the frightened woman at the hospital, not the carefree girl at the park, but a proper Ubecan widow in black, with her hair done in a severe bun. Curiously, the starkness enhanced her grace and beauty, calling attention to the curves of her body.

"You did not like the lechon?" she asked softly, with an amused twinkle in her eyes.

"I beg your pardon? Oh, the pig—?" He shook his head, embarrassed that she had witnessed that charade. They were alone and he hoped that someone would join them.

"What do Americans eat, Dr. McAllister?" She was studying him, eyes half-closed with a one-sided smile that was becoming.

Gerald pushed his hair from his forehead. "Pies -- cherry pies, boysenberry pies -- I miss them all. Frankly, I have—"

She drew closer to him and he caught a warm, musky scent coming from her body.

"—I have lost ten pounds since I've been here."

"In kilos, how many?"

"Around four and a half."

"Santa Clara! You must get rid of your cook. She must be an incompetent, starving you like that. It is a shame to the people of Ubec!"

Gerald watched her, aware of his growing infatuation.

"I like you," she said suddenly. "You and I have a kinship. Come to my house and my daughter and I will feed you." Pausing, she reached up to stroke his face with her fan. His cheeks burned. "Nothing exotic," she continued, "just something good." Her eyes flashed as she smiled. "You know where I live?"

He hesitated then shook his head. His knees were shaking.

"The house at the mouth of the river. I see you swimming during siesta time. I like to swim at night, when the moon is full." She looked at him, closed her eyes languidly and walked away.

***

After dinner, Gerald hurried home and paced his bedroom floor. He should have been flattered by Agustina's advances, but instead he was angry and confused. She was enchanting and desirable and he was upset that he should find her so.

Once he had been unfaithful when Blanche was bedridden. The surgical nurse who laughed a lot had been willing, and he had wanted even for just a few hours to forget, to be happy. Blanche had known, just by looking at him. "Oh, Tiger, how could you? How could you?" After her death, he had not given this side of himself a thought. Yet now, he found himself recalling that indescribable musky-woman scent emanating from Agustina.

There was something else. It bothered him deeply that Agustina, widowed for only a little over a year, would laugh, be happy, even flirt outrageously with him. Why was she not consumed with grief? Why did she not sit at home crocheting white doilies? Why did she not light candles in the crumbling musty churches, the way proper Ubecan widows did? He was outraged at her behavior. He condemned her for the life that oozed out of her, when he needed every ounce of his strength just to stay sane.

He strode to his desk and stared at the album with photographs, which he had not looked at in years. The wedding picture showed a vibrant smiling young woman with a ring of tiny white flowers around her blonde curly hair. His face was unlined then, and his mustache seemed an affectation. Anxious eyes peered through round eyeglasses, as if he knew even then that the future would give him anguish.

He studied the other pictures—serious daguerreotypes—that unleased a flood of emotions. He found himself weeping at some, smiling at others. He remembered Blanche's soft voice: "Oh, Tiger, I adore you so." Blanche in bed, waiting for him. And later, Blanche in bed, pale, thin, with limp hair. She had been eaten bit by bit by consumption; she had been consumed, until only a skeleton that coughed incessantly and spat blood remained. Gerald did not believe in God, but he had prayed for her death, just so it would end. When she died, he was surprised to feel another kind of grief, more acute, more searing.

After her funeral, his mind would go on and on about how useless he was—a doctor whose wife died of consumption was a failure. And always the soft voice: Oh, Tiger, how could you?

Returning from work each night, he had found himself waiting for her voice: How was your day, Tiger? He saw slight women with curly blonde hair and he had followed them. He plunged into a depression — not eating, unable to work, to think clearly, to talk coherently. He stayed shut up in his room with wine-colored drapes. At times he thought he was losing his mind. When he pointed a gun to his forehead, a part of him panicked and said: NO. That part had taken over and started running his life again. Eat, so you will gain weight; exercise, so your body will be healthy; work, so your mind will not dwell on the agony.

It was this part that had led him to the Islands, far away from slight women with curly blonde hair. It was this same part that now said: Blanche is dead, you are alive; you have the right to laugh and be happy just as Agustina laughs and is happy.

Gerald struggled with himself but would not allow himself to surrender his mourning. He decided not to see Agustina; he would not allow her to corrupt him.

***

Governor General William H. Taft's handwritten letter from Manila arrived that morning and Gerald reread it several times, trying to absorb the congratulatory words. He felt nothing. He would not have cared if the letter had never come. He realized that he didn't really care, nowadays. Work was predictable; there was little risk. He applied himself and the laurels came. But the successes, the commendations did not fill his emptiness. He picked up the conch shell that he used as a paper weight and tapped it, listening to the hollow ring that echoed in his office.

Gerald went to Jaime's office to show him the letter. Jaime appeared cross; he sat erect and immobile as he listened quietly.

"Well?" Gerald asked after reading the letter aloud.

"Well, what?"

"The letter—it's a fine letter, don't you think?" He hoped for an enthusiastic reply that would rub some life into him.

"The Mayor's mother is dead," Jaime said. "She choked on some food."

"Too bad. Well, at least it wasn't typhoid or anything contagious," he said.

Jaime's black eyes snapped at him. "You bastard!" he said. "All you think about is work. You have no soul."

Gerald could not work the rest of the morning. He felt a growing restlessness, a vague uneasiness that he could not pinpoint. No soul. Had he indeed lost his soul? Was that why he could not feel and why he didn't care about anything? In trying to bring order to his life, in restructuring it after Blanche died, had he lost a vital part of himself—his soul?

***

Funerals, Gerald thought as he walked to the Mayor's house, were dreary, maudlin affairs, where people wore long faces and tried to sound sincere as they dug up some memory of the deceased.

He braced himself when he saw mourners in black and the huge black bow on the Mayor's front door. Inside, he was surprised to see the number of people crowding the place. Some wept; others laughed and related stories about the old woman. A rather festive air filled the place.

The Mayor hugged Gerald, saying, "What a tragedy, what a tragedy! She was eating pickled pig snout when suddenly she choked. It was over before any of us could do anything. She loved you like a son and worried that you were too thin."

"I'm sorry," mumbled Gerald.

The Mayor brought him to the casket in the living room. "Mama chose her own funeral picture," the Mayor said as he pointed at the huge picture of a slim young girl, propped up next to the coffin. "She was a vain woman. The picture was taken almost half a century ago."

The Mayor continued, "Her mind was not clear. She wanted to be buried in her wedding gown but it was far too small. I had to hire three seamstresses to work all night. They ripped and stitched, adding panels of cloth to the dress. It was still too small. Finally we decided to clothe her in another dress and to lay her wedding gown on top, pinning it here and there to keep it in place. Family deaths can be trying," he said.

The old Spanish friar said a Latin Mass and spoke lengthily about her goodness and kindness. "She had a rich and long life," he concluded. Near the hearse, an old man riding a horse stopped them. He was dressed in a revolutionary uniform with medals hanging on his chest, and a gun in his right hand which he fired once. Gasping, the mourners stopped still. The old man ordered the men to open the casket. He got off his horse, bent over the casket and planted a kiss on the corpse's lips. Then, he got back on his horse and galloped off.

It took a while for the mourners to compose themselves and continue to the cemetery. A pair of scissors was placed under the satin pillow; family members kissed the body; the priest blessed the coffin and she was finally buried.

Everybody returned to the Mayor's house for a huge banquet. Jaime tried to explain the revelry by saying that a person was feted on his birth, his marriage, and his death. "It's the end of a good life, my friend," he said.

Agustina, who was there, walked up to Gerald. "It was a beautiful funeral," she said.

"I've never attended one like it," he replied and laughed. "I guess it was."

They were near a window and she looked out. "Ahh, the moon is full."

***

From his room, Gerald watched the large moon rise, shining on the star apple and jackfruit trees in his backyard. It was a warm night, even with all the windows open. He waited for even the slightest breeze to stir the silvery leaves, but there was no wind and a restlessness grew in him.

At last he decided to go to the river. Silence and oppressive heat dominated Ubec as he walked the cobblestones. He reached the path leading to the river and the sea. The moon was so bright that the air seemed to vibrate as he followed the trail that widened, then narrowed, then widened again, until he reached the riverbank.

After leaving his things under a coconut tree, he walked to the water and saw how clear it was. Little gray fish darted between colorful rocks. In the distance the river and sea shimmered brilliantly.

The water felt cool and silky. Gerald swam back and forth, marveling at the brazenness of the fish that brushed against him, some even nibbling his toes. He spotted a bright green rock and wondered about it. Diving to the river bottom, he fetched it. When he surfaced, he saw her standing next to his things. He was not surprised; he knew she would be there.

Moonlight bathed her, making her glow. A green and red tapis was wrapped around her, exposing golden shoulders and neck, showing mounds of flesh.

Gerald felt life stirring in him and, holding his breath, he waded to the shore. She walked toward him. The water splashed and the small gray fish skittered away when she slipped into the water. He watched the river creep higher and higher as her tapis floated gracefully around her, until they fell into each other's arms.

TRINIDAD'S BROOCH

Ubec had been blistering, cracking from the heat, when overnight it seemed the dry season was over and the typhoons came. It was the seamstress Trinidad's second rainy season in the seaside town and she could not get over the abruptness of change. The rains had always distressed her, even at the orphanage in Manila. Confined to the large marble-floored rooms with the children, nuns, and teachers, Trinidad had listened to the howling winds and lashing rain and had felt alone. Now as she and her assistant Josefa worked, Trinidad's heart pounded with the monotonous drumming of the rain. She was near the window and she peered out through a small opening at the acacia and mango trees in the park. As the winds whipped through, the trees bent and strained. Pausing in the middle of a backstitch with her needle held in mid-air, she wondered if the trees would snap in two.

As if reading her mind Josefa said, "Those trees were planted during the time of Legazpi the Conquistador. Their branches break but they recover and become whole again." Josefa, in her last month of pregnancy, shifted her weight and massaged the small of her back. She was a young, dimple-faced, and talkative woman. "A fisherman drowned last night," she continued. "His mother banged the doors of the rectory. She wailed and pulled her hair because she doesn't even have a body to bury. The old Spanish friar was too deaf to hear the noise. The young one talked to her, but he was so flustered, he forgot to belt his soutane."

Trinidad looked at the flooded streets and stiffened at the image of the foaming sea swallowing up the fisherman. Quiet and serious, she usually paid little attention to Josefa's chatter, but that June afternoon, she listened carefully. However, the pregnant woman turned to other matters: the Mayor was planning a political rally, his mother had dysentery but was better, her cousin Ligaya had grown taller.

Trinidad resumed work but as she made nimble stitches into the fine piña cloth, her bones trembled with the creaking of the tile roof and the groaning of the walls. No matter how tightly she shut the capiz-shell windows, rain seeped in. Water gushed from the sky. The very air smelled damp like rotten mushrooms. It was the rain, she assured herself that afternoon and for the rest of the typhoon season. It was the rain that made her soul flutter on the surface of her skin.

***

When the rains stopped and the streets dried and the children returned to the park, Trinidad discovered that her unease remained. It was a vague annoyance, like looking at a crooked sleeve or an uneven hemline. She ignored it and prayed but she could not get rid of the gnawing disturbance. Josefa, who had given birth to a baby girl with thick hair that stuck straight up, brought her infant to work. When Josefa nursed her baby one day, Trinidad watched the tiny baby root against her mother's breast until she found the brown nipple dripping with milk. Trinidad felt something inside her strain and pop like the unraveling of a stitch.

That night Trinidad rummaged in her trunk for an antique brooch with a floral design. She ran her forefinger over the jewelry, feeling the smoothness of the pearls and the coldness of the gold setting. Years ago, Mother Asuncion at the orphanage had revealed to her the story about the brooch. One rainy night, the old nun said, the orphanage bell had rung. Mother Asuncion left the chapel and hurried outside to the turning-cradle where she found Trinidad, an infant whose umbilical cord had not yet dried. The brooch had been pinned to the baby's woven blanket.

At the orphanage, Trinidad had studied the brooch and imagined that her parents were handsome and good. She had told herself that her stay at the Asilo de San Jose was temporary—her parents would return for her. But now, by the light of the flickering lamp, Trinidad stared at the brooch and was overcome with sadness. Her somberness lingered for days. "I don't know … it is nothing," she answered when Josefa asked what was wrong. "Nothing," and she forced herself to embroider the little flowers on a baby girl's gown.

***

It was her custom to awaken at 4:30 before dawn and walk to the old stone church. By the time the young friar said, "In nomine Patre," she was kneeling in the front pew, watching the candles glow before the statues, and smelling melted wax and incense. After Mass, as Mother Asuncion had taught her, Trinidad always stopped by the vigil candle stand to light a candle for thanksgiving—for her life, for her food, for the roof over her head, for everything.

One morning, Trinidad, filled with wordless thoughts and strange feelings, tried to center herself in prayer, but could not. Before Mass ended, she left. She walked past the market vendors, but instead of returning home, went to the seashore. The sun beat down on the desolate sheet of blue water. The bleached sand stretched out empty and forlorn. She sighed a long and deep sigh and continued walking until she found herself near the cemetery. She entered and went from one mausoleum to another, reading the names of the grave markers and counting the number of dead in each family: there were a dozen Santoses, twenty Floreses, and eleven Macaraigs. At the back of the cemetery near the enormous balete tree, she noticed a mound surrounded by abalone shells. It was covered with weeds and a huge rock stood on one end. Sighing, Trinidad knelt down and pulled the vines and grasses. She straightened out the shells. When she finished she wept over the solitary grave.

***

To force this disquiet from her life, she regimented herself so every moment of her waking hours was accounted for: housework, breakfast, work, lunch, prayers, work, Novena to Our Lady, supper, and prayers. The days and weeks merged one into the other as she possessively protected her spartan schedule. She went through her clothes getting rid of the white dresses with wide collars and ribbons. She sewed clothes of dark browns and blues for herself. She gave away her potted vincas and four o'clock plants, and she stopped adorning her hair with flowers.

Her impatience with Josefa's chatter grew. Trinidad found her and all other Ubecan's tiresome. When they intruded into her organized life, she bristled. She wanted to be left alone; she was not one of them. She found them provincial. They engrossed themselves in other people's affairs, gossiping at all times of the day. They indulged in feasts they could barely afford, for christenings, weddings, funerals. They were superstitious, talking about holy statues walking at night, of spirits and ghosts roaming at dusk, of black giants living in treetops. Although her business prospered, Trinidad regretted having left Manila for Ubec. She cloistered herself in her shop, seeing only those whom she had to. A numbness would occasionally creep inside her, and during these times, she prayed and welcomed even the sensation of irritation at the townspeople.

***

The rains fell once more and went. Looking around one September day, she realized that the typhoon season had come and gone, and she had felt nothing—no dread, no melancholy, nor annoyance. Even staring at her brooch did not elicit tears. She shivered, thinking she merely was—a woman sitting by the windowsill, sewing still another chemise, crocheting still another lace curtain, embroidering still another chicken into a girl's dress. She sighed—she was dead. She was just as lifeless as the Mayor's mother who had died earlier that day. Trinidad went to her altar to say the litany. During her prayers, the Mayor burst into her dress shop. "You must help," he pleaded. The small round man was very agitated. "Mama, may she rest in peace, wanted to be buried in her wedding gown. But years of content have made her too large for the dress."

Trinidad hastily called Josefa and her cousin Ligaya to help fix the dead woman's gown. They ripped and stitched, attaching panels to the sides, but the woman was far too big, and the dress too small. When the cock crowed and dawn's light filtered into the Mayor's house, they gave up and sewed a loose white shift for the corpse. After clothing the dead woman, they placed the wedding dress on top, pinning it here and there to keep it in place. Josefa arranged the flowers on the casket to mask this deception. Trinidad sewed a large black bow for the Mayor's front door, and another for a huge picture of a young girl. The Mayor explained that this was his mother's funeral picture. "She was vain and her mind had grown unclear. She chose a picture taken when she was fifteen." They propped up the picture beside the coffin in the living room.

They finished in the morning when the mourners in dark clothing were lining outside the Mayor's house to pay their respects to the dead woman. The three women, weary from working overnight left their homes. It was Josefa who, one block away, began chuckling. Ligaya shook her head, covered her mouth with her hand, and laughed softly. Trinidad felt her lips stretch and open as laughter escaped. They stood by the roadside, clutching their sides, laughing for a long time.

***

She found a spark that glowed in her core and she nurtured it, fanning it as one blows at the embers in the hearth. Shortly after the funeral, Trinidad bought a dozen clay pots in which she planted dahlias, violets, and orchids. She took down her homespun curtains, replacing them with delicate airy lace. While Josefa chatted, she listened, clucked her tongue, and raised her eyebrows at the current gossip. She observed with fascination the little girl who made endless games out of empty spools and polished coconut shells.

One summer afternoon, Trinidad watched Josefa playing with her daughter. The child chortled heartily as her mother tickled her ribs. As Trinidad stared, knowledge rose from the pit of her stomach, filling every part of her body. She would never see her parents, and she would never feel the touch of their hands. Turning away, she looked outside at the sun sinking slowly. Streams of red-orange sunlight sifted through the full sprawling branches of the mango and acacia trees in the park. Before Josefa and the child left, Trinidad went to her trunk to find the gold and pearl brooch. She handed this to Josefa. "It's for the little girl," she said. "Keep it and give it to her when she is old enough. Let her know it came from me."

When the mother and child were gone, Trinidad closed her shop and went to the seashore. It was a late afternoon and the dying sunlight made the sea shimmer like multicolored satin laced with the fine foamy waves. Trinidad paused—she had been an abandoned infant, she thought. She had been an orphan at the Asilo de San Jose; she was now a seamstress in Ubec. And tomorrow—? Trinidad stared at the hermit crabs skittering about on the sand. Tomorrow, in the morning, Josefa and the child would knock on her shop door, and they would have to finish a wedding gown. She had a pongee skirt to shirr. There were San Francisco cuttings to plant. She sighed and wrapped her arms around herself. Far away the laughter of the fisherman's children tinkled. She closed her eyes and took in the sea breeze. The air was clean, pure. For the moment, this was enough.

THE BALETE TREE

After breakfast, Tiya Remia started. "Pay attention, Milagros," she ordered. "A woman must know how to handle an egg properly—like this." She cracked a brown egg and with a slight twist, dropped the bright yellow yolk and slimy egg white into the blue enameled bowl.

"Save the shells for the orchids," her aunt continued as she threw the shells into a bucket and wiped her hands gingerly on her lace-trimmed apron. She moved in precise economical movements.

"It's a simple thing, but there are disastrous women out there who demolish the yolk or shatter the shells so you end up with shells in your food."

"Yes, Tiya," Milagros replied, but her mind was on the tadpole that had sprouted little legs. It was in a jar under her bed. Last week her older brother Melchor had caught hundreds of tadpoles at the river and had given her a jarful. Most of them had died and only a handful remained. This morning she discovered that one of them had grown legs.

"Cooking, cleaning, sewing, embroidery—all these are of utmost importance. If you expect to marry well, you must master these womanly arts." Tiya Remia beat the eggs vigorously with a fork. Her lips were two thin lines and she had a fuzzy mustache. Her sparse dark hair was pulled back in a tight bun at her nape. She wore black, as Milagros did, because they were in mourning. Milagros' grandmother—Tiya Remia's mother—had been eating pickled pig snout when she choked and died ten months ago.

"Milagros, I know what you are thinking, 'Well, why isn't Tiya Remia married if she knows everything?'" She paused, her face softening. "I had many suitors. There was one in particular …" Her voice trailed and her face hardened once more as she continued "… but, well, as God would have it, I have been called to a life of single blessedness. And a good thing for you. Mama—may she rest in peace—spoiled you. No doubt she felt sorry that you have no mother. And your father is far too busy to attend to you. When I moved in, you had lice …" Tiya Remia raised her thin shoulders and shivered, "… a mayor's daughter with lice! And you hang around with the boys near the balete tree. Just like a wild thing! A wild thing!"

Milagros pulled her braids and studied the ends, searching for the pearly white nits, remembering the burning sensation of kerosene on her scalp and the irritation of the fine comb running through her hair repeatedly. She thought of Melchor who had raced out of the house after breakfast to play and she felt her stomach grow sour.

The cook, fat and sweaty Menggay, had forgotten to stop by Agustina's place. Milagros was glad when Tiya Remia told her to run over and pick up two dozen chorizos. "And don't tarry," her aunt said. "That woman is bad influence altogether. Why a doctor's wife continues with this sausage business, I'll never understand. And I cannot comprehend her insistence on running around with her long hair flying all over the place. It is unseemly. And her American husband … well, I've never liked their kind. As far as I'm concerned, they can all go back to Kansas, or wherever they come from."

Milagros skipped down the cobblestones toward the river. It was only midmorning but the sun was already scorching the narrow, winding streets of Ubec. When the sea breeze blew, dust rose, whirled around, then settled once more. She was sweating hard and felt her cotton blouse sticking to her back. To catch some shade, she ran from tree to tree.

It was cooler by the river and she slowed down to observe the laundry women beating the clothes on the rocks. She recalled the story about Agustina's mother and the river spirit who sired her. Tiya Remia said Agustina had horns like Satan's, that she was a Jezebel, but Milagros was fond of the vivacious woman. Her husband, the American doctor, had golden hair on his head and even on his arms. He was learned, often talking about germs and modern medicine. Milagros hoped he would be home so she could ask him how the tadpole grew legs.

Agustina's house stood near where the river and sea collided and formed whirlpools. It was a two-story house with capiz-shell windows, carved wooden balconies, and a scarlet bougainvillea vine that crawled up one wall and spilled over the tiled roof.

Agustina, her daughter, and her husband were not home. After paying the cook for the chorizos, Milagros stayed to watch her kill a chicken. The cook wrestled with the chicken, pinning its wings to the side until she held it firmly. Then she took the machete and with one stroke, cut off the head. Blood spurted out of the neck. With a sudden burst of energy, the headless chicken fluttered out of the cook's hands and ran around the yard.

Milagros hiked her skirt up, ready to chase the chicken, but hesitated knowing Tiya Remia would be displeased to see blood all over her. The sight of blood distressed her.

The chicken flailed its wings as it ran aimlessly around, knocking over a huge clay jug, trailing blood wherever it went. At last, the chicken collapsed. The cook picked it up, dunked it in a cauldron of boiling water and proceeded to pluck its feathers. Milagros picked up a brown feather and reflected on how swiftly all that had happened. A little while ago, the chicken had been alive, now it was featherless and gutted, ready to be made into soup. Her grandmother too had been alive one moment, then dead the next.

***

Melchor with three boys were huddled together on the riverbank. The biggest boy was boasting about having seen the agta last night. He said he walked through the cemetery to the balete tree and saw the enormous black giant sitting on the top branch, puffing away on his cigar.

The boys were impressed, and Melchor said he went to the balete tree at siesta time and also saw the agta. Milagros glanced at him, knowing Tiya Remia did not allow them near the tree. Her aunt had such a dislike for the tree and had often spanked them with her slipper for playing in the area. "Stay-away-from-the-balete-tree," she intoned as she hit them in rhythm to her words.

Milagros gazed across the river to the cemetery and the balete tree on the riverbank. The tree was the oldest in town, huge with sprawling branches and thick roots that swelled around the base. The agta, an enchanted being, lived in the tree. A long time ago, the parish priest had wanted the tree chopped down because its roots were destroying the cemetery walls. Overnight, the priest had died mysteriously in his sleep. And once, a servant girl who walked by the tree daily, was snatched by the agta who had taken a liking to her. The girl was never seen again.

When she had the chance, Milagros told the boys about her tadpole with little legs. The three boys ignored her and jumped into the river. Melchor said he'd look at her tadpole, but he turned and joined the boys on their way to the balete tree.

***

It was gone. Her jar with tadpoles was gone. She checked under her bed and scoured her room carefully. She could not find it. Running into the kitchen, she asked the maid where the jar was. Just then Tiya Remia walked in and shivered. "Slimy, disgusting creatures," she said. "I got rid of them." Milagros went to her room and wept.

Later she watched the gecko climb up the wall to the ceiling right above her head. The crickets outside were humming. The yard was full of them and when the sun set, they made their sawing sounds. The gecko had bulging eyes and a protruding stomach. It looked a bit like her tadpole with legs.

She was lying there, holding her small blanket that used to be yellow, green, and orange. Now it was worn around the edges and the brilliant colors had faded. Since her grandmother died and Tiya Remia moved in, Milagros slept with it every night.

She was comparing the size of the gecko with the faster-moving gray lizards when it fell right on her mosquito net, above her face. Without the net it would have landed right on top of her. She jerked and shouted. No one came. Her father was in Manila; Melchor was out playing. Tiya Remia was in the kitchen scolding the servants.

The gecko scampered away. Milagros hugged her blanket. The windows were open and the night breeze blew her net gently. The wind seeped through her net, caressing her face until she fell asleep.

***

Dragging the wooden rake methodically, the gardener gathered leaves and twigs into a pile. He made a bonfire that flared then settled into mesmerizing glowing embers. Thin ribbons of gray smoke trailed upward and diffused into the afternoon sky.

"Thank San Antonio he got around to doing that," Tiya Remia said as she slapped a mosquito on her arm.

"The smoke will get rid of the bugs, Tiya," Milagros answered as she struggled to make another cross-stitch on her sewing sampler. Her aunt wanted her to finish the sampler—which she had been working on for months—so she could start embroidering her own mantle.

"A woman is judged by her future mother-in-law by the quality of her needlework," Tiya Remia grumbled as she carefully inspected the sampler. She sighed, showing dissatisfaction at the irregular stitches. "Milagros, you must concentrate on your needlework, housework, cooking, rather than your tadpoles and God-knows-what-else."

Milagros studied her sampler thinking it looked just fine when Melchor, who was on bamboo stilts, doddered by. Distracted, she pricked her finger. She squeezed it and watched the round drop of blood form. Then she sucked her finger, surprised at how salty her blood tasted.

"You've hurt yourself," Tiya Remia said. "I abhor the sight of blood." Shivering, she turned away. She was quiet for a long while then said, "Well, let's rest awhile." Her aunt put her crocheting hook and spool of thread down. "Why don't you come with me and I'll show you something?" she suggested.

Milagros followed her to her room where her aunt opened a handsome carved camphor chest. A musty pungent smell filled the room. Tiya Remia removed a white gown, which she laid on her bed. The dress was made of fine piña fiber, with exquisite embroidery of flowery designs on the skirt and butterfly sleeves.

Her aunt's face beamed and her voice took on a dreamy quality. "Take a look at that stitchery," she said. "The famous modiste, Pacita Alesna, made this for me. She used silk thread and real pearls from Jolo. She charged me three hundred pesos, which was an outrageous sum then. It still is. But my fiancé insisted. He was a poet and a revolutionary. Isn't that the silliest thing you've heard? He was pale and thin and trembled when he was near me. Well … but … of course there was no wedding. But it is still a beautiful terno and it still fits me perfectly."

Milagros watched Tiya Remia's fingers travel slowly over the fine embroidery. There was a distant look in her eyes, a kind of wildness mixed with sadness.

"It is perfect craftmanship," her aunt concluded, as she carefully folded the white gown and returned it to the trunk.

***

She waited until the house was quiet, then waited some more. Quietly, she crept out of the house. In the streets, she listened for the night watchman and hid behind the bushes when he walked by. Some dogs barked at her as she hurried across the bridge and walked to the cemetery. The moon was large and bright and she could see the crumbling crypts and the white crosses on the ground. When she heard a weeping sound, she crossed herself and held her breath. She listened carefully and was relieved that it was only the sea breeze whistling through the crypts.

As she passed by her family mausoleum, she said a quick prayer for her grandmother. At the end of the cemetery, to her right, against crumbling cemetery walls, stood the balete tree. It was truly enormous and luminous under the moonlight. Four strong branches sprouted from the trunk and these forked into smaller branches. They sprawled outward giving the impression that they could carry the sky if it fell down.

Her breath quickened and her knees shook as she approached it. She searched the tree. When the wind blew, the leaves trembled and the branches shook. The quivering shadows appeared like a strange face or an arm. Blood rushed to her head and her heart pounded against her ribs.

The sound of splashing from the river startled her. River spirits, she thought. Milagros stepped over thick roots that pushed up the dank earth. She touched the rough bark timidly. Then she started climbing. Higher and higher she went until she reached the top. The sounds were clearer now. Low voices, soft laughter, water scattering. She sat on the branch and looked at the river expecting to see enchanted beings. She saw only Agustina, with her flowing dark hair, and her golden-haired husband frolicking in the water under the full moon.

***

The morning sun warmed her arm then her face. She covered her face with the pillow and tried to stay asleep but she heard kitchen sounds and Tiya Remia's high-pitched voice berating the cook: "The proper household must use fresh carabao's milk and not these newfangled American canned things."

Milagros listened for a while. Then she sat up and decided she'd go to the river that day to catch some tadpoles.

FRIDAY EVENING AT THE SEASHORE

Padre Zobel locked the rectory and, leaving the center of town, headed toward the seashore. He was a young Spaniard from the coastal village of Mojacar and he felt a special bond with the sea. It made his soul echo; it was home.

He was an athletic man and as he walked, he swung his arms around and shrugged his shoulders to loosen his taut muscles. He had been sitting, hearing confessions for four hours and he was weary. A zealous man, he suffered with his parishioners the guilt, shame, and pain as they mumbled their sins in the dark confessional. True, he also felt the sense of release, of joy, when their sins were absolved, but hearing confessions wrung his spirit. Other priests had advised him not to be so involved, but Padre Zobel could not help himself.

That Friday afternoon, another thought preoccupied him. He was concerned about a girl from his parish. Ligaya often attended the six o'clock Mass and Wednesday novenas to our Lady of Perpetual Succor. In his two years in Ubec, Ligaya had never missed Friday confessions until that day. He smiled to himself recalling her concerns: I was distracted during Mass, I was late for the novena. He had often wanted to assure her that her sins were hardly those at all. Such an endearing child, he thought. But recently there had been mention of a man, and she seemed flustered and withdrawn. Ligaya involved with a man—it was disturbing.

It was almost suppertime. The tropical sun was dropping slowly and fishing boats that dotted the sea were returning home. He picked up a blue starfish stranded on a sandbar and threw it into the water. Then he sat on a coconut tree that had fallen from a past typhoon, and gazed at Ubec's bleached sugary sand and the frothy waves that curled up to the shore.

He sighed, absorbing the tranquility. In Mojacar, the beach had been rockier, more coarse, and the Mediterranean had been rougher and colder. But it was the same tangy sea breeze. He closed his eyes and took deep breaths. He pictured Mojacar with its whitewashed Moorish houses cascading down the hills. His home had been on the highest hill, and from his bedroom window, he used to see the flattop roofs, the ancient winding paths, and the sparkling sea.

When he opened his eyes, he saw the figure of a woman in the distance. "Ana Maria," he shouted, then wondered why he had called out his cousin's name. The line the woman cut against the horizon must have reminded him of his cousin—graceful, well-shaped, pleasing to the eye.

The woman turned his way. She hesitated and started walking the opposite direction. Then she stopped, turned, and walked toward Padre Zobel. He was surprised and pleased that it was Ligaya.

"Good evening, Padre," she said in that soft trembly voice. She was blushing.

"Ah, child, what are you doing here?"

"Just walking and thinking, Padre."

She stood there, eyes downcast, with an uncertain air so he said, "Sit down. Come, sit down."

Her skirt rustled as she sat on the log beside him. Her back was straight, her hands folded together like those of a schoolgirl.

"Walking and thinking," she repeated. She had a sprig of sampaguita flowers in her hair and the sweet scent filled the air around them.

"Were you sick today, child?"

She shook her head. "No … well … I helped Mama with the baking. The Mayor has a dinner tomorrow and the tortas and the mamons are tedious to make."

"Ah, I have been worried. You have never missed Friday confessions."

She blushed once more, her bronze skin turning a deep coral hue. She stared at her bare feet and wrapped her arms around herself. She took a deep breath, shivering slightly, and started to say something but hesitated.

"Something is bothering you?" he asked, feeling protective. How very much like Ana Maria's her mannerisms were. Ana Maria used to blush and hide her face behind her fan when embarrassed.

"Do you know what my name means, Padre?" Ligaya asked.

"Joy, is that right?"

"Yes, but I have never felt more joyless in my entire life," she whispered with pain in her voice.

She looked forlorn, so helpless, and he felt moved. "You had mentioned a man. Is it because of him?" he prodded.

She did not answer but studied her feet as they poked and dug into the white sand. Her silence gave him a sense of dread. He knew that her mother, a widow, was busy with her catering business.

"Perhaps there is no one to confide in," Padre Zobel said. "If you are involved … that is, sometimes it happens that a girl finds herself …"

He hesitated and she looked at him questioningly. "That is, a girl may be in a difficult situation and not have anyone to turn to."

"Difficult, Padre?"

"That is, with child."

Her head jerked up, her eyes widened as she stared briefly at him. "He doesn't even …" then she stopped, lowered her gaze, and gave a soft laugh. She shook her head and stared ahead. He could see her perfect profile and the dark hair in a bun with the star-shaped flowers woven in. It was a lovely face; in a few years this child would be a beautiful woman.

Far away the sun touched the sea and the sky was splashed with red and purple. A solitary boat sliced across the horizon. The enchantment of the moment brought another memory to Padre Zobel—Ana Maria in the deep water with seaweed entangled around her legs. He had been a champion swimmer and brashly he swam the choppy water to help his cousin. She had flung her arms around his neck and he had removed the snakelike vines. Ana Maria had clung on while he swam back to the shore.

Ligaya's voice brought him back to the present. "In a way I am deeply involved."

"Yes?" he asked, but she became quiet. He grew embarrassed for having brought up such an intimate matter. But it happened often: young girls getting pregnant; rushed marriages. Often the girls were sent to another town until the child was born. Then the baby was raised by relatives or given to an orphanage. This occurred all too often and he could not dismiss this possibility even with Ligaya. Why, Ana Maria had gotten involved with the English merchant who fortunately had been willing to marry her.

"He has possessed me," Ligaya said. She put her palms together as if in prayer. "I think about him constantly. When the cock crows at dawn and I awaken, he is on my mind. At the market or while polishing the floors, I think of him. Always. I struggle to put him out of my thoughts, but I cannot help myself."

Ah, a young girl's infatuation, surmised Padre Zobel. He wanted to smile, but appearing serious and choosing his words, he said: "These feelings are normal. One must pray. Chastity you understand is a virtue. If the boy loves you, he will respect your wishes."

She hesitated. "He is … the problem is …" then sighed deeply. She bent over and removed the tortoise shell comb from her hair. Long hair tumbled to her waist. The tiny white sampaguita flowers were almost blinding against that mass of black hair.

Turning, she fixed wide somber eyes on him. A tender wisp of hair blew across her face. "Have you ever felt so passionately about someone?" she asked.

Her words startled him but he caught himself and decided the best way to guide this young girl was to be honest.

"The young have intense emotions. I loved once, yes, but God called her to another life, and I, to mine. Continue praying. Say the rosary and attend the novenas. God will give you strength."

Ligaya cocked her head to one side and with a slanted smile said, "I stopped praying because of him. I think of him and wonder how his mouth would feel against mine. Would his lips be soft, or would they feel like the back of my hand?" She brushed the back of her right hand against her lips and closed her eyes slowly. "I wonder how his kiss would feel. I have never kissed a man before. I wonder how his body would feel against mine."

Padre Zobel had never heard such passion and he felt an odd sensation in the pit of his stomach. "Perhaps," he suggested, "marriage is the best answer."

"He is not free to marry."

Ah, he thought sadly, at least in Ana Maria's case, the man had been unmarried. "Does this man know about your feelings?"

She shook her head. "No, no, he doesn't know." Before he could say anything, she rose and said, "I must go." Then she departed, leaving his soul with strange echoes.

Padre Zobel studied the figure walking away, her waist-length hair flowing around her. There was just enough light to see the woman's silhouette against the dying horizon. Padre Zobel caught his breath—what will happen to her, he wondered. He sat there, pondering her, even as darkness came.

MIRACLE AT SANTO NIÑO CHURCH

Before the sun rose above the tiled roof of the ancient church, Tecla heard dragging sounds. She rubbed the sleep from her eyes and in the semidarkness made out the figure of a man with a bayonet walking toward her. She felt her liver grow cold. He had found her after all, and he would kill her just as he had killed Marcelo and the children. She was lying on a flattened-out cardboard box at the church entrance, and holding her breath, she plastered herself against the church door. Perhaps she would blend in with the carved saints on the massive wooden doors.

"Manang Tecla, wake up," the man said. He stood just three yards away from her. She rubbed her eyes again and squinted. It was Pedring, the street vendor, carrying some poles. Tecla realized it was Sunday and Pedring was setting up his stall. She laughed softly to herself.

"What's so funny?" Pedring asked kindly as he put the poles on the ground and placed a square plywood on top. He laid rosaries, religious medals and prayers books on his makeshift table.

Tecla sat up and wrapped her dusty black dress around her legs. "For a while there, I thought you were a Japanese soldier."

"Not me, just a poor man trying to make a centavo. The wife's pregnant again. You'd better get up. I saw Father Martin opening up the church." He offered his hand. She looked at him sideways and smiled coyly.

"C'mon, old woman. I don't have all morning. This place will be bustling soon."

She scowled. Old woman, indeed. Didn't he know that she was once a beauty queen? Miss Ubec, the gold sash across her chest had said. Her float had been decorated with rosal, jasmine, and dama de noche flowers. The profusion of scents and colors had filled her senses. A real fountain had spouted water below her throne. She grabbed Pedring's hand and got up. She shook her dress and dust billowed around her and fell like heavy fog. Tecla took the tortoise shell comb from her head, twirled her long white hair into a bun and shoved the comb back to hold it in place.

The church bells chimed a melancholy "Silent Night." With surprising clarity, she remembered that it was the eighth of December and the birthday of Marcelo. She walked around the stone church to the servants' quarters where she used the smelly latrine that was swarming with flies.

Later, she rummaged through a pile of trash until she found a rusty tin can. Walking to the front of the church, she started to leave the church grounds when a young girl stopped her. "Wait, Manang," she called. "Here's a hardboiled egg and pan de sal. Father Martin said to give these to you." Tecla took the food and stuffed it in her right pocket. The front of her faded, sheared black skirt had two large pockets. From the other pocket, she took out a pair of blue knitted booties. She studied these for a while, then put them back.

After the young girl left, Tecla stood under the carved wrought iron gate, trying to remember what it was she had to do. The blistering tropical sun was up and beggars and hawkers rushed past her to claim areas next to the church walls and under the cool shade of sprawling acacia trees.

She retraced her steps, back to the latrine and the garbage. She was shaking her head, looking at the rusty tin can when she remembered. Tecla chuckle softly, thinking how silly she was to have forgotten.

Holding the rusty tin can in front of her, she passed the sour, grimy woman who laid a skin-and-bones baby on newspapers next to the church gate. The woman placed a chipped plate next to the sleeping infant and she scattered five coins on the plate. She sat down with the hard look of resignation.

As Tecla walked down the street, rainbow-colored jeepneys—blaring multi-noted horns—drove past her, leaving clouds of dust and exhaust fumes. She wrinkled her nose at the smell. When she saw the red, green and gold shimmering garlands that decorated the department stores, she clapped her hands. She smiled at the paper star lanterns that decorated the slum houses. Traffic was heavy on M.J. Cuenco Avenue because the horse of a tartanilla stopped in the middle of the street to urinate. The half-naked children on the sidewalks pointed and laughed heartily and Tecla laughed with them.

Near the corner sari-sari store, she saw three boys pinching off the lower bodies of black ants. She raised her arms and howled at them. The boys scattered, then regrouped and followed her for half a block, chanting, "Cra-zy woman, cra-zy woman." She looked down at her calloused feet. She was barefoot, her toes spread out, deformed. Her feet plodded with quick determination until at last she reached the old cemetery.

Thick cadena de amor vines crawled and entwined on the cemetery walls. She snapped off some branches with pink and white flowers. Tecla put them in the rusty tin can, then went to a dripping fire hydrant and filled the can with water.

She proceeded to a crumbling mausoleum, stopping in front of three niches with fading inscriptions:

Marcelo Banaga, d. Jan. 6, 1945;
Josefa Banaga, d. Jan. 6, 1945;
Agapito Banaga, d. Jan. 6, 1945.

"It's your birthday again, Marcelo," she said aloud as she put the flowers in front of his niche. "I'll light a candle for all of you later."

She cleaned each niche, brushing off the cobwebs and crumbled plaster. She pulled nearby weeds and broke off the vines that threatened to cover the tombs.

When she finished, she squatted in front of the tombs. She took the egg from her pocket and cracked it on a nearby tombstone. She was peeling the egg when she saw a mangy, pregnant bitch cowering behind the tombstone. The dog wagged her tail timidly and looked straight into Tecla's eyes. "Poor creature," she muttered as she gave the egg to the dog.

She watched the mutt eat the egg, then she took the pan de sal from her pocket and broke it into four pieces. She put a piece in front of each niche and she ate the last one. Tecla had no teeth so she sucked and gummed the roll until it was gone. In a little while, she said, "I have to go back to church. I haven't checked the boy yet. It's Maria's day today and I think the miracle will be today." It was a year ago when she made the promise. She touched the inscribed names gently and left the cemetery.

She took the long route back to church, past Slapsy Maxie's bar near the pier, where the ugly prostitute worked. Once a month, the girl went to confession and she always looked for Tecla to give her money. Wearing a bright red or orange dress, the girl would smile but on her ugly face it looked like a grimace. Tecla couldn't find her. Only the tired-looking madam with smeared makeup barked at the servant boy to sweep the patio carefully.

Pedring greeted her by asking her to pick two lottery tickets for him: Tecla pondered on the tickets, finally choosing numbers with six, three and one. "Fifty-fifty if I win, Manang Tecla. Lintik, I need to win. The wife's going to have another brat," Pedring said as he paid the hare-lipped ticket vendor.

Tecla inspected the colorful wares displayed on the stalls. There were religious objects, clothes, rice and corn cakes wrapped in banana leaves. There were toys, too, her favorite being the plastic swimming dog. The vendor wound it, put it in a basin of water and the dog's giant ears did the paddling.

"Want to buy something, ma'am?" How about this medal of Santa Ana, blessed by the Pope?" a woman called out to her.

"Leave her alone," Pedring said and Tecla caught him pointing to his forehead and making circular movements with his finger. "Ever since her family died," he whispered.

"Oh," the woman said and looked at Tecla curiously.

Tecla glared at Pedring. Her blood boiled when people said she was crazy. Didn't they know she had been a doctor's wife? She once had servants, a nice house; she had run a smooth household for her husband and children. The image of their dead bodies came to her again. They had been sleeping when she left and she had not said goodbye to them. She had not kissed them goodbye. It turned out her cousin hadn't needed her because the midwife was in her barrio. If Tecla had been home, she would have fought like a wild boar until the damnable Japanese cringed in terror and fled. She had tried to blow life back into them but their bodies remained cold and stiff; the blood of their bodies, crusty. All she had now, the only one who understood, who forgave her, was Maria. Tears trickled down, making little crooked paths on her dusty cheeks.

She made her way to the stand with the vigil candles. She

reached deep into her pocket and took out the coin that the ugly prostitute had given her. Tecla put it into the collection box and lit a candle. The flame flickered and danced like a firefly. Once, she had seen a bush covered with fireflies and it looked like an enormous enchanted ball. She gasped at the memory and placed her tongue against her palate. She threw her head back and made a trilling sound. Her feet started shuffling as she began to dance. Churchgoers paused and pointed at her, but she didn't mind. She was in perfect harmony, dancing her prayer to Maria.

After a timeless period, her legs gave way and she fell into a tired heap near the candles. A drop of wax fell on her brown, gnarled hand and she jerked back in pain. It occurred to her that this was a divine sign that today would be the day of fulfillment. Father Martin helped her to her feet. "Be careful, Tecla. You'll hurt yourself," he said and walked away.

The church was cool and dark and smelled of incense and melted wax. A Mass was starting and people filled the pews and stood along the aisles. Ignoring the people who pressed against her, Tecla knelt in the middle aisle and started walking on her knees toward the altar. She prayed, "Santa Maria, madre de Dios ..." until she reached the communion rail.

She stopped and gazed at the back wall that was filled with statues. There were four dozen all in all — Tecla had counted them many times — and in the center was the statue of the Santo Niño. The Child Jesus was about as big as her arm, with a scarlet cloak and a gold crown. She narrowed her eyes to study his cloak hem. It was clean and dry; Tecla was pleased. It was only because of her militant guard that the Santo Niño stayed inside the church. She had heard the stories about the Santo Niño roaming the city at night. In the morning, people said, the friars would find the ancient statue muddy and dirty from his promenade.

"Libera nos a malo," Father Martin said. Tecla went to Maria's altar at the back of the church and gazed lovingly at her statue. She was dressed in white with a blue sash around her waist. Her long curly hair peeked out of her white veil. Her face shone with love and understanding. Maria's son, after all, had been killed by soldiers.

Tecla told her that the Santo Niño was fine, that he had not wandered around Ubec. No telling what would happen to a mere child like that, walking the streets at night. There were women in tight dresses with Norwegian sailors doing God-knows-what in bars and massage parlors. Many houses reeked of opium. The incessant clicking of ivory mahjong pieces echoed through the narrow streets of Ubec.

The coolness of the church gave way to an oppressive heat. Tecla wiped off the beads of perspiration that sprouted on her forehead. "Please move," a woman said. "Our granddaughter has to be near us. She's sick, you see." Tecla opened her eyes and saw a plump woman in rich clothing and a thin old man. She closed her eyes once more and centered herself on her prayers.

Father Martin's sermon was long and the heat filled the musty corners of the church. Tecla was wiping her salty sweat from her eyes when she heard a woman exclaim, "Madre mia, she's fainted!" Then, "Jesus! She's not breathing; she's dead!" The plump woman stood there, one hand to her throat, staring at a girl who lay in a white heap near her feet. The girl was around sixteen, pale and thin.

From some corner of Tecla's mind, a memory surfaced. She went near the girl. The plump woman screamed and clutched her throat tighter, but Tecla continued with what she knew she had to do. She looked at the girl's face. White and still, just like her husband and children had been. She passed her hand in front of the girl's nose and there was no breath. Tecla pushed the girl's chin back and forced her mouth open. She put her mouth on hers, stubbornly resisting the clawing hands on her shoulders and hair. Tecla blew air until she felt the girl's chest go up. She pulled away and her chest went down. She continued doing this until the girl's chest rose and fell on its own. Only then did Tecla allow the people to pull her away.

"She's dead. The dirty beggar killed her," the plump woman wailed.

"No, no, she's all right," the thin old man said as he helped the girl to her feet. The girl leaned against her grandfather, one hand to her forehead. She wore a pure white dress with a blue ribbon around her waist. Her hair was long and curly. When the girl smiled at Tecla, Tecla thought—just for a brief moment—that this was Maria's apparition. The miracle.

The plump woman crushed the girl to her enormous bosom. People crowded around them until Tecla could not see the girl. Tecla chuckled to herself. How could she have mistaken the girl for Maria? What a silly thought. She went back to Maria's altar, counted the number of flowers in the huge bouquets, and wondered when Maria's promise of a miracle would be fulfilled.

CASA BONITA

1

In the center of the city, which is now rundown but which used to be fashionable, there stood a large house called Casa Bonita. The house sat on a corner property that used to be a cemetery, and evil spirits reportedly lurked in the house. People claimed that because of these spirits, a young bride threw herself into the well on her wedding night.

The tragedy left the groom reclusive and obsessively meticulous. A widower until he died, he kept his two-story house in perfect order. He also developed a passion for gardening, and he filled his courtyard with tropical plants of the most vivid colors. He had a magnificent mango tree famous for its bright yellow fruit, "like golden breasts," the people said. Despite all these, the house had a somberness, an atmosphere of strangeness that made passersby say a quick prayer.

After the man died, Casa Bonita was vacant for seven months. Just when neighbors thought the house would be abandoned forever, a man and his wife arrived. They spoke with an accent that the people could not immediately place. One thing was certain, they were wealthy; onlookers could tell from their belongings that were carted into Casa Bonita that day—porcelain lamps, carved desks, silver-framed mirrors, enormous wooden beds, chairs and tables, an altar for their private chapel, trunks full of dishes and silverware, linens and clothes.

Across Casa Bonita an old woman and her son watched. Part of the bottom floor of their house had been converted into a store, and from there they observed the wife giving directions from the verandah. Beside the wife stood a servant girl who held a black umbrella over her mistress' head.

"Such airs. Look at that, she can't carry her own umbrella," said the old woman, Epang.

Her son Ricardo, who was nineteen years old, did not answer. He watched, transfixed; he lost all notion of time. Against the grey sheet, the wife's fine figure was perfectly outlined. She was considerably younger than her short and plump husband with a drooping mustache. Her head was gracefully tilted to one side; her long hair and long skirt fluttered about. Once her hand flew to her mouth in fright when one of the men almost dropped a side table; and when she recovered, she threw her back and laughed, her white teeth flashing. She reminded Ricardo of a porcelain figure that he had seen at the Indian's shop downtown.

That night after Ricardo closed their store and carried his crippled mother to her room, he opened his bedroom windows. A damp smell like mushrooms filled his nostrils. The rain had stopped and a faint moon shone through the tree branches. Ricardo peeped through the branches, through the mandevilla vine that crept up the side of her verandah. He hoped to see her; the memory of her fluttering on that verandah burned in his mind. But he saw only the glistening raindrops on the verandah and tile roof. He went to bed with a strange restlessness that kept him awake for a long time.

2

Her name was Zenaida. She had been raised by nuns in a Manila orphanage, and it was there where her husband, a childless widower, found her. Her husband, an import-export businessman, moved to Ubec to start life all over with his young bride. Every day and night Richard looked for her, but several days passed before he saw her again. She stopped by one morning from church. Her veil was still around her shoulders; she carried the faint scent of incense.

"Do you have gugu for the hair?" she asked, pushing her hair away from her face. Her voice had a mesmerizing cadence. She stood erect, holding a pearl rosary and a purse. Her dress of delicate piña fiber floated around her like a mist.

Epang grunted a reply. Ricardo walked to the sheets of gugu bark on a table.

"It's for my hair," Zenaida explained as she went to him. "With all the unpacking, the servant forgot to buy some at the market.

"Nothing better for the hair than gugu and lemoncito rinse," Epang said.

"I don't care much for lemoncito rinse." Zenaida selected three sheets and opened her purse.

"Oh, don't you?" retorted Epang.

"The nuns made us use lemoncito. No, I don't like lemoncito rinse at all." Looking at Ricardo, she asked, "And you, do you think lemoncito rinse is good for the hair?"

"Well, I-I don't know, señora, that is, it-it must be so, señora. Yes, I-I suppose so, which does not mean that gugu is not good."

She laughed, little wrinkles forming on her nose. "What's your name?" she asked.

"Ricardo."

"Ah, Ricardo. And how old are you?"

"Nineteen."

She lifted an eyebrow. "Ah, not such a boy after all. I knew a boy once, who was nineteen, like you." Her eyes took on a dreamy look and for a while she seemed to be someplace else.

"Anything else, señora?" Epang said, rolling the last word.

Zenaida snapped back to reality. "No, nothing else. But I'll be back if I need something." She paid Ricardo and smiled. "Ricardo—nice name."

When she left, Epang sniffed. "Slut! All my life I have borne my cross, worked myself to the bone, and there was your good-for-nothing father, and here's this Jezebel who never worked a day of her life. Did you see her purse and shoes? Embroidered with pearls. Real pearls, I tell you. And the jewelry on her fingers and ears, and here we eat salted fish!" She slammed the coconut dipper into the jug. Her elongated ears quivered. The lines on her leathery skin deepened.

Ricardo took his switchblade knife and began cutting sugar cane into small segments. His hands were shaking and he almost cut himself. A memory came to him: his father stumbled home late one night. Epang met him with a ferocious verbal attack. His father had hit her and she had tumbled down the stairs and broke her legs. Her bones had not mended properly. Ricardo had wanted to become a priest, but he had to take care of his mother. Now he felt an urge to hit her; but he knew his commandments well, and the fourth commandment said, 'Honor thy father and mother.' He grasped his knife tight and continued working.

3

Ricardo saw her one night when the moon was full and the swollen fruit on her sprawling mango tree shone like golden breasts. Her bedroom windows were wide open. Looking like an angel in her filmy white gown, she combed her hair, her right hand moving front to back in slow motion. She swirled her hair over her shoulder to comb the ends. Ricardo felt lost in some kind of eternity, but then the light in her room went out, and he was left staring into darkness. He muttered to himself: she's there, and yet she's not there. A sense of hopelessness rooted in him. He closed his bedroom windows and swore he would keep them shut every night. He abandoned the store to his mother, spending time out in the carpentry shed instead. He built benches; the physical effort of cutting, shaving, carving occupied his mind, kept him from dwelling on Zenaida.

One siesta time, while the people rested, Ricardo continued working on a bench of an old fashioned design with elaborate carvings on the back and arms. It was November, but hot; even the breeze that occasionally blew through the nearby flame tree was oppressively warm. Ricardo's damp shirt clung to his back and he removed it and used it to wipe the sweat off his face and neck. He was running his hands over the bench to feel the wood's texture when he heard several raps on the wooden gate.

Zenaida stood by the half-opened gate. Her hair was tied loosely with a white ribbon; damp tendrils of hair curled near her hairline. Zenaida's simple cotton dress made her look like a young peasant woman; she even smelled of unhusked rice.

"I'd like to order benches for the verandah," she said, as she entered the gate.

Ricardo stepped back. His sudden movement scared the chickens who had been scratching the ground near him. They squawked and flew away.

Laughing, she tossed her head back. "I've frightened them, and

I've frightened you. I'm sorry. It was so warm, I could not sleep. I saw you working and I thought I'd talk to you about the benches. My husband is away and I want to surprise him when he returns."

She approached him. He stood still, not knowing what to say or do.

"I want one just like that one, with the carvings. Where I grew up, we had benches like that. They're sturdy; they'll last a lifetime."

Ricardo shifted his weight.

"Is it a bad time to talk to you? I can come back later. I know it's siesta time, an ungodly time to be roaming around, but I just could not rest."

He shook his head. "I was surprised, that's all."

Tilting her head, she lifted an eyebrow. "Why? Don't people order benches from you?"

"Yes, yes, they do. But you—"

"Oh, because I'm here. The señora is here. Really, I am a very simple woman." She paused and took a deep breath. "I love the smell of wood shavings. Will you make the benches? I need four."

"Yes, of course."

"Well then, I'll have Pedring pick them up next week."

He nodded.

"Just tell Pedring how much. I better go." She smiled and started walking away. Then she stopped, turned, and looked at him with a mocking expression. "I have not seen you. You've not been at your store."

He did not answer.

"You remind me of someone I knew. He was also terribly shy. Well, do a good job with the benches," she said and left.

That night he paced his room. Around and around he walked, like a trapped animal. He thought of Zenaida's hair. He wanted to smell it, feel its silkiness. He thought of her mouth, how soft and moist it would be, how hard her teeth would feel. He pictured her throwing her head back when she laughed, and he wanted to kiss the base of her neck right where it throbbed. His restlessness grew until the room could not contain him. He left for the pier where the women walked the streets until dawn.

For a while the sea breeze calmed him, but later the sight of a woman made him anxious. She had long hair like Zenaida's. Her movements stirred the air, and the smell of salt gave way to the subtle scent of gugu. He took a sharp breath and closed his eyes. He should have reached for Zenaida's arm, held her. He should have buried his face in her hair and kissed her. He should have led her to the wooden cot in the shed and there—a hand brushed his arm. Briefly he thought Zenaida was beside him. He opened his eyes and saw a painted woman, a mechanical doll of sorts, an insult—and his right hand formed a fist and it flew smashing at her face. He fled home and whipped himself with a length of frayed Manila rope.

Lying on his bloodied mat, he knew that some malevolent spirit, green in color and foul in odor, occupied his soul. This evil thing came from the old cemetery and it lived in Zenaida's house; it was responsible for the drowning of the young bride in the well; it planned Zenaida and Ricardo's meeting. It was trying to destroy them. And Ricardo would not allow that to happen. No, he loved her too much.

4

On Christmas Eve, Zenaida and her husband threw a big party. The important people of Ubec showed up—the foreigners, the fat politicians with their richly adorned wives, the old families who flaunted their names and influence.

Epang and Ricardo were finishing a batch of sticky coconut jam when commotion erupted in front of Zenaida's house. The French consul, flamboyant and new in town, had just arrived when a young woman holding a long knife rushed to him. She leaned against the carriage door and began slashing at the startled consul. The driver tried pulling the woman away, but she was too strong. Fortunately the police arrived to drag her away.

Zenaida rushed to the carriage. "You're hurt!" she cried. The French consul, tall, handsome with red hair, threw his arm around her, and as he did so, his blood stained her dress and hair. When they staggered into her house, some women shrieked.

The excitement ebbed, and soon music and laughter drifted from Zenaida's house. Ricardo could not get rid of the image of Zenaida and the consul standing side by side. Ricardo's breathing became difficult when he thought of how the consul flung his arm around her, as though he owned her, as though he had a right to do so. Ricardo watched Casa Bonita until dawn, and when the red streaks of light smeared the dark sky, he began to weep.

The next day, Epang asked Ricardo to crawl into her hiding place to get her bundle of jewelry. She wanted to wear them to Mass. As she unwrapped each piece from the tattered tissue wrappings, she talked of her widowed mother who sold salt to the mountaineers to make a living. "Look at these, Ricardo, all from salt. The mountain people needed salt otherwise they'd get goiter. She saved a centavo here, a centavo there, and she bought these one by one. She wanted me to have an heirloom."

Ricardo stared at the gold necklaces and bracelets that had faded into a sickly green. There was a set of crudely-cut diamonds mounted on flimsy gold. And Ricardo remembered Zenaida's jewelry, enormous stones of varied hues set in heavy gold and platinum. A realization came to him: It was not just a matter of shiny stones and cold metal that separated Zenaida from him, it was an entire world—no—an entire universe.

This thought festered in his mind like a fungus. He wallowed in darkness, not doing a thing, sulking, staring at his wall, at the unkind God hanging on the cross. He felt lost, uncertain. He had wanted to be a priest; and that dream had been taken away from him. He loved Zenaida, and she could never be his. Was he doomed to a lifetime of carting an old woman around? Yes, his sour mother who scowled at him accusingly as she crawled around the house like an ancient tail-less reptile, hissing, "Ricardo, you are possessed! Possessed!"

And yet the sight of her moved him. She was old; he was the only one she could depend on. She needed him. Honor thy father and mother. Bit by bit he forced himself to do things. The roof needed repair, the bushes and trees were overgrown, the store needed a fresh coat of paint.

5

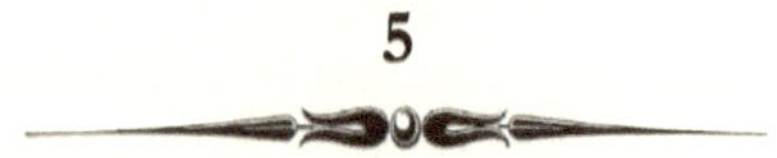

In the yard Zenaida appeared once again. "You are avoiding me," she accused. "Why? What have I done? Am I so ugly that you cannot stand me?"

His blood froze; he broke out in a sweat. He stood petrified with the wood shaver in his hands, a curl of wood quivering at the end.

She had been pouting, but now she looked worried. "You look pale. Everything is all right, isn't it?"

He nodded.

She approached him and stroked his left cheek. "You're so much like him; but he's gone now. Everything's different. If only he had not abandoned me to him." Her voice was low, her mouth slightly open, and she ran her tongue around her lips. For a while, she hesitated but then she turned and walked away.

Her visit had been so brief that he wondered if he had made it up, that it had been some kind of vision. For days Ricardo felt feverish, but he would suddenly turn cold, so cold that his teeth chattered. Feeling the spirit's eyes behind his, he resumed watching and waiting for her once more. He sensed the green spirit growing inside of him, taking hold of him. Night after night, when the lights in her house dimmed, he took his rope and whipped himself.

6

It happened suddenly and for a few days Ricardo did not know how to react. But a week after Zenaida started hearing evening Masses instead of morning Masses, he decided to follow her. As though it were a child's game, he trailed behind her as she entered the church. Before Mass ended she left and she meandered in the opposite direction of her home. When she hailed a carriage, he found one and instructed the driver to follow her.

Her carriage stopped at the edge of an undeveloped park, the Plaza Libertad. Aside from the fountain in the middle, the park was a jungle of trees and shrubs. Ricardo instructed his driver to move on until thick bushes hid them, then he told him to stop. The driver narrowed his eyes with suspicion but Ricardo paid him well and sent him away. It was dusk when the driver whipped his horse and his carriage disappeared around the bend. In the distance church bells chimed to signal the angelus. Crickets were buzzing. The air was turning cool. Shivering, he traced her steps along a narrow trail. He thought to himself that this was no place for a lady like Zenaida. Well, he assured himself, I'm here to protect her. Ricardo pulled out his switchblade knife—how it glistened even in the growing darkness.

When he heard a voice, he crouched down and looked around.

The voice was so low, he could not tell if it belonged to a man or a woman. The hair on his arms prickled as he crept forward. The whispering came from a small clearing in the midst of the bushes. He heard a soft moan. Hurrying, frantic now, he peered through the branches and saw Zenaida with the French consul. They were lying on a blanket, and his face was pressed against her bosom. Her eyes were closed, head flung back; her mouth was partly open. The Frenchman's hand was under her skirt.

There was a low click in Ricardo's brain. He gripped his knife tighter and flew at the man. He stabbed him. A jet of blood spurted into Ricardo's face when he yanked out the knife. For a moment, the Frenchman clawed at the air, but he slumped down with the death rattle on his throat. Zenaida froze, staring at Ricardo (how like a porcelain doll she looked, he thought). A slight breeze blew a lock of hair to her face and he reached out to brush it away. She shrank away from him. "Oh please, please don't," she pleaded.

It was laughable; he had to suppress his laughter. All he wanted was to hold her, tell her that he would never hurt her, that he loved her. But she stumbled away, shouting, "Oh God, oh God, you're crazy! Help me!"

He chased her to tell her that he only wanted to protect her. "Thou shalt not commit adultery"—he did not want her to sin. She was not a cheap whore like the painted woman at the pier. Zenaida was a lady, a fine lady. But she ran to a mango tree and tried to hide behind the trunk. He caught her, caressed her, but she scratched his face. He hit her, saying, "Can't you see—?" But she only screamed louder as her nails dug deeper into his cheeks. He struck her with the knife, once, twice, thrice, he lost count. Her white dress turned scarlet. Her hair felt slippery as he ran his hands through all that abundant hair.

The police found him, rocking her in his arms. "This mango tree," he whispered, "doesn't have any fruit. Have you noticed, Zenaida? Look up and see. Your tree has fruit, like golden breasts." But she remained silent and still.

7

Sometimes in prison he sang the Tantum Ergo, but most of the time he thought of her. In his mind, her mouth is half open and he can see the tip of her pink tongue. A warm breeze blows, carrying the fresh smell of gugu. The sunshine filtering through the flame tree dapples her face. He removes her hair ribbon and her abundant hair spills around her. As he strokes her head, a faint shiver runs through her body. She does not resist when he kisses her at the base of her neck (right where it throbs) and on her mouth; nor does she resist when he pulls her to the cool shadows of the shed and there make love to her.

THE VIRGIN'S LAST NIGHT

Four months after Petra Santiago died, and the night before her own death, Meding Santiago got out of bed, reached for her rosary by the side table and started reciting the Creed. It was almost midnight, and she was saying the rosary that Thursday for the second time. Since Petra died, she slept poorly, her mind fixed on the image of her younger sister on the hospital bed, waving her bony fingers in front of her face before she finally stopped breathing. Sometimes she would forget that Petra was gone, and she would pour another cup of hot chocolate or turn to say something to no one, and she would be surprised at the depth of her grief.

She was on her knees, with her eyes closed, when she heard a soft knock on the door. She rose and walked to the door. She opened it, expecting one of the servants, and was surprised at the figure of an old man. It took Meding a second before she caught her breath and said, "Mateo, what are you doing here? You're dead."

"Here to see you, Meding. It's been a long time," replied Mateo, standing first on one foot, then shifting his weight to the other, a man embarrassed.

"Well," Meding said, clutching her nightdress at the collar, uncertain about what to do, what to say, uncertain about her sanity at the moment.

"You're not crazy," Mateo went on. "I'm dead. I know, it's strange, but that's how it is sometimes. I have to get back before sunrise."

"Oh," Meding said, accepting this explanation with some kind of relief. Ever since her sister's death, life had taken on the quality of a dream, and Mateo's presence was just another strange event. She squinted at the figure by the doorway. "You've gotten old, Mateo," she said, "and paunchy too."

"You're just as beautiful." Mateo hung his head the way he used to as a young man, many years ago.

Meding laughed and walked over to the armoire mirror to study her image. "Mateo, you and I know I'm no spring chicken."

Mateo walked timidly to the armoire and leaned against it. "You're beautiful to me," he insisted.

"How'd we get old Mateo? We used to be young, remember? Now, look at us." She fingered her long flowing white hair, felt the rough weaving on the skin of her face. She closed her eyes and traveled back to the summer when she was twenty and she wore a white voile dress and her brown arms shone under the hot summer sun. Mateo, tall and lean and looking like a movie star, had stood behind her. They were at the annual carnival, and had marveled at the woman with the python son. The snake-son had undulated slowly around her shoulders and down her arm. The story went that the woman had given birth to twins, one human, and one snake, but the boy died in infancy, and she and her snake-son became closer than ever. People at the carnival had shoved and pushed and Mateo stood behind her, so close, she could feel his warm breath against her nape.

She sighed and opened her eyes to catch Mateo studying her intently as he had done so many times in the past. "I love you more than ever, Meding," he said, and Meding blushed.

"Don't be foolish," she said, in the gruff manner she had acquired through the years; but for the first time since her sister died, and perhaps far longer than that, Meding felt her spirit turn light, airy, like the lace curtain fluttering by the window. She moved so the bedroom light didn't fall directly on her face. "Don't be foolish," Meding repeated, feeling the heat spreading over her face and down her throat, thoroughly embarrassed that she was blushing, and what a silly, girlish thing for an old woman to do. She walked over to the antique rocking chair by the window and sat down.

Keeping a respectful distance between them, Mateo followed. He took a deep breath and looked around. "What's that sweet smell?" he asked, in a boyish way, and Meding thought that Mateo really hadn't changed that much.

"Jasmine," she replied, as she rocked slowly, back and forth.

He peered outside the window. "My goodness, it's the same

vine that used to be there when we were young," he said.

"The trellis had to be rebuilt because of wood rot," said Meding in a practical voice. "All those years, the typhoons, even though the wood was treated it finally fell apart."

Mateo leaned out the window. In the distance an enormous full moon hung in the sky, and Meding smiled as she looked at his silhouette against that backdrop.

"We kissed for the first time under that trellis," he murmured, turning to look at her.

She, avoiding his eyes, shook her head and said, "Don't bring that up now," but in her mind they were young and alone in the garden, and he had bent down and kissed her on her mouth. She had felt as if she would run out of breath, as if she would faint, and she pulled away. They looked at each other and again he kissed her, and this time she did not pull away. She had discovered that by tilting her head slightly to one side she could breathe, and besides she was so lost in the softness and moistness and wonder of the kiss, that she could not have pulled away if she had exerted her entire will. She had even felt—very briefly—the tip of his tongue, and she had become so heady, she could hardly find her way back to the house.

"I was so mad for you," Mateo continued. "I loved you; I wanted you."

"This is foolish talk, Mateo. Besides if you loved me so much, why did you marry Carlota? That was a rather disastrous marriage, wasn't it? I understand you weren't married a month when she threw you out of your matrimonial bedroom."

"Carlota knew I loved you, and she never forgave me. Not for the rest of her life."

"She outlived you, didn't she? I hear she died only a few years ago."

"Yes, she lived to be seventy-nine, and she spent all those years in bitterness, hating me, you, all of mankind. She told me once that she could feel your presence with us at all times. On my deathbed, she begrudged me for loving you."

"Well, that was very foolish of Carlota. I always did think she was a foolish woman. Like I said I never understood why you married a foolish woman like that. And then you had other women, equally foolish I'm sure. Don't be surprised that I know. My sister and I may have lived quietly in this forgotten corner of the world, but believe me, we heard news about you."

"What was I supposed to do? I wanted to marry you; you turned me down. Carlota was there; she distracted me from my pain, at least for a while. When we got married, she changed and became prickly and shrill. She became even worse after the fire."

"What fire?"

"You probably didn't know, but we had a fire at home. The boys were almost grown by this time. Do you know what I saved first from the fire?"

Meding shook her head.

"Your letters and pictures."

"What letters and pictures?"

"Your old letters and pictures. I never returned them, remember?"

"You saved those?"

Mateo nodded. "I had kept them locked in my desk. When the fire broke out, I brought them outside, to safety. When the commotion died down, Carlota saw those letters and pictures laying on the ground. She wanted to destroy them, but I wouldn't let her. It was over from that day on." He lifted his shoulders and shivered.

"Don't you think that was a bit foolish, Mateo? Saving those silly letters and photos when you knew there was nothing between us?"

"I loved you still; I wanted a part of you with me, always. You should have married me, Meding. We could have been happy."

"In the first place, you make it sound like it was my choice not to marry you, Mateo. You know I loved you. It wasn't my fault that Papa dropped dead and you knew perfectly well that Petra was ill. I couldn't abandon her, could I? She already had this idea that Mama had abandoned us when we were children. Now what would have happened to poor Petra if I'd up and married you? Why, she would have been so lonely, and she would have felt no better than a dishrag. I couldn't do that to my sister."

"She could have lived with us."

"And be a second banana? That poor girl was already losing her hair and had scabs all over her legs from her eczema; can you imagine how she would have felt, to have been a glorified servant in our household?"

"Nobody said she'd be a glorified servant in our household, Meding. She would have been my sister-in-law. We would have been a family together. And she would have been the aunt to our children. Our children, Meding, remember we used to talk about them."

"You and Carlota had children, didn't you?"

"Two boys, who took after their mother. When they got married, they never visited us. They hardly spent time at my wake. One was late for my funeral."

"I'm sorry to hear that, Mateo. Children should be a source of joy for parents. I know I've found great joy in my dealings with the children at the orphanage. Petra and I spent a lot of time with those children. Some of them were abandoned at infancy, placed on the turning cradle at the orphanage. Maybe because we lost our mother when we were young, my sister and I considered it a calling to make life brighter for those orphans."

"You would have been a wonderful mother, Meding. Our six children, Meding. The dreams we had; we had beautiful dreams; and they're all gone. If only you had married me. What kind of life did you have, running the household for your father, then taking care of Petra all her life? You never had a life of your own."

She stood up from the rocking chair and began pacing the floor. "I want you to know, Mateo, that I've had a good life. Just because you did a fine job messing yours up doesn't mean I wasn't happy. Petra and I have done our part serving the church, society, doing the best we can. No one can ever say this or that about us about me. I've been happy, Mateo, on my own, with Petra, I've been happy. Don't ever think that my life was in any way lacking because we didn't get married and I never had children, and that I've wasted my life taking care of my sister, may-she-rest-in-peace. You should have seen how she suffered, Mateo. If I could have eaten her suffering, I would have, right there at the hospital. No medicine could dull her pain, my poor sister." Meding sat at the edge of her four-poster bed and began weeping.

Mateo sat beside her and put his arm around her. "Don't cry, Meding. Nothing pains me more than to see you crying. Don't cry."

She did not stop. She could not. There was the loss of Petra, and here all of a sudden were old matters that rose up inside of her, old wounds of her soul that opened up once again. "The truth of it, Mateo, the real truth, is that I was afraid. I loved you so much, too much, and I was afraid."

"Of what?" he asked.

"Of being hurt. It seemed to me that love begat pain. And love is terribly unreliable. Papa loved Mama, and she died. Mama had Petra and me, and she left us. Then Papa died. You know he died in his mistress's bedroom; the shame of it. Love wasn't real. Pain was, and suffering; and I was terribly afraid that one day you would stop loving me. Don't protest, Mateo, I've seen it happen too many times, men falling out of love; and what would I have done if I had loved you so completely, with my body and soul, and you had abandoned me? What would have happened to me?"

Mateo pulled her closer to him and hugged her tight, as if comforting a child. Her tears dampened his shirt, and she felt this dampness on her cheek the same way she did years ago when she had told him that they could not get married, that it was all over, that she could never see him again, that same cool dampness on her face. Mateo pulled back, and she felt his mouth on hers, soft and moist as Mateo's kisses had always been. His kiss grew bolder and she felt herself yielding, as if there would be no turning back; but then he pulled away.

"What's wrong, Mateo?" she asked, wondering if she had done something wrong. She pushed her long hair away from her face.

"Nothing."

"What do you mean, 'nothing'?"

"Come, let's walk in the garden," he said. He stood up and held his hand out to her. "The moon is large. Let's go to the trellis."

"The trellis, of course." She got up, as if in dream and she felt lighter and younger as she glided with him down the stairs and out the verandah to the trellis with the jasmine vine entwined in it, the star-shaped white flowers casting off their delicious sweet scent. There, they assumed the pose they had taken in the past, and as if picking up the strand of that thread, they kissed. She was twenty once again, and Mateo was twenty-two. His hands stroked her back, his body pressed against hers. She could feel him, feel him against her, as their mouths explored the other with abandon. Her head was spinning; her mind was off someplace where she had never been before, some wonderful world of sensation, of smelling the flowers, of hearing the breeze rustling the leaves.

The melody of a waltz started in her head, and she swayed gently against him. He moved with her, and before long, the two of them were waltzing in the garden under the huge moon. Up and down the walkway they danced, past the rose garden, past the calla lilies, past the gazebo, then right by the gardenia bush, Mateo paused. He plucked a flower and handed this to Meding. She smiled broadly, happily, as she tucked the gardenia in her long, flowing hair. They sat on a bench and contemplated the moon. She leaned against him and rested her head against his chest. To her surprise she could hear and feel his heartbeat.

"Your heart is beating," she said. "Why is that, Mateo, when you're dead?"

He shrugged and stroked her hair.

She continued listening to his heartbeat; and she thought to herself how warm and comforting it was to be near him like that. "Mateo, I'm very happy right now. This is the happiest I've been for so long. I'm happy but I'm also sad. I remembered the children, the house that we planned to build by the sea, our dreams. It's sad to think that we lost a lot, even moments like this when I could just listen to your heartbeat, Mateo. So much, and we can never have them again."

"I know. Our dreams," he said, wiping away her tears.

"I've always wanted to lay down beside you and put my head on your chest and listen to your heart. Just listen to the rhythm of it. It must be soothing to do that. It must be nice to do that every night. Did Carlota do that? No, don't answer, I don't want to know. I've always wanted to do that. I just had Petra, you know, and there was so much fussing with hot-water bags and ointments for her before bedtime."

He said nothing, just continued caressing her hair, just continued pressing her head against his heart.

From far away, a rooster crowed, then there was stillness once more. She knew that the night was ending and dawn was almost there. They were quiet for a while, knowing that he would have to leave at sunrise. Mateo stood up and extended his hand to her. "Come."

She looked up, and she did not hesitate. She felt no fear as she placed her hand in his, and together they walked into the house, up the stairs, to her bedroom, and they lay on her bed. She rested her head first on his shoulder, then pressed her ear to where his heart was, and she could hear the pulsing of his blood, and she could feel her own blood pulsing through her veins. When his lips touched hers, they both knew that neither would pull away, knew that this was the only time they had for each other.

WAITING FOR PAPA'S RETURN

When Reverend Mother Superior tells Remedios her father died, all she can think is how ugly the nun looks. Remedios stares at the mustache fringing the nun's upper lip; Reverend Mother Superior stares back with pale watery eyes.

"This morning, child. Heart attack," the nun says.

In the distance the three o'clock bell rings as if repeating the nun's words. It is an October Thursday, warm and humid. The sound stays with Remedios as the nun brings her to the chapel. "Let us pray so your father will go straight to heaven," she whispers. They kneel on the front pew and Remedios closes her eyes. The ringing that echoes in her head fades and she hears her father's voice loud and clear: I'll be back in two weeks.

She clings to those words, mulling over them. I'll-be-back-in-two-weeks. That means next week because Mama and Papa have already been gone for a week. She pictures her father with his oval face, his gold rimmed glasses, and his balding head. Leaning on his cane, he asked, "What do you want me to bring?"

"Mama says she'll buy me shoes, clothes, candies, and chocolates."

"But what do you want?" his gentle voice prodded.

"A walking doll and a tea set like Mildred's. Not the plastic tea set, I want the kind that breaks."

"All right," he replied, tousling her dark hair. "I'll scour all of Hong Kong and I'll bring you your doll and tea set."

Those words her father said and he never lies. Remedios is confused: Reverend Mother Superior is the most important person in school and she doesn't lie either. She must have made a mistake. Papa and Mama will be back next week from their vacation.

Remedios thinks things over, trying to find a reason for this misunderstanding. Was it because she and Mildred giggled in church at the fat woman singing in a warbling voice? Mildred elbowed her in the ribs and they were bad, no doubt about it, snickering in the back row instead of paying attention to Father Ruiz's novena.

The chapel smells of melted wax, and when Remedios opens her eyes, she studies the bleeding Jesus nailed to the cross. "I'm sorry for having been bad," she prays over and over, until Reverend Mother Superior stands up and says, "Your aunt is picking you up, child."

They find Tiya Meding in the office. She is wearing a brown dress; her face is pale, her eyes, pink-rimmed. "Poor, poor child," she mumbles. In the car she looks at Remedios in a way that makes Remedios think her aunt is trying to discover something in her—and Remedios does not know what.

Feeling awkward, Remedios rolls down her window and watches the hawkers selling lottery tickets, boiled bananas and soft drinks. Her aunt delicately blows her nose and sniffles.

"Look, there's the woman in black, dancing in front of the church," Remedios points out.

"Crazy woman," Tiya Meding answers.

"Papa says she's pathetic."

"Pathetic, my food. She's as loony as they come."

Remedios keeps quiet; pathetic is how her father describes the woman in black.

Her aunt's chauffeur—that is what Tiya Meding calls her driver—brings them to Vering the Dressmaker. Remedios is surprised that she will have a dress sewn, and she nods approvingly at the design: puffed sleeves, boat neck and shirred skirt.

"And pockets, two square pockets," Remedios says.

Vering sketches in the pockets.

"And I don't want this black cloth. Yellow organdy would be nicer."

The two women eye each other.

"But the dress has to be black," Tiya Meding insists.

"I don't like black. Papa says I look prettiest in yellow."

"The dress will be black, Remedios." Her aunt sets her jaw and Remedios knows there is no use arguing.

Before leaving the dressmaker's shop, Tiya Meding asks for

pieces of black cloth the size of postage stamps, and she pins one on Remedios' blouse, right above her heart—a little bit of black cloth that flutters when the warm breeze blows.

At school she is the center of attraction, like the actress Gloria Romero or the one-eyed freak with the Chinese Acrobatic Troupe, stared at by everybody. When she picks up her schoolbag, the children glance curiously at her. The visitors streaming into Tiya Meding's house look at her, and when she and her aunt go to the funeral parlor and church "to make arrangements," people study her. Remedios feels as if her nose were growing from her forehead. Pairs of glassy eyes follow her around and she does not know what they want, how to escape them.

At her aunt's house, she tries to amuse herself by inspecting the numerous porcelain figures in the living room—pretty dainty women with ducks beside them, little angels kneeling down in prayer, but her aunt snaps: "Don't touch those. They're breakable." She goes to the piano and plays "Chopsticks," but her aunt lifts a reprimanding finger in the air. "The noise," she complains. Tiya Meding is on the phone and Remedios listens to her.

"Thank you," her aunt says. "Heart attack. Isn't that too bad? I warned my sister. An older man like that." Tiya Meding's diamond earrings dangle from her elongated ears and a huge diamond solitaire sparkles on her finger.

"Baubles," her father often says about Tiya Meding's jewelry. "She is a silly woman who likes baubles."

Remedios leaves the main house thinking to herself: Silly, silly woman. She goes to the dirty-kitchen and has a second lunch with the servants. Using her fingers, she makes a ball of rice and eats that with stewed fish. Later, she helps the cook peel cassava and grate coconuts.

"Your father was a good man," the cook says. "He made my son the foreman at the road construction."

"Yes," Remedios replies, "I can't wait until he comes home."

After speaking, she wonders why she said those words at all. She understands what Reverend Mother Superior said, what all the commotion is about, yet deep in the very core of her, she knows her Papa will return.

The kitchen is sooty and smells of grease and bay leaves. The cook, standing next to the huge wood-burning stove, looks at her. Remedios continues grating. She watches the curly slivers of white coconut meat fall into the basin. The kitchen smoke seems to engulf her and she feels warm. The pungent smell makes her temples throb. She begins to feel weak, just as she felt when her cousin told her she was adopted. He had lost in a game of checkers, and angrily, he told Remedios that her parents picked her up from a pile of trash, that she had been covered with fat flies. She did not cry; she crawled into bed to sleep off her tiredness. Her mother called the boy an idiotic pervert. Her father placed her on his knee.

"See this bump on my nose?" he said.

"Yes."

"Don't you have a bump on your nose like mine?" His warm finger traveled down her nose over the slight protrusion.

She nodded.

"That means that you are my very own little girl. We didn't adopt you."

The darkness lifted, and the next time she saw her cousin, she stuck her tongue out at him. But now the tiredness stays and she drags around until bedtime. It seems she has just tucked the mosquito net under the mattress when she falls asleep and has a dream.

It is Sunday, and she, Mama and Papa are driving over bumpy, dusty roads to Talisay Beach. Remedios is happy because she enjoys clamming in the small inlet. But when they arrive, the sea is blood-red and smells foul. Remedios cries and her Papa asks why.

"Something terrible has happened," she says.

"It's all right," he answers. "I'm right beside you."

She dries her eyes and, noticing that the water has turned blue and the air is clean once more, laughs and hugs her Papa.

"Don't cry. It makes me sad," her father says in her dream.

She wakes to Tiya Meding's voice telling her the plane is arriving in less than an hour. Trying to get excited, she bathes with her aunt's Maja soap and dabs Joy perfume behind her ears. Like a sleepwalker, she puts on her new black dress, white socks, and black patent shoes. Remedios ties yellow ribbons at the ends of her braids, but Tiya Meding removes those. "Not for a year," she says.

Heavy-faced people wearing somber clothes crowd at the airport. They stare at Remedios and she tries hard to figure out what they want from her. She laughs. "I can hardly wait to see them," she exclaims in a high thin voice. Pairs of eyes follow her, letting go only when the noisy plane arrives with a loud screech. The special cargo plane stops near the terminal, and some men open the side doors and struggle to bring a casket down. When Remedios spots her mother walking down the ramp, she runs shouting, "Ma!" The mourners around her pause. "Ma, where's my walking doll and tea set?" Her aunt tells her to be quiet. "She's just a child," someone says. "Just a child."

Her mother appears dreary in her black dress—Remedios really hates that color—and she weeps constantly. She will not talk, will not tell Remedios that everything will be fine.

A hollow feeling roots inside Remedios and sometimes she feels like a conch shell sitting on the writing desk. Other times it seems she is hanging on a thin thread, like the gray spider that swings back and forth from the ceiling. She feels odd, as if waiting for something to happen so all the staring will end, so the strangeness that has invaded her life will disappear.

The next day there is a Mass, then the men carry the coffin to the funeral car, so black and slick. When it starts raining, people scramble for umbrellas or newspapers and they mutter: Ah, a good sign, heaven is weeping. She, Mama and Tiya Meding walk behind the funeral car to the old cemetery with gray crumbling crypts. Some women hold umbrellas over them to keep their heads dry. Remedios trudges along, splashing in puddles, watching the slum children playing in the rain.

At the cemetery, the men pick up the coffin, carry it to the family crypt, and open it. The priest sprinkles holy water inside. Her Mama, who emits wailing sounds and whose shoulders are shaking, bends over to kiss the man inside. Remedios has not looked, but she knows that a man is in there. She had heard people talking: "Looks like he's sleeping, doesn't he? They sure did a good job."

Her Mama turns to her and Remedios walks toward the casket. Tiptoeing, she peers in. The man's face is a waxy mask. He doesn't wear glasses and his tight little smile is a grimace. There is a smell like mothballs. Remedios feels faint. She wants to giggle, but stopping herself, she bends over and plants a kiss on the wax-man's cool cheek.

The men close the coffin and slide it into the crypt with a grating sound. There is a dull thud when the marble slab covers the niche, and briefly, Remedios feels a lurching inside her stomach. She closes her eyes and hears that voice loud and clear: I'll be back in two weeks. I'll bring you our doll and tea set.

When she opens her eyes and sees the mourners crying, for

just a brief moment, she understands that they want her to weep, that they have been waiting for her to cry. But soon she is thinking of dainty tea cups, the smooth feel of delicate china, the clinking sound as the cup hits the saucer. She is seeing her father smiling broadly as she hands him his cup, and they make a toast pretending to sip tea under the cool shade of the lush star apple trees.

THE BLUE-GREEN CHIFFON DRESS

Summer vacation started off badly with my favorite guard dog getting killed. I was heading for the hammock with my *Lady Chatterley's Lover* tucked under my arm, and a plateful of green mangoes and a Coke in my hands when Sultan walked up to me, stiff and hostile. His eyes were giant marbles. I called him and he bared his teeth, growling a little. His mouth was foaming. I ran, sounding an alarm, and the next thing I knew one of the men shot him. I saw him writhing, blood gushing to the cracked brown earth. There was something other than blood that oozed out of his gut. I touched him; he was warm and became very still.

Sultan had been a sickly puppy. The servants had talked about drowning him but I took him under my care. He used to race to the gate when I arrived from school, and he'd jump up to lick my face. His death left me nauseous and sad.

To make me feel better, Mama took me to her couturier, who was famous in Ubec for his expensive high fashion clothes. We caught him peering out of his shop at the American soldiers walking by.

"That one looks like James Bond," he said, pinching my arm enthusiastically. "Oy, love those bushy eyebrows," he cooed with a roll of his eyes.

Eventually, he got around to me, scrutinized me and said I had grown. He sketched a few dress designs and he and Mama discussed the drawings, material and cost while I roamed his shop.

I was studying his ready-made dresses, frowning at the price tags, when a blue-green chiffon dress caught my gaze. The color was stunning, bringing to mind the deepest part of the sea. The soft billowy cloth was draped across the bosom making a deep V-neckline. The skirt was generously gathered and flowed in the same draped effect.

I showed the dress to Mama who said it was too sophisticated for a teenager. The couturier prodded me to try on the dress.

"Go ahead, Gemma," he insisted, and to my mother in an admonishing tone, "This is 1965, we must keep up with the times."

Before entering the fitting room, I glanced at him gratefully, our eyes locking briefly.

The bodice was loose so I stuffed Kleenex to fill it out. It was an enchanting dress and even my mother begrudgingly agreed. The couturier gushed over the blue-green hue.

"It makes your skin glow," he said. "Put your hair up in a French twist. We'll have to take in the tucks at the bust. And please wear a good padded bra," he added.

***

My cousin Yolanda and I went through the definitions of kissing, French kissing, petting, and intercourse again. Our favorite pastime was locking ourselves in the bedroom, slapping on makeup and discussing sex.

"I still don't know exactly how it enters the woman's part," I said.

"Idiota, it just goes in," she replied in exasperation. She had this superior attitude since Tristan danced slow drag with her and became aroused—she said.

When our eyelashes were curved and stiff with mascara, we decided to iron our hair. We had read that it made your hair straighter and shinier. I spread my hair out on the board, warning her not to singe it. She lightly ran the iron over my hair, then I did hers. After, we swished our hair around our shoulders to see a difference.

"Manolette smiled at me at church yesterday," I announced. "He's so sexy, I think I'll make him Number Two.

We proceeded to work on our crush-lists, shuffling the names of the boys in order of their appeal. I demoted Mandy to Number Ten because he had gone out with Mercedes.

"They were necking. Why else do people park in Magellan Hills?" Yolanda said. "No big loss, Mandy has no imagination."

She added that her Number One was Ruy who claimed to have had an out-of-body experience. "At least Ruy has imagination," she insisted. "Who's your Number One?" she asked.

I told her it was Jose Marie, a senior engineering student—5'11", lean, intelligent, much older at twenty-one. I fancied myself IN LOVE with him and got sweaty palms when he danced with me

***

During the summer, Ubec was pleasant. It was not as humid as Manila because the cool sea breeze blew through the ancient acacia and flame trees. There was so much color at that time of year: the sparkling blue sea; the brilliant clear sky; lush hibiscus, begonias and fuchsias; and bountiful fruit—yellow-green custard apples, luscious red mangosteens, succulent pink tambis.

The days flowed with little care. In the evenings, we attended parties or watched stocky Basque players hit the balls at the Jai-a-lai. Sometimes we went to the Sand Trap Club to dance to Amapola's music. There were movies, swimming parties and afternoon gossip sessions. And there was smoke-filled Eddie's Log Cabin, owned by an expatriate New Yorker, where we had greasy American-style hamburgers.

Our routine was disrupted when one of the local girls, Elena, suddenly left for Hong Kong. In minutes, stories about her mysterious departure flew all over Ubec and continued flying for weeks. Her family insisted she needed extensive allergy tests. Gossip mentioned an illegal abortion and the American captain she had been dating.

Ubec's matrons immediately stepped up their campaign against the American soldiers from nearby Mactan Air Force Base. From their mahjong tables, they lectured: "Madre mia, stay away from those soldiers, you'll catch Vietnam Rose. They're trouble. Look what happened to Elena."

I had already heard World War Two stories about American G.I.s spreading V.D., getting girls pregnant, ruining lives forever. We knew a girl who stood 5'9"—a giant to our eyes—with fair hair and skin. She stood out like an aberration beside the rest of us with our small frames, black hair and brown skin. "A G.I. baby," she was called behind her back.

"Stay away from those soldiers," the matrons scolded as they shuffled the ivory pieces.

We, good girls, stayed away.

We watched—from a distance—the dazed, short-cropped strangers wandering around our city. We made up stories: that one was a CIA-agent; that brunet was on R&R; the slight one with a nervous laugh was flying to Vietnam the next day on a bombing mission. We read about Diem, napalm, deforestation, and body counts. We saw photos of Buddhist monks burning in fierce self-immolation. We drove by the Base, saw the runway, tower, barracks, and the numerous planes. Several times a day, we listened to those planes flying overhead. We were scandalized by the shanties, claiming to be bars and massage parlors, which mushroomed all over the place. We clucked our tongues at the girls in tight colorful clothes who hung around with the soldiers.

We watched—from a distance.

***

Eventually, we tired of talking about Elena's disgrace. I resumed my crush-list, with Jose Marie maintaining his Number One place. I was glad he was invited to my cousins's End-of-Summer party. For days I fretted about the affair. I dieted, painted my nails pink, dyed my hair Jet Black with some cheap dye called Bigen that I later heard made some women blind.

On the night of the party, I stared at my blue-green dress as if it were some talisman. It would transform me into an enchantress, a goddess, and Jose Marie would be smitten and ask me to go steady with him. I kissed the back of my hand, imagining his lips on mine.

I tugged at my padded bra and put on the dress. I applied another layer of mascara and reddened my cheeks and lips. Then I slipped on my gold heels and studied myself in the mirror. I smiled, pleased with myself. Ordinarily I appeared average-looking with a pleasant round face—no bones to speak of, no strong facial characteristics that made people say: Oh, what pretty eyes, or, what a lovely mouth. Normally, I was just average. But that night, I actually looked beautiful. I was glad I had saved the dress all summer, for the right moment, for that night.

The party was slow. The band, called "The Magnificent Seven," was off-key and the boys stayed in the patio drinking San Miguels, Rum Cokes and a beer-gin-Coke concoction dubbed Virgin Coke. The girls were huddled in the living room—which served as the dance floor—gossiping about Carla and the two American soldiers with her.

"I didn't want to invite her but her mother and mine are second cousins," Yolanda explained.

"Papa's going to whip me when he hears about this," whined Dolores, whom we called Turtle Face.

"They're just sitting outside, not doing anything," I ventured.

"You will end up like Elena, Gemma," Turtle Face said. She stared at me. "So, that's your new dress by the famous Mario. By the way, where's Jose Marie?"

"He'll be here," I answered smugly, as I fussed with the folds of my skirt.

"I heard he and Mercedes are parked up in Magellan Hills. That Mercedes can probably find her way to those hills blind." Dolores' turtle mouth twisted into a little smile.

In my mind, Jose Marie plummeted from Number One to about Number Twenty. I felt angry and humiliated, and I consoled myself by thinking he would surely go to hell for necking with that cheap Mercedes.

I was forcing a smile, trying to save face, when someone asked me to dance. The band was terrible, no one was dancing, and someone was asking me to make a spectacle of myself. I glared up and caught a flash of red hair and wide grin on an oval face. An American soldier.

The girls stared at us with unhinged mouths. I didn't know what to do so I got up to dance slow drag with the stranger. I thought I heard giggling in the room.

The American said something but the music was too loud. His mouth moved up and down, then he looked at me quizzically. I tapped my right ear and shrugged my shoulders. He tried once more and I heard, "... nice dress." Aside from Yolanda, he was the only person who had said my dress was nice. I smiled and he grinned wider. When the music ended, he walked me to my seat and left.

"What did the Americano say, Gemma? How'd it feel dancing with him?" Dolores asked.

I felt my chest constrict and I shouted, "Do I have to wash my hands so I don't catch anything deadly?" I waved my hands in front of her like a magician. "You are very provincial, do you realize that? Pro-vin-cial!" Then I left.

Outside I took a couple of deep breaths. I walked around the patio, past the boys who were getting drunk, until I found the American with another soldier and Carla.

Carla was wearing red with black net stockings. She worked as a secretary at the Base. We tagged her "fast" because she sported hickeys on her neck and dated American soldiers. It was rumored that she went "all the way." That night her date was Marcus, a good-looking Mexican-American. Peter, who had danced with me, was his friend.

When I joined them, Carla was showing Marcus how to do butterfly kisses. She shoved her face close to Marcus' cheek and batted her eyelashes rapidly. The two boys laughed and I laughed tentatively. They were drinking Virgin Cokes and I started drinking. I was sixteen, Jose Marie and Mercedes were necking, and I could drink if I wanted to. The iced sweet drink flowed down my throat.

I was feeling like a ripe mango when Carla started telling jokes.

"There was this bar called Sally's Legs," she related between giggles, "and one afternoon, a cop stopped a bum outside the bar, 'What are you doing here?' the cop asked. 'Waiting for Sally's Legs to open so I can have a drink.'"

They laughed while I tried to figure out the joke. Carla whispered an explanation in my ear and I laughed hysterically.

"Sally's Legs! I get it—Sally's Legs!"

"You're drunk," Carla said.

"Am I? Am I? I've never been drunk before," I said, still laughing.

But soon I felt depraved. I was drunk, sitting there with American soldiers, laughing at dirty stories. I was truly lost. Trying to look dignified, I sat up, pulled my skirt over my knees and folded my hands together. I studied the white-wrought iron chairs that we sat on, the jasmine vine covered with sweet-smelling flowers that climbed the trellis.

I watched the two soldiers whose arms and legs flopped all over the place. They were nice-looking, with strong bodies and boyish ways. I was surprised to realize that they were only a few years older than I. Still with milk on their lips, my mother would have said. They were talking now, their voices sounding like distant rain.

Peter said, "I'm tired. I just want to go home. First day in 'Nam I see these huge bundles stacked up near the plane and I lean against them. I'm smoking a cigarette like nothing's wrong, then later I find out those were dead bodies."

"Jeez!" exclaimed Marcus.

"No kidding, Marcus. Dead bodies."

"Peter, you've gotta be cool, man, or else you're not gonna make it," Marcus said. "You're feeling shitty 'cause you're going back tomorrow. Gotta be cool, man. Be like the NBC guy standing in front of a pile of gooks saying, 'This is Walter Bullshit reporting from Da Nang.'" He held an imaginary microphone in front of his mouth, as if he had actually seen this happen.

It's the waiting," Peter said. "It's draining. Like we're on a sweep last month and we're being real careful. You know somebody's going to get it and we watch our step carefully. Sweep and sweep, and you're waiting. You're so tight, then Boom! This poor guy beside me loses his leg. Just like that."

I became sad listening to them and my mind latched on to the image of Sultan's body on that dry earth. They could die too, I thought, on some brown earth someplace, far away from their homes.

"For me it's the food, man. Boy, do I miss Mama's carnitas and tamales. I'm sick of that shit they feed us." Marcus ran his tongue around his lips. "One more month, man, and I am through. I'm going home! I'm gonna stuff myself with enchiladas, rellenos, and I'm gonna cruise down Colorado Boulevard and just have a good time, you know."

"One more month, that's great, Marcus," Peter said.

"How much longer do you have to stay in Vietnam?" I asked Peter, when Carla and Marcus went dancing.

"Six months."

He became quiet and I was feeling uneasy because we were alone. But he sighed and sat back to look at the sky. "Back home," he said, "the Big Dipper's over there." He waved his hand vaguely in the air.

I tilted my head and located the Big Dipper, wondering how the constellations could move when one was in another place. A multitude of stars shimmered in the sky; the moon was a mere crescent. A soft breeze was redolent with jasmine, gardenias and dama de noches.

Peter took a deep breath and said very softly, "That feels good." He paused then spoke in a distant voice. "It's real funny, but sometimes, in the middle of nowhere, I'll think of my baseball cards. When I was a kid, I collected baseball cards—Willie Mays, Mickey

Mantle, Ted Williams—I had them all. But I don't remember what happened to them. My mind starts going through the entire house. I'll search my room, my sister's, my parents' room, even the garage. I rummage through all the desks, drawers, and cabinets. It's crazy. I've even written my Mom to ask about those cards."

He sighed, then he turned to me and said, "That's a real pretty dress."

"My friend doesn't like it very much."

I laughed remembering Turtle Face. He grinned and ran his hand through his hair. I had never before seen hair as red as the mangosteen fruit. My apprehension left me and I watched the stars with him. He liked the night and things of the night. These made him feel safe, he explained, in a way that implied he didn't feel safe too often. When we saw a falling star he gave a quick low whistle. "Now I can make a wish," he said.

As he was pointing out Orion's Belt, he put his arm around my shoulders, his fingers brushing my nape. My heart pounded against my ribs, but I didn't move or say anything. He was so close and I could smell him—a strange, musky scent. He was quiet for a while then with his other hand, he turned my head toward him and he kissed me. His mouth was warm and yearning. There was a sadness to his kiss. It made me think of Sultan and how warm he had felt before he became still.

When Carla and Marcus returned, Peter kept his arm around me, but the spell was broken, the magic moment lost.

The next day, I listened to the American planes blasting overhead. Was Peter in one of them? I wondered. Would I ever see him again? I looked at my blue-green chiffon dress lying on a chair—it was magical after all.

Another plane zoomed overhead, making the windows rattle, leaving my soul with strange reverberations. I thought: Summer vacation was over. School would start. The rains would come.

THE DEAD BOY

When I was fourteen, Bill Lowry died. He was murdered one night in Magellan Hills where he and Bebop Villarama were necking. Although Sister Candida made us pray for the repose of his soul, the underlying message to the entire student body was such sinful acts merited that kind of punishment.

I had a serious crush on Bill. Before his father died and before Bill went steady with Bebop Villarama, he used to be an altar boy at Redemptorist Church where I attended many six o'clock Masses just to see him. I used to tingle with embarrassment when I stuck my tongue out to receive the Host. I was sure I appeared retarded and Bill would never love me. Once I caught him studying me in a mischievous way; and he flashed a smile that lit up that church and made me stumble on a pew. I spent all day at school writing "Mrs. William Lowry" on sheets of paper, which I later shredded and disposed of with great care.

Soon after this incident, Bill met Bebop Villarama who was seventeen like him, an "experienced girl" we called her because she reportedly had a passionate affair with a twenty-five-year-old pharmacist when she was only fifteen. Any religious devotion in Bill's heart evaporated the night he saw Bebop Villarama in her red mini-skirt, doing the twist so she looked like a pretzel at Lorna Lardizabal's coming-out party. I hated Bebop Villarama. She had interfered with what I prayed would be a budding romance. I had hoped that after the smiling incident, Bill would talk to me. But what could he have said to me—I see you in church often? Do you know that your neck turns the color of coral when you receive Holy Communion? Not the stuff for romance.

I should have put Bill Lowry out of my mind, but for some reason talk of Bill's and Bebop's Saturday trysts in Magellan Hills only made him more desirable. A Catholic boy gone bad—I was torn between wanting to save him and sharing forbidden pleasures he and Bebop knew.

Bill's family was one of four American families in Ubec. I'd seen him around for as long as I could remember, not only in church, but in movie theaters and local hangouts populated by the young people. I knew, through some kind of osmosis, everything there was to know about the Lowry family. His father was an American logger who fell in love with his laundrywoman, a rather ugly woman who came from the interior of Palawan. He actually married her. They had two children, Linda and Bill, who fortunately favored the father's looks. Mr. Lowry looked like a movie star, tall with red hair and a commanding presence. The Lowry family lived in an enormous sprawling bungalow on a hill overlooking Ubec City. During a rare moment, Mama gossiped that Mr. Lowry surprised them all by not being the heathen protestant they took all Americans to be; he was a devout Catholic who led his family to Sunday Masses. It was he who encouraged Bill to become an altar boy.

The times I saw them at church, I thought they were the perfect family; I had only my widowed mother and an aging German Shepherd who had belonged to my father. I used to daydream that I had a father, a brother, and a lovely airy house like theirs. I daydreamed a lot.

Unfortunately when Bill was fifteen his father died in a car accident near his logging camp. His car plunged down a steep cliff and it had been impossible to disentangle body parts from the metal. The rest of the family unraveled at the seams after the father's death. Before the traditional year of mourning passed, Mrs. Lowry started putting on lots of makeup and dressed in outrageously loud colors, prompting people to refer to her as the "merry widow." People were unkind to her except Mama, who was widowed when I was nine, and who sometimes said grief makes you do strange things. Then she would sigh and gaze away at invisible images that I could not conjure.

Linda, who was a year older than Bill, also got involved in some scandal. It was never clear exactly what happened but a story circulated that their driver raped her and she became pregnant, and her family dispatched her to the States for an abortion. Another version said

Linda became involved with the driver, a version that floated around during many merienda sessions as people sipped their coffee and speculated on how a well-bred girl like Linda Lowry could cavort with someone from the lower class.

While the Lowry women became topics of conversation, Bill himself transformed from the meek somewhat aloof handsome altar boy to the playboy running around with Bebop Villarama. It had gotten to the point where people kept a watchful eye on Bebop's waistline to see if it had thickened somewhat because after all the young couple were spending too much time together, alone, in dark forbidden places. And everyone knew that sort of thing amounted to nothing else than unwanted pregnancies and early marriages.

Bill's murder came right around the time people's tongues itched for something new to wag about. In our small-town minds, his death marked the depth the Lowry family had sunk to.

It was my best friend Mildred who called at seven in the morning. "Have you heard?" she asked.

"What?" I had been rushing through my breakfast.

"About Bill Lowry?"

"What about him?"

"He's dead."

"Dead!" I gasped.

"Shot six times with a rifle. Magellan Hills."

"Dead!" I repeated. Ubec was so small you kept track of births, marriages, and deaths. Either event was Big News. "What happened?" I asked.

"I'll tell you later." She hung up.

I bolted down the rest of my rice and hurriedly told my mother what happened. Making the sign of the cross, she raced to the telephone while I took off for school.

The principal called a school assembly since everyone talked of nothing but the murder and Sister Candida figured she might as well confront the matter and put it to rest. Besides, Linda was a graduate and when Mr. Lowry was alive, he gave hefty donations to the nuns. Voice shaking, the principal announced over the microphone that an unfortunate incident had occurred last night. The brother of our alumna, William Lowry, was killed by an unknown assailant. She urged us to pray for the repose of his soul, then she led prayers for the dead. Some high school girls started sobbing, which I found embarrassing, although I felt like crying myself. We had all fallen in love with Bill at one time or another. Bill was tall, angular with brashy hair the color of some exotic fruit. He could be stand-offish at times, and flirtatious at other times. He bewitched us. When he and Bebop became a twosome, Miriam, who had the most beautiful, sleekest black hair that fell below her waist, cut it to show her sorrow. She even wore dark colors for weeks.

I had laughed at Miriam then, but later I envied her for her gumption. I could never have done anything that dramatic. Perhaps it was because I grew up fatherless, but I preferred being invisible. I never told anyone that I had a crush on Bill. No one. And when Bill himself had been around, I hardly acknowledged his presence. He was too old for me, too out of reach, a demi-god. Even when Mildred told her biggest secret (she had seen Jojo Katigbak's penis when he changed into his trunks at a picnic) I never revealed a thing.

Sister Candida's assembly made no dent on our high emotions. Girls walked around sniveling and crying. They blamed Bebop Villarama for seducing Bill, for dragging him up the hills, for causing his early death. Miriam swore she'd shave off her hair; she said Bebop should have died, not Bill.

Bebop had survived. The way I tailored the shreds of information, this was what happened. After a party, Bill and Bebop had driven to the hills and parked in an area above the Police Constabulary (PC) headquarters. Someone, most likely a PC, crept toward Bill's car to spy on the couple. Catching the peeping tom, Bill called out, startling the man who started shooting. Bill was shot twice in the face and four times in his chest. Bebop managed to scramble out of the car and run all the way down the mountain to civilization.

***

After the initial shock of Bill's murder subsided, a kind of fascination gripped me. Death had always attracted me. Ever since my father's death, I'd ponder on dead animals—dead piglets and puppies—poking at their corpses, wonder how rigor mortis happened. How could they be so still? How could they be so empty? Had their souls (if animals had souls) actually gone to heaven? And what about my father? When he had that heart attack and died as quickly as the snap of a finger, did his spirit hover over his body? And did his soul fly to me to bid me farewell, as I imagined he did? There was much to consider about death.

I wanted to see Bill Lowry for the last time before they buried him. I told Mildred we should go to Everlasting Funeral Home downtown. Usually, corpses were laid out in their coffins at the Redemptorist Church, but Mrs. Lowy chose Everlasting Funeral Home. It was more Americanized, she reportedly said. Everlasting Funeral Home sat across Flower Drum Restaurant which was cheap but was considered the worst restaurant in town. After eating in Flower Drum, you were ready for Everlasting Funeral Home, people said. You weren't supposed to eat meat products at Flower Drum because there was no telling where the meat came from in the first place; it could have come from Everlasting.

Mildred dared me to eat at Flower Drum; I bounced her dare back and she accepted. We sat in a booth and she ordered a Coke and pork bao. I had a Coke and bean cake and we kidded about her pork boa. We were still laughing when we jaywalked in front of jeepneys and cars to Everlasting Funeral Home. Near the enormous double doors, our smiles froze at the sound of organ music and thick scent of dama de noche flowers. The heady sweet smell of the flowers gave me the sensation of being back in time when my own father was laid out in his coffin at the Redemptorist church. I experienced it all over again, that unreal floating feeling as if I were a mechanical doll. Walking down the marble aisle of Everlasting Funeral Home, I counted in my head: one-two-three-four-five. "Five years," I muttered.

"What?" Mildred whispered.

"Nothing," I said, not knowing how to tell her that I'd just realized that my father had been dead for five years.

She looked at me quizzically and shrugged her shoulders. I shrugged mine.

A rhythmic sobbing echoed in the room as we approached Bill's coffin. I glanced at the front row and located the source of the sobbing—Linda Lowry. Her face was drawn and wet from tears. Arms folded across her stomach, she heaved up and down as if struggling to breathe. Beside her sat Mrs. Lowry in absolute silence. She wore a low-cut black mini-dress and three-inch black stiletto heels. Her cheeks and lips were bright red; her hair had been dyed a terrible auburn. She was such a sight, I did not dare greet her.

When I reached Bill's coffin, I was feeling as light and fluttery as an angel. My breathing had turned so shallow, my legs felt like buckling. Bill had a magnificent coffin, bronze in the inside and mahogany on the outside. The idea was that the bronze would protect the body so it would stay intact for many years. My grandmother Filomena's corpse had not decomposed after twenty-five years, proof, my mother declared, of her sainthood. I'd heard stories about dead people growing hair and fingernails even as they lay in their coffins. The worst story was about the priest whose remains showed great distress: his fingernails clung to the coffin's lid. He had been buried alive and upon waking in the coffin, struggled to try and get out. Horror stories like these swarmed in my head, and at that moment, I was greatly relieved that my father had been embalmed; he was definitely dead when we buried him.

The two bullet holes on Bill's face left no doubt about his being irrefutably dead. One on the right cheek and the other closer to the ear. Poor Bill Lowry. Seventeen years old, and except for the bullet holes, resplendent in his dark navy suit. Even with his grotesque little smile, he was handsome. I sighed, remembering that wonderful smile Bill had given me at church. What promise in that smile. You are the prettiest fourteen-year-old, that smile said.

The oppressive feeling lifted when I remembered the times I had written "Mrs. William Lowry" while my mind traveled far, me and Bill honeymooning in Hong Kong, me and Bill in a sparkling house with our six children—three boys, three girls—and two German Shepherds, and one white cat, living happily forever after.

Mildred nudged me. "He looks terrible," she whispered.

I started to shake my head; I had not thought so. But when I studied him again, I agreed that this dead boy really didn't look like Bill. It was a mannequin—stiff, unyielding, expressionless. I could not help crying. Perhaps the contagious sobbing got to me; or perhaps I cried for my shattered fantasies. Maybe I cried for my dead father, or maybe it was for the realization that someday I'd end up in a satin-lined casket with strangers checking me over.

We left in silence, Mildred and I. We took the jeepney home in total gloom. But later, we gossiped about Mrs. Lowry's low-cut black dress, so low you could see her cleavage; and we giggled at Linda Lowry's smeared eye shadow; and we wondered if Miriam did have the nerve to shave her head; and we laughed at how shook-up Bebop was, she was contemplating entering the convent. But he hovered around, this dead boy, as a feeling of incompleteness.

A few weeks after Bill's funeral, when Mildred and I were in the bamboo grove in back of the school, we found a dead baby sparrow. It already had feathers and still felt warm. We could not figure out how it died. Mildred speculated it fell from its nest and starved, but it didn't look emaciated. We finally buried it under some leaves. Even while we stood there, ants started crawling toward this makeshift grave. I felt incredibly sad. I remained silent for a long time, then wanting to say something, I blurted out, "I had a crush on Bill Lowry."

"I know," Mildred said.

"You did?"

She nodded.

I told her how I filled a piece of paper with his name and slipped this under my pillow so he'd dream of me. I also related the smiling incident; and I told her about writing "Mrs. William Lowry" on paper. We giggled over my silly daydreams.

She confessed that she liked Bill too, and we shook our heads like two old women and muttered, too bad, he's dead. We didn't say much else.

THE DIRTY KITCHEN

My favorite room was the outdoor kitchen, which we called the "dirty-kitchen." It was a separate structure in the back of the house, a place with a huge cooking hearth, a place where the servants sat around, talked, and ate.

The main house was huge, Spanish-style, with marble floors, crystal chandeliers, very formal. My mother ruled the main house, and she shouted a lot. The dirty-kitchen felt like another world. The floor was simple cement; the roofing was made of corrugated sheets that threatened to blow off during the typhoon season. It always smelled of fried garlic.

I enjoyed my visits there. Sometimes the driver would play the guitar, sad songs full of longing for home or a loved-one. The servants liked to discuss the "Big Dance," an outdoor affair open to the public, which was held across the river. Friday nights I'd hear the loud music coming from the "Big Dance." They also talked about the Amateur Hour, a talent show open to the public, which was held at the Fuente Osmeña.

Every night, they switched on the transistor radio to listen to the evening soap operas. Sitting on the wooden bench, legs swinging, I got lost in the dramatic stories that involved infidelity, out-of-wedlock children, lost loves, every twist and turn in the human drama that one could imagine.

I listened until it was time to return to the main house for supper. Before opening the door to the main house, I often took a deep breath to brace myself.

FLYING A KITE

One summer day, many years ago, my brother did the finishing touches on the kite that we made. It was diamond-shaped, and bright yellow, with an impressive long tail. Assuming my father's tone, he said, "Tomorrow, we'll launch it."

I nodded. I was ten, perhaps too old to be flying kites, but this kite was a debt due me. Every summer, for as long as I could remember, my father made a kite and flew it with us kids—my brother, my two older sisters, and me. But the October of my ninth birthday, he died suddenly of a heart attack. Our household was thrown into chaos and gloom. After the required period of mourning, my brother and older sisters returned to Manila to resume their schooling. I remained in Cebu with my grieving mother in a dark, dark house.

Death was a mystery. Despite the rituals and prayers for the dead, in the back of my mind was the feeling that someday my father would return, and life would be normal again. It got me up in the morning, and made me do my homework and face the serious Belgian nuns who strove hard to mold our minds and spirits.

Six months after my father died, I looked out and saw that the leaves had turned brown and the earth was parched. It was summer, and I stared up at the bright blue sky and had a vision of my father leading his children to the backyard. I, the youngest, held the kite and released it into the air. When the wind caught the kite, the string grew taut, and the kite snapped up and sailed into the sky, above our house, above our street, above all of us.

I felt a sharp twinge inside when I realized my father would not be there to fly a kite with us. Soon after that, I had my first flying dream; and in my dream I was like a kite, hovering above the world.

By this time, my mother had ended her silent grief and started screaming at the servants. When my older siblings returned home for their summer vacation, my mother took to relentlessly nagging them. I stayed out of her way, filling my time by reading. I used to climb our star apple tree and I would wedge myself in the branches and read for hours. I also took walks to the nearby cornfield where I would pull out the silk from the young corn.

Around this time, I caught my brother talking to my mother, saying I had turned into a silent and invisible child. He was only eighteen but had the authority of a grown man. He took me to Alemar's bookstore and bought me all the Nancy Drew books that I wanted. One day, he bought balsa wood and thin construction paper, which we called Japanese paper, and he started building a kite. He asked for my help; and the two of us whittled and cut and pasted until we created a diamond-shaped kite much like the kite Papa used to build.

Before summer ended, he and I went to the backyard, and he held the wound-up string, while I hung on to the kite. I walked a distance away from him and positioned the kite in front of me. When a breeze stirred, my brother told me to release the kite. I did, and that wonderful kite snapped up and soared above us, above our house, far above our sorrow.

THE ARTIST

Tell me who the artist is, please," Gertrudes begged. She and Santi were studying a mural on Santi's living room wall. It was a famous image of Colon Street, the oldest street in Ubec. The mural occupied the entire wall with two supporting logs cleverly imbedded on either side so you felt you were looking out onto a quaint street with Spanish colonial houses. The picture tugged at her soul—the graceful street curved down the middle so your eyes were drawn into the picture. Two-story stone and wood houses unique to the era, called bahay na bato (stone houses), stood on either side of the street. The houses on the right side had awnings made of red tile, and there were shops under the awnings. A dog lay on the sidewalk scratching itself and two horse drawn carriages stood frozen in their timeless journey. It was an image from the past—and the thought of her ancestors walking along Colon Street enthralled Gertrudes.

"Like it?" Santi ran his hand over his five-o'clock shadow and smiled. Even though he shaved meticulously, he couldn't get rid of the dark fuzz, which he called a curse from his Castillan forebears. "I am a living remnant of Spanish colonial days," he liked to say.

"I love it, Santi. I promise I won't have a mural made. A mural is too big … too bold for me. Only *you* can get away with murals. Just a painting. A small one. Is he expensive?"

"But darling Gertrudes, I want this masterpiece to be unique. I don't want duplicates. I had this made deliberately so the mural is married to the house—coupled—note 'coupled' darling—as in forever. No one can ever take it away. I love this house. I can't get enough of the history, the drama that had taken place here." Santi stretched out his right hand and caressed a wall. "Imagine what this wall has seen and heard—truths, lies, babies' cries, lovers' promises, husbands' and wives' lovemaking, quarreling—everything." He swept his arms and glanced at his huge living room that had had carved antiques, Venetian mirrors, and the enormous mural.

Santi was doing an excellent job coaxing his house back to its seventeenth century colonial glory. When Gertrudes had first seen it a year ago, Santi's house had been gloomy and dirty but now the large rooms had been freshly painted and tastefully accented with expensive antiques. And now here was this dramatic mural. There was nothing muted about Santi. Gertrudes, who was on a limited budget and who considered herself conservative, decorated her house with few pieces of antique furniture and mirrors; she painted the exterior and interior of her house stark white. Everything was subdued, nondescript. When Santi first toured Gertrudes' house, he wrinkled his nose and said, "Too bland. Remember, Gertrudes, the people who lived here were wealthy. They washed gold and silver coins and spread them on the rooftops to dry. There was galleon trading here and this place was the hub of commerce. Goods from Asia and from Europe ended up here. Darling, do be a bit more eclectic and extravagant with your décor."

Santi had inherited his house from his father, just as Gertrudes had inherited her grandmother's bahay na bato. She loved her old stone house; she truly did. She had no regrets selling her Makati house to move here; in fact it had been a relief to let the Makati house go. She felt she was severing all ties with her husband with whom she had been separated for ten years. He had left her three years after she was diagnosed as infertile. When he eventually moved-in with a woman, Gertrudes didn't put up a fuss. Fortunately he gave her their Makati house and some solid stocks and bonds. But living in the Makati house always reminded her of him and her failure to bear him a child. In her grandmother's house however, Gertrudes felt unencumbered, free to sleep late if she wished, to garden the afternoon away if that was what she wanted to do.

She was also a history buff who knew her district's background. Called the Parian, it had its beginnings in the 1590s, thirty years after Legazpi founded the Spanish settlement in Ubec. Galleon trading encouraged Chinese traders to build combination houses-warehouses in a section adjacent to the cathedral and Spanish Fort. This was the Parian, which became a thriving community of wealthy Chinese mestizos. The place declined in the seventeenth and eighteenth century, but had another boom in the 1900s during the time of American occupation. It remained a high-rent district until World War II, when the retreating USAFFE bombed the city. After the war, most wealthy families of the Parian District moved inward to modern subdivisions, abandoning Parian to turn slummy. A handful of old families continued to stay in Parian and they did their best to maintain their ancestral homes. Gertrudes wanted to be like them—preserving Ubecan history, gentrifying an area that was the heart of Ubec; the Cathedral, Basilica of Santo Niño, Magellan's Cross, and Fort San Pedro were walking distance from her house.

"Santi, look at it this way, the painting will be another link between us: two writers with houses in the Parian, with paintings of what their houses looked like over a hundred years ago." Gertrudes was a novelist. She and Santi had become good friends after Santi had written about her in his newspaper column; she knew Santi admired her work.

Santi lifted an eyebrow. "Mural, darling, I have a mural not just a painting. I didn't realize you're a romantic after all. Come to think of it your early books had romance in them. Although, I must admit, and don't get angry darling, your recent ones have been depressingly sad with a strong dash of bitterness. What was the recent one? Something about a woman abandoned by her husband for a younger woman, and she seeks solace with some babaylanes in the foothills of Mt. Banahaw where she finds healing, except the end is quite sad because she discovers she has cancer and will die."

Her face flushed. "The book got decent reviews," she muttered.

"Now let's see the one before that was about a woman whose husband was in a plane crash and his body was never recovered so the woman spent years looking for him because she was convinced he was still alive, and meantime she passed up an English anthropologist who was madly in love with her.

She felt a surge of anger but controlled herself. There was truth to what he had said. She sighed. "Is it that obvious? All that fiction really isn't that fictional is it? We hide behind the lives of our characters, and our characters come right out and reveal our own lives."

"Forgive my sharp tongue, darling. I make more enemies because of my bluntness. I didn't mean to offend you—not you, darling Gertrudes. If it's any consolation, despite your depressing stories, for a woman your age, your skin is great, your figure not bad, if you would only smile and perk up and dress with some verve, you'd still be very attractive."

"Thanks, Santi. Your kind words overwhelm me. But you're not very generous about this artist. Are you hiding him all for yourself?"

"Oh, darling, forgive me." Santi hugged Gertrudes. After releasing her, he stage-whispered, "He's a foreigner, darling. I'm helping him, poor dear. I just found a beach cottage for him to rent. He's still feeling his way around."

"So why don't you give me his name, this way he'll have another job."

"I'm just not sure I want a duplicate of my mural. It'll lower the value."

"Santi, no mural, I promise. A painting. A small one."

"Let me light a candle to the Santo Niño and pray on it, darling. I'll let you know."

***

Her grandmother had been a lifelong devotee to the Santo Niño and she used to tell Gertrudes numerous stories about the venerated statue. The Santo Niño was a replica of the Infant of Prague that Ferdinand Magellan and the Spanish conquistadores had brought in 1521 and had given to the natives during Christianization. Magellan was killed; the Spaniards were driven out by local chieftains, but the Spaniards returned in 1565 under the leadership of Legaspi. When the native people saw that the Spaniards had returned, they burned their town and fled. The Spaniards found the statue of the Child Jesus under smoldering embers; it was intact, and ever since, the statue was said to have miraculous powers. Scholars claimed that the pre-Spanish native people had taken care of the statue because it gave them rain during dry seasons. What they reportedly did was bathe the statue, and rain followed.

On first Fridays, her grandmother used to visit the Santo Niño church; she'd get down on her knees and move down the long aisle to the altar. She sometimes danced a prayer to the Santo Niño. Her prayers were for Gertrudes' mother who had died of cancer when

Gertrudes had been three. Gertrudes had no memory of her although she had seen pictures showing her mother as young, good-looking, and healthy. Those pictures remained; but the images that hinted of her illness had been destroyed. Even the father of Gertrudes said little about her, so that in time, her mother became some kind of fictive character, someone beautiful, someone perfect, an angel distant from her.

***

One afternoon, Gertrudes took a walk to the Basilica of Santo Niño. From kindergarten on, she attended convent schools. The nuns had taught her religious rituals and prayers, but despite all that, she never felt religious. True, she had prayed to God during stressful times, in particular, during the frantic years when she tried to get pregnant. God had denied her that, and for years Gertrudes had been irritated with Him. She had even developed a suspicion that perhaps there was no God, this despite the fact that she continued to do the Catholic rituals—Mass on Sundays and holidays; it was mostly cultural, she decided.

Now, she found herself inside the baroque Basilica, staring at the ornate altar, chandeliers, and statues. She headed toward the statue of the Santo Niño in a separate side altar. A long line of people waited to venerate it. She stood at the end of the line and watched the people's faces rapt in prayer. She was enchanted to see worshippers enter the church and wave at the statue, as if to say hello; and some of those leaving waved goodbye at the statue. How childlike, how sweet, she thought, to wave as if to a real person, to a friend.

When she was nearing the front of the line, she felt self-conscious and wanted to leave. It had been years since she had done this sort of thing, but she forced herself to approach the statue. She observed how small it was, not longer than her arm, and she noticed its endearing smile. How interesting, she thought, a God-Child. Nothing big, nor complicated, nor fierce—just a sweet smiling Child. People dumped all their problems on this Child, and they loved Him like a friend. She prayed: My grandmother loved you. She prayed to you for my mother whom I never knew. Have mercy on both my mother and grandmother. Have mercy also on my father and on me."

When she left the church, she found herself humming the

Latin hymn: "Tantum Ergo, sacramentuum," the long-buried words flowing as if the nuns had just taught her the song.

She decided to walk to Fort San Pedro, to check out the current exhibit of galleon treasures. It was late afternoon and the fierce heat of Ubec had dissipated and a nice sea breeze blew. She liked this small triangular fort which had undergone numerous transformations since Spanish times. Under the American regime, it had been the American barracks; and in the 1960s, a zoo. Now, it was a small museum that focused on Ubec's history. The exhibit showed Chinese plates and jars and other artifacts covered with barnacles. There were dioramas and pictures of Spanish galleons.

As she went from one room to the next, she noticed a young man, a European she guessed, who was also studying the artifacts. He was tall and lean with auburn hair; he was very intent in reading all the signs and handouts.

Near the exit Gertrudes overheard him asking the curator, "Can you tell me there the statue of Pigafetta is?"

The curator pointed east. "Not too many visitors are interested in Pigafetta. May I ask why you are interested?"

"I am Italian," the visitor said. "I know Pigafetta travelled with Magellan and chronicled their journey. Who built the statue?" the young man asked.

"An Italian Filipino group," the curator replied.

Gertrudes watched the young man walk to the east side of the fort, and from a distance, she saw him taking pictures of the looming bronze statue of Pigafetta. How interesting, she thought, that foreigners would know more and have a better appreciation of her own country. She was well aware that many Filipinos hoped to get a visa to escape the Philippines for other countries with better job opportunities.

***

After seeing the movie about the Mexican artist Frieda Kahlo, Gertrudes felt the urge to paint the walls of her house with vivid colors: yellow, red, and green. She mentioned this to Santi who said the colors were too primary and too Mexican. "What's wrong with that? Our connection was Spain was via Mexico. There was the Acapulco trade for over 300 years," Gertrudes countered, "Wouldn't some of the

Mexican culture have ended up here? They gave us chile and avocados; we gave them mangoes. Wouldn't it have been possible that they gave us yellow, and red, and green walls?"

Santi relented, "Do what you want, darling. I have to agree that your white walls are boring beyond belief. I'll give you the name of a housepainter. And speaking of painters, I was in the Basilica the other day and the Santo Niño told me to give you the artist's name and cell number. Don't look so surprised, it's true, I prayed and this voice said, 'Give her what she asked for.' Seriously, darling, He did. So, I'll give you his contact information, but in return you must promise to attend the fashion show at the Casino."

Gertrudes groaned—fashion shows were not her thing.

"Now, darling, it's not that bad. It'll be great. Everybody who's anybody will be there. Ubec's high society. The consular people, our billionaires, our top models. You must attend."

Gertrudes sighed, "Fine, just give me the artist's name."

***

Carlo was his name. Gertrudes phoned to ask if he could make a painting of old Colon Street, and that same afternoon, he was at her place. To her surprise, he was the same young man she had seen at Fort San Pedro. He too recognized her. "Did you enjoy the exhibit?" he asked.

"I did. It's small and simple, but it had heart," she replied.

"I thought it was fantastic. One day, I'll make a painting of the Fort and of the statue of Pigafetta," he said. "Imagine a crazy Italian had already been here many years ago."

They laughed. They were in the upstairs patio which had huge potted ferns and heliconias, dripping with red birdlike flowers. They were sipping jasmine tea in translucent white cups. Usually Gertrudes was shy and stand-offish, but now she felt curious about Carlo. "What are you doing here in Ubec, Carlo? It's a long way from Italy."

"I came for the diving. I'd heard that Ubec has the best diving spots in the world. Then I fell in love with the place. So here I am. I paint to pay for my rent, food, my motorcycle, what I need. I enjoy painting your historic sites, your old churches and buildings. I like painting the Filipina woman—the woman bathing in the river, the women dancing in front of the church. You—you would be an interesting subject." He stared at her, and embarrassed, Gertrudes changed the topic, "And your family? Where are they? Do you not miss them?"

"My father is in Siena. Have you heard of it? That's where I was born and raised. It's a small medieval place. Centuries ago, it was a wealthy place, but after the Black Death, it declined. My mother is dead. My father and I do not get along. We are very different. Well … that's not all true, because we are both painters. He taught me how to paint. But he does modern art. I am not fond of dots and splotches of paint on canvas. I like to capture images on canvas—interesting images."

"I like your mural at Santi's place," Gertrudes said.

"It took forever to finish," he replied. "Now he wants his portrait." He was still studying her.

"I'd like one, no I don't want a portrait, nor a mural … I'm going to have the living room painted yellow and I want a painting over there, on that wall, just a small one, nothing big, nor elaborate. I promised Santi."

His eyes glossed over her hair, her eyebrows, her chin, her mouth. It was disconcerting; she felt self-conscious. She paused, searching for words, then suddenly he laughed, eyes sparkling, and threw his head back tossing his hair as he did so. "Ah, now I know. I was wondering where I'd seen your face. It was a picture in the paper. Santi had written about you."

"In his column, yes, about my work," she said.

"Yes, you are a writer. What do you write?" he asked.

"Stories, I make up stories," she replied.

"Writing is another form of art. My mother wrote poetry. My father has her notebooks. I tried to read them once, but I am not fond of flowery words—raindrops, moon, stars, sunsets …" He paused, before continuing, "I'm sorry, remembering my mother makes me sad. She died shortly before I came here. Where do you want to hang the painting?"

Gertrudes pointed out the dining room wall.

"Thirty by forty inches should do. The canvas comes in standard sizes. Thirty by forty is a good size for this space."

"How big is that?" she asked.

"Thirty by forty inches?"

"I have this spatial problem, I can't imagine size, volume. Is it as big as the dining room table?" She pointed at her dining room table in the adjoining room.

He looked amused when he walked to her dining table. She noticed how tall and lean he was, how easy his manner of movement. "Let me show you," he said, and showed her it was two-thirds of her dining table.

She gasped. "Santi will kill me. That's too big."

"It won't look nice if the canvas is small."

"And what is the price?"

"The gallery sells my large paintings for 40,000 pesos."

She took a deep breath.

"I'll do it for 20,000, with a nice frame."

"Let me think about it. My budget is limited."

By this time, he was standing in front of her book case, studying her books. "I'd like copies of your books. I need reading material. There is nothing to do at the beach house. I do not have TV. I'll do a partial trade. Fifteen thousand plus signed copies of your books."

She was flustered, flattered, that someone would think her books were worth that much. "That would be fine, I guess."

She gave him 10,000 pesos advance payment and the signed first editions he wanted. They agreed the work would be done in a month's time.

***

When the housepainter finished painting her walls, Gertrudes loved the vivid colors. She felt energized by them. The rooms took on separate personalities; the yellow room was cheerful; the red room was lively, intense; the green room felt hopeful. She invited Santi over for bibingka and chocolate-e so he could see the paint job. He surveyed the rooms, stared at walls and muttered, "Bold … but it's all right, at least this has life, personality. And Carlo's painting, where are you going to hang it?"

She pointed to the dining room wall.

"Your wall is crayola yellow, darling. Don't you think your painting will be swallowed up by all that yellowness?"

"Carlo said he'll hang it. Carlo will know what to do."

"Carlo-this, Carlo-that, hmmm, I seem to be hearing a lot

about him from you, darling. It seems to me that you and I can form a Carlo Fan Club."

"He's an artist, Santi, whom I commissioned to make a painting."

"The next thing I know you'll commission him to make a mural here, so he'll hang around here forever."

"Like you're having him do your portrait, so he can hang around your house forever?"

"He's not sure he'll have the time to do it. The gallery's selling his work like hotcakes." Santi paused. His mood suddenly shifted.

"What's wrong?" Gertrudes asked.

Santi weighed his words before saying, "We exchanged words."

"You and Carlo? What happened?"

"Last Sunday I stopped by his place to bring him something. There was a young woman there—sassy, not pretty at all, but well-built. She asked me about my family background, and when she found out about my Spanish blood, went on about how my family had taken part in subjugating the Filipinos. Her exact word—subjugating. I asked what she was doing for Filipinos, and she said she was an artist who was documenting the sufferings of the Filipino people. I said, 'Bullshit!' And she said, 'Bullshit' back to me. And while all this was going on, Carlo did nothing. He just sat there, reading a book—your book, by the way."

"Your verbal exchange was with the woman, then."

"But he didn't do anything."

"What did you expect Carlo to do? Defend you?"

"She shouldn't have been there in the first place."

"Why not? Why shouldn't he have friends?"

"She was a slut, Gertrudes. I wanted to scratch her eyes out."

"That's not very rational, Santi. Did you apologize?"

"Of course not! I told her what I told you, that she's a little slut."

Gertrudes groaned. "Oh, Santi."

"Oh, you should have her seen her smug little face; I wanted to scratch her face. But I left in good terms with Carlo. He promised to go to the fashion show. And you are going too, aren't you?"

"I'll try, Santi. I'm not crazy about those high-society socials."

"Darling, I'm one of the organizers. You must be there."

***

Carlo and his male friend delivered the painting. The friend held the painting while Carlo directed him, "Two inches from the top, center it, a little to the right …"

Carlo turned to Gertrudes for her approval but she shrugged her shoulders and gave a helpless look. "Gertrudes has a spatial problem," he explained to his friend, with a half-smile. "It's a good thing she's a writer because she'd have a heck of time being a painter."

Gertrudes laughed with them, although she felt her face flush. Changing the topic, Gertrudes asked, "The wall isn't too yellow? Santi said the yellow would swallow up the painting."

"The yellow makes a nice background. Your husband will like it." Carlo looked at her, waiting for her response.

Embarrassed Gertrudes lowered her eyes. "He's not going to see this."

"Why not?"

"He's in Manila."

"That's too bad. He would like it," Carlo said. "Santi talked about a fashion show. Will you be there?"

"I promised him. He's one of the organizers."

"I'll see you there, then," Carlo said, before leaving.

***

When her marriage had been falling apart, Gertrudes had a dream, one that continued to pop up now and then even after her husband had left her. She finds herself in a dark and gloomy warehouse. It's pitch black, impossible to see a thing, and she wanders around the huge place, bumping into things; she can't find her way out. She had the warehouse dream again, but just as she started to feel afraid, two huge doors swung open and bright light and sparkling fresh air spilled into the warehouse. Looking around the warehouse, she discovered it was quite harmless; it had some of the furniture from the various homes she'd lived in, the walls were white; everything was well … bland … nothing frightening there at all, but what caught her attention was the brilliant light outside. Its brilliance was irresistible, demanding; it beckoned her. Like a sleepwalker, she stepped out and—

to her delight—found an incredibly beautiful garden filled with chrysanthemums, roses, daisies, orchids, gardenias, hibiscus, and many other colorful plants. It was a vibrant and cheerful image, one that lingered with her when she woke up.

She surprised herself when she started fussing about what to wear to the fashion show. Ordinarily, Gertrudes avoided such Ubec socials, preferring the company of writers, artists and academics. If she had to attend, she threw on any old thing, a black pantsuit perhaps. But now, she scoured her wardrobe. A long dress—no too frumpy; pants—no too old. In the end, she decided to go shopping. She selected a classic black silk dress, with a low cut neckline to show off her South Sea pearl necklace, which had belonged to her mother. The dress fit perfectly, hugging her body in the right way, showing off a bit of cleavage. She squirted some perfume at the base of her throat and put a bit of makeup on, and she wondered if Carlo's artist eyes would notice the foundation and powder that tried to hide her age, cover the lines of disappointments and weariness. And all this time she knew she was behaving foolishly—like some desperate woman, that was how she was behaving, some lonely old woman. The Manilans had a term for someone like herself: nag-mumurang kamatis—an ageing tomato—a woman, once beautiful, but past her prime. But a recklessness possessed her as she fixed herself that night.

***

One of the founders of the Casino Español had been Santi's great-grandfather. The Casino was an exclusive club that had served as a watering hole for the Spanish families in Ubec. Architecture, décor, food and activities tried to recapture an old world effect. It even had a smoking room with plantation chairs, just like colonial days. As time went on the Casino Español welcomed non-Spanish members, as long as they could afford their steep fees. In short it became a place where Ubec's high society and social climbers gathered.

Indeed everyone who was anyone was there: the old families, the new-rich, the young and beautiful, the middle-aged and wealthy. Gertrudes found Santi running around breathless, greeting guests and attending to the slender models who complained about the dim stage lights. He was arguing with a technician about the spotlights. "Do your best!" he shouted at the flustered technician, before turning his attention to Gertrudes. He paused when he saw her. "You look smashing, darling! Black—usually, I detest black, it's just too dreary and too safe, but you look … what is the word? … mysterious!" He led her to a table where Carlo sat. "I'll join you two as soon as I can. Gertrudes, darling, you must protect Carlo from all the predators around," Santi raced off, barking orders to the technicians and waiters.

"I will tell you a story," Carlo said after greeting her with a kiss on the cheek.

"And what is the story?" Gertrudes asked as she settled into her chair.

"First let me get you some wine. I hear they carry good Spanish wine here."

Gertrudes watched him make his way to the bar. He had a white suit on, an outfit that would have looked pretentious on someone else, but on Carlo, it was dazzling. Some art students and models flirted with him. The wife of the American Consul greeted Carlo with a kiss on the check. Gertrudes caught snatches of their conversation: "I saw your paintings at the gallery … they're beautiful … what are you working on now? … we were just in Siena, how we loved the plaza … the view of the Palozzo Pubblico and Torre del Mangia is breathtaking … we have pictures, stop by sometime …"

When he returned, he had a glass of white wine for Gertrudes. "I'm sorry it took so long," he said, "everyone has something to say. All very important, you understand, it can't wait." He laughed. "By the way, you look stunning."

Gertrudes waved her hand and said, "That is what we writers call a cliché."

"Is it still a cliché if it's true?

"Writers try to use other words, fresh words to say the same thing."

"I am not sure what to say—you are magnificent. Your skin against that black, your hair, everything," Carlo continued.

She smiled. "And you look nice yourself, Carlo. And you're famous, Carlo," Gertrudes teased him.

"*You* are famous," he countered.

"But nobody knows me here."

"Perhaps they do not read," he replied, and at this they both laughed.

"The story—you have a story to tell me," Gertrudes said.

"Ah, so you are curious about my story. I should keep you in suspense so I have you in the palm of my hand."

"Is that what you want, Carlo? To have people in the palm of your hand?"

"Not all, just you," he said with a smile. "Here, let me tell you the story. It is not much of a story, just a memory that came to me when I first saw you this evening. When I was a boy in Siena, there was a young widow, named Irena, very beautiful, always in black. All the boys were in love with Irena. I was madly in love with her. You could say she was my first love. I spent many nights dreaming about her, you know, those painful yearnings of a young boy. You remind me of her," he said.

Gertrudes didn't know how to respond to this kind of conversation. She had never flirted with men; and after her husband left her, she became more distant when it came to men. She never gave men the chance to talk to her about her good looks or to ask her out. She was grateful when the lights in the room dimmed for the fashion show to begin. The models appeared wearing designer clothes that were too short, too tight, or had too many ruffles. After a while the models and clothes started to run together and Gertrudes stifled a yawn and was embarrassed to see that Carlo had caught her. He smiled and continued watching her. She could feel his eyes on her. It was not an unpleasant feeling; it felt as if some energy was exchanged between them. When she met his eyes, he would smile and turn away; but after a brief moment his eyes would be riveted on her once more. Finally she tapped his hand and whispered jokingly, "Don't do that. Stop staring at me. Watch the show."

"I'm sorry. I can't help myself. I want to paint you. I enjoy looking at you, every bit of you. I am thinking of the colors to mix, to capture you, to make you mine. You are incredible. You are the most beautiful woman I have ever seen. More beautiful than the widow Irena. But you two have the shadow of some tragedy in your faces; that is what you share with her, but you are far more beautiful." His eyes scanned her face once again.

She blushed, uncertain about how to handle this matter. It was the writer thing, she decided. Sometimes people fell in love with the writer, not the person. Perhaps this young man has fallen in love with the idea of me, she concluded. And now what was she going to do with a lovesick Italian? she wondered. How young he was, she thought, young enough to be her son, if she had had a child. And remembering once again her childlessness made her pensive and quiet. She watched the models come and go; the fashion show was interminable. She could feel Carlo watching her all this time and mid-way, he said, "You are bored with all this. Neither do I like this. I prefer the ethnic events—fiestas, parades, authentic Ubec—not this pseudo-Western charade. I'm going to the Waterfront. There's an exhibit there. It includes my work. Would you like to go? I have paintings of churches. I've done all the churches of Ubec. Someone wanted to buy them but I didn't sell them because I wanted to exhibit them. After the exhibit the gallery will sell them all. Come see them with me. You have become sad here. I want to see you laugh. I want to see you happy. Come with me." He rested his hand on her, and she could feel its warmth. She felt the urge to turn his hand over to see if he had calluses. And she wanted to touch his arm, his hair, stroke his face. She bit her lower lip—it had been a long time of aloneness, a long time in the darkness of the warehouse.

"Will you come to the exhibit, so you can see my work? After, we go to my place. I have a bottle of good French wine; we can talk." It was he who turned her palm upward, and then he bent down to kiss it, his warm breath lingering on her skin. "Come with me," he urged.

To avoid his eyes, she looked down at the marble floor, and briefly studied its pattern.

"I'd like you to come with me, please."

She wondered what harm there would be in going to the exhibit. There was nothing wrong with that. The Waterfront was a public place. And sipping a bottle of good French wine sounded good; she did that with Santi sometimes. The problem was she understood what Carlo wanted, and she was old enough to realize that it was what she wanted too. She saw the yearning in his face. What a beautiful, promising young man he was, right at the threshold of his life. And in a sense she too was at the threshold of a new life, a beginning, even though she was no longer young. She would go. She could go. But what she finally said was, "I would love to see your paintings, but I'm sorry, I can't. Santi'll be looking for me."

A shadow flitted across his face, but soon he gave that charming laughter of his and kissed her goodbye on the cheek, and the moment of decision ended right there.

***

It was Santi and Gertrudes who drank a bottle of French wine at her place. Seated on plantation chairs with their feet up, they stared at Carlo's painting of Old Colon Street. "Carlo probably went to his little girlfriend," Santi said glumly.

"He said he was going to the Waterfront. There's an art exhibit there," Gertrudes said.

"He does not always tell the truth, Gertrudes," Santi said softly, in a measured way.

"He said his paintings are there."

Santi brightened, "That is true; his paintings are displayed there." Santi closed his eyes and tilted his head back so Gertrudes could see his profile. He looked very sad and tired; his voice sounded hollow. "I have not told you everything. You do not have to know everything. I've helped him; I've done everything I can for him. You see I have always seen his raw talent, his possibilities. He appeared here in Ubec like a magician. So beautiful, you know, like a magnet, drawing men and women to him. Do you know that he has broken many hearts?" Santi sighed. "For some reason, it's important for Carlo to be loved. And he has the ability of turning himself into whatever it is people want him to be. They all fall for him, you know, all of them, wives of important men included, all behaving foolishly."

Gertrudes swirled her glass of wine and stared deep into the redness of the liquid. Smiling, she nodded in agreement to what Santi said.

FLIP GOTHIC

DEAR MAMA,

Thank you for agreeing to have Mindy. Jun and I just don't know what to do with her. I'm afraid if we don't intervene, matters will get worse. Mia, her Japanese American friend, had to be sent to a drug rehab place. You'd met her when you were here; she's the tiny girl who got into piercing; she had a nose ring, a belly ring—and something in her tongue. Her parents are distraught; they don't know what they've done, if they're to blame for Mia's problem. I talked to Mia's Mom yesterday and Mia's doing all right; she's writing angry poetry but is getting over the drug thing, thank God.

There's so much anger in these kids, I can't figure it out. They have everything—all the toys, clothes, computer games, and whatever else they've wanted. I didn't have half the things these kids have; and Jun and I had to start from scratch in this country—you know that. That studio we had near the hospital was really tiny and I had to do secretarial work while Jun completed his residency. Everything we own—this house, our cars, our vacation house in Connecticut—we've had to slave for. I don't understand it; these kids have everything served to them on a silver platter and they're angry.

We're sure Mindy's not into drugs—she may have tried marijuana, but not the really bad stuff. We're worried though that she might eventually experiment with that sort of thing. If she continues running around with these kids, it's bound to happen. What made us decide to send her there was this business of not going to school. Despite everything, Mindy had always been a good student, but this school year, things went haywire. This was what alerted us, actually, when the principal told us she hadn't been to school for two weeks. We thought the worst but it turned out she and her friends had been hanging out at Barnes and Noble. It's just a bookstore; it's not a bad place, but obviously she should have gone to school. We had to do something. Sending her to the Philippines was all I could think of.

She'll be arriving Ubec on Wednesday, 10:45 a.m. on PAL Flight 101. Ma, don't be shocked, but her hair is purple. Jun has been trying to convince her to dye her hair black, for your sake at least, but Mindy doesn't even listen. Jun has had a particularly difficult time dealing with the situation. It's not easy for him to watch his daughter "go down the drain," as he calls it. He feels he has failed not only as a father but as a doctor.

It's true that it's become impossible to reason with Mindy, but I've told him to let the hair go, to pick his battles so to speak. But he gets terribly frustrated. He can't stand the purple hair; he can't stand the black lipstick—yes, she uses black lipstick—and the black clothes and boots and metal. I've explained to him that it's just a fad. Gothic, they call it. I personally think it looks dreadful. I can't stand the spikes around her neck; but there are more important things, like school or her health. She's just gotten over not-eating. That was another thing her friends got into—not eating. Why eat dead cows? Mindy would say. She was into tofu and other strange looking things. For months, she wasn't eating and had gotten very thin, we finally had to bring her to a doctor (very humbling for Jun). The doctor suggested a therapist. One hundred seventy-five dollars an hour. She had several sessions then Mindy got bored and started eating once again. She's back to her usual weight, but well, the hair and clothing might scare you, so I'm writing ahead of time to prepare you.

Thanks once again, Ma, for everything, and I hope and pray that she doesn't give you the kind of trouble she's been giving us.

Your daughter,

Nelia

***

Dear Nelia,

She had blue hair, not purple. Arminda explained that she had gone out with her friends and found blue dye—obviously you were unaware of this. She brought several boxes of the dye, including bottles of peroxide. Can you just imagine—peroxide—what if the bottles broke in her suitcase? Apparently, she has to remove color from her hair before dying it blue. The whole process sounds terribly violent on the hair, but I didn't say anything; I didn't want to start off on the wrong foot.

Arminda arrived an hour late—PAL, you know how that airline is. She was not wearing boots; she had left them in New York, she explained, and was wearing white platform shoes instead. It's an understatement to say that operations at Ubec Airport came to a halt when people caught sight of her. People around here like to say Ubec is now so cosmopolitan, with our five-star hotels, our discos and our share of Japanese tourists, but it will always retain its provincial qualities. When I saw Arminda—blue hair, black clothes, sling bag, platform shoes—I was not sure Ubec is ready for Arminda. I had to remind myself that I survived World War Two and therefore will survive Arminda.

Indeed she is rebellious. It does no good to tell her what to do; in fact she goes out of her way to do exactly the opposite of what you say. I have placed her in your old room and have stopped entering the room because the disorder is too much for me to take. Clothes all over the bed and dresser chair, and scattered all over the floor as well. One cannot walk a straight line in that room. There was also the business of blue dye all over the bathroom. The maid Ising spent one whole afternoon scrubbing the tiles with muriatic acid to remove the stains.

Her language is foul, her behavior appalling. I will not pretend that it's been easy having Arminda here. I try to give her a lot of leeway because she is just fifteen and doesn't know any better, but having her here has been purgatory.

Frankly, Nelia, I blame you and Jun for all this. If she had been trained properly, if she had been taught right or wrong from the beginning, she would not be this incorrigible brat. Forgive me, but I don't know what else to call this willful, mouthy, and arrogant child. I have repeatedly called your attention: I have warned you that that child will bring you to your knees if you don't discipline her. But all I heard from you and Jun was: Ma, don't be old-fashioned; this is the American way. Here now is the result of your American experiment. My words have proved prophetic, have they not? There is some poetic justice in all this: your daughter has finally shown you the pain parents endure, as I have endured on account of you. I am still trying to figure out why you left for America when you had a good life here. You parroted all the cliches about America—freedom, equality, human rights, opportunities—well, obviously you have learned that cliches are just that.

I am not enjoying rubbing it in and pray she can still be saved. And I also pray that you and Jun can alter your ways. You two have become too American for your own good. This has contributed to the problem. You have spoiled her. You yourself admit you have given her everything. Every material thing perhaps, but not a good sense of herself. It is clear this child is terribly insecure, that she does not like herself. Coloring her hair, this outrageous get-up—she is simply hiding behind all these.

Another thing, you do not even keep an altar in your home; and even though you go to church when I visit you in New York, I am well aware that you do not always go to Mass on Sundays. Despite all your wealth your family does not have a solid foundation, so there you are. But let us drop the matter for the moment. After all, you and Jun are paying for your mistakes, and I can only hope that it is not too late.

Let me resume my report on Arminda.

Arminda has been so disagreeable, the kids of Ricardo dislike her intensely. I had hoped they would all get along and that therefore Arminda could spend time with her cousins. I *am* old, and my interests and hers are very different. Miriam and Oscar are close to her in age. Unfortunately things didn't work out. In her New York accent Arminda called her cousins backward and ignorant, and therefore they boycotted her. She has only me and the servants who barely speak English. She does not really talk to me but does extend standard cordialities: good morning, Lola, good evening, Lola—at least you have taught her that much.

She is restless; she does not know what to do with herself. She roams around the house and yard. She likes helping the gardener build bonfires in the afternoon; of course her playing with fire makes me nervous so we keep a close eye on her. There is just no telling what will enter her mind. In the evening, she watches television. She is constantly flipping the channels, from Marimar to CNN, my head spins when I watch TV with her. The maids say she reads and writes when she is in her bedroom. I have suggested that she write you and Jun but she says she will never talk nor write to you.

Obviously, she cannot hang around here forever. I've visited schools around here so she can go to school soon. She will not do at St. Catherine's. The nuns there are as strict today as they had been half a century ago. Ricardo suggests enrolling her in American School. Your brother says American School is more liberal, less traditional; perhaps Arminda will not be so different there.

Oh, another thing, she insists on being called Arminda, not Mindy. She said she has always hated that name; that it reminds her of some dumb television show "Mork and Mindy."

I will let you know how her schooling goes.

Love and kisses,

Mama

***

Dear Nelia,

Arminda is not in school. I had enrolled her at American School, but the night before she was supposed to go school, she shaved off her head—the whole thing except for the blue bangs. Even the liberal Americans will not have her. She hated school in New York and will never go to school again, she insists.

I was very angry but have decided not to force her. At any rate, there is no school in Ubec that will take her. The Christmas holidays are almost here, then there's the Sinulog festival; nothing much will be happening in school any way. I have told her that she must spend a few hours reading in our library; your father had many history books and there's the entire collection of the *Encyclopedia Brittanica* besides. For once she agreed to something.

Frankly I feel she is unhappy about having shaved her head. She has been wearing that black fedora hat of hers with the veil in front. When she is not in the library, she sulks in her bedroom. I have raised six children and have eleven grandchildren; I know better than to give her attention.

Mama

P.S. I forgot to mention that it had entered her head to dye the hair of my Santo Niño. Since you were an infant, that poor statue has been standing at the landing of our stairs, unmolested; we offer it flowers, we light candles in front of it; we take it out for the Sinolug parade; the artist Policarpio Lozada carved it from hard yakal wood, which is now impossible to find, and here your daughter comes along and colors its hair bright blue. It looks ridiculous, Nelia—the Child Jesus in red robes with blue hair. When she saw how upset I was, she offered to dye the hair black, but I told her to leave it that way as a reminder to all of what she has done.

I am saying the novena to the Santo Niño, patron of lost causes, for your daughter.

***

Dear Nelia,

I don't know if the Santo Niño had something to do with it, but she has discovered the animals. I have three pigs, one enormous black female and two small males that I've earmarked for Christmas lechon. She releases the small ones from their pen in the morning and chases them around. Sometimes I catch her talking to them. The runt, the pink one with freckles down his back, cocks his head to one side and stares at Arminda, as if he is listening. She gets the water hose and hoses them down. The piglets root about and roll around the mud near the water tank, then afterwards, they march back to their pen.

She also plays with my two hens. Abraham had given these to me several months ago, but one day, they started laying eggs and I could not kill them. The chickens run around scot-free and they never learned to lay eggs in a regular place. I'd tried to make nests for them near the garage, but they prefer the many nooks and crannies around the yard. Arminda hunts for the eggs daily. She says the hen that lays brown eggs favors the place under the star apple tree, whereas the hen that lays white eggs lays under the grapefruit tree. She asked the cook to teach her how to prepare the eggs properly so Arminda now knows how to fry eggs, scramble them, and make omelets. This morning, she made me a cheese omelet and she arranged it on the plate with parsley garnish to make it look pretty. She was quite delighted at her creation.

She is really still just a child. I cannot help wondering if your lifestyle there has forced her to grow up too quickly. Your way of life is horrible; when I am there my blood pressure rises from all that hurly-burly. Life does not have to be such a rat race. One ought to "smell the flowers"—as your kitchen poster says.

Love and kisses,

Mama

***

Dear Nelia,

We did not have lechon for Christmas. I had seen it coming. Christmas Eve, when the man I contracted to slaughter and roast the pigs arrived, Arminda begged me not to have the pigs killed. She was in tears. She said she would grow out her hair once again; she promised to behave—anything to save the pigs. Like Solomon I weighed the matter: Christmas meal versus the pigs. I could see that the pigs meant a lot to her, that in fact, the pigs are partly responsible for her more mellow behavior. In the end I decided to save the pigs. For the first time since her arrival, Arminda kissed me on the cheeks.

She was actually charming to her cousins. We joined them for midnight Mass at Redemptorist church, then later we gathered at home for the Noche Buena meal. Even without the lechon, there was plenty of food. It's always that way every year, even when you were small, too many rellenos and embotidos; and Ricardo always makes his turkey with that wonderful stuffing. The desserts are another whole story: sans rival, tocino del cielo, meringue, mango chiffon cake, maja blanca, all the way to the humble saba bananas rolled in white sugar.

I don't know if it was a joke but Miriam and Oscar gave her a black wig. Arminda removed her hat, tried on the wig and kept it on the whole night. I was surprised to see that she looks a lot like you.

Arminda gave everyone poems written in calligraphy on parchment paper. I do not know what mine means but it says:

I fled from you
A world away
I turn and
Find you
All around me.

As usual, she wore black, but this time it was a dress sewn by Vering. It had a nice flowing skirt, and instead of a zipper, the dress had black ribbons that criss-crossed and tied into a ribbon. She wore black net stockings and black chunky shoes. She continues to wear black lipstick but we have become used to it. Actually we have become used to Arminda and her drama; and I believe she is getting used to us.

I hope your Christmas has been as lovely as ours.

Love and kisses,

Mama

***

Dear Nelia,

Arminda wanted to know more about the Sinulog festival. People are getting ready for the Sinulog and the Christmas decorations have given way to the banners with the image of the Child Jesus. I explained that even before Christian days, Ubecans have always celebrated during harvest time. When Christianity was introduced, the statue of the Child Jesus, called the Santo Niño, became the focal point of the festivities. People dance to honor the Child Jesus. In parades, people dance to the beat of drums. Some people blacken their faces and they wear costumes and dance through the streets of Ubec. People do get drunk and it can get wild sometimes, so one must know where to go; I told her this because I could see her eyes sparkling with interest.

We visited the Child Jesus at the Santo Niño Church. I could not help myself—I pointed out to her that this original statue does not have blue hair. Embarrassed, she looked down at her shoes and mumbled that she had offered to dye my statue's hair black. I explained that if we dye the statue's hair from blue to black to God-knows-what-other-color, it will lose all its hair. She apologized once again for having touched my statue. She said this sincerely and I decided to let the matter go.

I related stories instead about the Santo Niño: how the Child roams the streets at night; how the Child gives gifts of food to His friends. And I told Arminda of how you were born with beri-beri and how I danced to the Child Jesus so that you would be saved.

The last item fascinated her.

"What is beri-beri, Lola?" she asked.

"A disease caused by a lack of Vitamin B," I said.

"What happened to my Mom?"

"She was born near the tail-end of the war, and I had not eaten properly when I carried her. Your mother had edema and nervous disorder. Her eyes were rolled up; she was dying."

"I didn't know my Mom almost died."

"I prayed to the Santo Niño for her life."

"She never told me she was sick when she was a baby."

"Perhaps she did and you didn't listen."

She furrowed her brows and thought for a while before asking, "How did you pray?"

"I danced my prayer."

"Show me," Arminda said.

And so outside the Santo Niño Church, we held candles in our hands and we shuffled our dance to the Child Jesus. It was mid-day and quite hot and sweat rolled down our faces as we swayed to the right, then to the left. People gathered to watch us. I am usually shy about these matters, but this time I did not mind. Both of us were laughing when we finished.

She also wanted to see the old Spanish fort, so we drove to Fort San Pedro and later we stopped by the kiosk with Ferdinand Magellan's cross. This got her interested and she scoured the library for information on Philippine history. She was pumping me full of questions; then this morning, she expressed interest in going back to school. After the Sinulog, I will meet with the principal of the American School.

I think, Nelia, that Arminda's problem has been basically a

question of identity. I know Jun has talked to Arminda, telling her she has Filipino blood but that she's an American citizen. I am not sure that is enough for that child. At the hospital where he works, Jun is treated like a god; he is a doctor and is not subjected to the "looks" and the questions: where do you come from? Or worse—*what* are you? He doesn't feel the discrimination, not as much as Arminda may, in your American world.

These past months, she has immersed herself in our world—granted it is not her world because one day she will return to America—but in the meantime, she has a better understanding of what it means to be Filipino. It is important for one to know where one comes from, in order to know where one is headed.

Love and kisses,

Mama

***

Dear Mom and Dad,

I need six packages of blue dye and three bottles of peroxide. If you call Mia, she can tell you where to buy them. Tell Mia, I'm glad she's well and that I wish she were here with me. She'd like this place; it's cool. Tito Ric has brought us to the beaches here, and he's promised to take us to the rice terraces this summer. He said the place is very old, and there are mummies there, and there are fireflies at night. He also said some of the people there, especially the older ones, have tattoos on their bodies. (He's already told me I can't have a tattoo, so you don't have to worry.) I can't wait for the summer.

Last week we had the Sinulog. It wasn't as fancy as the Rose Parade nor the Mardi Gras, but there were numerous parades all over the city. Day and night for a week you could hear the drums beating. People from other towns came to the city and many of them slept along the sidewalks. The city was crammed with people, celebrating and eating and dancing. I went around with Miriam and Oscar. They were such dorks before, but they're not that bad any more.

For the main parade, we wore costumes—Lola lent Miriam

and me some of her old sayas; Oscar blackened his face and wore a huge feathered hat. The three of us had blue hair. People stopped us in the streets to ask about our hair. They fingered our hair and wondered how we turned it blue. We just laughed. We did not tell them we used dye from New York. It was like a secret— our secret.

But I've run out and need more. Be sure and send it; but don't rush because the school does not allow blue hair. I'll have to wait until summer vacation before I can dye my hair blue again.

Love,

Arminda

THE TURKISH SEAMSTRESS IN UBEC

I've never experienced pain like this in my thirty-five years of life. I'm talking about this slash on my neck; I'm talking about the contact of the knife against my skin. It's agony that doesn't just smolder where the flesh and bones have separated; it courses through every part of my body from my toes all the way to the very tips of my long hair. The millisecond the serrated metal touched my neck, I heard my skin rip like satin and what followed were the worst sounds I've ever heard: neck bones crunching and snapping reminding me of the awful sounds made by a butcher hacking away at a dead cow. And now the knife lies next to me, cold and slippery from my own blood.

I smell something foul. Am I near the wet market where heads of pigs hang on hooks, their fetid intestines displayed on wooden tables? Where does that stench come from? I try to move but can't. A breeze shakes the nipa palms overhead and the sun slants through, hitting my face, making me feel its warmth. I remember now: I'm out in the field near the creek. It must be morning. What am I doing here? I should be in my shop, with a hot cup of chocolate sending off tendrils of steam while I arrange the clothes on the mannequins, and oil the sewing machines, get ready for another day.

The smell of my own blood disgusts me—how could I have such foul-smelling blood? Isn't this the same blood that turns my skin a faint coral when a man stares at me? Doesn't this blood race through my veins when a man makes love to me? Love, love, love that makes me want to get up in the morning. Yes, love more important than stitchery. The look of a man, his touch sends me far away, makes me forget the deaths of my parents and brothers, the hunger and lack with Achmed in that hovel in Constantinople, the humiliation Pierre inflicted on me in Paris. How did I survive those cruel men? How did that skinny frightened girl grow plump and voluptuous, someone envied by women, desired by men? What a long journey it's been from the Sultanahment to St-Germain to Colon Street. Constant movement, like the salmon that swims upstream, except I'm running away from where I was spawned.

If I had learned my lessons, I would have been fine. I would have many more years of sewing and stitching, and sipping hot chocolates and aperitifs with my wealthy clients, but I could not. The men that catch my eye know how to weave nets with their soft words, piercing looks, trembling touches, fruitless promises; and always I find myself entangled, caught—in love again—spending sleepless nights, waiting for their visits, weeping buckets of tears, watching the clock on Sundays and holidays because no matter what their promises are, no matter how good at lovemaking they are, they always spend Sundays and holidays with their families. One lonely Christmas day in Paris, I understood what being a mistress was all about.

The worst one was the cruel man in Manila with the heavenly touch and golden words who made me suffocate, took my breath away. I had to pack, leave. If I wanted to survive, I had to flee.

That was how I ended up in Ubec. A backwater that I chose, arriving with a bag and a handful of coins. I thought, here no one will find me. Here I will be safe. I hid my shame behind my toothy smile and good figure, and in a year's time I had my own dress shop on Colon Street. Here the women clamor for me to design their dresses. To have a dress made by me, Nurten, is something to brag about. The people here allow me to live the way I want to; that's more than one can ask for. This life is far better than the ones I had in Constantinople and Paris. I'm no longer the underdog here; here I'm somebody.

I can sew; I can design clothes. Tuck folds here and there to slim down the fat ones, lengthen the short ones, make buxom those without breasts, turn frumpy women irresistible. I am a magician with cloth and pattern, needle and thread. I think of my dress, this dress that has turned red from my blood. I remember sitting by the window of my shop, embroidering this same dress, weaving in silk thread in fine and regular stitches, creating what looked like blue green peacock feathers. The embroidery was perfect, it was reversible—a difficult task. How happy I was creating this dress, dreaming of romance with still another young man.

I should have confined my life to stitching dresses. I tried to do that. When I moved to Ubec, I did my best. But the cruel man sought and found me. And the dance began all over again: last night I walked to the International Hotel, talked with some clients who glowed in their silks and satins. Look at me, several said, you have made me beautiful. I smiled and shrugged my shoulders. At 10 o'clock I slipped away and walked to the park where he waited in the shadows of the acacia tree near the grandstand. When some people walked by, we parted and hid our faces. When they were gone, we kissed and he led me down Mabini Street toward the creek, which reflected a full moon. I looked at the sky and at the water, at the two moons, and I felt hope building inside me again. Then I felt it, that metal slicing my neck.

I feel my head wobble and I realize that my head is not completely severed. Maybe I'll survive. I'll pick myself up from this riverbed and make my way through the dimly lit streets to my dress shop. After climbing the stairs to my apartment, I'll scrub all this blood from myself and sleep off this nightmare. In the morning, the sun will burst through the milky glass panes and I'll get ready and throw open my doors for my clients with their parcels of cloth and dress designs. Everything will be as it was.

But I'm dreaming, because here I am, body sprawled on the riverbank, head dangling by silky thread-like matter. I don't know whether to laugh or cry at my predicament. There's no picking myself up from this muck I'm in. My body is riddled with slash wounds and drenched in blood. It looks like a bloody sack of something foul and ugly. My dress with the exquisite embroidery might as well be a butcher's rag.

On top of everything, I hear scratching near the clump of palm trees and I wonder if it's a tree rat and if it'll start chewing on me. I feel my entrails turn cold from fear. I try to remember prayers my mother taught me, but the words are gone, buried under years of trying to forget. I can't ask a single person, and I can't ask God for help, for consolation, for hope. There is no help, no consolation, no hope, no God. I'm a corpse on this riverbank. The only thing I'm grateful for is that I'll stop running now.

Part 2

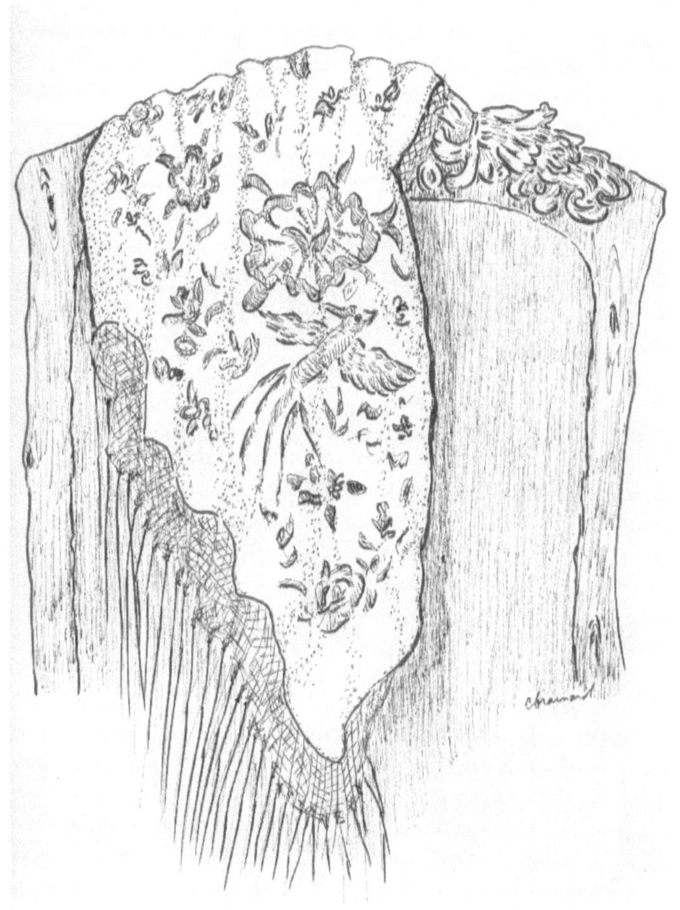

ALBA

Malate, Philippines (July, 1763)

I set the bundles of thread near me and I pick up the dead boy. He is seven, maybe older. It is difficult to tell. He is extremely thin and his head is too big for his body, making him look like a shriveled old man. His rags reek of urine and feces. The wounds on his legs had festered until the poison travelled throughout his body. There is a huge gash near his right eye.

Other street urchins cower behind the battered, moss-covered church walls. Before the English came, there were stalls laden with Chinese silks, European brocades, and Mexican tapestries against those walls. Under that sprawling acacia tree, a toothless man sold copper cuspidors and silver-framed mirrors.

I remove my cotton panuelo and clean the boy. I lay him down and pick up my thread. His corpse will be carted away and burned along with the other bodies that litter the Walled City of Manila and its surrounding villages.

As I walk toward the seashore, I curse the English and Spaniards. To think of it—you carry a child in your womb for nine months, you nurse him, watch him grow, only to have him killed before he is even a man. If the child's mother saw her son, she would feel the anger I have when I remember my grandmother's corpse.

The sharp edges of the nilad grasses scratch my legs and arms as I go through the swampy shore. I recall my grandmother, Lola Juana, pounding herbs with her marble pestle, saying life is a silver cord connecting us to a maker. A gift, she said. Life must not be wasted.

Turning, I see the galleons and English ships tossing on the blue-green bay. The air is damp and the sparrows flutter excitedly, seeking refuge in the coconut trees. A storm is coming. I hurry to my hut next to huge rocks. The strength of this bamboo and nipa hut, Carpio once said, is its ability to bend. The strong typhoon winds will not destroy this home.

My chickens and pigs scurry from the bushes to greet me and I herd them under the hut. Before climbing the short ladder, I give them water and I light a lamp. The wind is blowing and I feel my hut swaying. Below, the animals grunt and run around. I picture the bay foaming and the ships thrashing like coconut husks.

After eating some fish and rice, I work at my loom, alternating the colorful thread I bought today from the sly pockmarked peddler. I look with pleasure at the intricate bird pattern which I have created with blue, green, and red thread. Lola Juana taught me this design. The magnificent bird, she explained, became jealous of the first man's beauty and thus tried to peck out his eyes. But the first woman grabbed the bird's long and beautiful tail, scaring him away. I will give the finished blanket to Carpio. When the planting season is over, he will return. I smile, thinking of his fine brown body on this blanket.

The rain falls and its heavy pounding drowns the animal sounds. I finish a row on my loom and consider unrolling my mat when a clapping sound startles me. A girl's shrill voice rises above the whistling wind: Alba, Alba.

I open the window and peer out. Cold rain hits my face; there is only blackness outside. Who's there? I call out. Epifania, she answers. Doña Saturnina sent me. I ask her in. The young girl's black hair is plastered wet on her skull making her look like a crow. She flaps her arms excitedly as she explains. Her mistress is in labor and has asked for me. There are problems, she adds.

I throw a blanket over my head, wondering why Doña Saturnina wants me and not some European-trained doctor. There are many of them in Manila. We hurry through the swamp and I remember Doña Saturnina's visit a year ago. It was before the English came; it was drizzling, unusual for September. I handed her a piece of cloth to dry herself with, but she did not stop shivering until she saw my plants, my baskets, and my weaving loom. She said, My servants speak of your special powers.

There are fantastic tales about me, I answered. Some say I can turn into a dog or bird, or that I eat unborn babies. A woman accused me of making all the coconuts on her grove fall by merely walking nearby. My grandmother was murdered because of those stories. I am a simple healer. I use herbs and things of nature to help people.

Her eyelids flickered and I knew she had indeed heard those stories. I hold her father responsible for Lola Juana's death. He called himself a Catholic Defender and accused many of being heretics and witches. He incited the people to such a state that one night, Lola Juana was hacked to death by the village drunk. A black dog with glowing eyes attacked him, he related, and he was only defending himself when he used the ax. He was acquitted.

Lola Juana was my only relative. My parents and two sisters died of the fever when I was an infant. My grandmother raised me and taught me everything she knew.

That rainy September, I eyed Doña Saturnina with contempt. She sat erect next to my loom, looking like a typical Manileña. She had clear brown skin and her silky black hair swirled up and was held in place by a finely carved ivory comb encrusted with pearls. The jewelry on her fingers flashed red and green. I felt a coldness as I stared at her. I wanted to say I could do nothing for her; I wanted her to leave, but Lola Juana often said that healing is a gift from the Maker and one so gifted must use it.

Doña Saturnina's voice was low and sad. Her somberness reminded me of the black Madonna of Antipolo. Her husband, Don Diego Torres, had a constant buzzing in his ear, she murmured. This began after his brother died of the pox.

Without seeing him, I could do nothing. I told her this, but she insisted that I must have something for him. Finally, I gave her herbs from the enchanted forest and explained how to make tea from the dry leaves. She handed me a gold coin. At the door, she hesitated. The truth is, she whispered, I am here because I am barren. Help me, she pleaded in that melancholy voice.

She had seen midwives and European-trained doctors. She had made numerous novenas and pilgrimages, but she remained childless. Once, she said softly, she had thought of throwing herself into the Pasig River, so her husband could marry a fertile woman. He wanted an heir. His brother's death made him the last of the Torres family. I had heard of the Torres haciendas and galleon investments. They were almost as rich as the Spanish friars, the people said.

Doña Saturnina's hips were slightly narrow, but she appeared to be in good health. Her breath was sweet and her eyes clear. I gave her powdered bones of the flying lizard and told her to take a pinch, mix it with water and drink it every day. I made no promises, but she was grateful.

Now, Epifania leads me to the carriage at the end of the muddy trail. The driver beats the horse as we splash through the roads of Malate. We pass the church where I saw the dead boy. In the darkness, I can make out the beggars huddled against the walls. We turn a few streets and enter the Torres estate. The enormous house looms in front of us, surprisingly undamaged by the war. The English, Epifania explains, used the house for their living quarters. There was plenty of food and we were untouched by the war, she adds with pride.

Shortly after Doña Saturnina's visit last year, there was a freak storm. I was at the rectory giving the old Spanish friar ointment for his rheumatic legs. He was telling the story about the Madonna and Child when news came that thirteen English warships were at the bay. The English were demanding the Spanish authorities to surrender, but Archbishop Governor Rojo insisted on defending the Walled City. Rojo had six hundred poorly equipped soldiers; the Englishmen, Draper and Cornish, had five thousand men.

I watched the villagers pile their belongings into carts as they fled for the mountains. In just a day, the English captured the villages surrounding the Walled City. They used the solid stone structure of the churches for garrisons, and from there they bombarded Manila.

There was bloodshed everywhere—men, women, and children, maimed if not killed. Women were abused by the English. Houses burned down in a few minutes. Manila—the Pearl of the Orient—was destroyed in a few days.

Epifania guides me through the huge and elegant rooms with high ceilings. We walk past elaborately carved furniture. There are Persian rugs on the polished wooden floors and European damask draperies hang in front of capiz-shell windows. Don Diego Torres grasps my arm when he sees me. He is a wiry, graying man, much older than his wife. He has the furtive look of a forest creature. He leads me to the room, begging me to do everything I can to help his wife. She is all I have, he says. Help her; she asked for you.

The room has the sour smell of sweat and foul air. I instruct Epifania to open all the windows. A spray of water hits the windowsill and a crisp breeze fills the room. There are clean blankets on a chair and there is plenty of hot water. I wash my hands in the pink-flowered basin near the bed.

Doña Saturnina is curled up on her side. If not for her huge belly, she looks like a girl with her dark hair spilling around her. I put pillows behind her back and help her to a sitting position. She stares at me. Her brows are deeply furrowed. I feel her stomach to check the baby's position.

The bags of water broke this afternoon, she says. Labor began this evening at sundown. The furrows between her eyebrows deepen as a contraction takes hold of her. Was your grandmother a midwife? she asks. I nod. She says nothing else.

The baby is a footling breech. A good-luck child—if it lives. I have never assisted in such a birth, but Lola Juana talked about such a delivery. Be very careful, she warned. Pull one foot, then the other, and the rest of the baby will slide down. If the mother is narrow, the baby may get stuck and both will die.

She tenses and winces. A contraction. Take a deep breath and let it out slowly, I tell her. I show her how and she follows me. Her body relaxes.

Later she says: I had nothing to do with your grandmother's death. I was only a child like you then. The memory of Lola Juana's mutilated corpse flashes in my mind. The men found pieces of her body in the plaza. Like a giant puzzle, they put her together. Swirling darkness swells inside me.

Once, she continues, I saw you. You were just a girl, walking to the river with a bundle of clothes on your head. You were with the other laundry women. I had my porcelain doll from Sevilla and I wanted to give it to you. But I could not.

Another contraction comes and she holds her breath and bears down. Not yet, I say. I look at her face and realize that she was indeed a mere child then.

She stares at me, her dark eyes flashing like that of a mad dog. Kill it, she hisses between her teeth. I feel her forehead, thinking she is delirious. If it's not dead, kill it, she repeats. Her skin is damp and cool. She cringes; there is another contraction.

So this is why she wanted me here, I think. I remember Lola Juana—she smelled of herbs; she was wise and warm—and darkness rises to my throat. I feel tired. If I do nothing, they will die. The tiredness fills my joints, the tips of my hair. She is drenched with sweat, her enormous stomach heaving with a life of its own. If I do nothing, they will die, my mind repeats. But Lola Juana's voice silences mine: Life is a gift; she is a woman in labor; and I am a healer.

The baby will be born feet first, I explain, as I reach for the infant's feet. I continue: When the head passes through the birth canal, the pain will be terrible. Then it will be over. Push with all your might when I tell you.

The baby slides down, then stops. Push, I instruct Doña Saturnina. She strains but the baby does not move. I tug at the little body and its head pops out. The infant is bluish in color and its mouth is wide open as it cries lustily. Doña Saturnina's eyes are closed as she breathes rapidly. It's alive then, she whispers.

I wait until the umbilical cord stops pulsating, then I tie the cord. I tell her to push one last time and the placenta comes out. I check this thoroughly, heeding Lola Juana's warning. A woman bled to death because a piece of the placenta was left in her womb.

I wipe the blood and cheesy covering from the baby boy. He is swiftly losing the bluish color and he appears strong and perfect. I hand him to her. The very fair skin of the child next to her brown skin startles me, and then I understand. She looked hesitantly at the infant. Her eyes become watery and tears spill down her cheeks. He's small, she says as she looks at me sadly as if seeking forgiveness. It's not his child, but he is mine, isn't he? she asks.

I help her hold the baby against her breast. The infant roots wildly until he finds her nipple and he sucks contentedly. This one will live, I think. An English bastard and a good-luck child.

I wash and comb her hair into a bun at her nape. If you wish, I will take the child, I tell her softly. She does not answer. She is stroking the baby's face and body.

I clean the bed and room before calling Don Diego Torres. He rushes to me, eyes wide with anxiety. She lives? he asks. I nod. His sharp features soften and he weeps. Holding his breath, he walks slowly toward the bed. Don't be afraid, I say, your wife has a boy. I close the door and wait, fearful for the infant, but all I hear are hushed cracked voices.

The carriage is waiting but I prefer to walk home. The rain has stopped. There is a soft dawn and a mild sea breeze. I breathe in the cool, tangy air as if to cleanse my spirit. I look back at the huge house and see a morning star shining faintly above. I am surprised that I feel no rancor. Some birds fly past me to their nests in the battered church walls. I think of Carpio. I must finish my blanket so it will be ready for him when he returns from the fields.

VIGAN

When I was ten, a year after my father died, my mother decided to return to Vigan, back to her grandmother who had raised her after her parents died. We left Manila for the sleepy town with crumbling stone houses, cobbled streets, watchtowers, and other vestiges of colonial days. Vigan boasted of having been founded in the sixteenth century by Juan Salcedo, the Spanish conquistador who conquered Manila. In its heyday, it was the port of entry of the Spanish galleons coming from China and headed for the Walled City of Intramuros. The ships sailed up the river and moored at the edge of Old Town, near the Cathedral and Archbishop's Palace. The merchants' houses and warehouses clustered near the river. Here, traders exchanged items such as indigo, cotton, silk, pearls, tobacco, porcelain, hemp, for silver and gold.

Our family house sat in the middle of a row of ancient merchant houses, crumbling relics of limestone blocks and wood. Our house had massive wooden double doors fronting the street, which my great-grandmother said allowed carriages in and out of the family compound during Spanish times. The lower portion of our house had a shed with two pigs, four chickens, and one mean-spirited goat. A section in the back served as the servants' quarters, but since my great-grandmother had only one servant who slept upstairs, this section was unoccupied and was in total disarray. An elaborate staircase led to the second floor, which had the kitchen, dining room, living room or sala, the music room, library, a verandah, and bedrooms. There were four bedrooms, but huge, with high-ceilings that allowed the air to circulate thus cutting the oppressive tropical heat. Except for the room occupied by my great-grandmother, the other bedrooms had several four-poster beds, lined up dormitory-style, and covered by yellowing crocheted bedspreads.

I'd only heard about this house from my mother. We had never visited it when Papa was alive. So even though I was unhappy about our move, I was impressed by the surprises the house offered. The walls of the rooms, for instance, had hand-painted murals: musical instruments were painted all around the music room, the dining room had a border of grapes on a vine with a hunting scene on the wall nearest the dining table, and the bedroom my mother and I shared had a picture of Cupid sitting on a cloud and shooting his arrow at a young woman in a forest. Although the paintings were flaking and faded, my great-grandmother, whom my mother and I called Lola, was very proud of them.

What interested me most was the coffin at the foot of the stairs. An old sheet covered it and on top were all sorts of junk: newspapers, empty glass jars, and a huge vase with dusty fake flowers. I had mistaken the coffin for a table until Lola removed the sheet to reveal a bronze casket with gold decorations. She struck the metal with her fingernail and declared it was our family coffin. Apparently old families in the area kept family coffins, which were used only for the wake. For the actual burial, the corpse was wrapped in an Ilocano woven blanket and buried directly in the family vault. The coffin was cleaned, then stored, in this case at the foot of the stairs, ready for its next temporary occupant.

The idea sent me into hysterics, considering my own father was buried in his own bronze casket—cost had been no object as far as his parents were concerned. He had been their only child.

I asked my great-grandmother what happened when two family members died, like my mother's parents for instance. She said they lay side by side.

"But what if more than two die?" I persisted.

"It's never happened," she said. By that time, she was clearly annoyed with me, and so I kept quiet. Lola had not liked my father and his family, and I suspected that dislike extended to me. People said I looked a lot like my father. He was tall and thin and had a lot of Chinese blood in him, unlike my mother's family, which had a lot of Spanish blood.

Even though Lola spoke enthusiastically of the house (this remnant of our family's glorious past), I found it depressing. There were cobwebs everywhere, and at night, I dreaded going to the bathroom because I usually ran into the sticky strands. There was dust all over the old furniture. Ceiling plaster was peeling, the wooden floors creaked, and there was one section near the kitchen with wood rot. I could peer through the holes and look down at the animals. Sometimes I would spit on the goat that had butted me once.

Before we came, Lola's solitary companion was another old woman named Manang Gloria. I was never sure who took care of whom because half the time, my great-grandmother was the one in the kitchen cooking bitter ampalaya to strengthen Manang Gloria's blood. There were men workers who came during the day to take care of the animals and yard, but by late afternoon, they were gone.

By six in the evening, the only sounds you heard were the two old women rattling around in the kitchen, some lonely crickets outside, and my mother sighing by the window. Times like that, I would ache for my father and my old life.

***

My mother had never worked in her entire life. After college, she'd married Papa and moved into his house. In Vigan, she spent many nights crying, cursing my father for dying, and wondering how she could support the two of us. We had left Manila in the first place because she and my father's parents did not get along. They disliked her from the start, accusing her of being pretentious. It was true that my mother carried with her an arrogance that old families from Vigan had, even if their ceilings had caved in and their floors rotted. My mother, likewise, scorned my father's family, calling them "new rich" and accusing them of having no culture. While my father was alive, he kept the two warring parties apart, but after he died, nothing stood between his parents and my mother. Like cats and dogs they went after each other; of course my mother was always on the losing end. After a year of strained silences, sharp words, doors slamming, and countless tears, my mother grew weary of the quarreling, took whatever she could, and we left.

It was Lola who suggested that she open an antique shop downstairs. "Manang Gloria knows some carpenters who can make replicas," Lola said. "Have them copy our antique furniture. Price them low. City people will buy them." She was right. Antique dealers traveled far to buy Mama's bentwood chairs and love seats, drop-leaf tables, armoires, chairs, and wooden statues of the Virgin Mary and Jesus on the cross. The most popular item was the plantation chair, an enormous lounging chair made of mahogany and rattan, that harked back to days of sitting around the verandah, a leg resting on one arm of the chair and a drink in one's hand.

***

I hated school. I did not fit. I was used to the stimulating environment of my school in Manila. The school in Vigan was dull and provincial. I spent most of my time in Mama's antique shop, doing my homework on the table, reading old books from the library, rearranging the display in the showroom, or bothering the workers who were carving the reproductions in the back. "Look at that," I would say, "antiques made-to-order."

I was there the afternoon Ramon arrived. He was an antique dealer from Manila. I overheard him ordering a lot of furniture and so I was not surprised when Mama invited him for dinner. Mama's clients usually lived in one of the four hotels in town, none of which served decent food. When Mama invited clients to dinner, Manang Gloria would come to life and prepare local recipes, crispy mouth-watering bagnets, steamed prawns, fried fish, and that bitter vegetable stew that local folk loved so much.

Ramon praised Manang Gloria's food, and she giggled like an idiot. She was really quite fresh, behaving more like a peer than our servant. When I tried to put her in her place, Lola always defended her, saying she was the fourth generation to work in our house.

Lola ate and left the dining table early. When she was gone, the conversation between Mama and Ramon livened up. It seemed they had mutual friends in Manila, and they discussed them one by one, Mama gushing over the good fortune of some of them, and clucking at the misfortune of others. Later (they must have forgotten I was there) Ramon talked about his wife. He had married his college sweetheart, a journalist who had gotten involved in the anti-Marcos movement. She had written many daring exposes of the oppressive dictatorship. She even wrote articles about the "disappeareds" until one night she herself disappeared. Ramon spent years looking for her until his family convinced him she had been "salvaged" so not a single trace of her body could be found. Ramon had gone into seclusion until Cory Aquino came into power. He said that after the EDSA Revolution, he discovered he was still alive after all. "I found out," he said, "that I could laugh again."

My mother grew teary at Ramon's story, then told Ramon about Papa. She described how Papa started dropping things, that we thought he'd had a stroke, but that it turned out he had brain cancer. The doctors had said he had six months to live, and that they had been right almost to the date. She did not tell Ramon of her quarrel with my paternal grandparents. When he pressed her about why we left Manila, she said Lola needed her.

It was a conversation, nothing more, but I was disturbed by it. I hated how she shared a piece of our lives with him. I hated being reminded of Papa and our old life, and I hated how happy Mama seemed with Ramon.

***

Ramon would come around every two weeks. He would talk to Mama at great length—"business" they called it. He would dine with us; and sometimes he and Mama would ride off someplace. I would interrogate Mama as to where exactly they went, and reluctantly she would confess they visited the old church and rectory in Santa Maria, or the beach of Vigan, or the Luna Museum in Ilocos Sur, or the open market to buy Ilocano blankets. She said this blithely, as if I should not care. But when I thought of the two of them in these places, I would feel a heaviness in my chest, a sorrow that lingered for days.

Ramon tried to befriend me, bringing me books, which he recognized as my weakness, but even though I hankered to read them, I would deliberately abandon them in the shop, on the same table he had set them on, so he could see, so he could understand that he could never bribe me.

Once he told me, "You are very different from your mother."

I glared at him. "I am my father's daughter," I said, thinking I sounded very smart.

My mother blushed when she heard me, and later that night she scolded me for being rude. I told her I wanted to go home.

"There is no other home," she replied softly. "This is it. Those people don't want us. They have cheated us of your father's inheritance."

She was crying now. "They are the people who killed Ramon's wife. They were cronies of Marcos; that was how they made their money. They killed her; and I suppose, we are guilty too."

Her hair was disheveled; her makeup smeared. I saw how much older she had become since Papa died. I saw how vulnerable she was, how spineless, and I told myself I would never be as weak as she was.

***

In the middle of that summer when the heat left you breathless, my great-grandmother decided she was going to die soon. She called Manang Gloria and instructed her to have new satin lining made for the family coffin. After inspecting the shiny pink lining and checking the hinges of the coffin, she went back to bed and refused to get up. In a few days her legs started cramping, and it became my job to massage her with Sloan's Liniment. I would pour the liniment into my palms, vigorously rub my hands together, and massage her spindly legs. That was when I learned about my mother's bad luck.

Lola said, "There are some people who attract bad luck, and your mother is that way. When your mother was four, her parents died in a car crash on the zig-zag road to Baguio. Then of course your father died. It's just bad luck, that's all. There is no other explanation."

I felt kinder to my mother after that—until I caught her and Ramon kissing. It was afternoon, and Lola had told me to call them to the verandah for merienda. I ran down, paused by the family coffin, and lifted the sheet so I could feel the coolness of the bronze. Then I went to the door of the antique shop. I caught them locked together in a tight embrace—my own mother with this man. Ramon saw me, pushed her away, and cleared his throat. Calmly I told them Lola had hot chocolate and pastries waiting for them.

Mama closed the front door of the shop and headed for the stairs. "Are you coming, Rosario?" she asked.

I shook my head. "I have to finish something. I'll be there."

I waited awhile then I opened his briefcase and went through his things, looking for something, I was not sure what for exactly. Just when I was putting his papers back into the briefcase, a picture fluttered out. It was Ramon and Mama standing happily in front of the town plaza. I took it and stuffed it into my pocket.

***

I had heard Manang Gloria talk of Sylvia, a mangkukulam who lived on the edge of town. When Manang Gloria was twenty, Sylvia had read her cards. The witch had predicted that a man would fall in love with her, but that they would be separated. A young man did come along, and for a long time, Manang Gloria tortured herself by wondering when the man would drop her for another woman. The man, however, was steadfast and asked her to marry him. They picked a date, made preparations; Manang Gloria had her white gown made. The night before their wedding day, the man walked by a sari-sari store where two men were fighting. He tried to stop the fight, but in the scuffle, ended up dead.

Aside from reading cards, Sylvia made potions. The most popular were love potions and potions to exact revenge. She could also cure sick people by catching their illness and transferring it into a rooster whose head she would chop off. If convinced it was right to do so, she could harm people. She could even turn into a ferocious black dog at night, which was why people avoided walking around after dusk.

One Saturday in June, I went to Sylvia's house. I was afraid; I did not know what to expect. I found her planting seedlings in front of her hut. At first glance, she appeared ordinary-looking, with a simple native dress and her gray hair tied in a knot. When she looked up, I noticed her sad, sad eyes. I told her I knew Manang Gloria. She stared at me, with those sorrowful eyes, until I too felt like crying. I was about to leave when she invited me in.

She led me in front of an altar with numerous statues of saints and burning candles. She took my hand, turned it over so she could see my palm. "One day," she said, "a man will fall in love with you, but you will be separated."

This sounded like Manang Gloria's fortune; I felt disappointed.

"I'm here," I said, "for my mother."

She said nothing.

"I have to save her."

"Ah, does your mother need saving?"

I nodded.

"And whom are you saving her from?"

"From a man. A wicked man. I have a picture of him. Do you want to see?"

She glanced at the picture. Her eyes became darker and sadder still. "A handsome man. Once, I knew a handsome man…" She trailed off, but then recovered, "Handsome men…well, what can I say? Yes, they can be dangerous. Tell me more."

"He is hurting her. He is hurting us. I want him to go away. I want him to stop seeing her."

She sighed. "Your father is dead," she said. "You miss him."

This pronouncement impressed me, and I wondered how she divined this truth.

"Everyone talks in this town. You and your mother live in the Pamintuan Mansion, with Doña Epang."

Again I felt disappointment.

She stared into my eyes until my eyes burned and I felt like blinking.

"I can give you something that will attract good. You can give this to your mother, so only good will go near her. If this man is bad, he will stay away."

"Mama's a bad-luck woman. Lola says so. Nothing you can give her will attract good. I need something so he will never come back. He is evil. He has hurt her; he has hurt me."

She turned her sorrowful eyes to her altar. "All right," she finally said, "just because of Manang Gloria I will help you." She went to a corner and returned with a bottle of Coke, only it didn't have Coca Cola in it, but some amber-colored liquid with herbs and flower petals. "The morning after the full moon, rinse with this. Then go to Mass and pray that he will no longer return. Pray hard, especially when the bells ring at the Consecration."

"Is that all?" I asked.

"That is all. Leave your money in the pot near the door."

***

Back home, I hid the bottle in my closet and left it untouched until the first storm fell. Mama was in bed staring at the Cupid painted on the wall. She whispered, "It is so cold to be alone in bed."

I found a calendar and figured when the full moon was. I bathed with Sylvia's water, went to Mass, and prayed as she had taught me. When the bells tinkled at Consecration, I stared hard at the white host and repeated: "God, keep Ramon away from Mama, keep him away from us, drive him far away, separate them, God, please, God, please. You've taken my father away, I'm asking you now, God, to keep him away from us. You owe it to me, God, because Papa's gone and not only have you taken him, you've taken me away from my house and planted me in this miserable place, the last place on earth I'd like to live in God. I have no friends, no one, except my Mother. Please God, don't let her leave me too because when she's with Ramon, that's how it feels God, like she's left me too."

On and on I rambled, venting my sorrows and miseries, and pinning them all on Ramon, blaming him for them, and wishing for him to disappear from our lives. When I left the cathedral, my hands were shaking and I felt flushed. My mother and Lola asked me if I was all right. I kept quiet. Something had shifted in me and I knew that things would be different.

***

It did not happen right away. From the time I saw Sylvia in June until December, Ramon continued to visit Mama every two weeks. When I saw his happy face, my chest would tighten. He would smile, white teeth flashing; and he'd give Lola a box of American chocolates or bag of hot chestnuts, and he would kiss her on both cheeks. And Mama, standing by Lola's bed, would beam proudly at Ramon as if he were some genius-child who had done his homework right. He would greet me too and give me a book or puzzle. With a stony face I would thank him, then put his gift down and run off to wash my hands, scrubbing them hard until my skin hurt.

When he was around and I felt desperate, I would beg Manang Gloria to tell me the story of her dead lover once again. Other times, I would go to the family coffin, remove the things on top, open it and run my hands on the pink satin lining, feeling its coolness, imagining the dead people that had occupied this coffin, and thinking that one day it would hold Lola, Mama, and even me. Once I climbed into it and lay down as if I were dead, with my eyes closed and my palms together as if in prayer. I was drifting off to sleep when Manang Gloria happened to see me and screamed so loud, Lola ran down the stairs. "You are a strange, strange child," she said. "You must take after your father's family."

***

And so time passed in Vigan, until finally it happened, in December. Ramon arrived with Christmas gifts. By this time, I had almost forgotten my visit to Sylvia, and I must admit, I'd gotten used to his visits. Lola's house was so dark and full of decay, and Ramon's visits added some sparkle to our lives. Manang Gloria would cook; Lola used her Sevres China and Baccarat crystal; and Mama would dress up and look happy and young.

He insisted that we open our gifts immediately: an expensive bottle of French perfume for Lola, a sweater for Manang Gloria, a pearl necklace for Mama, and an antique music box for me. We were like children, fingering our gifts, and I saw him beaming happily that he had found the right gifts for us. Lola and Mama kissed him on the cheek. Manang Gloria kissed his hand, as if he were a "patron" of colonial days. And since everyone was looking my way, I went to him and planted a kiss on his cheek. He looked surprised and stood there for a long time touching his cheek where I had kissed him.

We were happy that night. Lola walked with us to the cathedral for Midnight Mass. Later we had the noche buena meal at home. Numerous carolers stopped by our house, singing about Christ, love, and joy. It was a clear and beautiful night. From the verandah I looked up at the stars, and I could feel my soul expanding. Since Papa died, I had not felt happiness like that.

It was almost dawn when he said he had to drive back to Manila to have Christmas dinner with his parents. After a lengthy farewell to the women, he said goodbye to me. I felt a flutter at the pit of my stomach. "Ramon..." I started, then lost my words. "Merry Christmas," I finally said.

In bed, I thought of Papa in the hospital and how he struggled to speak but could not. I thought of our big house in Manila. I thought of the malls that my friends and I used to frequent. I remembered my third grade nun who lectured once about charity being the most important virtue of all. I knew that I had done something terribly wrong. I wept silently in bed; even my mother did not hear me.

***

Years later, my mother blamed herself for Ramon's death, saying she was bad luck. His car had turned turtle on the highway, heading back to Manila. I did not tell her that in this matter, she was wrong.

THE LAST MOON-GAME OF SUMMER

Summer vacation is ending. While the moon is still large, we decide to play another moon-game, the last this summer. Jorge offers to go to his house to get buckets filled with water. As he's leaving, my cousin shouts, "Go help Jorge!"" She's been teasing me ever since our last moon-game when Jorge held my hand. I'm burning with humiliation, but Jorge simply smiles.

We're walking down the cobblestone street when a warm breeze blows stirring up the dry leaves, whipping my long hair around. I reach into my pocket for a rubber band to tie my hair back, confine all that wildness. I'm struggling with my unruly hair, when Jorge stops me. "It's nice like that," he says, taking away the rubber band from my hands. I feel embarrassed; I feel grateful. This attention makes me feel funny, and I start running. He runs after me, and together we race down the street.

Jorge's house is tall and dark, reminding me of an abandoned cemetery. The first floor is made of mossy bricks that need patching so badly. The upstairs is made of wood and the windows are the old-fashioned sliding kind, made of capiz. The white squares of capiz shells give off a strange luminescent glow.

The front doors were originally carriage doors, very wide, with a smaller door cut-out on the one side for people to use. There's an antique brass door knocker colored green from age, which amuses me greatly, I pound it several times until a servant opens the door.

It occurs to me that finally I'll see the inside of his house. It's two blocks away from our house, but until Jorge held my hand, I've dismissed this house as another decrepit mansion in Vigan. These past nights I've slipped away from my bedroom to head for the verandah.

Standing on tiptoes, I stared across our neighbor's backyard to study the peak of Jorge's roof. I wondered where his bedroom was, how it looked, if he had a desk with books, or a side table, if he kept his books on the side table as I do mine. And I wondered if he was already asleep, or if he was reading, or if he was thinking of me as I was thinking of him.

When we're in the house, Jorge's demeanor changes. He becomes solemn and serious, and I wonder if I played with the knocker too long, or if I said anything wrong. He whispers, "Papa is sick."

People in Vigan say his father is a descendant of a man from Canton, China who made a lot of money from cotton. But Jorge's father and his brothers fought over money and inheritance. His father drove away the brothers, and for that, God punished him and he developed a rare disease and has been bedridden for years.

I, too, assume a serious face. Jorge leads the way upstairs. There is a huge living room, which is dreadfully quiet. The windows are shut and the only source of light comes from double doors that are ajar. "Wait here," he says and he disappears behind the doors. The room is really quite dark and I feel frightened.

I see a huge framed picture of a Chinese man in Mandarin garb. The portrait hangs on the wall from a long cord attached to the ceiling. The man has a drooping Fu-Manchu moustache, his eyes are piercing, and his expression so stern that I think this man never laughed. I wonder if this is the man from Canton, Jorge's ancestor. He reportedly came to Vigan in the late 1700s with a bundle of clothes and his abacus. With the cotton boom, he was able to build this house and marry a Spanish mestiza. His imperial glare makes me sit on the edge of a plantation chair and fold my hands on my lap. I look around at Viennese mirrors, marble-topped tables, and other portraits of people long dead. When Jorge returns, I point at the man's portrait, and he acknowledges he is a great-great-grandfather.

"I'll show you around," Jorge says. He leads me to another sitting room with a grand piano and harp. Pretending I'm a famous harpist, I stand next to the harp, my spine exaggeratedly erect, and with great flare I run my fingers over the strings. "Bravo!" Jorge says, clapping, "You look good doing that." I give a little curtsy and we both laugh.

"I'll show you something," he says. He takes me to the library, which has enclosed lawyer bookcases. He opens a case and pulls out a book. He lays it on a desk and opens it. I catch the title: *The Discovery of the Moluccas and the Philippine Islands*. Then he points out a date: 1708. I've never seen a book that old. "Can I touch it?" I ask, in great awe. He hands me the book. As I reach for it, our fingers touch. Flustered, I almost drop it.

I remember the night he held my hand. We were playing the moon-game on my aunt's driveway. We had created a huge circle on the ground, using water. The "It" ran along the circumference and diameter, chasing the others who raced in and out of the circle. I stayed outside the circle, where I felt safe. "Come in," the others shouted in sing-song, "Come in. Don't be afraid," and reluctantly I ran into the circle. I was breathless with laughter and fear that I would be caught. The "It" singled me out in his pursuit. Like tentacles, his long arms waved toward me. My heart knocked against my ribs as I shrank away. The others shouted at me to run out of the circle, but I was afraid I'd get caught. I stood there, paralyzed. Jorge ran back into the circle, grabbed my hand, and pulled me out. He continued holding my hand. We were safe. I was safe.

"It's very old," I say, trying to hide my thoughts from him. I run my fingers over the old parchment paper. Avoiding his eyes, I fix my gaze on the book; I know he's watching me.

"Look at this drawing," he says, his hand brushing mine as he flips the book. He singles out an illustration of some natives next to a tree. He's standing close to me and I can feel the length of his body near mine. Our heads are so close together, I can feel his breath. We continue to pore over the book, but all I'm thinking about is Jorge next to me. I've spent nights dreaming something like this would happen; and now that it's happening all I can do is stare at an old book.

After we've scrutinized all the drawings, he leads me to a chapel full of antique ivory statues. The statues are dead-white with movable glass eyes and dark brown wigs made from human hair. I shiver and tell Jorge I don't like statues and dolls with real hair. He laughs.

"Do you want to see my room?" he asks. Without waiting for my answer, he leads me past the dining room to a room that must have been a smoking room in the past.

While the rest of the house has a dusty and moldy quality, Jorge's room is airy and light. The brightness comes from a wide window that opens out to the upstairs verandah. There's a bed, side tables, large desk, armoire, and cabinet. I walk past his bed and study an oil painting on the wall—a landscape painting of women threshing rice. "It's by Juan Luna," he says. I nod in recognition of the master painter's name. He tells me he used to have another room, beside his parents' bedroom, and that he moved into this room recently.

He sits on his bed and moves over, as if to make room for me. It's a four-poster bed with rich green velvet bedspread. I'm thinking we should hurry back to the park, but it feels right to be with Jorge. I sit beside him. We stare out at the verandah. There's a dry fountain in the middle, and scattered all around the tiled floor are Chinese dragon pots crammed with aloes and sword plants, tenacious plants that need little care.

All this time, we have been talking in whispers, but here in his room, his voice becomes normal again. He tells me about a sparrow that built her nest on the fountain, and how he watched her lay her eggs, how she sat on them until they hatched, took care of her babies until they were old enough to fly. "It was wonderful," he said, "Life just yards away."

And then I do something strange: I throw my head back and laugh.

"Why are you laughing?" he asks.

"It's silly, the bird with her babies, right in the middle of the verandah where everyone could see them," I reply, still laughing. I'm not making sense—I know that—and I wonder what's come over me. I look at Jorge wondering if he thinks I'm being foolish, but he takes a strand of my hair and pushes it back. He says, "I like to hear you laugh."

He lies back on his bed, closes his eyes. He's smiling; he appears content. He runs the palms of his hands on the bedspread as if rubbing the fur of an animal. "Of all the colors, I like green," he says. I remain seated although I'm tempted to curl up beside him, rest my head on his chest, listen to his heartbeat.

"Why do you like green?"

"It reminds me of Abra," he says. And he continues to tell me about the forest that he visited when he was seven. The caretaker of Jorge's house brought him to the mountaintop of Abra, where the forest was so thick there was hardly any sunlight. I have not been to Abra, but have heard of its remoteness, of its strangeness. Many years ago, the people there were headhunters; I have seen sketches of tattooed warriors holding human heads.

In this perpetual green, he looked around and felt God. "Do you believe in God?" he asks.

I pause, uncertain how to answer him. I hear running water and the rattling of pans from the kitchen. I know what he wants to hear. A part of me says I ought to tell him, yes, and in the Holy Trinity. Be done with all of that. Instead I say, "I'm an atheist." I say this softly, but with some defiance. I'm certain he will find me repulsive; he will never see me again.

He is not shocked. He watches me. "Why not?" There is curiosity in his voice, not judgement.

"I can't say; it's too much to explain."

"You go to St. Catherine's, and I've seen you in church."

"I do all that, but I just do them, I don't believe." I check his face and find a furrow between his brows.

Fingers pressed together as if in prayer, I add, "But I was a good Catholic before my father died. I said all my prayers and went to Mass." I describe the Sacred Heart at the landing of the stairs and Our Lady of Perpetual Succor in the hallway. I tell him about the holy cards I collect, some of which I keep in my missal. Before the First Friday of each month, the nuns herd us to the Redemptorist Church. "I learned to invent sins for some man I couldn't see eye to eye," I tell Jorge.

"Ah, I know about your father," he says, "the plane crash in Mount Manuggal. With President Magsaysay."

I fidget. I don't want to talk about *that.* It's too difficult to even think about all that. I hear sizzling and smell fried garlic. I didn't cry when the nun told me about the plane crash. I dug my nails deep into my flesh as I clenched my fist. Dear God, I prayed, let there be a mistake, let him have missed the flight. I made deals with God: I'd hear Mass every day for the next month. But it didn't matter. Pieces of his body were sent to us in a closed coffin. I never saw his body before the burial, never saw what God did to him.

After the funeral, I used to play near the gate with my father's two police dogs. When a car drove by, the dogs barked and we raced to the gate, expecting my father.

"I didn't become an atheist just like that," I explain, snapping my fingers. "I didn't just say, now I no longer believe in God. Things just didn't make sense. The nuns talked about purgatory, which is temporary. Then there's hell, which is forever. Then there's another place called limbo, where unbaptized babies go. I see no justice in placing babies in such a place. Could God be so unfair?"

Jorge sits up. He strokes my hair back. I can feel the warmth from his hand. "You've been hurt," he says. "You're angry at God. One day you will realize that He loves you. And one day, I'll take you to Abra. It was there in Abra, that I knew God exists." Then he adds these words, softly, but I hear him: "I felt it inside, as surely as I know I love you."

He lifts my chin and I let him. My eyes are open; I do not know what to do. He presses his mouth to mine. I am surprised at how soft and moist a mouth is. It makes me think of that green forest in Abra, that mountaintop of Abra where he found God.

It makes me realize that even though we'll go back and play the moon-game, and later my cousin and I will walk back to our house, and I'll sleep in the same four-poster bed, and wake up in the morning and do the same things I've been doing all summer, that somehow things will never quite be the same ever again.

THE RICE FIELD

Tiya Octavia has died and we are on our way to Vigan, a cavalcade of cars and a funeral hearse carrying her body. Octavia died in Makati Med, but she must rest in our family mausoleum in Vigan.

From the main highway, we turn left to a long stretch of dirt road that winds up a hill until we reach a high gate. Two guards holding armalites scrutinize the funeral hearse and the cars that follow. It is only my mother's insistence that she is the older sister of Señora Ceres that convinces them to open the gate and allow us in.

After driving for hours, we need a break. We head for the main house where Tiya Ceres is ready for us. It is not quite dawn, but she has breakfast ready — hot chocolate and coffee, rice cakes, steamed rice, fried eggs, and sliced Spam with caramelized sugar. She tells me the Spam is for me, and she stirs Nescafe Instant Coffee into a cup of hot water for me. It is her way of showing affection to me, her godchild. When I was small, she used to give me envelopes with money or pieces of jewelry.

My mother has three sisters: Aurora, Ceres and Octavia who just died. Aurora and Octavia, both unmarried, had lived in their ancestral house in Vigan. Ceres lives here in Pangasinan. She is a small, frightened-looking woman whose only visible sign of vanity is her dyed red hair, a color that looks frightful with her skin tone. She was what Tagalogs called, "kayumangging kaligatan," a brown-skinned beauty. But that was when she was young. Now she is in her sixties, and she has the weary expression of an old woman. Her shoulders cave into her shrunken chest, as if she wants to disappear, to remain unnoticed—except for the red hair, which screams for attention. Her hair has always puzzled me. She used to have black hair streaked with gray, until her husband brought home one of his many mistresses and ordered Ceres to serve them. Soon after, she dyed her hair this crazy color. Her husband, one of Marcos's generals beats her. We have known this for a long time now, and my mother and Tiya Aurora have been prodding Tiya Ceres to leave her husband, but she refuses.

The electricity is down—brown-outs and black-outs are now ordinary occurrences under the Marcos regime. A few scattered candles and candelabras on the dining table illuminate the room. Tiya Ceres and Mama sit at the end of the dining table. She holds my mother's hand and talks to her. Octavia was their baby sister, and now they talk about her. They recall how she was born during the year of the great earthquake, which buried a neighboring church bell tower. They murmur about how she did not talk for three years and how fearful they were that she was retarded, but that she surprised them all by one day reading the labels on English tins filled with crackers and chocolates. Octavia loved food, especially fried plantains—and here the sisters wept hard and were silent for a long time. But after a while, they rehashed Octavia's last days and how she died. It was her heart; finally it gave up. She wasn't strong to start with, and the war incident made her more frail. In her last days, she remembered the awful things that had happened to her, but thankfully, just before she died, she was happy, talking about calla lilies which she loved. The sisters cry together. They talk of everything except the obvious, that is that she was the birth mother of Jorge, that Jorge and I had been in love, but when he learned my aunt was his mother, he left Vigan for Sagada.

After eating enough to please Tiya Ceres, I step out to the patio for some air. Even though a bit of golden light fringes the sky, the huge moon is still up. I take a deep breath. Even now, after all these years, it's still difficult for me to comprehend that Tiya Octavia was Jorge's mother.

Tiya Octavia was like a child; or I should say, she was childlike. I recall the time we spent a morning together; this was in Vigan. I was around nine years old. It was early in the morning when we descended the marble stairs to the huge backyard, which was a riot of plants. We walked past the back wall, a section that is wild like a jungle, green and mysterious. We walked through the orchard of lanzones, chicos, star apples, balimbing and other fruit trees. We checked the orchids and herb garden next to the dirty kitchen. We lingered along the rows of

Tiya Octavia's beloved calla lilies which stood against the mossy brick walls.

She placed a shovel and trowel near the calla lilies, and before tilling the soil, she handed me the garden hose and motioned for me to water the plants. Typhoon season or summer, my aunt watered her garden at dawn and at sunset. Twice a day, every day, even when the monsoon winds were blowing so ferociously the tiles fell from the roof.

She was a creature of habit, my aunt. Before dawn, when the stars were still out, she said her prayers. After, she filled the dragon-pot with water for her bath. She used strong laundry soap called Perla, not Ivory nor Palmolive. A devotee to Our Lady of Carmel, she wore a stark brown dress and a scapular. She also wore white socks to hide the eczema on her legs.

After we worked in silence, she led me to the kitchen where she took out an antique copper chocolate pot. She rummaged in the cupboard for chocolate tablets. She special-ordered the tablets made from the fattest cocoa beans. To make our chocolate drink, Tiya Octavia used the gas range, not the open hearth. She melted the chocolate, whipped in fresh milk and sugar, and she poured two cups—one for her and one for me. We went to the gazebo, and there she removed her white socks to dry them under the morning sun. After, we sipped our chocolate. Surprisingly she became talkative. For the first time, she alluded to me what had happened to her. Pointing at her calla lilies, she said:

"Calla lilies are beautiful. I dream of them all the time. I first dreamt of them when I was a prisoner. It was the second night. The first night I could not sleep. I simply lay on the small bed and watched the gecko on the ceiling. It had fat little toes that made it stick to the ceiling. There were lizards too, scampering about. One of the lizards fell down beside me but I did not move. It slithered over my leg and down the bed. It didn't hurt me. I heard my breathing so I knew I was alive. That was how I spent the first night. But the next night I dreamt of calla lilies, a long row of calla lilies with gigantic fan-leaves and long graceful stems topped with white flowers, like these, only bigger. It was all in bright color, like a Technicolor movie. They were amazing calla lilies; they stood waist-high. The leaves were like banana leaves, and the white flowers shone like something pure. Each flower folded over in exactly the same way, right over left, with delicate folds on the petal, making it look like shirred white satin."

***

From where I stand, I can see beyond the high walls with barbed wire. There was no barbed wire in the past, only crumbling walls, mossy from age. An enormous rice field stretches out as far as I can see. Under the moonlight, it glimmers like some strange watery patchwork. The water beneath the rice stalks catches the moonlight, flashing light here and there, reminding me of fish moving through water. The rice is incredibly lush and green. I leave the patio and walk down a gravel path toward a rice paddy. The tall rice stalks are bent over, heavy with grain. A white mist rises from the soil, so that the rice stalks look like they're floating.

Once Jorge, I, and four others were here for the fiesta. We walked single file along the bank of the rice paddies. I was terrified of falling into the watery seedbed squirming with leeches. I walked gingerly along the narrow bank, trailing far behind the others. Jorge helped me. "Put your hands on my shoulders," he said. I followed him. Slowly, we negotiated the rice paddies. In the distance, someone started singing the rice planting song, and we all broke out in song:

Planting rice is never fun,
bent from noon 'til the set of sun,
cannot stand,
cannot sit,
cannot rest for a little bit.

Then suddenly Jorge stopped, "I know a story about a rice farmer and a star maiden."

"Tell me the story," I begged.

"It's a long story, a nice one," he said, "I'll tell it to you sometime, when we have time."

But that time never came.

I thrust memories of Tiya Octavia, of Jorge back into my mind. That was long ago. It was time to put all of that to rest, to let matters die with Tiya Octavia.

***

Something glitters in the distance, next to the acacia tree. Small tongues of fire dance about at the base of the tree trunk. Strange, flickering light, like shards of steel that make my breathing rapid. Could this be St. Elmo's Fire? Barrio folk talk about coming across St. Elmo's fire, usually in remote places, a forest, or lonely road; St. Elmo's fire has always been associated with death and tormented spirits walking the earth.

I walk toward the tree. Yellow tongues of flame quiver when the breeze blows. A dozen votive candles are clustered near the tree. The place feels like an altar overflowing with unheard prayers. Another breeze blows making the hair on my arms prickle. I make the sign of the Cross and say the Our Father.

In the dark living room, I tell my aunt how lovely their rice field looks, and I mention the votive candles. Instantly there is a hush in the room. I look around, not understanding what this silence is all about. People avoid my eyes. I realize I've said something wrong. My mother quickly announces we have to get back on the road, that we have another two hours ride. My aunt races to the kitchen and asks the servants to wrap up the leftover rice cakes for us. She says she'll be leaving for Vigan within the hour. Soon we are all in our cars and heading back toward the highway.

In the car, the driver explains that the rice field is known as a killing field. The military regime of Marcos dumped bodies there. The relatives of the dead leave lighted candles for their loved ones.

We are driving by the rice field when he tells me this, and it is then I see the funeral hearse turn left at the highway. The rest of us—four cars in total—have trailed behind and are still negotiating the dirt road. In the distance, and as if moving in slow-motion, the hearse vanishes behind a wall of rice stalks.

1943: TIYA OCTAVIA

You dream of fried bananas, sizzling hot in bubbling coconut oil, golden brown, its sweet aroma bringing back childhood memories of your mother in the kitchen—happy times. With a metal spatula, you lift the banana-halves from the wok and roll them in a mound of precious sugar. The irresistible sight of the white grains of sugar clinging to the red-brown surface make your mouth water, pushes your sister's words out of your mind: "No matter what happens, don't leave the house." Ever since the Japanese occupied Vigan, you have not eaten fried bananas. Meals consist of sweet potatoes, cooked with mongo beans, dried fish, and coconut milk. You're fortunate, you realize that, because many have only watery soup to drink.

You slip on your wooden clogs and sling the woven basket unto your right arm. The plants still have dew when you wrap three silver coins in your handkerchief. You pin the bundle to your bosom, and pat it. With the image of fried bananas shining in your mind, you open the gate and head for the open market. Along the way you run into a skin-and-bones dog rummaging through a pile of garbage. The image unsettles you, but soon you wonder what the banana vendor will say today. He's an old widower who likes to talk. Maybe, if he has them, he'll show you the small bananas called fingers of the Datu; and he'll point out the sweet stubby kinds; and of course he'll bring out the starchy kind, perfect for boiling or frying. You'll buy six of those, hurry back home, and fry the bananas, just on time for breakfast.

But near his stall, you see two Japanese soldiers. They're in their stiff khaki uniforms and they're clutching rifles in their hands. They're shouting at the banana vendor. You consider turning back, but they see you. Besides, it's too late, your feet can't stop; you're headed toward destiny.

The loud guttural voices reverberate in your chest. A soldier pushes the vendor to the ground. He falls near a black puddle. Enormous fruit flies alight on his face. The soldiers laugh. They prod him with their rifles. He's an old man; it isn't right for him to be treated that way, but townspeople stay back. They're remembering the seven men beheaded by the Japanese. They were simple farmers, accused of being spies. People slink away, hide behind mounds of wilted vegetables and decaying entrails. In the distance, a horse neighs. There is only one thing to do. While the soldiers laugh, you bend down to help the banana vendor. The fingers that he plants on your shoulders dig like claws. Both of you turn to walk away. For a few seconds, it seems the two of you will make it, but suddenly the soldiers are pulling you away. The old man pushes you, disowns you. Now, you're the undesirable one. He runs and disappears among the cowering spectators. The soldiers drag you behind the banana vendor's stall. Years ago, you found two boys playing with a coconut beetle. They tied a string around its neck and twirled the string around to force the beetle to fly. When the beetle's wings whirred, they laughed. The laughter of the soldiers reminds you of those boys.

Someone throws you down so you lay sprawled on the dirty cement floor. A huge bunch of yellow-green bananas, the kind you were looking for, lies just a foot away from you. You can almost touch them. You try to get up, but one soldier pins your arms to your side. A soldier's face looms in front of you. He has pimples on his face, a boy playing war. You struggle, and he hits your mouth. You start to scream, but the other one holds your chin. The young one kisses you, a salty, foul kiss that forces vomit up your throat. He lifts your skirt.

"Help!" you shout, but people step back.

He pulls down your cotton underwear on which you embroidered "Thursday," a long time ago.

Santa-Maria-Santa-Maria, you think.

Then you hear a man scream, "Baka!" It's a third soldier carrying a long curved saber, an officer. The two soldiers release you. The officer slaps them. "Baka! Baka!" he shouts at them. Briefly you think he will save you. You cling to him, and then, too late, you see lust in his eyes. He struggles with the buttons of his pants, then he gets on top of you. He forces his way inside you. It's like being cleaved in two. You hear the heavy breathing of the two soldiers who are standing nearby, who are watching. When the officer finishes, he turns you over to the other soldiers.

There's so much blood and pain, you shut your eyes, there is nothing else to do. They have you; they own you; they defile you; and there's nothing you can do except shut your eyes.

JORGE IN SAGADA

Sagada. I'm in Sagada, a place I do not love. Nearly two decades ago, I visited this place. Then and now Sagada has a mournful quality, an aridity despite the bitter cold especially when the sun goes down. These past nights, I have listened to the whipping of the wind and the slamming of the shutters, and once I heard the cry of some desperate farmer, perhaps weary of coaxing sweet potatoes to grow on the dry rocky soil of this bitter place. Or perhaps it was just the shrill cry of a desolate bird. I am no longer sure, because here in Sagada I am sure of nothing.

I came here when I was young; it had entered my head that I would find peace in Sagada. I have always been drawn to mountaintops, their images etched in my mind as cloudy mystical lands the old people talked about, places that their ancient gods and goddesses visited, a ladder or rainbow connecting both worlds. Sagada had something more than misty mountaintops; I had heard about the caves, and some primal instinct to burrow deep into the belly of the earth drove me here.

Mama who did not believe in the folklore warned, "It is not a hospitable place." But I insisted. I had just learned the truth about myself and felt a longing to go someplace far away. I took the long dusty bus-ride and stayed in the only hotel, a rundown place without running water and electricity, and which smelled of mushrooms. Right away, I sensed the decay in Sagada.

At the time I thought the feeling of death came from within me, not from Sagada. Papa had just died, and Mama told me her secret. She talked about the night the doktora came to the house carrying a baby swaddled in a rainbow blanket. "He needs a home," she told

Mama. "His mother was forced into prostitution, his father was a Japanese soldier," the doktora explained.

While Mama told me this story, she traced the contours of my face: "Your eyes were closed, and a bit of saliva trickled down the corner of your mouth. You were making sucking motions. The second I saw you, I knew I had to hold you and no one could take you away from me." Her fingers traveled over my cheekbones, my eyelids, my nose.

And so having learned the truth about myself, I discovered I knew nothing about myself. I had been stripped of every knowledge about who I was and where I came from. I hankered to know something about my real parents. I harangued Mama for information about my real mother, until weary of my relentless attacks, she revealed her name.

I had seen Octavia Villanueva around town. She was a small, plain woman who always wore brown. She must have loved shredded coconut sweet because I saw her several times buying sweets from the market vendor, opening the wrapper and eating the sweet before the transaction was completed. Her gestures were slow; her face had a placid expression. At some point in my childhood, I had dismissed her as a simpleton, but now I yearned to see her as if seeing her would give me back my sense of self. I walked a thousand times past the Villanueva mansion. I ached to see if she carried any trace of the shame she had when she carried me in her womb. One early morning I climbed a tree and peered over the Villanueva fence and caught a glimpse of Octavia, walking about in her slippers, with lifeless socks dragging on the earth. She pored over the calla lilies and mumbled to herself. Her short skimpy hair stood out in all angles, and her placid face revealed nothing about me.

I decided to stop seeing Isabel. I could not tell her, "Listen, by the way, we are cousins after all, your aunt is my mother." I should have, if I dared, but the lie that was as old as I was sat within my throat, a screen that twisted words of sorrow and confusion into words of hate. I told her I did not love her; I said I loved someone else. I told her we could no longer see each other, and she crying could say nothing, not even that she hated me, because I deserved her hate.

I fled to Sagada, where the caves turned out to be ancient burial grounds, where dark shriveled mummies resembling desiccated coco lumber curled up in the fetal position rested like pods in the centers of hand-hewn tree trunks. The lids of their sarcophagi were made of dark wood and carved with birds and serpents. Inside the cave, I felt the world turn inside out: I saw three women huddled together, arms outstretched, palms facing upward. Bent forward, they stare at a baby boy swaddled tightly in a faded blue blanket, his face chalky white, his mouth wide open as he roots about trying to find something to suck. A woman picks him up, turns to hand him to the woman beside her. She accepts him, then, she too turns and hands him to the third woman. Three women in a circle, passing this baby from one to the other until I became so dizzy, I almost lost my way out of that dark cave. That night, I dreamt of wandering around faceless with little demons jumping around me. I awoke with an incredible thirst. I could not go back to sleep. Every night hence, I had trouble sleeping. If I did catch some sleep, I had the same nightmare. I was becoming mad, and the only thing that kept me from going completely insane was prayer:

Oh God, my God, my refuge and my strength look down in mercy on me who cry to Thee — have mercy oh God; and by the intercession of the glorious and Immaculate Virgin Mary, Mother of God, of Saint Joseph her spouse, of Thy blessed Apostles Peter and Paul, and of all the Saints, in mercy and goodness hear my prayers—hear me, oh God, hear me.

It was all I could do to hold myself together, here in Sagada, this awful place of death. I knew I had to leave Sagada or go mad.

1973: RECRUITING

I didn't know it but the retreat scheduled in Valencia was cancelled. Valencia is a remote town in Negros Oriental, and Father Neil the parish priest of Valencia, was unable to contact me. For most of the night I struggled to find the right words to make the people understand their exploitation. I planned to tell them how the Spanish friars turned this fertile land into haciendas, how landowners used the fruit of this land to buy Cadillacs and all kinds of caprices while they, the workers who planted and cut the sugar cane, had nothing more than their one-room nipa hut and constant hunger in their bellies. I was going to tell them about the cronies of Marcos who tried to manipulate the market but ended up with soft sugar market and sacks of sugar rotting in rat-infested granaries. I was ready to teach the people in order to gather more recruits—this was what we really wanted to accomplish, gather more recruits, increase the number of those who opposed the government. It took five hours to get to Valencia, and when Carding told me we couldn't do anything now because of a dead infant, I felt great disappointment.

We attended the funeral—Carding and I. It was a good opportunity to be part of the people, to know them, to understand their psyche, and to better prepare for them.

It was not your usual funeral. I'm comparing it to the funerals in Luzon where the wake lasts a week, the bodies lying in open caskets for the entire town to see, more of a social affair where there's food and men gamble. The funeral in Valencia was different.

It was one of the saddest I'd ever witnessed, worse than Papa's own funeral. In Papa's case, he had been sick for two years and Mama and I were prepared for his death. Even though Mama and I mourned, we had felt relief that his suffering finally ended. But in Valencia, we buried a week-old baby who died overnight from beriberi, an infant girl who didn't have the chance to see the seasons, who only witnessed a hot week in May, so hot the earth cracked and birds were found dead along the dry riverbed. Carding said the parents of the infant had gone to the landowner to borrow money to pay the hospital, but the landowner had declined. The baby died. Even with medical care, the baby would still have died because she was very frail.

I didn't see the body. By the time I arrived, the people and priest were gathered outside the chapel. Usually, villagers noticed me upon my arrival. The men especially would look me over, sizing me up as to whether I'm a government man or not. But yesterday, the funeral consumed them.

The priest stood in front, muttering prayers. The young parents of the baby stood behind him. The father fiercely clutched in his hands what looked like a shoebox. It was made of cheap plywood, and flowers of all colors were piled on top of it. It took me a while to comprehend that this box was a coffin. So small—I have never seen a coffin that small. It was smaller than Mama's carved ebony jewelry box. In some other place, some other time, this young man could have been carrying a present, a gift, perhaps for his wife who stood beside him and who looked no more than eighteen. But in this place of hunger, this man carried his dead infant daughter.

The mother of the dead child was very shy, and she appeared embarrassed for upsetting other people's lives with this funeral. She cowered beside her husband; her left hand constantly touching the side of the small coffin. She wore a faded billowy navy-blue shift, which looked like a maternity dress. Her belly was still rounded from her recent pregnancy and her young breasts still swollen with milk for her dead child.

The hands of the father of the child shook as he grasped the sides of the box, hugging it against his chest. Every time he exhaled, his breath made the soft petals of the flowers on the coffin quiver. There was a strange stillness around us; not a single dog barked; not a single pig or chicken made a sound. There was only the priest, this couple holding on to their dead child, and the rest of us trailing behind.

It was May and if not for this funeral a nice summer day. I was astonished at how nature could contradict human reality. It seemed to me that sadness like this called for a dreary wet day, but yesterday, as we walked along the dusty trail, the sugar cane fields shimmered like a sea of green. The tall emerald tops rippled when a breeze blew. But the wind was dry and hot.

The procession snaked its way through the narrow trail in the midst of the sugar cane fields and stopped in an old cemetery. One of the men dragged a shovel over to the area near the acacia tree. Despite the dryness of the earth, it did not take him long to dig a shallow grave. The priest sprinkled holy water on the grave and on the coffin. Little drops of the water clung to the face of the father carrying the coffin. He took a deep breath and shivered, and I wondered if he could ever let go of the coffin. He did so with grace. He knelt down and laid the small coffin in the middle of the grave. Tenderly, he arranged the flowers on top, and then he got up and stood there like an altar boy waiting for the priest to give him instructions.

I felt I had slipped into a dream. It was the smallness of the coffin that made everything seem large and strange—a small mound of flowers in that shallow grave. It was easy to forget about the infant inside.

After the priest finished praying, the mother of the child released one prolonged sob. Then she fell to her knees and clawed at the flowers on the coffin. I thought she would open it. I wondered what I would see. I have seen malnourished children with wrists like matchsticks, stomachs bloated from kwashiorkor. Would the baby look like that or would she be rigid and gray? Or maybe she would look like a little doll?

The father of the dead child pulled the mother up and held her steady. She crossed her arms across her breasts. I wondered how she and her husband met. Watching the two of them, I made up the story that she minded her father's little store where she sold soft drinks, beer, Chicklets and cigarettes. He sauntered to her store one afternoon after a hard day's work at the sugar cane fields. While the other men asked for San Miguel beer, he asked for a Coca Cola. Every six o'clock for a month he sat just six feet away from her while he bantered with the other men about what happened at work, which men cut themselves while cutting the cane, which ones lost fingers while operating the huge presses at the sugar central. While talking and laughing, he would tilt his head to the side, the dying sun casting red-orange highlights on his dusty hair, and his eyes would catch hers. At first she quickly lowered her gaze, but as the days passed, she met his eyes and smile until a bond grew between them. One night in October when Typhoon Alicia blew, he stayed to help her close the store. When they finished propping up the corrugated sheets over the flimsy windows, they walked together, huddled close under a small black umbrella. They struggled against the wind and rain until they reached her home, a nipa hut that leaned when the wind blew.

"You need the umbrella," she said as she started to climb up the ladder to the hut.

"Wait," he said, and he held her arm and pulled her back and kissed her lightly on the lips.

That was how it all began, that was the beginning of this sad funeral.

The people placed more flowers in the grave, and someone threw in a small plastic rattle. It lay on top of the coffin. Then soil was thrown over all this until we could no longer see the coffin. Someone stuck a small wooden cross in the fresh mound of earth.

When people started to leave, I motioned to Carding that we too should go. "Next week," he said, "Come back next week. It will be better next week."

I nodded, thinking I had driven five hours through PC territory for nothing more than this funeral. But in town, near the jeep, the father of the dead child caught up with us. With the same hands that grasped that incredibly small coffin, he held my arm. "I want to join," he said. "I want to fight."

We signed him up and told him where to go for meetings.

It had not been a useless trip after all.

CHRISTMAS EVE

By the time Christmas decorations appeared in Manila, Nadia insisted we see Miguel. He needed us, Nadia said. It didn't matter if Marcos himself killed her, she had to see our son. We never raised him. The last time we saw him was eight months ago, in a movie house where Nadia's mother brought him. It was the safest place we could think of, and so in the back row of the balcony section near the lovers seeking refuge in the dim theater, we hugged him and gave him some sweets from Bulacan. That was all we could do to show him our affection; but even then I felt him withdraw. We were strangers to him. He had lived with his grandmother since he was two. Nadia said she wanted us to live together like a normal family. The longer she'd lived underground, the more she yearned for a conventional life. I had to remind her how impossible it had been to move about underground when Miguel had been with us.

Every time Nadia heard a Christmas carol over the radio, or saw twinkling lights in the department stores, she spoke of Miguel. All this sentimentality surprised me because Nadia had always been stoic. In fact, she was more than stoic: Nadia was the kind of person who was bred on hate; she hated her domineering father, and she hated her mother for allowing her father to abuse her. She had a brittle quality, which she disguised as practical. There was something almost mechanical about Nadia that frightened me at first, but which I found reassuring as the years passed. She was the kind of person you wanted with you during a raid—calm and quick and seething with rage that she could turn on the attackers.

I agreed we'd see Miguel but only on Christmas Eve, and only near Malate Church where there would be many people. It was always safer to meet in crowded places. Salvagings happened in isolated fields.

I wore dark clothes and I told Nadia to dress simply; nothing should call attention to us. She insisted on wearing a dress with a floral pattern; she said she wanted to look her best for her son.

Billy accompanied us, and we traveled in a jeepney with psychedelic decorations. Even though it was almost midnight, the streets were filled with people. I wished I were one of them, anonymous, lost in that human mill. I was getting tired of our fake identities, the constant hiding, the tension. Too many friends had been killed or had betrayed our cause. I was starting to wonder what our cause was all about. It had been for freedom, for a better life for the majority. Once I believed the NDF could make a difference. But now after over a decade what have we to show for our all our work? We had splintered into numerous bickering groups. The names of our groups sounded like alphabet soup: NDF, CNL, CCP, ND, KAAKBAY, MABINI, ATOM, SAPAK, AKKAAPKA, KOMPIL. Had it all been a game for us, playing heroes and martyrs, and meantime Marcos stayed in power, and after him, another dictator would step forward? I felt lost.

We parked near Los Indios Bravos Bar, and the three of us waded through the crowd toward church. I kept expecting armed men to jump out and arrest us, or shoot us the way they shot Evelio Javier in downtown Iloilo.

Nadia's mother and Miguel stood next to a cotton candy cart. Miguel was plucking bits from the airy pink mass and popping them into his mouth. Nadia ran toward him and thankfully the boy hugged her back. He was nine; he'd grown an inch since we last saw him. Nadia had not known she was carrying him until she was four months along, and she hadn't taken care of herself. Even when she did know she was pregnant, she was unable to eat properly. We were constantly moving, and oftentimes the food we ate was not cooked properly. I thought Miguel would die when I first saw him—yellow from jaundice, eyes lifeless. It was good to see he'd grown and looked healthy. I could even see my face in his. I wanted to hug him but felt awkward. I hardly knew my son. Nadia's mother urged him to give me a kiss. He smiled shyly and approached me carefully. He took a deep breath, as if giving himself courage, and stood on tiptoe to kiss me. I smelled the sugar on his breath, and felt his sticky lips on my cheek. I felt past longings, felt like weeping. I wanted to hug him tight, tell him how sorry I was that we were never there for him, but my feelings did not translate into words, and all I could do was pat him on the head, like Papa used to do to me.

***

We should have left, but Nadia wanted to spend more time with Miguel and her mother. We walked to Max Fried Chicken, the group of us, like a family having a midnight meal after Christmas Eve Mass. The briskness of the December air reminded me of another Christmas Eve years ago, when Mama, Papa, and I walked from church back to our house. I was between them, holding both their hands, and all the way we greeted people: Maligayang Pasko! Merry Christmas. And back home, we had our noche buena meal. There had been such serenity and happiness then, but this time, I felt uncertainty and fear.

The restaurant had not changed much; it still boasted of the small roasted fryers, red-brown from the ketchup-baste. Tables were filled with families dressed in their best. We sat in a table chosen by Billie in the back of the restaurant. I wondered how life would have been if we *were* just another family. Would Nadia and I be professors? Would we live in a project near the U.P.? Would we have Sunday family gatherings at our home? Would we have been content with a life like that? Would I?

Nadia asked her mother how Miguel was doing in school. He's an honor student, her mother reported, his test papers are 100% most of the time. Nadia ran her hand over Miguel's head; the boy beamed proudly. He said, "Lola says you got 100% also."

Nadia nodded, then she turned her head to one side to hide her face. I caught her wiping away tears from her eyes. She got up to go to the bathroom. "Are you all right?" her mother asked, following her.

I was alone in the table with Miguel and Billie, and awkwardness rooted in me. The boy looked at me, as if waiting for me to say something. I searched my mind for words, trying to recall what Mama said to me when I was young. "Do you have friends?" I asked.

His eyes sparkled and he raised one finger. "Tony," he replied.

"That's good," I said, "it's good to have a best friend. I had a friend once."

"What's his name?" he asked.

I shook my head not wanting to remember. "It was a long time ago," I said.

"Tony lives down the street. We meet at the corner store sometimes, to buy candy. But Lola doesn't want me go out."

I detected loneliness in his tone; and I looked hard at him and saw in his face weary days of trailing behind his grandmother, watching the television programs she watched, conversing with a woman forty years his senior. The house I grew up in was big and quiet. Mama and Papa were considerably older and I learned to converse with people who were old enough to be my grandparents. The other school children used to laugh at the formal way I spoke and behaved.

Making conversation, Miguel offered to say the multiplication table from 11 on: 11 times 1, equals 11; 11 times 2 equals 22, and so on. His thin voice rose and fell rhythmically, hypnotically.

He was multiplying 13 times 13 when Nadia and her mother returned. Nadia was smiling, excited about something; her mother looked somber. "Jorge, listen Mama has agreed to have Miguel visit us just for a week this December," Nadia said.

Billie glanced at me. The boy looked at his grandmother, uncomprehending what was going on, but sensing he was part of the discussion.

"From now until New Year's eve. We'll bring him back to Manila on New Year's eve. Isn't that so, Ma?"

"Nadia …" I started to protest.

"It'll be all right. Nothing will happen now. It's Christmas time. Just for a few days, Jorge, that is all, that's all I ask. I have never asked you very much these past years; you can't deny me this."

She was right, of course. Nadia never asked for anything.

"We'll pick up some of his clothes, and we can leave now. We'll get there by mid-day tomorrow. We can have Christmas together," she continued, her face glowing with her dreams.

Sensing a family quarrel brewing, Billie excused himself, saying he had to check the jeep. I looked at Nadia's face, happy for the first time in the two years we'd lived underground. Christmas—with her and with our son—It sounded like a dream, something from the fairytales of my youth. I could feel myself being drawn to the idea of the three of us, together, just for a few days, but I could not rid myself of the image of the dead bodies of Lenny and Cris, not to mention the numerous missing friends of ours, all dead no doubt. I would have to say no. "Nadia …" I started again.

But before I had to say the cruel word, she placed her finger on my lips, then heaving a deep sigh, she turned away from me and whispered to her mother. They started crying, and Miguel started to get agitated. I picked him up, hugged him tight, and said, "Be a good boy, don't give your Lola a hard time. We love you."

Nadia recovered before her mother did, and wiping away her tears, she hugged and kissed Miguel. "We'll see you soon," she said. The corners of her lips quivered, and her eyes looked like those of a very old woman.

We joined Billie near the jeep and left. The tears had stopped. We waded through the crowd once again, away from church.

ALMOST FORGOTTEN

Before the Second World War and when my father was still alive, our Manila house was as grand as the mansions in the then-fashionable Malate District. Japanese and American bombs, grenades, bullets destroyed all that.

After Liberation, my parents found their house in rubble—crystal chandeliers smashed to pieces, enormous airy rooms flattened to the ground, marble floors broken, rats scurrying about. They even found a dead nun rotting out in the backyard. Papa speculated she was a Paulist nun from nearby St. Paul's College, who got caught in crossfire. They buried her unceremoniously in the backyard. Postwar Manila was littered with countless putrid corpses like hers.

My parents decided to construct three smaller houses, one for the family and the other two to rent out. It was a prophetic move because my father died in 1957, and the rentals provided reliable income to my frazzled mother.

Our place was a three-bedroom, two-bath concrete structure, very functional, and within walking distance to the market, church and school, just what my widowed mother wanted. In the 1950s we had upscale tenants. For years a British ambassador lived in the house fronting the street. He was very pale and spoke in a monotone impossible to understand. An American businessman named Mr. Selsby, whom my mother kept calling Mr. Sells, lived in one of the houses. There was a Spanish family with a tiny grandmother named Abuelita who fed the sparrows daily.

By the 1960s, we had less-affluent renters. Squatters settled in nearby empty lots. When I was in high school, the neighborhood was downright pathetic. It was a source of great embarrassment to my older sister, especially when she started dating and boys had to drive past rickety lean-tos and piles of foul garbage to get to our place. She and my mother had big fights about this. They shouted at each other, my sister insisting we should move to a better neighborhood, and my mother reciting her litany about how she'd lived there since pre-war days and my father himself had built our house, earthquake proof at that, and we would not leave.

Even though I mentally sided with my sister, I kept quiet. After losing my father at the age of nine, I was dependent on my mother. I wasn't about to enter a shouting match with her. Besides, my mother and sister's high drama only annoyed me. I developed a personality that tried to please, to stay out of trouble. I never complained even when one day, as I was walking to Pasay Avenue to catch a jeepney, a thief yanked a gold bracelet from my wrist.

My mother had shrugged, saying it was a shame because my bracelet was made of Chinese gold, and I should be more careful. And she went on with her work. I don't know if she ever noticed the decay of our surroundings. Widowed at forty-seven, she threw herself into the family business to insure that my sister and I would be fed, clothed, and educated properly—her basic goals for us.

She never admitted how dangerous the neighborhood had become even when a man slashed my sister's purse off her arm, right on our street at 11 o'clock in the morning. Nor did she acknowledge the area's downward slide when a robber entered our house one night and stole jewelry and money, a frightening experience since we were all asleep at the time. Even when local residents were clearly prostitutes and bartenders, my mother bull headedly declared they were secretaries and accountants. "And they all work the night shift?" my sister sarcastically noted.

There was an incident that happened to me during this time. It has suddenly surfaced, like a drowned body that comes bobbing to the surface of the water after enough time has passed. I have been thinking, wondering why now after some twenty-five years, I should remember this.

In my senior year of high school, a classmate of mine was turning eighteen (she was two years older than most of us). Melisande, the daughter of a congressman, was going to have a debut, a big affair at the Manila Hotel. We were giddy with excitement. We had only attended a few parties of the jam-session/soiree variety; here was an honest-to-goodness coming-out party, at the fabulous Manila Hotel no less. The press built up this Debut of the Year. *Women's Magazine* and the *Philippine Graphic* featured Melisande. We talked of nothing else but "the debut."

On the Saturday of Melisande's birthday celebration, I woke up early. I looked at my new pink lace dress. Beside the dress stood my new pink high heels. I was almost breathless with excitement. I don't know what thoughts crowded my mind, what expectations I had, but one thing—I was convinced that something magical would happen that night.

Skipping breakfast (since I was crash dieting anyway), I told my mother I'd go to Carmen's Beauty Salon to have my hair done and to get a manicure. She sighed and gave me twenty pesos.

Carmen's was four blocks away. I walked past Willie's apartment. Willie was a boy my age who had cerebral palsy and who spent his days at home. I saw him four times each weekday, every time I walked by their front porch. I'd wave at him and his mother. Willie would be so happy to see me, he'd contort his face and flail his arms. That Saturday, only his mother was outside.

"Where's Willie?" I asked.

"Resting," she said. "And where are you going?"

"To the beauty parlor," I said proudly.

"Growing up, aren't you?" she said, giving me an added lift.

I hurried on past Antok's corner market that sold all sorts of items from coarse sea salt to dried squid. If you forgot to buy something at the outdoor market, you ran to Antok's to get it. He was a Chinese immigrant who favored shorts and sleeveless T-shirts. Every day he sat behind the counter with a flyswatter in his hand. I always smiled even though he never returned my greeting. That day Antok's eternal frown didn't bother me one bit; my mind was spinning fantasies—I would be the loveliest girl that night, the envy of my classmates, and boys would flock around me. I wondered what dresses my friends would wear. I'd heard that some of them had originals by Manila's leading couturiers!

Manila is hot at ten in the morning and I tried to catch the shade of trees and high walls. Before getting to St. Paul's College, I turned left then turned right towards Carmen's. I was on the left-hand side of the street when I spotted a man on a bicycle. He was on the other side of the street. No one else was around. I suspected nothing until he veered to my side of the street. We were facing each other and I clutched my bag close to my body, an instinct I'd developed from living in Manila. I avoided eye contact, another trick I'd learned. Eye-contact was a sure invitation to the men hanging around street corners who called you names and blew unwanted puckering kisses.

The man and I were now rapidly approaching each other. I took several steps to the left to create more space between us. The street remained deserted and I desperately hoped for passersby. He pedaled faster, then he screeched to a stop beside me. I froze. He flashed a smug smile. Something glinted in his hand—it was a foot-long knife. My mind crowded with news accounts of bludgeoned corpses found in back alleys. I wondered what to do if he'd attack me. He was not very big, but he looked wiry and strong. And the knife—well, that definitely made matters swing in his favor. While these thoughts flew through my head, the man leaned over and grabbed my right breast. It was a rough and painful touch, shocking like a sudden clap of thunder. I gasped, pulled away. He brought his knife close to my face, made a slicing motion, then laughed. He quickly got back on his bike and sped away.

I looked up and down the abandoned street, not knowing what to do, not comprehending what had happened. Folding my arms across my chest, I turned to go home. I wanted to take another shower and lock myself in my bedroom. My legs were shaking. I thought of St. Maria Goretti who was stabbed to death as she resisted her attacker, to protect her virginity. I felt inadequate, guilty somehow.

After taking a few steps, I stopped, remembering Melisande's party. I didn't even want to attend it now, but friends would be picking me up that evening. I headed back toward Carmen's. Despite the tropical heat, I started shivering. By the time I entered the beauty parlor, I was crying.

"What's wrong? What's happened?" Carmen and the other beauticians asked as they gathered around me. I shook my head and tried to compose myself. When I could speak, I said I wanted my hair set in large curlers and my nails painted pink. At home, I did not mention the incident to anyone. I was too ashamed to bring it up and acted as if nothing unusual had happened. For over two decades, I kept this a secret.

It was a small matter. Worse things have happened to people; and yet it was something that happened to me. I don't think the attack affected me in a strong way; but in a subtle way it did. I felt responsible for what happened. Had I walked seductively? Had I invited trouble? Perhaps my skirt was too short, my blouse too tight?

When I grew older, I became suspicious of men, although my father's sudden death or those careless infatuations over undeserving young men may have something to do with this. I'm not sure. What I know is that I am angry for not having kicked the man off his bike. He was just a puny coward picking on a young girl after all. I should have screamed until my tonsils quivered and the whole world knew his crime, and he would have gotten caught and punished. My passivity infuriates me. I'm angry for having felt shame and guilt over some wrong done to me, not by me.

As things turned out, Melisande's debut was enjoyable. I felt elegant and beautiful in my pink lace dress. All my accessories were pink—shoes, bag, even my handkerchief. Carmen had swept up my dark hair and placed tiny pink flowers on top. Frankly, I wasn't crazy about pink. It was my mother who liked to dress me in pink. But I had to smile when someone said, "How lovely, you look like cotton candy."

My classmates and I sipped exotic fruit drinks, and we gossiped and giggled and shyly eyed the boys. At the Manila Hotel ballroom, under the glittering crystal chandelier, I forgot what had happened earlier that day. Or so I thought. The memory just sat inside of me until the time I was ready to look at this bit of ugliness.

MANILA WITHOUT VERNA

After a quarter of a century of living in America, I have turned into some kind of bird, a sparrow perhaps, returning to where I come from, once a year. One of the so-called "balikbayans" (which some people say with a sneer). Indeed we have become strange creatures, we balikbayans, not quite Filipino, not quite American. And still I do my annual trek, as if searching for something, what exactly I do not know, cannot pinpoint why exactly I return. I say it's to visit my mother. I say it's to visit my roots. But it's something else, something vital to my soul. Is it something from my past? Perhaps. So much of the present is linked to the past. Therefore this year, like the year before, and the year before that, I shut down my studio, say goodbye to my agent, and endure the 25-some hour flight from New York to Manila. And this year, I say the weather isn't too bad although Manila is getting smoggy. And my mother says it's the lahar, it has been such since Mt. Pinatubo exploded in 1991, the lahar, diverting rivers, drowning towns, filling the air with blackness that we inhale, that my mother inhales and which sends her and many others in Manila into coughing spells. Bronchitis and asthma, ordinary day-to-day illnesses, this is Manila now unlike the Manila that I knew in the 60s, long stretches of fields between Malate and Quezon City, stretches of nothingness, a canopy of blue sky, now there are houses and buildings, and traffic that can try a saint. Manila.

My school friends still remember me. Tess, especially, who was my best friend in high school, and who has remained a special friend always. "You must come to dinner. It's for the February celebrants," she insists. In their middle-age, my Theresian classmates have bonded and hold monthly dinners for their birthday celebrants. "It'll be at the clubhouse at my apartment. And we'll have a program, poetry reading! Bring your favorite poem to share. And you must tell us about your recent show. I heard it was a success."

Tess lives in Pacific Plaza, where Imelda Marcos has moved in recently; and when I arrive the women are huddled gossiping about the former first lady—something about Imelda forgetting to pay her phone bill and PLDT cutting her line. Twenty women whom I barely recognize, laughing giddily as if it's 1964 again, young sixteen-year-olds, giggling without any care. A memory comes to me—our high school graduation night. After the ceremony, we returned to our classroom to gather our things for the last time. Someone started sobbing (was it Verna?), and a spell was cast, and all of us sat still and began crying, for no specific reason at all, just some vague sadness at the recognition that a chapter of our lives had ended, and that there was something out there for us, what exactly we didn't know.

Sister Agnes is present, a treat I understand because she doesn't usually attend these gatherings. There she sits looking very much like Sister Agnes of the past, large eyes with a startled expression, that tentative smile, that low clear voice recounting details about all of us. How does she do it? She must have had thousands of students, and still she remembers my Hong Kong-bought black shoes with Cuban heels, and she recounts with a laugh how much Tess loved cucumbers in her sandwiches. When we were freshmen in high school, Sister Agnes frightened us so much, we'd jump when she walked up to us. She was known as the terror. But she became our teacher in our junior year, and even though she was strict, she loved us. We "belonged to her" and she tolerated our foibles. Once, standing in line for a long time; Tess and I became bored and we left the line to peer down some pipe. There was nothing there really, just a pipe shoved down the earth; and there we stood, with a vacuous expression, staring at the pipe and earth. Sister Agnes approached us; we jumped, ready to be punished. Instead she stared at the pipe and earth and declared, "Well, there's nothing there. Get back in line."

They ask how I'm doing; they say they've been reading about me, that they're proud of me, so glad that I've "mainstreamed" one of few Filipino artists who have done so in the States. I smile, answer their questions, but do not go on and on about my work. It's taken me over two decades to learn my art, to make a name, to build a reputation—how can I sum up what I've done in a few minutes? How can they truly know the difficulties I've faced as a so-called "minority woman" in White America? How can they understand how much I put into my art, that it must be more than good, that it must stand out? How can they know the politics involved, the networking to gain whatever edge I can? How can they know the dry spells, the times when there's nothing, nothing worthwhile coming out on the canvas, and the panic I feel over this aridity? I smile, say things are just fine, that yes, my recent show went well, and yes I'll do one in Manila soon, perhaps at the Manila PEN. I avoid revealing to them the private details of my life—that I have no children, that in fact my husband left me because I did not want to have a child. Details—mundane, painful—that add another texture to the picture I have created of myself these years.

After the explosion of greetings and remembrances, we settle down to chat and eat. I'm in a table with Araceli, Darn, Carol, Aida, Henedina, old friends, so we have an easy time catching up. Tess is in her element, flitting about, playing hostess. After dinner, she emcees the program. She cajoles everyone to get up to read a poem or recall favorite stanzas. Everyone hams it up in front of the mike, even shy Monina dares to read a poem. It's as if Sister Agnes's presence validates our youth—if she's around, surely we couldn't be that old? Silly young girls this balmy February night.

When the poetry reading disintegrates to nursery rhymes, Tess recovers the mike to read a poem by Maya Angelou. Her voice is soft and seductive like the night outside:

The caged bird sings
with a fearful trill
of things unknown
but longed for still
and his tune is heard
on the distant hill
for the caged bird
sings of freedom.

She pauses (as we all feel a pause in our hearts); then she invites others to continue the program. But we've run out of poems. Everyone who has brought a poem has shared it, and there is a lull in the program. The mike is passed around like a hot potato—here Carol, you emcee, no, you do it Araceli, no you do it.

Sister Agnes gets up, takes the mike from Tess's hands and says: I would like to say something.

A shadow flits across her face, and briefly I wonder if we forgot to say our prayers before eating. Sister says, "Tess's reading of 'The Caged Bird' has reminded me of someone close to my heart, to our hearts. There is one of you who is not present here, and I want to remember her."

I know whom she is talking about—Verna. Verna, the other class artist aside from myself. Verna who did vivid water colors and oils that brought me to rain forests and the Cordilleras. Soft-spoken Verna, who unlike the other "artsy" ones in class, was most conservative in appearance. We dared wear clunky boys' shoes, she wore dainty black shoes that looked like ballet shoes. As the class artists, she and I were often pitted against each other. In our junior year there was an art contest and she and I knew we were the only serious candidates. I won the two-hundred-peso price; and I was afraid that she would stay away from me. But no, when the winner was announced, Verna was the first to congratulate me. We became friends, meeting during recess and for lunch.

Verna talked me into joining the Sodality, and Sister Agnes got us started on visiting the sick at Philippine General Hospital. The very first time we went, we ran across a nurse carrying a basin filled with blood. I almost threw up. I hated that hospital, hated the indigent patients who clung to us with a desperation that took days to wash away from my skin, my soul. Verna did not mind talking to the patients, consoling them, giving them hope. "They're poor," she explained, as if I were unaware of that fact.

Verna fell in love with a boy of eight with kidney problems. Every Saturday, we visited the hospital, and she saw that boy. She brought him little gifts, toys and candies. He lit up when he saw her walking toward his bed. There was something I did not approve about that relationship, something that disturbed me. "He really likes you," I said, in a tone that was more reprimanding than I had wanted it to be.

"I like him too," she replied.

"But is that all right? Is it really all right for us to like these patients? We won't be members of the Sodality forever and then we won't be back, and then what will happen to them? We can't be friends with them, have them expect things from us, then abandon them?"

"They'll go on without us."

She said this so calmly, it infuriated me. Verna had a way of being self-righteous sometimes. She had a way of knowing black from white; whereas I always had too many gray areas in my life. Even now, there are a lot of gray areas in my life.

One Saturday—it was March, almost the end of the school year—we visited the hospital. I was edgy because I figured it was time for Verna to say goodbye to the child, to explain to him that finals were coming and summer vacation would soon be here, that we would not be back to see him. "You must tell him, Verna, otherwise, he'll go on waiting for you."

"Don't worry," she said.

When we entered the children's ward, his empty bed loomed in front of us. Verna and I glanced at each other. Without being told, we knew. The dayshift nurse confirmed that the boy was dead. All we could do was walk to the chapel and pray. Verna cried. I cried with her, but inside I felt that I had been right after all, that she shouldn't have gotten involved with that child. I picked up the idea then that relationships need to be measured in terms of the toll on one's self or one's goals. I don't believe Verna learned that lesson.

Sister Agnes's voice brings me back to the clubhouse, to the present. "Do you know what happened to Verna?" she is asking.

We nod. Someone says, "She died in a car accident."

Tess wrote me about Verna's car accident in Mindanao. I'd just finished a huge painting of a "Mother and Child," in an Ifugao motif. I knew it was excellent, and I was feeling fuzzy the way I do when I create something really fine. The mailman came, and I spotted Tess's handwriting on an envelope. I opened her letter and found out about Verna. It was strange, but one of the first emotions that went through me was resentment that Verna had never even dropped me a postcard.

"There's more to the story than that," Sister continues.

"What?" we ask. What more could there have been except for the fact that Verna died at thirty?

"After graduation, Verna continued to visit me," Sister Agnes said. "She went to art school and I even helped get her a teaching position. She was an excellent art teacher. Things were going just fine for Verna until she met a man named Hector. Verna's greatest mistake, in my opinion, was falling in love with Hector. The political situation was very bad at that time, and Hector was an activist. Verna followed him wherever he went. I saw them in Negros where they were conducting teach-ins for farmers. You recall that land reform was a big issue then. Verna and Hector were against the Marcos government and were deeply involved with the more radical political elements.

"In Negros, Verna told me that she loved Hector and would marry him. I wondered about this because I noticed another young woman who kept following Hector around. It was clear, at least to me, that Hector was keeping both Verna and this woman in tow. But Verna loved him too much and either ignored the situation, or believed that Hector's infatuation over the woman would pass.

"Apparently, Hector's affection for the other woman did not fade because even when he and Verna were married, this woman continued to hang around them. This hurt Verna of course, and she mentioned this to me during her visits. But she could not leave him. That's what she said to me, 'I can't leave him. I love him.' By this time, she had given up her art. She was fully devoted to Hector and his causes.

"When the Marcos government started cracking down on anti-government elements, Hector and Verna went underground. I didn't hear from her for several years, but one day, Verna, with a baby in her arms, came to see me. She said she, Hector, and their baby would be leaving soon for the States, that things would be better, that they could work for the people over there. The baby was beautiful, clear-skinned with slanted eyes, like Verna's. There was one brief reference of that woman friend of Hector. Verna said it calmly, but I could imagine her pain over the situation. It seemed to me that all she wanted was a quiet life with Hector and their child. For years, she and Hector had lived a harsh life, hiding from the government; working for what they believed was good for the people. So you see, in many ways, Verna was a caged bird.

"Well, you know how the story ends. One day, Hector, Verna, and their baby were in a car, near Davao. The military ambushed them; Verna was killed. Hector and the baby escaped. Why only Verna died, I'll never understand. A part of me says that she died because she wanted to die. Maybe loving Hector was too much for her. That was her biggest mistake, you know, loving that man.

"So now, since we are gathered here, let us remember Verna for just a moment and pray for the eternal repose of her soul."

After saying prayers for the dead, we mumble to one another

surprise at Sister Agnes's story. None of us knew about Hector; none of us knew about the other woman; none of us knew about the ambush.

I am left with emotions so turbulent; I do not know where to begin to sort them out. I feel guilty that Verna is dead while I survived and am an artist with some measure of success. But at the same time I envy her political involvement and nobility to the end. I was not even in the Philippines when things were bad, when people like Verna were getting killed; I was in New York, making compromises to get where I am now. Again that huge expanse of gray in my life, while Verna knew what black was and what white was. I look at my life and my accomplishments and the price I've had to pay for all this; and I look at Verna's brief life; and I wonder who of us won this time. That art contest in high school—how simple it had been to win that two-hundred pesos. It has never been as simple ever again. Never. A sadness starts to gnaw inside me and will not leave. A pain that probably has been there for so many years I do not when it began.

When the others leave and only five of us remain, we ascend to Tess's apartment on the fortieth floor. It is a magnificent apartment, surrounded by picture windows that make you feel as if you're floating on top of Manila. We immediately gravitate to the enormous picture window in the living room that reveal to us Manila as we have never seen it before—a sprawling metropolis, a-glitter with multicolored lights. It's like staring at Hong Kong from Victoria's Peak at night. How glamorous Manila looks. Even with its smog, its poverty, its traffic, its turbulent history, Manila lays before me like a mysterious and beautiful woman. Manila moves me.

I can feel a stirring in me, an urge to capture this picture on canvas; (and always with that creative urge is a sense of excitement, of life.) It will be more than the sprawling city scene before me. The challenge as I see it will be to capture the evening on my canvas, maybe capture my sadness, maybe even capture Verna there.

I will call my creation: "Manila Without Verna."

ROMEO

It's Sunday evening and my mother has just returned from the 5:30 Mass at Malate Church. In the past, after Mass she and I would have walked to the Chinese restaurant on Remedios Street where we sat on the table against the mirror, away from the crowded doorway. Mama would have ordered fried rice, sweet and sour pork, pancit, and a crab and lobster dish swimming in white sauce. While we ate, she would ramble on about the Indonesian tenant in the house in Bel Air complaining about a roof leak, or her court case with her uncle, or she would complain about my brother and sisters needing money from her. While she talked I would daydream about going away after graduation, to America or Europe.

But this particular Sunday evening, I'm not in Manila and my mother is alone and so she has walked the six blocks to our house, bypassing the Chinese restaurant. In the dark shadows of the foyer, she fumbles with the locks on the front door. There are four sturdy American-made locks and the dog is barking. "Romeo, quiet!" my mother shouts. The dog whines in recognition. "Quiet!" She sounds stern, but the sternness is not because of the noise, but because of her alone-ness. Her children—we—are all gone: I in America, a sister in Venezuela, another sister in Spain, and her only son in Cebu. She had a live-in maid who used to sashay up and down the driveway, but my mother fired her after some money and jewelry disappeared. "It's safer to be alone," she wrote me. Years later, after the fall of Ferdinand Marcos, during my visit to the Philippines, she told me about an old woman whose throat had been slit by her servant. My mother was afraid that would happen to her, so she let the girl go, preferred to be alone in the house, protected by the numerous door locks and the dog outside. "At least a dog is loyal to the person feeding it," she said.

So it was the dog that became her only companion. He lived in the garage that was filled with old furniture and boxes with empty jars and bottles and old newspapers. He liked to sleep on the tattered "Welcome" mat made from rags, which he dragged as close as he could to the kitchen door but where he remained dry if it rained. The garage opened out to a side yard that was seven feet wide by thirty—a very narrow space with room only for a couple of clothes lines and a row of San Francisco plants against the high cement wall. The dog patrolled the area diligently, round and round, took in all the odors of the neighborhood—dried fish frying, piles of rotting garbage along the street, the occasional whiff of Manila Bay. He listened carefully to everything that went on in the three-house compound: the creaking of the iron gates, the quarreling of the gay couple in the front house, the squalling of children in the back house. He could even hear the plaintive cries of balut vendors walking down our street at night, vending their ducks' eggs, echoing throughout the night until dawn — "Penoy-baluuut!" Every little sound made him bark. What drove him foaming mad were the huge ugly gray rats that paraded on the cement wall above him, taunting him, sassing him, wanting his leftovers that sat in his chipped Melmac bowl. The dog had some German Shepherd blood in him and his barking was ferocious; when I read about my mother's decision to let the maid go, I thought that at least the dog was with her. Manila in the 1970s during the Marcos dictatorship had an increase of holdups, of burglaries. Once during this time my mother walked along our street, Luis Maria Guerrero, when a man rushed to her and ripped off her earrings from her ears. Her ears bled and the ragged ends needed to be stitched back together by a doctor. It was my brother who told me what had happened, not my mother. "She's sixty-five, she should not be alone, but she insists," my brother complained. "Manila is too dangerous; she should be here in Cebu, with me, with her grandchildren. She should retire now, rest." That was what my brother and I talked about often when I visited—my mother and how hardheaded, how impossible, how unreasonable, how difficult she could be. But after my visit, I would leave, cross an ocean, go to my other life. It was easier for me but not for my brother.

***

The dog's name was Romeo. We had been studying Shakespeare at Maryknoll College when I gave him the name; *Romeo and Juliet* had made me weep. For some reason, people talked to him in English. Even neighbors and visitors who only spoke Tagalog would call out: Romeo, come here, or Romeo, quiet. Once, my mother's best friend and dancing companion, Mrs. Quintos whom we called Anday naively wondered why the dog in our household was English-speaking—"Naku, pati aso English-speaking."

I got him when I was in my sophomore year of college. Saturday mornings, I visited my orthodontist, Dr. Polintan in Escolta. On this particular Saturday, I was there with my ten-year old niece, Lisa. After Dr. Polintan tightened my braces, Lisa and I left his office and waited for a taxi. Lisa spotted a man holding two puppies. They had large dark eyes and brown fluffy fur with German Shepherd markings. The sight of them brought me back to my childhood when my father had raised a couple of pedigree German Shepherds, Prince and Beauty. Our cook used to fix ox tail for them; and Papa used to inspect their food, cutting up the meat and mixing in rice. Prince used to jump up and lick me whenever I got home from school. They were happy times. The markings on the puppy that Lisa was playing with reminded me of those days. I asked the man how much. Thirty pesos at the time could buy a nice pair of leather high heels, but I paid it and the dog was mine.

When my mother saw the dog, she screamed and said she did not want a dog in Manila, that we did not have the space for a large dog, that a dog like that would run away or turn rabid and have to be shot. When my mother went into a screaming tirade, I usually kept quiet, went to my room and picked up a book, but that day I held the dog tightly in my arms and firmly said, "I'll take care of him." My lack of hysteria silenced her then. Later there were arguments about the dog, and at some point, there was talk that he would be dispatched to Cebu. But this never happened, and after a while we stopped talking about what to do with Romeo. He became part of our life in Manila. In fact, as the Marcos regime entrenched itself and the economy worsened, crime increased and Romeo became something of an asset. And as the months passed, Romeo became less my puppy and more of the family guard dog. I was too busy then with school and if I recall right there was a boy who had broken my heart and that consumed a lot of energy right there.

***

This Sunday, my mother is in her bedroom with the two beds. The bed she sleeps in is neatly covered with a blue and white Ilocano woven bedspread which Anday had given her. Making her bed every morning is something Mama learned from the German nuns of St. Scholastica, along with eating potatoes and cleaning your plate. A crucifix and a statue of the Blessed Virgin Mary stand on her headboard. The other bed however is in total disorder with piles of folded clothes, documents, letters, and pictures which I have sent her. Thursday nights, my mother clears this bed so Anday can sleep over after their dance lessons. Long before ballroom dancing became popular in Manila, my mother and Anday took tango, mambo, paso doble, foxtrot, and cha-cha lessons with dance instructors. One of their dance instructors was named Diko, a tall serious family man who took his dips and turns seriously. Once when I was moping around in my upstairs bedroom, my mother and Anday called me to dance with them. There in our living room, Diko held my hand and walked me through the steps—one-two-three cha-cha-cha—he chanted but I kept messing up the cha-cha-cha and Mama and Anday laughed so hard they were clutching their bellies. You are too stiff, they said and you should stop looking down at your feet but just feel the music. Meanwhile outside Romeo started barking and howling because he could hear the record player and the laughter.

***

In my mother's room, there is a dusty wooden dresser crammed with makeup and bottles of perfume and a one-legged ceramic musical ballerina that would suddenly start up for no reason at all. And this Sunday night, it suddenly starts playing its brassy tune (*Somewhere My Love*) while the one-legged ballerina twirls around. My mother stops and stares at her and sighs remembering her husband and children, remembering the noisy happy household they used to have. She waits until the song is finished and the ballerina is once again frozen in her pirouette and then my mother removes her Sunday dress, bra and slip, and she hangs these over a chair near the TV. She slips on her housedress with the floral pattern—little yellow flowers with a green background. It's loose like a tent and made of cotton because cotton is cool and it's always hot in Manila. Even when it rains the temperature rarely gets below seventy degrees. She removes her shoes and searches for her rubber slippers. She's tired tonight, but the dog is waiting. She switches off all the upstairs lights. My brother has repeatedly told her that it's not energy-efficient to be switching lights on and off, but she likes to turn off lights and appliances that aren't used; it makes her feel she's saving money.

She goes downstairs to the kitchen. Romeo starts to whine and he wags his tail so it hits the kitchen door in a rhythmic thump-thump. My mother ignores him; she opens the refrigerator to find food to heat up, her supper, also Romeo's supper. If it weren't for the dog, she'd toast a slice of bread and eat that with some margarine and strawberry jam; but the dog needs more than that, and so my mother heats up kare-kare—beef stew—making sure there are bones for the dog. While the food is heating, she searches the refrigerator for forgotten containers of food, which she can give the dog: last week's pork chops, chicken adobo, rancid pancit. She opens the door to the side yard and is met by the overjoyed dog that jumps up to lick her. "Down, Romeo!" My mother picks up the dog's food basin and gets back into the kitchen. She throws in the leftovers. When the kare-kare is hot, she picks out the bones, ligaments, meat, some vegetables and adds that to the dog's food. She picks up the rice pot, dishes out what she needs, and scrapes the remaining rice into the basin. She pours hot soup over all these, mixes these up, and then she opens the screen door and places the basin on the ground. "Eat, Romeo," my mother orders. The dog wags his tail and licks her hands and her feet before eating. The dog worships her.

***

What the dog wants most of all is for my mother to touch him, rub the fur on his back. His fur is clean. A neighbor woman comes in every Saturday to clean the house and to wash him using a strong bar of sulfur soap to kill his fleas and ticks. He loves the feel of the woman's strong hands working the soap through his thick fur; and the gushing of cold water down his back makes him moan. He never barks, never whimpers, but he stands perfectly still near the garden hose which the woman uses to wash him.

But he rarely feels the touch of my mother's hands, and so in the early mornings while she's hanging her clothes to dry, he makes it a point to do his rounds so he'll brush against her legs. And then she says: Go, Romeo. Sit down. But sometimes she talks some more: I heard the children playing, and I forgot and thought they were mine. I forgot that they've grown and are gone. But they'll come back home. They always do. They'll be back. And the sound of my mother's voice echoes in Romeo's mind, creating strange longings, yearnings for wide fields and open skies which he has never seen.

***

By the time my brother told me about Romeo's death, my brother was drinking. He liked brandy and preferred Napoleon. He could go through a hundred dollar bottle in three days. The day after I got in from the States, we went shopping at the Duty Free Shop so he could stack up on his brandy. He was drinking brandy that afternoon. We were sitting on the verandah between the old house and his house. During the first few glasses of brandy, he talked about Cory hiding in the Carmelite Convent in Cebu during the EDSA People Power Revolution, and the dramatic fall of Marcos. But with his fourth drink, he talked about our mother, about Romeo's death in particular.

"Romeo couldn't get up," he said. "He'd been dying for several days before Mama finally called and asked me to go to Manila. He was lying on that dirty mat and he could barely move, but he wagged his tail when he saw me. The typhoon season was starting, and he was constantly wet. I told Mama we had to call a vet. She didn't want to put him to sleep; she insisted he just had a cold. We argued for a long time until I finally convinced her that a vet could give him medicine to make him feel better. She was in her bedroom when the vet arrived. She was looking at a dress catalogue. I was with Romeo when the vet gave him a shot. I didn't even know he'd died. He had a peaceful death."

My brother and I recalled how good natured Romeo had always been, how willing to please, and how as a puppy he looked so much like a German Shepherd, but that as he grew older, his legs grew lanky and his chest filled out while his rear remained lean so his shape was more like a dingo; but he was always big and always sounded fierce, just like a German Shepherd. I told my brother how happy Romeo had been to see me as a grown woman with my first-born son—this was back in 1972, right around the time of the Plaza Miranda bombing. It was as if the years had not passed between us; and he had jumped up into my arms and licked my face, and he wagged his tail as he stared curiously at my son. He was terribly polite when my son yanked his tail—all he did was whimper and turn to look for my mother. It was clear to me then that it was my mother whom he now loved. I had become some kind of pleasant memory, one he cherished, but I was no longer part of his life; I was no longer part of the universe of that garage and backyard in our Malate house.

***

There is one more thing: long before Romeo died, on Monday morning, at 5:30 in the morning, my mother picks up her the bra, slip and dress which she had worn on Sunday. In the semi-darkness, she makes her way down the wooden stairs. Romeo hears her, and he quickly stands up from his mat and races to the kitchen door. He wags his tail expectantly as he listens to my mother picking up the plastic basin and filling this with water at the kitchen sink. She drops her clothes into the basin, sprinkles Tide over them, and proceeds to wash them. Romeo hears all of this and his heart is beating fast as he stands by the kitchen door waiting, waiting. At last, before the sun is up, the door opens, and my mother with basin in her hands, steps out into the small backyard. Romeo looks up, rushes to her, jumps up and whines his greeting. "Down Romeo," she says, pushing him away. Undeterred, he wags his tail and starts his patrol of the small backyard, round and round he goes and the dripping from the clothes fall on Romeo's back as he does his rounds of the seven-feet-by-thirty back yard. And then, and then, as he squeezes past my mother, he brushes up against her legs, and then my mother reaches out to touch him, "Come here, good dog, Romeo, good dog, you're all I have now," she says. The sun is up and it's morning finally when Romeo licks her hand and shivers with delight.

MY MOTHER IS DYING

My mother is dying and I'm not by her side. She's in a hospital room in Makati which was painted white six months ago, but which already has gray smudges from Manila's smog. The film of dirt is darkest near the window where an air conditioner hums. The only other noise in the room is the life support machine which purrs constantly and which gurgles every few seconds. My mother is attached to this machine via a long rubber tube and mouthpiece. Tape around her mouth keeps the mouthpiece in place. The mouthpiece fills her mouth and makes her face look different, her mouth thrust out like a snout, and the wrinkles on her face pulled forward. Her short white hair crowns her head. Even though you can see some of her scalp, she still has hair. She has always been proud of having hair, and she used to dye it black. But now it is white, and sticks out, wiry from a forgotten perm.

She's wearing a hospital gown with blue and white stars. The gown opens in the back, but since she is unable to move, the nurses have left the gown untied and they tuck the hemmed edges underneath her body. A starched white sheet covers her bony legs.

Even though her legs are thin, there are some muscles left. She was a dancer all her life. The rest of her body is skin and bones; her skin hangs loosely. One could pick up the skin under her arms and move this about. But you couldn't do that with her legs; the skin is still taut. The skin still hugs the remaining leg muscles.

Aside from the bed and the life support machine there is a small cot in the room. The night shift nurse is dozing on the cot. She worked all night from 5:30 p.m. and now she is waiting for the morning shift nurse to replace her. It's December and she's planning to go shopping for Christmas gifts today.

At 5:20 a.m., the morning shift nurse catches the night shift nurse snoring. She shakes her awake and she checks on my mother. The nurse fusses with the dials of the life support and makes sure the IV is dripping properly. She and the night shift nurse have taken care of my mother for three weeks now. Since my mother is brain dead and immobile, only the machine pushes her chest up and down. It is this that gives a semblance of movement, of life. When the nurses are together, they clean and massage my mother's body. First they turn her to her left and when they are done, they turn her to her right, trying to get all parts of her. This morning they discover a pink sore on my mother's buttocks, and there are three black and blue marks on her legs. My mother's skin tone has a grayish cast, and her breath is more foul than it was yesterday. If you add up the years they've worked in ICU, it'd come up to thirty-nine years, and they've never seen anyone cling to life like this. They wonder how a ninety-year old woman could last this long. What is it that keeps her going? Why doesn't she let go? And where are her other children, her grandchildren?

***

My mother is a continent away and it's early afternoon in California, a crisp Saturday in December, quite pleasant until I feel a strange unease that drives me upstairs to pray. I'm in bed, clutching my rosary, feeling the crystal coldness of the beads, saying, Hail Mary, full of grace, the Lord is with thee … when she comes to me like a waking dream. I sense her presence. I do not actually see her. It's a darkness, a heaviness, something like urgent sadness. I'm not surprised. I'm comforted but I'm also worried. I understand she must see me before she dies. My mother never told me—never told us—"I love you," but I know that now.

My dying mother comes to me as a voice: I'm sorry, she tells me, the words slipping through my brain so fast I think I've made it all up. My heart knows what she means, and really, it is too enormous a matter to explain. She does not have time for that. There are not enough words to explain: I'm sorry.

Don't worry about those things, I say. I love you. Go on. But she *is* afraid. She wants to die but cannot die. She struggles, continues to be sad and confused. She is frantic, anxious, in agony. I remember how she used to pray to the Sacred Heart of Jesus and to Mary, their alabaster statues sitting side by side on the table on top of our stairs. I remind Jesus and Mary of those days of prayers and ask them to stay with her, to help her. In my imagination, they come, Jesus with His Sacred Heart exposed, Mary with her long white robe and veil, and they stand on either side of her. I can't see my mother, but Jesus and Mary reach out to hold her hands. I want to see her, yearn to see the mole on her check, the same mole I used to touch when I was a child and she carried me in her arms, my face against her head, and I touched her ears, nose, her eyebrows, the mole.

It is timeless, my mother's dying, something that could go on and on, or something that could be finished with one breath. As suddenly as it began, the urgency subsides. The fear and anxiety dissipate. I realize she has died. There is nothing dramatic about this conclusion. It is a certainty, like looking at a sunset and saying, look there, the sun is gone.

THE CHE GUEVARA NIGHT

It was the night I call the "Che Guevara Night"—my last night in Manila, so a couple of girlfriends and I went out to Malate, now a hot spot in Manila, to the Café Havana de Manila to be exact, Friday night it was, when streets were blocked off and the rotunda teemed with people, not just the baklas of long ago, although I understand Remedios Street still has gay bars—I am always amazed at how crowded places can get in Manila: malls, streets, packed with people night and day—and so at 8:30 we were seated in a corner of the Café, the Remedios side, looking out at the very same street my mother and I used to walk on every Sunday on our way to Malate Church—and oh, the bittersweet memories of that time of my life when I was sixteen and living in Malate with my mother—but that night the three of us sat in that café which is not really a café but a high-priced restaurant packed with Che-memorabilia: framed pictures of the charming delicious Che smiling, smoking a cigar, and staring down at us, and waiters and waitresses looking cool with their red Che-berets, as we had our paella and lengua and two pitchers of Margarita, and because I'd be leaving the next day, we didn't have enough time to tell the stories, by women past their prime, two still looking for Mr. Right, and talking about the Mr. Wrongs of their lives, now told with humor, although fifteen years ago the same stories were told with tears, three women huddled together, laughing, with Che listening to every word and smiling, smiling, smiling.

Part 3

ACAPULCO AT SUNSET

1790, Acapulco

The spider spins her web—up and down, around and around she races. Ysabel and Renato giggle at the marvel she has created—the twins have joined me on the verandah this afternoon. They know this spider. She moved underneath the arbor two weeks ago. She is very diligent in building her web, away from the children's reach, in just the right spot where the breeze carries unsuspecting insects straight to her gauzy trap. I have been keeping an eye on her since she first appeared in mid-September; and I've instructed Pedro the gardener to leave her alone. Pedro looked at me and the cobwebs, then back at me again, and shook his head—why would the señora want cobwebs in the verandah? No molestar, I insisted. And when the twins spotted her, I talked to them as well. She is a magical creature, let's leave her alone. They have obliged. Besides they are not tall enough, even when they stand on stools and stretch out their skinny arms.

"Mama, it's lace!" Ysabel exclaims as they continue studying the spider web. It billows with the breeze, reminding me of Mama's sinamay cloth, that gauzy creation that she used to spin, that fine tediously-wrought fabric that we lived on. It was our life, that sinamay cloth and the enormous wooden looms downstairs that the women shoved up and down tirelessly, in the heat, the whole day through. During my siesta, I used to hear the rhythmic slamming of the wood against the frame. And sometimes late at night, in the half-darkness, Mama would work at the loom—a rush job for a wedding dress or a First Communion dress.

Clouds fill the sky and soon a drizzle falls. The children remain on their stools, laughing and pointing upward, their little faces catching the raindrops. "You better go in," I tell them, "you'll get wet and get sick." They jump down and start running indoors. Near the doorway Ysabel pauses: "Mama, and you? You'll get wet and get sick and die. I don't want you to die, Mama."

"Come in, come in Mama," they shout in singsong.

I nod. "I'll be in soon. Go on ahead."

And then they are gone, their footsteps echoing on the tile floor, echoing like the fragments of memories that cling to my mind, like I cling to this verandah, waiting for the letters and things that bring these memories back to life.

The rain falls gently; the drops are light fingertips on my face. The spider web catches little shards of the slowly setting sun. It is a marvelous afternoon. The salt air feels clean. Everything is sparkling — my whitewashed house, this verandah with the wooden chairs and potted plants, my favorite spot in all of Acapulco. From here I can see the city; I overlook the bay with its blue, blue water.

Mama loved the sea; and the few times she could get away, she would take me to the seashore. There we would swim and gather seashells and eat the rice and fish that roaming vendors sold. We lived on Calle Morelos in Jaro, in a two-story house, quite decrepit—the foundation poles stood askew. The bottom floor was used for Mama's sinamay business. Near the door, Mama displayed sinamay cloth of various patterns. In the back portion, near the wide doors, her weavers worked. Midday we shut the doors to keep the stifling air out, and later in the afternoon, we threw them open to welcome the cool breeze. Weaving was painstaking and Mama knew how quickly her workers' backs and eyes ached. She herself continued weaving until the day she became thin, tubercular, and died.

She was always busy, especially before Papa's visits. Papa lived with his wife in Calle Santa Clara, but twice a year he came, in the summer and before Christmas, to visit us. Mama ran about scrubbing walls, wiping mirrors and furniture. One thing she liked to do for my father was cut white and lavender orchid stalks and arrange them in the antique blue and white Chinese vases. Those vases were some of the prettiest things in the house. Our house was simple, unlike this one—how I wish Mama could have seen this house. She would like it, this house, on the hill overlooking town and the bay. My house is impeccable—cracked tiles are immediately replaced, potted plants brighten dark corners, the children are clothed and well-behaved, the servants diligent and obedient. I could ask for nothing more.

The rain falls harder and I plaster myself against the wall under the eaves. Through the drumming rain Santiago calls, "Maria Soledad, come in out of the rain." I plant wet feet firmly onto the tile floor; I will not leave the verandah. From here I can see the bay, all of it. From here I can watch the galleon, the Nao de Manila, enter the bay. It arrived on the first day of October last year. Santiago had said the galleon would not arrive until late November; and I believed him. I had gone about my business, and others did not know that inside I was dry and hollow, like a floating ghost, smiling emptily at Santiago and his business associates, watching the children as if from behind a screen. This heavy screen always surrounds me weeks before the Nao de Manila arrives. It surrounds me now. I wait and wait. And all sorts of fears grip my soul—perhaps the galleon has sunk near some reef, perhaps the galleon will be terribly delayed, perhaps there are no letters from home. Last year I almost went mad with these weavings of my mind; then like a burst of light the Nao de Manila appeared in the horizon. October first it was.

It is October once again; the Nao de Manila will arrive this month, today. For weeks my soul has been a shriveled raisin; since dawn I have been scanning the water for the galleon. From the right side of the bay, near Roquetta Island, the tip of the sail will appear, so small you cannot tell if it's merely a bird skimming the surface of the water. But bit by bit the galleon will take shape and traders will grow frantic. Already, anxious merchants have filled the Parian for over a month. Surely the galleon will arrive today.

When the galleon arrives in Acapulco, it is fiesta time—bright colors, music, laughter, vendors bartering, people milling about. Here, in this house, it is Three Kings all over again. Santiago has his goods, trunks and trunks of them. He will have his silks, carved saints, pearls, rubies, and diamonds for me. Santiago always has gifts for me. Papa had told me that with Santiago as my husband, I and my children will not lack anything; he was right. (He could not say the same about Jaime.)

The children will have their toys and clothes and multitude of knick-knacks. They'll marvel at the wondrous things from China and from Filipinas—mantillas, carved nacre chests, clever toys made from molave and pure silver. And even the servants will have their treasures—cottons, tortoise shell combs. There will be plenty. But what I want, all I really want are the letters from Papa, Tiya Edyong, and Marietta. They are usually packed in a pungent smelling camphor chest filled with clothing, porcelains, their gifts to me. In his letters Papa writes about his business and his gout; my aunt gives her spare account about the servants and her embroidery-work. Marietta's letters are longer — about the hacienda, her husband and children, their Arabian horses, her endless intrigues with relatives and friends. From their words I can create their world once again, imagine the cobblestone streets, hear the watchman's mournful cry at night, taste Tiya Edyong's cooking, be a giddy girl with Marietta again, picture Jaime in church craning his neck to see me, smell the champaka flowers that he secretly handed to me and which I kept by my bedside until the white flowers turned red-brown from age.

When I was new in Acapulco, Marietta used to write about Jaime — about his return from Sevilla, his marriage to the Chinese mestiza, the daughter of a jewelry vendor. Marietta wrote about what a disaster their marriage turned out to be, how Jaime had taken to other women and the wife remained barren all these years, and she grew fat, so fat she could barely move about. I laughed hysterically when I read about this. I used to lock my bedroom so I was completely alone; how could I have explained my hyena-laughter to Santiago and the children? Marietta stopped writing about Jaime when I had the twins. Perhaps she decided it was time for me to forget Jaime once and for all, time to get on with my life. I had to read between the lines or make up stories about Jaime and his corpulent rich wife.

But enough—I have Santiago and the children. Jaime was a young girl's fantasy, a ghost. I would not know him as a man; like his wife, he may have bloated up from drinking and eating and womanizing. No, I would not recognize that man at all. I remember him only as the slender dark-haired boy-man, who used to go to church to see me. He wanted to marry me, but Jaime was a tailor's son; I did not want to end up like Mama, so poor, weaving until she was half blind. No, I wanted more.

Sometimes now, when I dress for company, I open my jewelry boxes and stare at the luminous pearls larger than my thumb, at the gems and gold and silver, and I think I have more rings than I have fingers, more earrings than I have ears, more necklaces than my neck can carry. Jaime could never have bought me these things. I have so much, so much, and yet this nagging little pain will not go away, this wondering what kind of life Jaime and I could have had. Basta ya! It was my choice not to marry Jaime after all.

The rain has stopped and the sky is brilliantly clear. The sun is above Roquetta Island's gray and brown rocks, and it is turning bright orange. Sunsets in Acapulco are precious. But Manila sunsets more so. From the third floor of Papa's house, Tiya Edyong and I used to watch the sun sinking, while the world blazed in vivid colors, until at last the sun touched the water and the sea swallowed it. Then my aunt would urge me to finish sewing. We were constantly embroidering endless supplies of pillowcases, sheets, towels. We embroidered RCS, my father's initials. It was fitting, she often said for such an important man to have his linens embroidered with his initials. Once I asked why we branded my fathers' things. She is hard of hearing, my aunt, and she said, "Eh? What?"

I said, "Branding, branding, like a horse."

She sighed. "I don't know what you're talking about. What is this about brandy?"

"Branding," I shouted. "In Marietta's farm, they brand their horses so everyone knows they belong to the Montinolas. But towels, beddings don't need to be marked because they never run away. Unless the breeze blows them off the line and lifts them all the way to Calle Santa Clara." I laughed then, thinking of huge bed sheets sailing across the sky and landing in the middle of the busy street—what would the horse carriages have done, the pedestrians, the vendors?

My aunt sighed and folded her needlework. "I don't know what you're talking about, first brandy, now horses."

Even though I made fun of my aunt, I loved her. In her own strict way she was good to me. My mother had just died in Jaro when my father sent for me. At that time, my father's wife ran the household in Calle Santa Clara. She was a sickly woman who fortunately stayed for the most part in her bedroom, the only reason I survived that year. She despised me because I reminded her of my mother whom my father loved. I stayed in the kitchen with the servants, but when my father's sister Tiya Edyong moved in, she pulled me out of there and taught me how to cook, sew, and say my prayers in grammatical Spanish so one day I could run a decent household.

Indeed I now have a fine household, one of the best in Acapulco. Santiago and the children are content. Everything is in perfect order; one could not wish for more. No, one should not wish for more.

In Acapulco the sun sets slowly. It is a lazy sun. I once mentioned this to Santiago who replied it is the same sun all over. He is a good businessman, but always preoccupied. Papa was glad when Santiago wanted to marry me because Santiago is also a merchant. During my despedida de soltera, they talked of how to corner the tobacco market in Manila and Acapulco. Marietta and I sat in the corner and wept.

Basta ya! I will not talk of sad matters this afternoon, this lovely October afternoon. I will think of the cool rain that washed the palm fronds green and left quivering raindrops on my hair. I will think of the busy spider and her elaborate web—I too am creating a web, am I not? I will hold in my mind how the baby can now say ma-ma, pa-pa; how Renato and Ysabel are growing so tall, they are taller than the cacao sapling in the side yard. I will picture the galleon hugging the shoreline as it sails south toward Acapulco, and that little tip of the sail, no bigger than a bird, will suddenly appear in the horizon, over there, right near Roquetta Island.

Now there is only a finger between the sun and the ocean. With one eye shut and my finger in front of me, I watch the sun slide further down until there is a bite mark on its lower part. The ocean continues to eat the sun.

The ocean, dark blue, and deep—what if it swallowed up the galleon? It has claimed many galleons, taken them into her bosom. She is like a woman this ocean and she speaks. I found this out on my way here. During the four-month journey, I was constantly seasick. I did not care when we were running out of food and ate nothing else but salted fish and mongo beans; I did not become afraid as others did when there was talk that drinking water was running low and the men had to catch rain water on the sails. Near the "place of death" where a countess had jumped overboard years ago, I stared at the dark ocean. That's when she spoke: I am deep and dangerous and can swallow you up, annihilate you. I am distant and foreign. I am a prison. I can engulf you, take you into my warm pulsating depths, destroy you. Its voice softened as it said, I am a seductress and can give you solace.

I wondered what sort of peace it offered me. I thought of throwing myself into that swirling water, but the men spotted some dark seals and we knew land was in sight, and the ocean became silent and still.

The sun is dying; the day ending. Perhaps Santiago is right and the galleon will not arrive today. He said it was too early—the weather pattern, the prevailing winds, on and on he talked. I protested, "Last year—" "I am too busy to argue," he replied as he shrugged his shoulders and resumed his bookkeeping. He is always doing something. Business cannot wait, he explains. Buy this, sell that, earn gold and silver. He is one of the wealthiest men in Acapulco, and yet he wants more. He works and works. It has crossed my mind that Papa and Santiago are the same man after all, and I, like Papa's wife, will one day shrivel up and die.

The sun is gone. Roquetta Island and the water have disappeared into a black wall. I and the spider are cloaked in still darkness. Nighttime in Acapulco is whispered stories in the kitchen by the cooking hearth, children swatting mosquitoes, lanterns flickering, sounds of my breathing rattling in my head. Santiago calls me from inside the house: Maria Soledad, donde esta? The children need you. It will be dinner time soon. His voice so loud and urgent, I am sure the spider is cringing in her web.

But there is no other place to go to. It is time to leave the verandah; Santiago was right about the galleon not arriving today. But tomorrow, surely the Nao de Manila will arrive?

WELCOME TO AMERICA

I know you're wondering why a graduate student at UCLA is in an airplane headed for San Francisco. Summer vacation's started, and to be perfectly honest with you, I don't like Los Angeles. It's huge and smoggy, and the people are rather snippy, like the old saleslady at the Westwood drugstore who was real snotty with me. I suspect she treated me badly because I'm Filipino. They're like that even in Westwood Village, which is supposed to be cosmopolitan and all that, what with UCLA being right there and everything. My Biafran classmate at film school had a difficult time finding an apartment near campus because he's black. Eventually, he found a dinky little place after making it clear to the manager that he's African, not American Black. As if that should make a difference. You'd think it's 1950 instead of 1970.

Anyway, I rather like San Francisco. Several months ago, on my way to Los Angeles, I spent a few days there and became enchanted with its steep hills, the lovely Victorian houses, the thick fog that rolls in the afternoons, and the flower children hanging around the Haight-Ashbury. I made up my mind that I'd check San Francisco out.

And here's the other reason why I wanted to leave Los Angeles. I lived in a board and lodge place called "Hilgard House," a sprawling structure a stone's throw from the campus, which initially reminded me of a charming Spanish convent. It didn't take me long to realize there was something, well, peculiar about the place. I couldn't quite put my finger on the problem, until one night, one of the older female residents ran screaming down the hall — stark naked, mind you. "What *is* this place?" I finally inquired. I learned it was a half-way house. True there was a handful of UCLA students grouped in one wing, but the majority of the residents who drooped over their meals and mumbled to themselves came from UCLA's neuropsychiatric ward.

All right, I said, once the quarter's over, I'm going to San Francisco; and I contacted a college friend of mine, Susie, who's up there.

I packed all my belongings in two suitcases, took the Airport Bus down Westwood Boulevard, and here I am in United Airlines heading north.

***

There's Susie, waving at me near the gate. We've been out of college for over a year, and she still looks like a freshman. She always did look young: petite with a pert nose and curly hair. Susie looks sixteen instead of twenty-one. Oh well. Who wants to look sixteen when you're twenty-one anyway? I mean, I rolled up my skirt to make it more mini, and I spent a long time brushing my hair and putting on makeup to look like a woman, not a teenager.

Suz busses me on the cheek and announces we're taking a cab to her uncle and aunt's Mission District apartment.

"Susie," I say, "I told you to find me a hotel room."

"Just for a few days, until you find a place of your own."

The cab takes us past Daly City, into San Francisco. It's late Friday afternoon and thick white fog is frothing all round the tall Victorians with red geraniums on the window sills, and I'm feeling real glad I'm in San Francisco and not at Hilgard House. I mean this sense of adventure's building up inside of me — I'm a stranger in this city, and I have no history, no one knows me (except Susie), and there are no expectations of me whatsoever; I can be anyone I want to be.

"The—ah—place isn't really—" stammers Suz, and I know she's trying to tell me that the apartment isn't as elegant as the houses we're seeing.

"Suz," I say, "I appreciate all this, your picking me up and everything. And really, I've got to find a place of my own as soon as possible, and a summer job."

"I wish I could have a place of my own," she says.

"Why don't you get one?"

"My uncle and aunt—they want me to stay with them. They've

petitioned for me, and until I get my green card, I have to stay with them."

"I'm sure it won't take long."

"It's taking so long—" She pauses then adds, "And Lillia, I want you to know that my aunt's an ex-nun."

"An ex-nun—how—ah— interesting."

She shakes her head and rolls her eyes up and I laugh, and she laughs too. Then she relaxes and asks me about UCLA and Los Angeles, so I'm able to give her a blow-by-blow account of the odd place I lived in and the interesting people I met at the university.

Her uncle and aunt are standing side by side like quaint porcelain dolls when we arrive. He's around seventy, an O.T. (old timer) if I've ever seen one—small with a heavy accent, baggy pants, floppy hat. The aunt, thin and austere, has her head bowed down; she avoids eye contact even when you're talking to her.

They've prepared this authentic Filipino food—bagoong, adobo, rice, atchara—which I welcome after all that rubbery chicken at Hilgard House. After supper, in the bedroom that Suz and I share, we discuss what we'll do the next day. She wants to take me around; I want to start looking for a place and work. Saturday morning after breakfast (rice and fried fish!) I give in and tell Suz we can go wherever she wants. Union Square, she announces, and Chinatown.

The uncle—get this—follows us to the bus stop, rides with us, although he doesn't sit with us. He acts as though he's going someplace on his own. But when we get off, he also gets off, and he trails behind us, wherever we go. Saks, I. Magnin's, Chinatown, and when we eat at Louie Gooey's, he waits by the doorway until we exit. It's creepy, and finally I ask Suz what's going on.

Out it comes: the uncle, who lived in America for something like fifty years without any kin whatsoever, was overwhelmed at having a niece, an honest-to-goodness blood kin, and feeling protective or overjoyed or something, he follows her around.

"Everywhere?" I ask, incredulously.

"Hindi naman—no," she replies. "It's like this kasi, Tiyo had a hard life in America. He's been poor. I think he worked in the farms. And the sad part is that he couldn't marry. There were no Filipinas in America and the Filipinos weren't allowed to marry American women— white American women. He just married Tiya three years ago, after she left the convent. I feel sorry for him."

The next time I see the old man, I sort of understand why he's hovering around Suz constantly. Suz was the daughter he never had.

Sunday night, the aunt has a tantrum. Suz and I are watching "Star Trek" on TV, eating See's Candies that the uncle gave us. The aunt passes right in front of us three times. She's bristling and her skirt rustles around her like electricity. Then she goes to the kitchen and bangs pots and pans around. This is all very disconcerting to me, but Suz just ignores her. Which is probably one of the reasons why the aunt's slamming things around. I mean, here's her husband doting over Suzie, and suddenly, she has to compete for the old man's affection. She's not happy about the whole thing. As far as she's concerned, she might as well be back in the convent. And as far as I'm concerned, I left one odd place for another.

The next day, the first thing I do is go to the corner store and buy a *San Francisco Chronicle.* There's an ad mentioning an apartment-to-share with a view of the Golden Gate Bridge. I call the number. The nurse who lives there answers the phone. Yes, she'll be in that morning—she works the night shift. It's a two-bedroom flat, with a kitchen, balcony, sounds real nice, and I'm over there in no time at all.

The nurse is plump, around twenty-nine, and she makes a big issue about allowing male visitors in the apartment. But the place is great. Expensive, but great. My share would come up to $280, a substantial chunk from my $500 allowance. I look at the stained glass windows, the lush hanging plants in the gorgeous living room with fireplace, the beautiful wood panels and later I stare at the Golden Gate Bridge from the available bedroom, and I blurt out, "I'll take it."

The same day, I move in—I only had two suitcases, remember? Suz is all sad and upset, and I'm feeling a bit sorry for her because she's stuck with that weird uncle and aunt. But I tell her she can spend nights at "my place." We laugh, remembering our sleepovers in Manila, with the rest of the group, and how we used to phone boys, slap on makeup and be silly.

***

The next few days I wake up first thing in the morning, buy the *Chronicle*, and scour the classified ads for temporary work. I make some phone calls but the positions are filled. The jobs I'm looking for are office type positions, because that's the only kind of temporary work listed in the classified. Frankly I've never worked in an office before. Well, that's not true. I worked a summer in my father's office, which hardly counts because I was messing around most of the time. My best typing speed in college was 45 wpm with 20 errors.

I'm still job hunting when I meet this Filipina in one of the Filipino parties.

"Anong visa mo?—What's your visa?"—asks Betsy, an accountant who has been in San Francisco for five years.

"Student," I reply.

"Ay, you can't work, ano?"

"I have a summer job permit."

"You won't find summer work now. It's easier to find permanent work," Betsy advises. It is clear that Betsy considers herself a mentor to newcomers like me. "It's late June, all the temporary jobs are gone. Look for permanent work, then quit in September."

"I—I can't do that," I say. "That's—that's lying." I was raised by Catholic nuns and the sense of right and wrong is real strong in me.

"You have a summer permit, 'di ba? That's not really lying. Lillia, this is America. You're on your own here. No one's going to baby you. You have to watch out for yourself." Betsy whips out her permanent resident card and flashes it in front of my face. "Just say you have a green card. They don't always check."

I stare at this highly prized card. "Green? It looks blue."

She looks at her card and chuckles. "Oo nga ano—yes—it's blue. We always call it the green card."

***

I dismiss her suggestion. Like I said, I have this strong sense of right and wrong, and that kind of deception is wrong. And yet, when I look at my bankbook and note my expenses—well, what I mean is that $500 can only go so far when more than fifty percent of it goes to pay for a second-story flat on Green Street. And I can't very well ask my father for more money when I know the whole family's making a sacrifice so I can get my master's degree.

Then the thoughts come to me, bit by bit: It's not really lying, is it, to look for permanent work? I do have a summer work permit. Betsy says a lot of students do that sort of thing. It happens all the time. Businesses are used to it. They don't go bankrupt from employee turnover like that. That's just part of the game.

One morning, when there's absolutely no job prospect of any sort, I study the ad for Kelly Girl Employment Agency. I catch the bus and head toward Market Street, to check the agency out. See what it's all about, see how it goes.

A chipper redhead greets me. "Can you type?" she asks, in a cheerful high-pitched voice.

"Yes," I reply, hoping she won't ask for my speed.

"Oh good, we have a lot of listings."

She's so impressed that I have a Bachelor of Arts and have done some graduate work. Without asking about my residence status, she gives me a typing test. I do 44 wpm with 19 errors. I expect her to say, "Don't call us, we'll call you," but she flashes a smile, flicks her carrot-colored hair back, and says, "You're just nervous. It's probably actually 60 words per minute. There, we'll put you down as 60."

She makes a few phone calls and schedules an interview for me the next morning at a dictating machines shop. Well, I think to myself, as I ride the bus back to my flat, I didn't lie.

The next day, I find a gray-haired man in a gray suit fiddling with the door of the dictating machines shop. I brush an imaginary lint off my cream-colored suit, take a deep breath, and am about to greet him when the door alarm goes off. He shouts above the shrill sound, "I'll be with you in just a second." The man turns locks until the buzzing sound stops. He turns to me. "Hi, I'm Bob Williams. Are you from the agency?"

I nod, give him my name, and follow him inside the office. We cross a large reception area with dictating machines displayed on the wall. A leggy philodendron, looking rather neurotic, stands in the corner of the room. An odor like lighter fluid hangs in the air. I sneeze—I have this allergy problem—and the man explains that their repair shop is in the basement. He invites me into his office, offers me coffee.

All this time, I'm getting real nervous. It's one thing when you're going for a job interview, and quite another when you're carrying the burden of a deception on your conscience. I'm trying to assure myself that there's no problem. I mean, I'm not an illegal alien or anything like that. My visa's better than a tourist; I've got an I-20.

"You're Filipino," he says. His lips stretch into a wide pleasant smile. He is around fifty, tall, with a gentle horsey face. There is a kindness about him that permeates the stark room.

"Ah—yes."

"Great people, Filipinos. I was there during World War Two."

We small-talk a bit about where he's been—Subic, Leyte —and he reminisces about the adobo and calamansi juice he had. Then he mentions some girl he knew. "A real nice gal," he repeats, beaming from the memory.

I get these funny pictures in my head sometimes and as Bob Williams is talking, an image flashes in my mind of him as a lanky young soldier standing beside a Filipina in a soft white dress. I know then that because of that girl he met almost thirty years ago he likes me, that he trusts me.

"We need a gal to answer the service calls and tell our repair people where to go." He describes the job, mentions the salary, and asks when I can start.

"Right away," I reply.

"How about tomorrow?" he asks. Then he throws this out: "You do have a green card, don't you?"

My heart freezes then does double-time knocking against my ribs. I pause, look him straight in the eyes and say: "I do, although I don't know why they call it a green card when it's blue."

As we walk to the door, my ears are ringing and I feel faint. All I hear are his fuzzy words saying I should be in at nine. My hand is embarrassingly clammy when we shake hands; but he's a real gentleman and doesn't let on like anything's wrong. Nothing—just the happy trusting smile, which is making me feel pretty bad. "See you tomorrow," he says pleasantly. I wave and walk down Montgomery.

It's about noon when I pass by Woolworth's and I stop and have a hotdog and a Coke. After lunch I buy some screen gadget that fits over a frying pan to prevent grease from splattering all over the place. Then I window-shop along Market Street and walk up to Union Street where I watch the pigeons until late afternoon.

When the working people rush by with their hands shoved into their coat pockets, I catch the bus back to my flat. That evening I peer out the window at the Golden Gate Bridge. Fog has gathered below and only the spires are visible. It is beautiful, truly elegant, and I think to myself: Here I am in America. And I become incredibly sad.

BUTTERSCOTCH MARBLE ICE CREAM

Friday night Mark wanted to go to Swensen's. "I need butterscotch marble ice cream," he announced.

I was eight months pregnant and wanted to stay home. The night before I hardly slept. I was so big that finding a comfortable position in bed was impossible. Changing position was a major production; getting out of bed was a task. It was depressing; everything was depressing, like the old woman hanging clothes from a line that stretched from one end of the building to the other.

I had seen her earlier that day after I finished scrubbing the thrift-store-bought bassinet with Clorox. The apartment reeked, so I opened the living room window. I spotted her then. She must have been sixty with chin-length white hair whipping around her hair. She was leaning out a window—her kitchen window I guessed—and she had some clothespins dangling from her mouth. The way she stooped—or maybe it was her scraggly hair—gave her a defeated look. She hung her laundry then pulled the line towards her, hung some more, and pulled. The entire line rotated slowly and the clothes swayed back and forth rhythmically. Underwear, nightgowns, pants, shirts, sheets, and towels wavered in the air; and for some reason they all looked gray. The whole scene looked bleak. As I watched her I had the feeling that years from now I would be doing exactly the same thing, hanging laundry from my fifth-floor apartment in the Mission District of San Francisco.

Our apartment was very small: a bathroom, a walk-in closet, a kitchen, a bedroom, and a living room. Accordion doors separated the living room and bedroom. The bathtub was the free-standing kind with claws from legs; and the kitchen had an unused icebox. Mark jokingly called them antiques, but that Friday they appeared simply old to me. Our dream was to buy a Volkswagen bug before the baby was born; Mark had already sold his Kawasaki motorcycle for seed money.

My mother's warning went through my head like a tape recording. "Hija, it's easier to marry a Filipino," she had said. "We have our own ways. Why marry someone different? And to live in another country—why leave home? In America they don't even take care of their old people; they put them in homes. What future will you have there?"

For the first time I felt the gravity of my marrying an American and giving up my life in the Philippines.

That Friday, Mark had no idea of the doubts floating through my head. He was happy.

"Aren't you tired?" I asked. He was a senior law student at Hastings. Four nights a week he sorted mail at the post office.

"I feel great!" he said.

"We can't afford it."

"C'mon, don't be a stick-in-the-mud." He put on his coat, grabbed mine, and stood by the door.

"We don't have the money. I wanted to go to Sears to buy T-shirts for the baby, but I only had seven dollars and fifty-five cents."

"I've got a few bucks. Let's go, let's go, they're going to close," he said.

Reluctantly I got up and walked to him. "I wanted to tie-dye the baby's shirts. Elizabeth taught me how. You use rubber bands. That's how you get the pretty rings. You can use several colors. But I didn't have enough money for the shirts and dye."

"Buy them next week. Tuesday's payday."

"I wanted to make them now. I want to get the baby's things ready."

"Move it along, move it along."

"What's more important anyway, the baby or your ice cream?"

"Right now, my ice cream. Everything will be all right." He grinned encouragingly.

"All right, all right—how can things be all right? We have cockroaches. Three ran out of the garbage chute. I stepped on one; there was this loud crunch. It was disgusting. Then this afternoon, I heard gunshots and ambulance."

"Firecrackers and a fire truck, that's all."

He always said that even though the next day's news reported some killing in the Mission District. I wanted to cry. I was so enormous, I waddled. It was cold and my coat wouldn't go over my stomach. I was still struggling with the first button as we got on the cable car.

"I want to get the baby's things together, then I'll cook some food and freeze it for you for when I'm in the hospital."

"You worry too much," he said.

That made me even more cross, and I kept quiet. He went right on about his pinochle game with Chun and Ross and how Able didn't know demur from demure and Dean Prosser said, "Young ladies are demure; in law it's demur."

I wanted to tell him to stop. I wanted to tell him how afraid I was. I was feeling very pregnant; I was feeling very alone, very foreign in this country; and I felt very uncertain about my future. Where I came from you knew the cycle of life: babies were born, they grew up, they courted and got married; they had children, grandchildren, great-grandchildren, and they died. Everyone knew where everyone's family crypts were in the cemetery. You knew where they'd bury you.

"I hope we're not late," Mark said. "I think they close at ten."

We hopped off the cable car, hurried to Swensen's, and saw the closed sign.

"Shoot!" Mark said. "It's not even ten yet. I really wanted butterscotch marble." He paused, shoved both hands into his pockets and sighed. "Well, c'mon. Let's go. It's foggy and you didn't really want to go out."

Some of that energy, that optimism faded from his face and I felt sorry for him. "Isn't there another Swensen's in Fisherman's Wharf?" I offered.

He smiled gratefully. "Want to try it? How do you feel?"

I rested my hands on top of my stomach—the shelf, he called it. "I'm fine."

Another cable car ride later we were at Fisherman's Wharf hurrying towards Swensen's. We could see a man at the cash register.

"They're still open," he said hopefully.

"Go on ahead," I said, as I tried to keep up with his long strides.

"Just c'mon, move it along. Move those stumps along." I was not very tall, but he was. That night, dressed in my yellow corduroy jumper (one of two clothes that still fit me), my trench coat that wouldn't close, white knee-high socks and brown loafers, I must have looked like a strange humpty-dumpty.

The man tilted his chin when we entered. "Closed," he said.

Mark and I exchanged glances and moaned.

The man continued counting money. "Sorry. Ten o'clock, closing time." He was very serious.

I located the clock on the wall. "It's ten," I declared, defeated.

Maybe it was my tone, but the man looked at me, his eyes resting briefly on my huge stomach. His expression softened. "You need it bad?"

I realized he thought I was the one who wanted the ice cream. I nodded.

"What kind?"

"Butterscotch marble, a pint please," I said. Mark winked at me.

The man dished out a pint and handed it to me. Mark reached into his pocket for his wallet, but the man shook his head. "It's free. Good luck."

I didn't know what to say. I smiled and committed his face to memory: harried-looking with a dark mustache, pale skin with a bluish tint, the kind that hadn't been under the sun much; he was around my age, twenty-two. "Thanks," I finally said, and we left.

Outside, the fog had lifted and the air was no longer damp. As the cable car inched its way up Powell, Mark said, "What do you know, free butterscotch marble ice cream. All because of this." He stroked my stomach; just then the baby kicked and we both laughed.

Back in the apartment, Mark got two teaspoons and settled in front of the television. *The Hunchback of Notre Dame* was on.

"Wow!" he said, "a classic. Come and watch and have some ice cream."

I shook my head. "I feel fat and ugly."

"You're beautiful," he said. "Besides free butterscotch marble is always low cal."

He ate the ice cream alone while I stood by the window, peering through the darkness to where the woman had been hanging her laundry.

"What are you doing?" he asked.

"Thinking."

"What about?"

My thoughts were still clicking around in my head; they hadn't settled into words yet. All I knew was that life wasn't as bad as it had been earlier that day. I said, "I hope she brought her laundry in."

"Who?"

"Never mind," I said.

The baby kicked once more and I shifted my weight. Something wonderful happened when I did that—the light fell on the window in such a way that I lost sight of the outside darkness and saw Mark's reflection instead. He was sitting on the couch, contentedly eating his ice cream, a gentle happy giant of a man.

I saw in that reflection my future.

SID LANSKY'S VACATION

Soon after Sid Lansky's wife tells him she doesn't love him anymore, that she loves another man, Sid moves out of their three-bedroom Redondo Beach house and into an apartment in Santa Monica. For a while he continues phoning his wife. She says things like, "We've never really connected, Sid. You're so distant; you were never there for me."

Her words hurt Sid's feelings; he suggests counseling but Cindy says it's too late, that he should have had counseling after he got back from 'Nam. She files for divorce and tells Sid to stop calling, to talk to her lawyer instead.

Sid's friend Jake, another Air Force pilot from Vietnam days, tries to help Sid through his depression. Jake recommends the best divorce lawyer in L.A. He explains everything about the dating game—the singles' ads, singles' dances, handling the AIDS-business.

During lunch downtown when Sid is relatively upbeat, they eye two women who are pecking at their salad. One woman, a giggler, is overweight with frizzy hair all over the place. The other has short blond hair—good-looking but aloof, the ice-queen type.

Jake dares Sid to go for the blonde.

Sid says he doesn't like blondes.

Jake persists and finally Sid asks the blonde if they've met before and he tells her how attractive she is—the point of all these is to ask her out on a date, a young man's game that Sid at forty-six now finds himself doing. The blonde, also in her forties, but fighting hard to pass for thirty, cocks her head to one side and asks for Sid's telephone number. "I'll call you," she says and smiles.

Later the two men have a good laugh; they don't expect her to call. Sid is stunned (and flattered) when the blonde phones to suggest they meet at Ocean's. They have drinks, dinner, and afterward they stroll on the boardwalk where she shows Sid a tiny birthmark like a little red spider on her right shoulder. He runs his finger over the birthmark, then he tentatively kisses her shoulder. She shivers and sighs deeply, so Sid kisses her on the mouth. She's receptive so he kisses her again, this time with more ardor, and kisses her again while his hands fumble for her breasts. She pulls away and in a breathy voice says "Ah, so horny" and invites Sid to her townhouse.

Since Sid has been married to Cindy for eighteen years, he doesn't know the etiquette of modern courtship and lovemaking. But the blonde knows and they have a night of intense lovemaking. In the morning he awakes with an incredibly dry mouth and a sad feeling.

They have a few more dates and everything is fine until the blonde starts— "You didn't call last night. When will I see you again? I want to see you. I want you." She doesn't stop and Sid feels hemmed in.

The next time they meet, he notices her dark roots, a quarter of an inch of dark hair all throughout. Ridiculous, the thought shoots through his mind, how women bleach their hair. That night he stares at the filet mignon on his plate and he hears the low mooing of a cow—a soft but definite moo. With his fork he pierces the piece of meat and blood oozes out. The image of the bloody corpse of his co-pilot flashes in his head, and Sid almost vomits.

He does two things after that: he stops seeing the blonde and he turns vegetarian. No red meat, pork, chicken; no eggs, no dairy products. He gets into tofu, beans, vegetables, fruit, and multivitamins. He hangs around Mrs. Gooch's health food store, and he works out five times a week at the Y.

Cindy and he intensify their fight over who'll keep the Toyota or the Taurus, and what about the vacation house in Arrowhead, and will Sid turn over the Redondo Beach house to Cindy in exchange for 50% of his retirement pension?

To top all this, his mother calls: "Thank God you don't have children because you'd be fighting over them too." Sid feels really bad because it was never clear who had the fertility problem—Cindy or he—and the suspicion that he's the defective one roots in him all over again.

He grows more vigilant about his diet and exercise. He worries about whether he's consumed any preservatives that day and whether L.A. smog will give him lung cancer. He spends a lot of time flossing and brushing his teeth, and he studies his gums at great length in a magnifying mirror to make sure they're not receding. At night he falls asleep exhausted and he dreams of rotting dead cows and sweltering jungles (like those in 'Nam). He wakes before dawn, sweating and feeling as though he's misplaced a huge part of himself. Without blinking he stares at the bleak white ceiling while the sky slowly pales into morning.

***

The dreams change when the divorce becomes final. In one dream he's in the Redondo Beach house, and he's racing through the house locking windows and doors because there're VC outside. The VC knock down a door; Sid runs to the backroom, locks the door, shoves the dresser against it, and waits. He's tense, then suddenly the window rattles. He didn't figure on the VC entering through the window. He backs off just when someone kicks the window. Glass shatters, then the scene shifts and he's in 'Nam, parachuting down to an open field with over a dozen VC waiting for him. When he lands, a VC rushes to him and shoots him. Sid doubles over; he crawls on the dirt, trying to escape. He's groveling on the ground when a VC shoves a bayonet to his mouth, then Sid wakes up.

The other dream involves a four by six cage and Sid whose six feet two can't even stand in it. In this dream five hundred and two days drip away like melted wax. When he wakes up from his dream, he goes to the kitchen and drinks glass-after-glassful of water.

***

"You're stressed out. You need to rest. How about a little vacation?" Jake suggests.

One day Sid spots a United Airlines billboard advertising a four-day special to New Orleans and right away he decides to go. He always wanted to see the French Quarters, he tells his mother.

"But you hate flying," his mother protests.

"I'll be all right, Mom," Sid says.

He drinks Scotch in the plane, and he's drunk when he checks into his room at Le Richilieu Hotel. From his bed he studies the balcony and overhead cast iron lace work, and he thinks of the high-ceilinged room he had in Bien Hoa back in '67. He remembers sultry nights with the rotating fan whirring above him. He thinks of the nurse Than, the OV-10 he flew, the crisscrossing canals of the Delta, the pockmarked U Minh forest, bodies, the wounded—he stops; he can't think further. An emotional overload weighs him down when he remembers that part of his life. He never discussed Vietnam with Cindy, his mother, not with Jake, not with anyone. He gets up, staggers to the bathroom and drinks three glasses of water.

***

Since Sid enjoys sports, he takes the bus to the Louisiana Superdome and joins a tour. The guide explains: "This is as tall as a twenty-seven story building. It can seat up to a hundred thousand people. It's so large that air conditioning must keep the temperature constant otherwise it rains inside."

All that space, Sid reflects. As he stands there looking all around him, the image of the four by six cage that was his prison creeps up on him. Perspiration beads on his forehead. He sucks in a deep breath and struggles to listen to the guide.

She's still droning on when the woman to the right of Sid turns to her companion. "How can it rain indoors?" she whispers in a soft accented voice. Sid freezes; he recognizes the accent; it's Vietnamese.

"Probably collects moisture," the man beside her replies.

The man and woman continue talking in hushed voices and Sid watches her, fascinated. Her sleek black hair falls down to her waist. She is lean, graceful. He can see her profile but can't see the rest of her face. He cranes his neck but she turns her head away. It suddenly becomes very important to Sid to find out what she looks like, so he trails behind them to the bus stop.

"Do you have to go to the meeting tomorrow?" the woman says, sounding disappointed. When she turns, Sid sees her face. He sucks in his breath at how beautiful she is.

"Just from ten to noon. I'll meet you at the Cafe Du Monde," the man replies. He puts his hand under her chin and kisses her.

Sid notices his wedding ring. He wonders if the woman has a wedding band too. Sid is staring so hard that he's surprised when the man turns to glare at him. Embarrassed, Sid lowers his eyes.

The bus pulls up in front of them and the couple gets on. Sid hesitates but can't help himself. He follows them and sits behind the woman. He wants to reach out and stroke the woman's hair. At the next bus stop when he thinks no one is looking, he shifts his position so he touches her hair. It feels silky, soft, and he imagines how it would feel against his mouth. The woman straightens up; she reaches back, gathers her hair, and twirls it over her shoulder. She has a gold band on her left ring finger.

They're married, Sid thinks, and he becomes melancholy. When the bus stops along Canal Street, the couple stands up. Sid considers getting off with them, but the man stares at Sid, this time in a threatening way, and Sid remains seated. The woman casts him a curious glance. He catches her gaze, but she quickly turns away.

The rest of the day he does the sort of things tourists do in New Orleans: he rides the St. Charles trolley, visits the Audubon Park, dines at K-Paul's, and listens to jazz at Preservation Hall. All this time, he's thinking of her. She reminds him of a delicate orchid, a fragile, fragile flower that he does not want to destroy. He keeps reenacting what happened from the moment he saw her until they got off the bus.

His mind is still on her when he stands on the balcony that night and runs his hands on the intricate iron grillwork. A mild sting makes him pull his right hand away and he notices a slender line of blood. He squeezes the flesh around the cut to make it bleed, and he stands there for a long time staring at the spreading redness.

A sense of growing, of expansion, comes to him. His mind fixes on a memory, then another, and still another. He remembers the time he cut his hand in 'Nam on a piece of metal. He ignored it until the wound became infected. The Vietnamese nurse Than scolded him. "This is the tropics," she said in her lilting voice. "Little cuts are same as big ones; they must be cared for." She swabbed it and gave him penicillin ointment. He asked her if she'd go out with him, but she smiled and walked away. He didn't see her for weeks until he and Jake went to Dalat for R&R.

Two women were having trouble navigating a paddleboat on the lake. When he looked closer, he saw that one of them was Than. He got on a boat and paddled out to help them. Later the four of them lunched at the restaurant in the Catholic convent where the nuns sang lovely French songs. It had been enchanting, sitting there in that restaurant with Jake and two beautiful women, as though they were in a magical place far away from the war.

In Bien Hoa he went to the military hospital to find her. She laughed when she saw him and the next night on the way to the movie theater they laughed some over the boat episode in Dalat. He put his arm around her in the theater; Than rested her head on his shoulder. She seemed so delicate, and he had been so afraid of crushing her. After the movie, they took a walk and later she pouted, "You do not like me?" They kissed, and the next time they went out he kissed her harder, and the third time they became lovers.

***

Sunlight crisscrosses his face and for a while he thinks he's back in 'Nam, in that bamboo-prison not fit for pigs. He sits up, squints at the dresser, the TV, the balcony, and realizes he's in New Orleans, that he's divorced from Cindy, that he's forty-six Then this slips in—he's past the midpoint of his life, and he's going nowhere but straight to his grave. The idea sinks to his marrow; it frightens him, saddens him so much that for the first time in many, many years, he starts crying. He tries to control himself, but the more he tries, the louder his sobs become. He gives in to his sorrow until crying becomes a tiring activity and he's merely making sounds, forcing tears from his eyes.

He feels better after he showers and dresses. He decides to go to the Cafe Du Monde. It's a foolish idea; he knows that. The woman is obviously married. He can't bother her; and yet he finds himself heading straight to Jackson Square. His heart is pumping hard; his hands sweating. He's feeling all that adrenaline flowing, just like parachuting down that open field straight into the hands of the VC.

At the Cafe, he decides to skip his healthy diet and he orders beignets and cafe au lait. From an outdoor table he scans the people in the square and around him; she's not there. He sips his coffee and waits. He feels tight, strung out. He considers leaving but something pins him down to his seat. He imagines her walking toward St. Louis Cathedral, her dark hair hanging loosely down her back. She'll cross the square to the Cafe Du Monde. She'll walk up to the counter and order a cup of coffee. Sitting down in a table near Sid, she'll open her purse, pull out a book and start reading.

Her cheeks are flushed; the fringe of her dark eyelashes are two crescents. When she reaches for her cup, she accidentally spills her coffee. Sid grabs some napkins and rushes to her table. The coffee is on her purse, on her book; it starts dripping down the table to her skirt. He helps clean up. She thanks him.

Then he says, "Excuse me, but were you at the Superdome yesterday?"

She smiles. "Yes."

"I was there too. This probably sounds like a line, but you remind me of someone I knew. You're Vietnamese, aren't you?"

She nods.

"Chao co," he says, "Toi o Vietnam."

And he talks about Than, how they met, their love for each other, and he describes Saigon, Cam Tho and the orphanage there, breathtaking Dalat, all the places he's seen in 'Nam; getting hit near the U Minh forest, his dead co-pilot beside him, the eternity it took for his plane to spiral down; the VC swarming around him when he hit the ground; the miserable four by six bamboo cage; the torture; the anger; the despair; the hunger; the thirst; the incredible fear; all the humiliating things he did to survive; trying to find Than in Bien Hoa when he's finally released. Not finding her.

He tells her all that. And opening up, finally confessing after twenty-three years eases his burden.

No need to go on about returning to the States, graduate school, and Cindy. Don't mention the fog he was in after the war (yes, Cindy was right; he never connected with her). No need, because what mattered, what was real, was 'Nam when he was twenty-three.

ON THE WAY TO KALIGHAT

When I was in India I visited Mother Teresa's Home for the Dying in Calcutta. It was my second morning there when I got into a taxi. The taxi driver studied me on his rear view mirror and asked why I was going to "Mother's Home for the Dying." I said I wanted to see how she had transformed the Kalighat into such a place. He smiled. "There are many like you who come to Calcutta just to see Mother's home."

"Tell me, was it a real Hindu temple before?"

"It remains a temple for the goddess Kali," he said.

"But don't the Missionary Sisters of Charity now run the place? Haven't they taken over?"

"They use the rooms for the dying; there are cots, and of course the dying. But the statue of Kali is still there. She still has garlands of skulls around her neck. Do you know that she is the goddess of disease, destruction, and death?"

I nodded. I could not imagine Kali there in Mother's Home, just as I could not imagine a place dedicated solely for the dying. A last resting place. I remembered the story I had read about how Mother Teresa had found a dying man and had brought him to the hospital, only to have the doctors turn him away because they could not save him. That night, after the man died in her arms, she went to the department of health and harangued them for a place for the dying. The same night I read the article I made up my mind I'd go see this Home.

"Tell me," the taxi driver said, "Why are you in Calcutta?"

"I've told you, I want to see this Home for the Dying. I'm a writer. I want to write about it."

"But why are you really here?" he insisted. "You could be in Shimla instead of here."

"Shimla is a British colonial place. What's there to write about there?"

"You could write about the memsahib places; you could write about British injustice, how they built their mansions on the foothills while people in Calcutta died on the streets." He paused. "I know why you are here. It is why everyone else comes to see Mother's Home. You want to see God."

"Is God there? Is God standing side by side with the goddess Kali?" I said somewhat lightly although my mind clung to his words about God, and started to turn them around in my head. Was that really why I was in India, to find God?

"If it's not God you want to find, then it's yourself," he persisted.

"You will not give up, will you? All right, I'll tell you. I'm here to find my mother and my father who are both dead. They both died at the World Trade Center on 9/11, and I had nothing to bury. I had nothing to convince me they are dead. Ever since I have been visiting hospitals, places where people die, hoping I see their faces in the dying."

"Ah, well, you will see them in Kalighat, no doubt about that. There you will see the faces of your parents, your brothers, your sisters, yourself," he said confidently.

And I sat back, watched him weave in and out of the narrow crowded streets of Calcutta past the slaughterhouse to the Kalighat.

THE CIRCLE OF LIFE

After two years, I think I've gotten over Tai, that I can look at any Asian woman and not think of her. But it happens once again at Thursday's performance of *Lion King*. At exactly 7:50 p.m. I step out on to the right balcony to check my instruments—an assortment of drums, cymbal, and other percussion instruments. The other musicians are checking their instruments as well, and a loud hum fills the Pantages.

It's October and even in Los Angeles the weather is starting to change. It's cooler now; summer has become a memory and I'm feeling out of sync. I do better when the sun is out and I can walk along the boardwalk where the crowds keep my mind occupied. During the fall and winter, I grow dreary and start thinking too much; and it's not good for me to do that.

I'm tapping out the beat of the *Circle of Life* on the drums, trying to get into the music, when she walks down the aisle, heads straight toward me. A woman wearing black, something long and sinuous, looking so much like Tai it makes me lose my beat. She is looking at the seat numbers. When her dark hair swings around her, I feel it, a sharp stabbing pain inside. I remember Tai, her long hair that she lost after chemo. "Tell me: if you were a tree, what tree would you be?" she asked me when she was already ill; and tonight for some reason, I remember her words.

The woman pauses in front of the right row and sits in the solitary seat directly in front of me. She is Tai; she is not Tai. She sits down, fumbles with her purse, and starts to read the program. I don't even realize I've stopped playing and that I'm staring at her, standing rigidly like a foolish gawking boy. She raises her eyes and stares directly at me. It's a questioning look as if wondering why I'm looking at her. Holding her gaze I feel a strange feeling of familiarity with this woman whose name I do not know but who reminds me so much of Tai it's as if we've shared a past together. I nod at her, and she gives a tentative smile. But quickly, she glances around to see if there's someone else I greeted. She lowers her eyes. She is not offended; I can see the soft expression on her face. It's a strong face, and intelligent face—like Tai's—chiseled, sultry, earthy, making me wonder what jungles look like, what dangers lurk in them.

She fidgets some more with the program, then looks up at me. "Am I in the wrong seat?" she asks.

Her directness surprises me. "No, it's nothing," I mumbled, embarrassed. I try to focus on my drums.

She continues to talk. "I didn't think I'd get in; it's sold out. It's very exciting!—her voice carrying Asia with it. She gestures around her, pointing at the stage and the huge overhead chandeliers. I glance at the gilt decorations of the deco-era theater. I remember how excited I'd been two years ago when I started playing. But I've been playing mechanically for a long time now. It's been just a job—playing twice a day, six times a week. My social life has been reduced to rehearsals and cast parties. Something has been missing for a long time. I know that, and I know that Tai's death has something to do with all this.

But tonight, there is something about this woman staring at the stage and sometimes at me that energizes me, makes me play exceptionally well. For most of the night I watch her—no, it's not really her; it's Tai I'm watching, Tai when she was well and we were happy. She used to listen to me for hours while I practiced in our apartment. She never grew tired listening to me play.

All throughout the performance an incredible urge builds inside me to talk to the woman, to find out if I can see her. I tell myself she's just one of the thousands of tourists who come to see the *Lion King*. I try to suppress the urge to go to her and make a fool of myself. But the more I try to do so, the clearer the words form in my head, "If you were a tree, what kind of tree would you be?" I want to hear this woman's answer. I want to hear Tai's answer. I never did get Tai's answer to that question.

But soon after the curtains close, before I have the chance to get to her, she's gone.

***

I wake up with the thought of going to the Huntington Gardens, to the tropical section, to search for the tree that Tai used to talk about—a tall Australian tree that flowered when the weather turned chilly. I figure it'll have flowers now.

By 11, I've paid the $10 entrance fee and I'm walking down the gravel path toward the desert garden. I'm remembering Tai in the hospital when I finally said, "An oak—if I were a tree, I'd be an oak."

"What does an oak look like?" she asked. She had a black scarf on her head; she didn't want anyone to see her bald. Losing her hair was one of the things that made her very sad about her illness.

I told her they were the big trees we had seen on the way to Central Coast. "Remember the trip we took to Hearst Castle," I reminded her. I reached out to hold her hand. How cold it was—I recall being startled because Tai had always been warm to the touch.

She beamed recalling that weekend. She stroked my face, "An oak is a big and strong tree; you could be an oak. But I think you're more like the tree in our backyard in Saigon." And she told me about the huge tree with pink flowers.

I never asked her: What do you remember about Saigon? How could you remember so much when you were only four when you left? How did you adjust to America? I never asked because I was afraid my questions would plunge her into the darkness she would sometimes find herself in. Sometimes, it took her weeks to crawl out of that darkness. We never talked about it.

After walking through the desert section, I find myself in the middle of tall trees laden with shocking pink flowers. I walk to the nearest tree, study it carefully. This is the tree that Tai said is me. The flowers are beautiful to look at, but the trunk is thick and the base is filled with thorns. The roots are large and push down into the earth. This tree will survive a drought, I think.

Was this how Tai saw me? I run my palms on the bark, search for an area without thorns and I press hard as if feeling for a pulse for the rush of blood, a life force. "I miss you, Tai. I wish you were here to tell me what you meant when you said I am this tree."

***

This was how Tai died.

One morning she awakes, shivering violently and her hands are cold. I spent hours beside her, listening to her breathing apparatus gurgle and hum. The rhythm of the sound is mesmerizing and there were moments when I actually dozed off. I wrap the blanket around her. She stirs and stares straight at me. She is back. Yesterday, she was drifting in and out, her mind unclear. Sometimes she talked of the past; sometimes she talked to her dead father. And when she did this, her eyes were closed or they wandered around aimlessly, ignoring me and the nurses. But now Tai is looking straight at me and I know her mind is alert and I smile bravely. She struggles; I hold her down. "No, don't," I say, pointing at the tubes hanging over her. She tries to turn her head and she lifts her right hand, points to the side table. She wants the pencil and pad of paper. I hand the pencil to her and hold the pad up so she can write on it. With great difficulty, she writes, "Whatever." I do not understand what she means. She motions for the pad, and I hold it up again. She continues writing, "it takes."

Whatever it takes: she means, whatever it takes to keep her alive. Before the doctors hooked her up to the breathing apparatus, she told me, "Don't worry about my looks, just keep me alive."

All her hair is gone. She is reduced to bones and skin, although her abdomen is large from the cancer. Her hunger to live hurts me terribly. I wish I could give her my own life, or twenty years of my life at least, enough time for her to grow into a woman like her mother.

"Don't worry," I say, stroking her forehead. "Try to rest, don't worry. They are doing everything they can." I almost say, "Things will be all right," but I know that would be a terrible lie. She and I know things are pretty bad right now, that she is close to death.

She closes her eyes and stops struggling. Encouraged I continue, "You have made me so happy. These past three years have been heaven." I expect my clichéd words to be comforting, but she opens her eyes and I see fear in them. No—not fear; it's more an accusing look, as if I've betrayed her. And then, tears well in her eyes.

"Don't, please, don't."

I wipe her tears from her face. It is difficult because of the breathing apparatus and the tubes going in and out of her body. She has a terrible smell; she has had this smell despite the diligent care of the nurses and her mother.

Her mother is taking it better than me. She is calm when she tells me it is the smell of the dying, that there is nothing we can do about it. She can talk to the doctors and nurses about Tai more easily than I can.

It is the mother who later informs me that the doctors will try to wean her from the breathing machine tomorrow. We're in a waiting room, not too far from Tai's room.

"And what if it fails? What if she can't breathe on her own?"

"I will have to discuss the options with the doctors," she replies.

"What options are there?" I say, my voice louder this time.

"Andre," she says, as if talking to a child, "the problem is not the breathing; it is the stage 4 cancer."

Bitch, I think, but inside I know she is saying the truth. I want to accuse her of being a cold unloving person, but I know she has spent days and nights in the hospital room with Tai, that she has done all she can to make Tai as comfortable as she can be.

But I still cannot help myself, "How can you be so unfeeling? She's your daughter."

She stares out a window for a long time, then says, "Tai and I are more than mother and daughter. We are like one person. It was that trip here in that boat that made us very close. We saw things; things happened, you see. We already died then, this is a second life, but if Tai wants to go on, that is all right. It is just for a little while. One day I too will go, as will you. The time is not so important; it's the sharing of experiences that count."

She is right, I know that, and not knowing what to do with my anger, or perhaps more accurately, my grief, I leave her and enter Tai's room again. Her eyes are closed, and she is talking softly to an imaginary person once again. I run my hands over her head, her face, crush her cold hand in mine. "Thank you, Tai, for everything. I love you."

And then I leave, knowing that tomorrow they will unplug the machines and Tai will die.

***

A year after her death, I visit her mother. I ask her questions and she answers me. Tai was born shortly after the communists took over Vietnam. The communists had killed Tai's father. After the father died, the mother sold all her jewelry to be able to take Tai and her brother away. She talked about the boat trip, about an old woman who died and whom the men threw overboard. After a circuitous trip, they made it to the Philippines, and eventually to California.

When I am ready to leave, she goes to an album and pulls out a picture. She hands it to me. The picture shows a young family of four standing in front of huge tree filled with flowers. It is an Australian tree, the tree Tai referred to when we were talking about trees. The mother says Tai loved that tree, that she and her brother used to play under that tree for hours. The picture is yours, she says.

I clutch it against my chest. For now, it is enough.

SAN MIGUEL DE ALLENDE

Just outside the Parroquia San Miguel de Arcangel, Susan sat down on a concrete bench, one of many scattered around San Miguel de Allende, and she glanced at the front door of the church. She had on her bright yellow dress, and she fussed with the skirt, then turned her attention once more to the front of the church door. She took a deep breath. She waited as she had waited two years ago. This waiting was something spontaneous—something that rose out of her heart or soul, certainly not her mind, because her mind knew that he was dead, that he had been dead for nine months. Time enough to make a baby, she thought, and then just like that she remembered the times she and Roland had lain on the magnificent bed of the Casa Veronica and sipping enormous glasses of frothy Margarita, they fantasized how their child would look—he would have his lively inquisitive eyes that seemed to sparkle with joy at all times; he would have her thick dark hair; he would his sense of humor; he would have her logical mind; he would have the skill of words like him, and be a whiz with numbers like her.

She paused—indeed she was known for her logical linear mind, her left-brain engineer's way of thinking. So why had she traveled all the way to San Miguel de Allende, to sit in front of their grand church only to wait for the impossible? She was on a holiday; that was true, but to come to San Miguel where she and Roland had honeymooned was madness. And why this sense of anticipation, as if he would come back to her, as if he would suddenly appear in front of the church, extend his arms out to her, tell her it was all a mistake, tell her he loved her more than anything, anyone in the whole world.

She had not seen his body, so perhaps this explained why even now she still could not fathom that he had disintegrated like many others in New York that awful September day. His business partner who survived 9/11 had told her how they were half-way down the long flight of stairs when they came across a heavyset man sitting on a step. The fat man was sweating and gasping, and Roland had stayed behind to help him. Both of them didn't make it.

Many nights when she struggled to catch some sleep, she would see in her mind the television scenes played over and over—first the one building bursting into flames, then the other, then both buildings disintegrating like sand castles. She tried to force her imagination to see close-ups of Rolando, not just those long shots of the buildings. She struggled to get a glimpse of his face—but nothing came to her; no image of Roland. She would have wanted to see his face, catch some hint as to how he was feeling as he helped the fat man—was he confident, was he worried, was he afraid, did he suffer much? But all she could see were the twin buildings burning, burning, burning ...

She had replayed the scene numerous times until it became engraved into brain. She was weary of it. Somehow nine months passed, and now here she was studying the concrete bench on which she sat. It was decorated with wistful angels. She ran her fingers over the face of one angel and wondered if she looked like that—face upturned, eyes wide open, mouth slightly open in anticipation. He always told her she was beautiful, but she knew she wasn't. She was plump with big arms which she hated; she always wore dresses or tops with sleeves to cover her arms. She tugged at her sleeves now, pulling them downward to cover more of the hated arms. She used to tell him exactly that: I hate my arms, and he would laugh and shake his head, and then he'd lean over and look her straight into her eyes and say, "I love your arms, your face, all of you."

It was almost 4 in the afternoon, and it was still hot. The bench she sat on was under a coral tree and she scrunched over to the side with some shade. Her face was dappled by San Miguel's brilliant sunshine, her yellow dress shimmering more vividly yellow. The warmth of the sun travelled through her body. She felt like—well—a fruit, hanging on a branch, absorbing the sun's rays. A thought seeped into her—*Today, I am a lemon, a bright yellow lemon.* The image of her shaped like a lemon bloomed in her imagination and she couldn't help but laugh a bit. Catching herself, she looked around, and thanked God no one was there. She needed to get a hold of herself; she was behaving poorly. Oddly, that was how she was behaving—oddly. How unthinkable it was for an engineer like her to behave strangely. She couldn't allow herself to just lose it.

But the image of her as a lemon remained, and laughing had felt good. She hadn't done that ever since … ever since … So for a couple of minutes she laughed—no one was around in any case; and when she finished, she brushed her bright yellow skirt, admiring the life and richness of the color. She spread her fingers on her skirt and observed how her skin glowed. He loved me very much, very, very much, but he's not coming, she concluded.

The thought gave her a searing pain, sharp but quick, like a razor-cut. It didn't even make her cry. It came, then went. She got up and straightened her back, wondering what she would do next. Quick as a flash it came to her to walk to town and sit in an outdoor restaurant with a mariachi band playing, and she'd order an enormous glass of frothy Margarita. He would like her to do that.

REMEMBERING CHE GUEVARA

I was nineteen when I met Che Guevara. This happened in Cuzco long before he was known as Che, long before he was killed in Bolivia. It was 1952; he was twenty-three; I was nineteen. I was in Cuzco with my cousin Tita. Cuzco had not been my first choice for a vacation. I had wanted to see Miami, or Barcelona, or Madrid, or Mexico City, places I couldn't afford but instead of some glitz, I got a sleepy town in a valley, an arid cold place riddled with Inca ruins, some 3,500 meters above sea level.

"Three nights in Cuzco is just right," Tita said in the bus, "there are museums I want to see, then we'll take the train to Machu Picchu." She was an anthropology major and had been wanting to visit this part of Peru.

"Will the museums in Cuzco have pointed skulls and mummies?" I asked, referring to the ancient malformed skulls and mummies wrapped in baskets, displayed in the museums in Lima.

"I hope so," Tita said.

I sighed. "Skulls and mummies just aren't fun, Tita."

"You know how they shape the skulls? By tying boards on babies' heads—isn't that interesting? It's all interesting. Cuzco is the oldest inhabited city in the Western Hemisphere. It's the capital of the Inca World."

"You've already told me that."

"Will you quit being a wet blanket?" she said. "Just because Antonio two-timed you doesn't mean your life has ended. You're only nineteen; you have your whole life ahead of you."

I sat back and sulked even more. We were in the back of a crowded bus. I didn't want to hear about Antonio again. For most of the twenty-four-hour trip from Lima to Cuzco (via Nasca and Anbancay), we rehashed what he'd done to me: that is, he dumped me for a socialite in Lima. Tita thought she was being funny when she talked about his new girlfriend. "Antonio says she's the daughter of the Minister of Health, and that her mother is the descendant of Mansio Serra. She could be a descendant of Pizarro himself, but you know what, her buckteeth are so large, she looks like a horse."

"I don't understand why anyone who's anyone in Lima society is either descended from a Spanish conquistador or Inca royalty—or both," I said.

"She is full-blooded Española, but you know why her teeth are so large? From inbreeding—cousin marrying cousin. And you know why they did that? Just to keep wealth in the family," Tita said.

"I heard she's very pretty."

"If you like horses." She parted her lips, stuck her upper front teeth out, and whinnied like a horse.

I had to laugh but later as I glanced at my reflection on the glass window and stared at my thick black hair and my brown skin, I realized how Indian I looked, just like my grandmother.

"Carolina, don't be insecure. You're pretty, so stop this whining," Tita scolded.

Sighing, I twirled my hair and touched my cheek, not feeling pretty at the moment.

When we arrived Cuzco, Tita and I immediately felt light-headed and nauseous from the high altitude. My mind was in such a fog, I almost forgot my purse in the bus. My grandmother, who came from this part of the world, had told us to drink coca tea before we made our ascent. We didn't, and consequently we spent our first day in our hotel room with the runs. I felt like I'd traveled straight to purgatory. Tita rang the front desk and ordered coca tea. "We should have listened to your grandmother," she said.

The coca tea was steaming hot and comforting. After the second cup, I could walk around our hotel room. I opened the balcony doors. Our hotel was at the corner of Avenida del Sol and Almagro, facing the Plaza de Armas and the cathedral. The Plaza was larger than I expected and surrounding it were two-story colonial buildings, now turned into hotels, restaurants and shops. Against the walls, Indian vendors rested on their haunches; they were selling weavings, knick-knacks, ears of corn, bags of coca leaves, live chicks and ducklings. The women were short and pudgy. Their long braided hair hung down their backs; and they had bowler hats perched on their heads. Their full skirts ballooned out around them; and their brown legs stuck out from underneath the voluminous skirts. They looked like my grandmother who lived with us and who spent most of her time in the kitchen and garden. She had been so happy about our visiting the Andes. "When I was small," she had said, and had proceeded to tell us stories about her growing up in Puno.

The sun was setting by this time. From the balcony, Tita and I watched the lights that flickered on as the darkness grew. The way the plaza nestled against the hills, the quaintness of the buildings and people made me think of a nativity scene. I have always loved Christmas, and for the first time in weeks, I felt a quiet inside, a calm.

***

I was almost asleep when Tita shook me. "I'm hungry," she said, "let's go find food."

"But I'm sleepy," I protested.

"You can sleep in tomorrow. Remember we're on vacation."

It was past ten when we changed and left our room. The hotel manager suggested their restaurant, which did not have a single customer in it. Tita declined, saying, "We want authentic Andean food." What she meant was, "We want something cheap." The hotel manager pointed down the street and said the Inka Grill served guinea pig, rabbit and alpaca steaks. Outside the hotel, Tita made a face and said, "Guinea pig? I hate guinea pig. There's hardly any meat on them. They make me cry," she said.

I was annoyed that she brought up the matter of guinea pigs, knowing precisely that my grandmother fixed and ate guinea pigs. I said, "I like guinea pig, especially the way my abuela fixes it."

It was a lie, of course, and she called me on it, "You do not. You've always told me you hate it."

"I like it sometimes."

"No guinea pig tonight, besides we can have your abuelita's grilled guinea pig anytime. Now where's the Inka Grill?" she asked.

"Over there," I said.

"Then we're going the opposite way," Tita said, and she extended her arms and danced down the cobbled street. Near the old

Jesuit Seminary, she twirled around, "Here, in this place, Pizarro captured the great Inca, Atahuallpa. Think of it, Carolina, we are walking where important historical events happened. Can you feel the history? Can you hear the voices of Huacar and Tupac Amaru? I can hear them, calling: come find your roots, know who you are." She raced down the street, and I ran after her. I envied Tita's excitement. For weeks, I'd been feeling as if I were crammed tightly into my body, like a flame tree crammed into a flowerpot.

It was chilly that night, and I buttoned up the alpaca sweater that my grandmother insisted I bring. It was gray with black Indian zigzag patterns; it was my least favorite sweater; but here in Cuzco, the soft fuzzy material felt warm and cozy. The moon rose above the hills and Tita said the fortress of Sacsayhuaman was out there someplace and tomorrow we would see it. The moon was large and yellow, and the old town of Cuzco seemed to glow from the moonlight. It was a Spanish colonial town, with narrow streets that meandered here and there. We followed a group of around six students who walked past the cathedral and up a cobbled street. They were loud and noisy and full of life. I hated how happy they were. They reminded me of the times Antonio and I went to movies or bars with friends. The students entered a crowded small restaurant-bar. Inside people were drinking chicha corn beer and smoking. I started to walk past the place, but Tita held me back and said, "Let's go in." Without waiting for my reply, she walked in.

That was another irritating habit of Tita, she always dismissed what I wanted. Begrudgingly I followed. "What are we doing here? I thought you're hungry. This is a bar."

"They'll have some food, empanadas or something. Sit down, relax," she commanded.

"I don't want to be in a noisy bar. I thought we were going to a small restaurant with home-cooked food," I shouted, above the noise.

"We'll have a couple of drinks then leave," she said.

I sat down beside her, feeling grumpy. It didn't take long for Tita to start a conversation with two Argentines, Alberto and Ernesto—Che, that is. They said they were doctors traveling through South America. Tita had her eye on Alberto and she asked him questions about Argentina, about Eva Peron whom she thought was beautiful. The two of them soon acted as if they'd known each other since elementary school. "From here, we're going to the Urabamba Valley," Tita said.

"Ah—Machu Picchu! We've just seen it. You'll love it! It's the most fabulous place in the entire world," Alberto said.

"You've been there! Tell me about it," Tita gushed.

He leaned toward her ear and started talking. Tita's eyes glistened as she listened. He stared at her with rapt attention, and again I recalled how Antonio used to do that to me, treat me as if I were the center of his life. I felt lonely, out-of-place.

Tita and Alberto became so engrossed with each other, it was as if they both vanished from our table. Tita had done this to me in Lima, but in Lima, it wasn't a problem because I had other friends to talk to or who could take me home. But in Cuzco, I only had Tita. I peered out the door and tried to remember how to get back to the hotel. I wondered how safe it was to walk around Cuzco

I was trying to decide what to do when Ernesto started coughing. "I have to leave," he said. He was wheezing badly.

"Go, make sure he's fine," Tita ordered.

"My friend gets asthma attacks," Alberto explained, "if he gets worse, call me."

It was now my job to babysit this sick Argentine. I wanted to go back to the hotel, but as I looked up and down the street, I didn't know which way to go. Ernesto was near the Inca wall, bent over, trying to catch his breath. I thought that if my grandmother were there, she would take care of him; my grandmother was always taking care of people. "Are you all right?" I offered.

He nodded, coughed and wheezed some more. He waved his hand, as if to send me away.

I shook my head. "I'll wait until you feel better. I don't know where to go anyway."

He coughed and wheezed a bit longer. After a little while he seemed better. He took some deep breaths. "It's the smoke," he said, straightening up and regaining his composure

"It was bothering me too."

"I'll take you back to your hotel," he said. "What's the name?"

"Plaza de Armas, across the cathedral."

"It's down the hill." He led the way, and as we made a turn, he stopped and pointed out a stone wall. "Have you seen this?" he asked.

I shook my head. "We'll go sightseeing tomorrow. We got in

today, but we were sick most of the day."

"The altitude," he said.

I nodded.

He spread his arms, as if to embrace the wall.

"The Incas built this wall," Ernesto continued. By now, he was well and was very animated. "Each piece is carved to fit the other pieces exactly. Look at how tightly the stones fit; you couldn't slip in a blade. It's a wonder how they moved them, and how they cut them. The Incas were fantastic engineers. The walls the Spaniards built don't survive earthquakes. These have. They'll continue to stand when you and are under the ground," he said.

Another romantic glorifying the Inca past, I thought, just like Tita gushing over skulls and mummies. It was a waste of time, I thought, focusing on a past that was no longer around. They made it exotic; they analyzed it from all angles, they dissected matters to the smallest minutiae. They spent their lives with their heads turned back, instead of pointed forward to the future. The things and people they talked about were no longer around. They were dead, gone. It was all academic.

"What do you think of it?" Ernesto said.

"It's old, from the past," I muttered.

"I beg your pardon?" he said.

The wall he studied was made of huge pieces of gray stones, of different sizes, some of them with jagged edges, but all fitted together, like a giant puzzle. "This wall, this culture is from the past, and it's finished, over. There's no point mulling over the past. When one is focused on the past, one cannot look to the future."

He scrutinized me and said, "Ah, you are talking of something else, of something close to your heart. It's true that simply looking at the past can turn one into a fossil. In that case you wouldn't even be living in the present. But the past can teach us about ourselves, which in turn can influence how we live in the present, and in the future. Consider that the Spaniards tried to destroy this civilization. Consider how poorly they treated the Indios, and yet, this wall proves that the people who built it were superior engineers, better than the Spaniards."

"But what good is it to spend so much time learning about ourselves?—we'll get left behind by the train, as the saying goes."

"I see what you're saying," he said, "if one dwells in the past—period—then it is indeed a waste of time and energy. One has to apply the knowledge gained to improve the present and the future. Without knowing history, one would be groundless. It's a balancing act. Am I making sense?"

I pursed my lips, nodded, and started walking down the hill. I understood what he said; I understood it in a deeper way than he imagined.

He caught up with me. By this time we were near the cathedral. "Here is another Spanish structure built on top of Inca foundation," he said, pointing at the great cathedral. "Do you want to go in?"

"Isn't it closed at this time?" I said.

"I know how to get in," he said. He led the way to a side gate, reached over and opened it. He entered and I followed. We were in the dark corridor that led to a side altar. Some lights shone on the old statues and huge silver crosses. Against the walls were huge oil religious paintings.

He stopped near a small altar with an elaborate silver altar. "Look up there," he said, pointing at a painting that hung near the ceiling.

There were numerous paintings hanging on the wall; he was pointing at the painting of the Last Supper of Christ.

"Do you notice anything unusual about it?"

I stared. It was like any other Last Supper scene, with Jesus and the apostles around a table. "It's old?"

"From the 1700s," Ernesto said. "Anything else?"

I shook my head.

"Look at the platter on the table."

I moved closer so as to get better lighting, and what I saw made me hold my breath. There on the platter was cooked guinea pig, on its back, with its paws sticking up. I was shocked. "Roasted guinea pig!"

I wondered if he was ridiculing me or the Andean culture and I quickly turned to look at him. He was beaming. "In the 17th and 18th centuries, there was a flourishing school of art here, and the artists created images that combined Andean and Spanish cultures. There are more paintings of the Cusqueña School at the pulpit of San Blas and the church of La Merced."

"Oh," I said, surprised. I was not the type to pay attention to history and art but now I felt curious to see more paintings like this strange one with the guinea pig.

"We better go," Ernesto said, "before the watchman finds us."

Before we left I gave the painting one last lingering look. Something about the guinea pig painting touched me. It made me think of my grandmother, of her Indian-ness, of my Indian-ness—and for the first time I felt proud of this heritage.

Outside, as we were walking toward the hotel, I said, "My grandmother cooks guinea pig. We live in Lima but she came from Puno"

"In the Andes?

I nodded.

Ernesto continued: "The people from the Andes get a significant portion of their protein from guinea pig. Guinea pigs are linked with food, celebration, and myth."

"Sometimes she cooks black guinea pig."

"Black?" he said.

"It's a cure for arthritis. She fixes it for my father."

"It's a good thing he lives in Lima. Cuzco would not be good for him."

"Why is that?"

"The cold," he said, pointing around. By this time we had walked past the Plaza the Armas. "Ah, here's your hotel," he said.

The neon light of the hotel sign shone on his face and I saw that when he smiled his eyes sparkled and his entire face lit up. He was not a bad-looking man. In fact he was quite a nice-looking man. And back then, young as I was, I paused to wonder what sort of future Ernesto Guevara would have. "Will you be a doctor, or a professor?" I asked.

He tilted his face upward, as if searching for the answer in the starlit sky. His words were measured. "Before leaving Argentina in January, I was certain I would become a doctor and that I'll marry and have four or six children. Before, life seemed simple, laid out in a straight line. But now I'm not sure. I can feel the direction of my life taking a curve. I can sense it in my bones, in my innards. I did not know it until now that life can do that to you, that is, that life can lead you, rather than you leading life. And you? What will you do with yourself? Ten, twenty, thirty years from now, who will Carolina be?" He smiled and chucked my chin.

Embarrassed, I turned my face and looked out at the darkness. "I don't know. Like you I'm not sure what the future holds for me. This was what I had wanted: to be married, like Mama, to live in an upscale neighborhood in Lima, and yes, have four or six children. But now, I am not so sure."

How did the evening end? Tita and Alberto appeared, laughing and singing, drunk, in short, and then we found a bar where the four of us drank some more chicha and wine. But eventually the sun rose and dawn came to Cuzco and we had to say goodnight—no, not just goodnight, but goodbye because despite the promises of letters and seeing one another again, I knew Tita and I would never see Alberto and Ernesto again.

And so we parted and I can still see clearly the two young men walking drunkenly down the street toward the cathedral, and beyond I saw the outline of the hills with the ruins of Sacsayhuaman, and Tita and I returned to our hotel room and went to bed to catch some sleep.

It was many years later when I came across a picture of Ernesto in the newspaper. He was now Che Guevara the Minister of Industry in Cuba. And then more news about Che but none more shocking than the one about his assassination in Bolivia. When I read this, my mind went back to that night in Cuzco when I was nineteen and he was twenty-three, and we had walked and talked about the America we loved.

THE SYRIAN DOCTOR IN PARIS

May 9, 2014, the last rebels leave Homs

He lives in a flat near the Ile Saint Louis. Today, he's up at four in the morning because he hardly slept and news feeds from Syria stream into the internet. His favorite sites are "The Syrian Revolution 2011" and the "Local Coordination Committees in Syria", which give up-to-the-minute news in Syria. The sites will warn: "Artillery shelling and mortars and heavy machine guns aimed at the country districts of Daraa Al-Balad's neighborhoods" Or: "Explosive barrel bombs targeting the village Guenitarat in Aleppo."

It's May and Paris is still chilly at this time of the morning. He glances at the velvety blackness outside and tries to make out the hulking outline of the Notre Dame. It is too dark but soon, when the sun is up, the Notre Dame will present itself with its turrets and gargoyles, a sight that used to enchant him and which still gives him some bit of solace. Quietly, so as not to wake his son, he makes a pot of tea and resumes his vigil in front of his computer. He has a couple of hours before he has to go to the Hopital Cochin.

The images today are of rebels in Homs lining up to board buses. He has seen dead children in white shrouds lined up after the chemical attack in Ghouta; he has seen piles of bodies barely recognizable as human beings. But today's news about the capture of the last rebels in Homs upsets him. He can trace his roots in Homs back to the sixteenth century.

Even though he has lived in Paris for decades, he calls Homs "home." Right now, even as he performs surgeries, does his rounds, deals with patients and hospital staff, home is Syria. It's home even though Assad has bombed and obliterated the schools he had attended, the mosques his ancestors had built, the streets and alleyways he had walked on. Most of the landmarks of his "home" have been ripped apart, shot at, destroyed by bombs, scud missiles. Some of the girls he had loved, the boys he had called "brothers" are dead, some from chlorine and sarin nerve gas. Some from barrel bombs.

He chews his lower lip at the sight of the men who have held out for two years in the Old City, burrowing like rats in the tunnels and pathways they have created. Assad's soldiers had surrounded the Old City, and for over a year the rebels and people who remained had been eating nothing more than grass, and if lucky, some unlucky cat—their imam had to issue an official permit allowing them to eat stray dogs, cats, even rats. The Syrian doctor looks at the drawn faces and hunched shoulders of the rebels. Some are younger than his son. That was another sorrow—the Syrian child soldiers—nine-year-olds, eleven-year-olds toting rifles—boys who ought to be in school, who ought to be playing instead of killing.

The news is not good, but there is nothing unusual about this. The situation has been getting worse and he wonders how a peaceful march could have spiraled into this awful war.

When the last of the rebels are bussed out of Homs, he remembers he's supposed to see Christine that evening. Suddenly he finds her tiresome. She's French, trim, perky and he sees her once a week for dinner and he has sex with her regularly. With Christine he can make love with a wilder abandon that he can with a Middle Eastern woman. He can enjoy her body fully, allow her to pleasure him as well. She is a social worker, divorced, and makes no demands for him to marry her, which to him is one of the attractions of Christine.

Today he performs surgeries in the Hopital Cochin and Clinique Blomet. He attaches bones together with pins and plates; he welcomes doing these because the activity pulls his mind back to Paris, away from Syria. He can lose himself in that work, forget for hours that some of the rebels were picked up for further questioning, meaning they would be tortured and killed.

He calls Christine after work. "Hello, Christine, good afternoon," he says, trying to sound cheerful. They met after Christine's divorce and he made her laugh and that was how their affair got started. With Christine, he always appears buoyant, light-hearted, optimistic. But tonight he can't put on this mask.

"Hello!" Christine replies, sounding happy, her cheerful voice grating on his nerves. He recalls the girl he had loved in Homs, wonders what their lives would have been if they had gotten married. His marriage in France had been a disaster; the only good thing that came out of that was his twenty-four-year-old son.

"Tonight—" he starts, then stops.

"The same café, yes?" Christine says in a voice less cheerful. "Is something wrong?" she adds. Then before he answers, she says. "I know the news is bad. I am sorry." Her voice trembles.

People have been saying "I'm sorry," and he's never sure how to answer them. He is tired of "I am sorry" while the world's governments have turned their faces away from Syria. Ignored Assad's crossing of red lines, reduced the misery of millions of Syrians into statistics. His head throbs when he hears "I am sorry." This afternoon, he decides to disregard Christine's sympathies, says instead, "Something has come up and I can't make it tonight." He's aware Christine will know it's a lie.

Christine sucks in her breath and is silent for a few seconds. Then recovering, "Of course, I understand. Don't worry. I'm fine. Take care of yourself. Next week …?" Her voice trails off.

He does not answer; he can't think about next week. He can't think of Christine, not of the weekly dinners and lovemaking. His mind overflows with images of faces of his countrymen filled with anger, desperation, fear, anguish, pain. He has been yearning to hear the musical call of the muzzeraine and he wonders if it still echoes through the streets of his youth. He hopes the perfume of jasmine still sweetens the night air of his family's open courtyard, even though he knows his parents' home has been reduced to rubble.

Christine continues, "I know it's a difficult time. If I can help, let me know."

"Yes, yes, thank you," he says. "I have to go. I have a meeting with Dr. Khatoud," he lies.

He hurries out of the Clinique Blomet, gets into his car, and drives toward his flat. But before he gets there, he turns and heads toward the Sorbonne. He stops the car and studies the white buildings which had frightened him when he was eighteen. He closes his eyes and recalls that long ago journey from Homs to Paris, his sad farewell to his father who died a few months after he arrived in Paris. As he starts his car he wonders how long his mother will hold out in Syria, wonders when she will accept that it's time to leave. He hopes she makes the decision soon, before things get any worse.

It is almost eight at night when he enters his flat. When he closes the front door, silence surrounds him. The hallway feels clammy and he smells the mustiness of his old books which fill the bookshelves. He thinks he should get rid of some of these books, save only the ones that had belonged to his father.

Later, he switches on his computer and he settles down to catch more images of death and destruction, to catch images of home, even when home is no more.

MELISANDE IN PARIS

Paris 1899

Spring was late that April '99, and Melisande and her Tante Juliette wore heavy woolen coats as they waded through the crowded streets of Paris. They delivered a gown to a client near Notre Dame and bought some sewing notions, after which they waited for a carriage. It took them a good half-an-hour to find one. Juliette, now cold and impatient, hurriedly lifted herself into the carriage, but both feet had not yet been planted firmly when a large crash spooked the horse—an overloaded crate nearby fell. The horse reared; Juliette teetered and fell. Some men grabbed the horse to keep him from trampling poor Juliette who lay sprawled on the street, her right leg and foot pointing the wrong way. Melisande sucked in her breath and froze, uncertain about what to do. It was Juliette who ordered her to align her own leg the right way.

Meanwhile curious onlookers gathered around them. Two men stepped forward, young and muscular workers with a wagon, who offered to take Juliette to the Hopital Dieu de Paris. "Before you move me," Juliette said, "wrap the leg with my coat. It hurts like the devil smashed it … Be careful … I'm as fragile as a Sevres. Carefully, my dears, this is how you should carry me."

Melisande walked alongside the wagon and kept a watchful eye on her aunt. The leg was clearly broken. The gravity of that situation was starting to sink into her. It had taken two men to move her aunt to the wagon. How could she bring her back home with the broken leg? How long would the leg take to heal? And would it heal properly? The father of Etienne, the boy she once loved, fell from the barn and became a cripple. Melisande had heard of amputations of broken limbs that did not heal properly. She was afraid for her aunt.

Juliette on the other hand showed no fear. She smiled and bantered with the men; in fact, she was flirting with them. Juliette was forty-four years old, unmarried, and always looking for her "Romeo," according to Melisande's mother. Juliette was reportedly the least attractive of her five sisters, and to compensate, overdressed, wore loud perfume, and heavy rouge. Juliette reportedly hennaed her mousy-brown hair to keep up with her red-headed sisters. But despite her mother's stories, Melisande found her aunt attractive, like a pretty butterfly, petite, with a nice figure, and full of energy. She worked hard and had made her dress shop popular. Further, she made her own rouge from grapefruit, butter, and beeswax, which sold briskly to her devoted clients. But what impressed Melisande as they hurried to the hospital was Juliette's incredible presence of mind. Had living alone in Paris for decades created this strong independent woman? Melisande's mother had depended on her father for many things.

The waiting room of the Hopital Dieu de Paris had patients with trauma and fractures—people with broken arms, wrists, clavicles, hips, and legs. A construction worker who had fallen off a church roof was immediately whisked to another room. Those with broken wrists and arms sat in chairs; the others, Juliette included, lay on hospital beds. The room smelled of antiseptic. It didn't have a single plant, not a bit of color; it was gray and sad. Melisande was getting depressed, but Juliette kept up her chatter: "that man's nose is as big as a turnip, and that woman is as wide as a door, oh, my goodness, can't they silence that bratty, funny-looking child," and so on. But soon enough, Juliette moaned because her leg was hurting. Melisande peeled back her coat and was shocked to see that Juliette's leg had swelled. She went to the nurse to ask where the doctor was.

The nurse curtly replied that the surgeon was taking care of a man with a broken spine, he would be along, please be patient Mademoiselle, sit down and wait. Melisande was twenty-three, from Lyon, and Parisians intimidated her. Parisians always seemed superior and arrogant—she had heard them say the Lyonnais were only good at making silk and sausages, and while indeed they made excellent silk and sausages, the statement was a put-down. Melisande retreated and sat quietly beside her aunt. There they remained for four hours without anything to drink or eat. (Melisande had offered to buy something, but her aunt didn't want to be left alone.)

It was mid-afternoon when Doctor Samir Martine burst into

the room with a brightness that was out of place in that purgatory. He had a broad smile, bouncy walk, and his face was animated as he talked to the nurse. Melisande told her aunt she would talk to him, but the doctor was soon heading toward them. He nodded, eyes fully on Melisande. "Mademoiselle," he greeted, before turning his attention to Juliette who fluttered her eyes when she had a close look of him.

"Madame," he said, "do not worry, you are in good hands. I am the best surgeon in Paris."

Melisande stared at him sharply. In Lyon such braggarts were shunned.

He glanced back at her, their eyes meeting. "Well, no, I am not the best surgeon, but I'm one of the best—" He bent over to uncover Juliette's leg before adding, "—in all of Paris."

Juliette warmed up immediately. "And what is the name of the fine surgeon taking care of me?" She reached up to fuss with her hair, wincing as she did so.

"Doctor Martine," he replied with a flare, sounding like a two-bit actor in a theatrical play; Melisande had to cover her mouth to muffle her laugh.

"How fortunate I am to be helping two beautiful ladies this afternoon. Madame, I have to apply some pressure, you might feel some pain." Juliette gritted her teeth as he pressed the swollen leg at certain points. "Hmmm, some puffiness, but don't worry, everything will be fine."

Before Juliette could say a word, before either of them could react, the doctor held Juliette's leg firmly—huge hands, with long fingers, the hands of an artist, Melisande thought—then suddenly, with a quick but precise movement, he pulled apart the bones and snapped them back in place. The ghastly sound made Melisande nauseous. Juliette straightaway fainted.

Unruffled, the doctor ran his hands over her leg. "I had to set her bones before the swelling becomes worse. She'll be fine. Your aunt will have to stay here, you understand, for perhaps two months. If there were no complications, she can go home. She'll need crutches, and she can't put full weight on the leg even after three months."

Melisande's head started throbbing and she pressed her temples. Aside from dealing with her aunt's condition, she would have to run Juliette's business, an overwhelming notion.

He added, "The hospital and treatment are free; she will be all right here. And you, Mademoiselle? Will you be all right?"

She paused, groped for words: how could she even start to explain the problems she had to face at the dress shop … clients … bills … rent to pay … she could not describe the flood of thoughts and emotions that gripped her.

His stared at her for a moment before saying, "There are some nuns who can help." He nodded toward the hallway.

This took her aback; he was referring to the Sisters of Charity. No matter how dire, her family never asked for charity. They worked; they coped; they survived. The idea that this doctor who had made them wait forever thought they were a charity case infuriated her—she had been smarting from the earlier exchange with the nurse in any case—and she snapped, "My aunt owns a dress shop on Avenue Bouquet, Doctor; I'll have you know we are not destitute." She should have stopped right there but didn't: "We waited half the day for you, Doctor, four hours, while my aunt's leg swelled to twice its normal size. She was in agony, and here we were in this God-awful place. Please make sure her leg is fine."

His face turned darkly serious. He lifted his eyebrows and chewed his lower lip for a second before speaking in the most clinical tone: Mademoiselle, be informed that there is still danger of bone necrosis although this is unlikely … the nurse will give you further information. And then he dismissed her: Well, then, good-day Mademoiselle, it was—he paused before continuing—a pleasure meeting you, I have to attend to others who have been waiting for longer than you have.

***

Melisande could have been petrified by the situation she now found herself in—alone to solve what seemed like insurmountable problems—but she knew she had to keep her wits about her. She had learned back in Lyon that when catastrophes happen, you have to deal with it. After her father died, she had helped her brother run the farm, and at night she and her mother stitched linens to make extra money. When her mother passed away, Melisande turned over the house and farm to her brother, and she packed her things into a bag and took the train to Paris. That April she did what she had to do: after making sure her aunt was all right at the Hopital Dieu de Paris, she went straight to their seamstress, Simone, and asked her to work extra hours. The next day Melisande informed their clients about Juliette's accident, and she sat down and figured out her finances, which fortunately were sound. Every afternoon she visited her aunt; and every morning and most evenings, she worked.

When life settled into a routine and was therefore less overwhelming, she felt guilty at having flung sharp words at Doctor Martine. She tried to find him at the hospital to apologize, but the few times she saw him, he was far away and very busy. On one occasion, she caught a glimpse of him, at a distance, saying goodbye to her aunt, and their eyes met, and she hurried toward them, hoping she could make things right, but before she got there, he had walked away.

That was when Juliette showed Melisande a charcoal drawing of a row of tulips. "Look Melisande, from Doctor Martine himself," she said, smiling happily and cocking her head to one side to admire the work. "He did this himself at the Jardin de Tuileries. Imagine Melisande, he is not only a surgeon but an artist." Juliette carefully propped it up on her side table.

Melisande studied the drawing and thought it was not very good; it looked like one of the cheap artwork sold by student artists on the Left Bank. She had to control herself from making a face and criticizing it.

More drawings appeared of gardens, parks, and the bridges of the Seine, and Juliette could talk of nothing but the doctor: Doctor Martine did the morning rounds at six … Doctor Martine took his time with each patient (with her certainly) … Doctor Martine was thirty-five years old and unmarried … Doctor Martine was an honors graduate from the medical school of the University of Paris … Doctor Martine was an excellent surgeon, very clever and absolutely delightful … and oh, Doctor Martine was very handsome … how very lucky she was. The broken leg seemed to have been forgotten.

Her aunt's adulation for Doctor Martine made Melisande wonder if something was going on between them. He was younger, true, but Melisande was aware that in Paris, age was not a hindrance to love. Parisians treasured the story of their King Henry's lifelong love affair with his courtesan Diane de Poitiers who was nine years older.

***

Two months passed and in late June, Juliette was well enough to return home with crutches. Melisande had prepared a room for her, at the back of the dress shop, away from the workers and customers. But her aunt flat-out refused to stay there. "What is wrong with my own bedroom, Melisande?" she said, referring to her room upstairs.

"You cannot climb the stairs. You cannot, not with those crutches. You must not," Melisande said.

"I can and I will," Juliette said and started climbing the stairs.

"Tante!" Melisande said as she watched her aunt ascend step by step, grimacing in pain, awkwardly struggling to keep her balance. Twice, Juliette stumbled but fortunately caught herself. All Melisande could do was trail behind her, ready to soften her fall if her aunt missed a step.

When at last Juliette was ensconced in her bedroom, Melisande insisted that she stay put. Melisande was strict—garrulous even—in forbidding her to use the stairs. Juliette reluctantly agreed, but consequently Simone and Melisande had to go up and down countless times a day to bring the older woman what she needed. There was no choice—her aunt couldn't afford another tumble.

Between taking care of her aunt and running the dress shop, Melisande could barely keep up. One Saturday after Juliette had returned home, Melisande was working on a bias cut skirt that required a lot of work space. She decided to use the floor instead of the cutting-table. She rolled out a bolt of silk moire, and after hiking up her own skirt, got down on her knees to lay down the pattern. She was cutting the fabric when she heard knocking on the door. It was late afternoon. It had been a warm day and Melisande had left it ajar. When she looked up, there was Doctor Martine studying her. "Mademoiselle, do you need help?" he asked.

He had caught her on all fours. Embarrassed, she clambered up and brushed the lint off her skirt.

"It's me, Doctor Martine," he said, as if it were necessary to identify himself.

She had only seen him with his white coat, which made him look washed-out and undistinguishable from the other doctors. Without it he looked different—younger and his features seemed more decipherable. Her aunt was right; he was attractive after all, with strong jaws and a faint five-o'clock shadow, which looked charming, not unkempt. Because her life revolved around fabric and stitchery, she noticed the fine quality of his suit, a cashmere-wool blend it seemed, which made him look elegant.

But his unexpected appearance had unnerved her and Melisande was unable to speak.

"I've come to check your aunt's leg," he said casually, pleasantly even.

"Come in," she managed to say. Her hair was in wild disarray with curls falling in front of her eyes, and which she tried to sweep back. Painfully, she remembered her compromising position of bending up and down and crawling on the floor—how much of her acrobatics had the doctor noticed?

To her relief, he behaved as if nothing were wrong. Inside the shop, he studied her project on the floor. "So this is how a dress is made?" he asked.

"I should have worked at the table," she said, pointing out the clutter on the floor.

Melisande was sorry she had not tidied up—there were bolts of fabric leaning against the walls; dresses on hangers or folded and piled high on tables and chairs; sewing notions and magazines scattered about; in addition, two of their mannequins were undressed.

His eyes swept over everything.

"I'm sorry for all the mess; I've been busy."

"Please, Mademoiselle, don't worry. I should be the one apologizing for barging in on you." He had barely finished his sentence when something caught his attention at the table. "Drawings. May I?" he said and he leafed through sketches of dress designs, which Melisande had done. Other dress designers used stick figures in their sketches, but she drew human figures.

"I sometimes pick up my mother's clothes at the Maison Orientale, but I had no idea what went into the making of those dresses." He held up some drawings, "Did you do these?"

She nodded. "Some summer designs."

"I have noticed your artistic bend but didn't realize you also draw."

She leaned over to have a closer look at the sketches. "That is part of what we do. We design dresses for our clients and get them done."

"What is that?" he suddenly asked, sniffing and lifting his chin to locate the source. "A pleasant scent, like citrus."

She had rinsed her hair with lemon juice that morning but it seemed an intimate matter to mention that so she ignored his question. "When I arrived Paris, Tante Juliette asked me to design some spring dresses. She handed me a pile of dress design books and magazines, told me to look them over, and gave me paper and pencil. I did as I was instructed. That was all the training I got."

"Hmmm ... the figures are well-proportioned and the drawing is well done," he said, sounding surprised. "Drawing the human figure is difficult, at least for me. I've never worked with models, but I understand one must first lay down the action line." By this time, Melisande was leading him to the stairs in the back of the shop.

He paused and tilted his head upward to size up the flight of narrow uneven steps. "Is Madame upstairs?" His voice had turned serious.

Melisande sensed the shift in his tone and demeanor.

"Her leg is not yet healed," he said with a frown.

She knew what he was thinking because those had been her thoughts exactly—it was dangerous for her aunt to be climbing stairs. His words sounded like a reprimand. Suddenly she felt tired, simply exhausted. She had been taking care of her aunt, catering to her clients, buying the groceries, supervising the seamstress, doing everything to keep things running, and here this man stood, suggesting she had maltreated her aunt. It was really too much to swallow, and her voice was shaking as she said: "She insisted. The minute she arrived, she started climbing the stairs. She defied me. I argued with her but she ignored me totally. You do not know my aunt, Doctor, she is hard-headed and impossible. She is like a child. I did my best; I am doing my best. It is not my fault that she is upstairs. It is not fair to suggest that I have neglected her."

"Mademoiselle, words flow out of your mouth easily ... recklessly in fact," he said in that clinical tone that she had heard once before at the hospital. And he went past her and ascended the stairs.

Melisande stood by the stairwell, uncertain about what to do. Certainly she was angry and wanted to be as far away from him as she could. She considered returning to her sewing project, but she was too upset to work. Her mind had latched on to his reprimand, and worse than that, his condescension. Her aunt's voice calling her upstairs reminded her that it was highly improper to leave Juliette unchaperoned with the doctor. Reluctantly Melisande went upstairs.

She slipped into her aunt's bedroom, just as the doctor scolded Juliette in a gentle voice. "Madame, I understand you climbed the stairs on your own?"

"All my things are up here, Doctor. I am more comfortable in my own bedroom." Juliette fluffed her hair and arranged the neckline of her dress to lower it. She was sitting on her bed, leaning against pillows. Her outstretched legs were covered by a white crocheted blanket. Her room was rose pink in color with a lot of lace and ruffles. It was usually tidy and spacious, but now there was an extra table with her food tray, some fruit and drink. Another table had been brought up for her sewing notions. Magazines were piled high on the chair beside her bed.

"You cannot afford a fall. The bone has not mended fully." His tone was cajoling.

"Doctor Martine, I did not fall, I will not fall." Juliette nodded toward Melisande. "My niece makes sure I have everything I need. I am very lucky to have her with me. For years I had begged her to leave Lyon and join me here in Paris, but she had all sorts of excuses. But now she's here. She ensures I do my exercises; she even massages my legs."

Doctor Martine turned to Melisande. He had an eyebrow up and a little smile as if he were surprised or amused or contemptuous—Melisande wasn't sure which. Words bubbled up to her throat, "Tante, Doctor Martine thinks I have been cruel to you."

Before Juliette could answer, he shot back, "That is not what I said, Madame, although indeed I was appalled at those dangerous steps, which you navigated in your delicate condition. Madame … Mademoiselle, I had a patient who traumatized his leg a second time and there were complications. I had to deal with this unpleasant business earlier today."

Juliette closed her eyes and flung one arm over her forehead.

"Not everyone is as fortunate as you, Madame. What I mean is your leg is healing beautifully, and therefore you must take good care of yourself." In the coldest clipped voice, he added, "People should learn to control their temper."

There was a long pause as Juliette stared first at one, then the other, settling finally on Melisande, whom she pierced with her gaze. Having done that, she turned her attention back to the doctor, and in a voice lilting with charm said, "I'm up here because I chose to be here,

Doctor. It was my fault. Please do not blame my niece. She is overworked, running here and there, and despite all that, succeeding in giving me excellent care. Frankly, Doctor, I don't know what I would have done without her. The truth is she is like a daughter to me."

"Like a sister, you mean. You are too young, Madame," he said, while Juliette giggled and patted her hair.

Melisande, who had felt the sting of his words, held her tongue for her aunt's sake.

"Madame, I need to check your leg." Doctor Martine cleared the chair and sat down near Juliette.

Juliette lifted the crocheted blanket to reveal not one, but both legs. He felt the bone of her leg and declared she was healing nicely. She went on to complain about some pain in her hip, and glanced up at him expectantly. The doctor did not check her hip, but said the discomfort was normal. He explained it was because of the uneven weight on both feet. Juliette went on to praise him and she kept up her coquetry, until finally Melisande had had enough. She turned to leave, but when she walked past him, he reached out and touched her arm. "Mademoiselle, stay. I need your opinion about something."

She shot him a glance, surprised at his request. But the truth was she was tired of the little game he and his aunt were playing, and she took another step toward the door. "Please stay," he said, softly. It was a plea not a command.

Juliette covered her legs with the blanket. "There is nothing important downstairs, Melisande. You can stay, can you not?"

Melisande sat on the stool next to the window. Outside, the usual din of Paris had quieted down.

"My niece is typical Lyonnais, Doctor," Juliette said as she smiled at Doctor Martine.

Melisande glared at her aunt who was oblivious. Juliette's statement echoed the Parisian put Hedown—Lyonnais were only good at making silk and sausages. If Melisande were not seated far from the door, she would have left, but she was trapped, and she would have to tolerate these two, for how long, she had no idea. Melisande remembered how vexed her mother used to be over Juliette. Her Maman had few good things to say about Juliette and would sometimes gossip about Juliette's many lovers and how eventually they always grew tired of her carping—where were you last Saturday … you did not visit me … you promised … and so on. One of them was a wealthy man who had given her money to start her dress shop, but like the others that one eventually took off with a more agreeable woman.

"I want to show both of you something," the doctor said, his words, bringing Melisande back to the room. He had picked up his briefcase and was rifling through his papers. He sounded buoyant, optimistic, and Melisande waited to hear what he had to say. "Ah, here it is," he said, his face lighting up. He pulled out a charcoal drawing of the Eiffel Tower and held it up for Melisande to see. "What do you think?" he asked, like a child proudly showing off his school work. "Your aunt says you are very artistic and I must admit that your sketches downstairs are impressive. I would like your candid thoughts. As well as Madame's of course."

"Indeed she is very talented, Doctor," Juliette said. "If you could see her dress creations and if you understood dress design at all, you would appreciate how cleverly she works with the principles of design: emphasis, harmony, balance, rhythm. For instance, Doctor, she chooses a point of emphasis so that the best body part of a woman is enhanced. The plump one becomes voluptuous; the rail-thin one sophisticated. Melisande works with texture, color and shape to give a feeling of oneness. My niece has extraordinary abilities."

Her aunt's praise took the sting out of her earlier Lyonnais-statement, and Melisande was grateful for her aunt's words. She was also glad that the doctor heard that she was not a mere seamstress. She was sick and tired of Parisian condescension, this doctor included.

"And that is why I would like your opinion of my work, both of you," Doctor Martine said.

Juliette spoke before Melisande did. "Pooh!" she said, with her nose scrunched. "I am not a fan of the Eiffel. It is too modern, Doctor Martine!"

The doctor looked amused.

Encouraged, her aunt continued, "I remember watching them build it platform by platform, from '87 to '89. I prayed it would get better—or topple down—but the higher it went, the more hideous it became. The skyline of Paris has been ruined by that ghastly protrusion."

"It's Gustave Eiffel's most famous work," he said.

"He should have stuck to making bridges. Oh, how I abhor his tower. I'm not talking about the drawing because you're an excellent artist and I love your work. I'm referring to the subject you chose, a monstrosity."

He remained mirthful when he said, "Blame Koehlin and Nouguier, Madame. They made the original design for Eiffel's company."

Juliette continued her lament. "The tower is useless. It's an aberration that does not fit the other structures in Paris. You heard of course that the writer, Guy de Maupassant used to have his lunch in the tower's restaurant daily to avoid seeing the structure?"

Melisande passed by the Eiffel Tower several times a day. It had a presence that could not be ignored. She had felt it the first time she saw it, looking gray and slick in the rain. When she was new in Paris, on many occasions she used the Eiffel as her beacon to guide her back to the shop. It was reliable, fixed. This was the first time she heard of its controversies and was interested.

"I can see the Eiffel from my window," he said. "I'm afraid, Madame, it has worked its charm on me. I find it most appealing. It has a certain beauty. Consider that it's made of metal and yet it manages to be delicate and graceful. And throughout the day, as the sun moves, its appearance changes. The shadows it casts alters the landscape as well. It is like a woman that way—changeable and seductive."

"The 'Iron Lady' they call it, Doctor, but tell me, what is feminine about a rigid structure thrusting up in the middle of Paris like a gigantic phallus?—"

Melisande covered her mouth in shock—her aunt could really be outrageous! No wonder she and her Maman did not get along.

"—Nothing soft, no folds, all angles and symmetry."

And there he was, laughing and watching her. "And you, Mademoiselle—what do you think? Not about the Eiffel, but about my work because that was why I kept you here. Feel free to speak your mind. I am certain that a brilliant woman like you will have a lot to say. I can take your criticism, Mademoiselle." He squared his jaw as if bracing himself.

Melisande oftentimes felt like a country bumpkin in Paris, and she didn't miss that he had explicitly asked for her opinion. She had also noted his words of praise for her earlier. She sighed. If she looked at the matter clearly; if she set aside the annoying flirtation between him and her aunt, well, he had done nothing wrong really. She was the one with the short fuse. He had taken excellent care of her aunt; and here he was, making sure her leg was healing, and amusing her with his art and chitchat.

"Mademoiselle?"

Melisande weighed her words so as not to offend him. "When I arrived, the Eiffel was already here, so to me it is part of Paris. It does not offend me, but neither do I love it as you do, Doctor. But about your artwork, I can see that it is—how do I put it?—well done." The truth was that she found his drawing simplistic and lacking in imagination. "Very well rendered," she added, to conclude the matter.

"And—?"

"It is a faithful copy of the Eiffel." She had nothing else good to say about it.

"Mademoiselle, please stop censoring yourself. Go ahead; tell me. You can see that I'm a grown man."

Her aunt knew Melisande could be blunt and she rolled her eyes and said, "Ooh la la!"

Melisande took a deep breath. "Forgive me, Doctor, I will try my best, but I don't always have the words to express myself. While your work is rendered very well, it seems to be … hmm … lacking something." She paused, wondering how to tell him that his work was lifeless.

"Please continue, Mademoiselle," the doctor said.

"When I look at something created by someone—a creation that is—I want to feel something. An emotion must bubble up inside me. You understand me?"

He nodded, listening to every word she said.

"My heart must be touched; my soul must quiver; memories must be unlocked or formed. Nothing of this sort happens when I look at this drawing. It looks like the other drawings sold near the Eiffel. Executed very well, you understand, but so are those other drawings."

As she talked, the expectant expression on his face slowly faded, and by the time she finished, he looked pale. She wondered if she had overstepped herself. Had she been reckless with her words, as he had accused her? She needed to learn to talk the way Juliette did, in a teasing voice, even as she ripped something apart. Melisande felt flustered … and … she felt sorry for him.

His voice was flat when he replied, "Interesting idea, about feeling. I never studied art. I was too busy with the sciences. I started drawing because I discovered it allowed me to rest."

With a weary expression, he opened his briefcase to return his work. (Melisande noted he did not give this to her aunt, not after hearing her vehemence about the Eiffel).

He continued, "You can imagine that some patients do not survive or that they end up badly. My patient this morning who lost his leg—I had difficulty dealing with that. His wife and children will also suffer. It's not just one life, but many lives affected by such tragedies."

Juliette, who liked to believe that everything should be sunny and nice, never dark and sad, said in a cheerful voice, "It's good that you have turned to art to keep from dwelling on such dreary matters, Doctor. You are one step ahead of Leonard da Vinci, Doctor. He studied anatomy to improve his art; you already know anatomy. But you must keep in mind that the judgment of your work came from two dress designers. Granted Melisande is an artist in her haute couture, but she is not an art expert. With a little bit of this and a little bit of that, she and I can create the illusion that a woman is beautiful."

That day, Melisande was wearing a raw silk dress, turquoise in color with magenta piping at the hem, understated but cool, perfect for a summer day, and he looked at it and said, "Yes, you have a good eye. The colors are interesting, and you play with texture too." He paused— "Now, feeling? Do I feel something when I look at your creation? Yes, I feel happy knowing we will have beautiful days ahead. In a flash, I recalled past summers, but it was not a full recollection, it was more like the scent of perfume, flitting, something that cannot be contained. And a memory has now been formed of my being here with the two of you this summer afternoon."

"Voila! You are learning," Juliette said.

He seemed to have recovered and his voice had a lift once more. "I like the idea that art should create feelings. It is profound, in fact. I have been preoccupied with acquiring the skills but did not consider creating feeling in my work; or should I say creating work with feeling?"

Her aunt continued her banter. "You are interested in the subtle changes of the Iron Lady. Clearly there is something in your mind and in your heart about the Eiffel. Let us see if we can get to it. Let's play a little game, Doctor. Close your eyes and tell me what you see."

Sometimes Juliette and Melisande did this before sketching a dress; it allowed their minds free reign to come up with fresh ideas. But imagination seemed contrary to the nightmare of broken bodies and pain and medicines. Melisande wondered how he would respond. She expected him to balk, but he closed his eyes.

The days were now longer, and through the window, the sun's rays slanted in and shone on his dark hair. His face was as still as that of a statue, and his eyelashes were crescent fringes on his cheeks. She felt like touching them with one finger as one touches a caterpillar—gently. He had talked about his Eiffel Tower changing but it was he who was always changing, from a doctor to an artist, from a jovial man, to a serious one, to one who brooded over broken people—what else would they learn about him? There was something hidden in that face, something exotic and different, something fascinating.

"Well then, Doctor Martine?"

It was as if he had left them for a long time, and it wasn't until the church bells tolled that his eyes fluttered open.

"Doctor?"

He took a deep breath and sat forward. "That was interesting. It's the first time I've experienced anything like that. It was very restful. I even feel I've recovered from the harsh criticism of my work."

Juliette moaned. "Oh, Doctor Martine, please do not take our words to heart!"

He smiled and waved his hand to indicate he was jesting. "I did not actually see anything. It was more of a feeling." He started gathering his things.

"You can't leave now, not until you tell us what you saw," Juliette said.

He paused, "I felt there was a woman in front of the Eiffel Tower."

"A woman? How mysterious! Then you must do the drawing so you can find out more about this."

"I have done only one portrait, in oil, poorly done, I'm afraid. I have books that teach me what to do, but I need to practice drawing live models. As you can guess, Madame, I am up early in the morning, I do rounds, surgery, and there is paperwork to complete. I also have my parents to attend to. Art lessons require time. I've looked into it, and it's impossible."

Juliette pursed her lips as if weighing matters. She finally said, "You know, Doctor Martine, we are here. When we are free, you can practice drawing us, my niece and myself. I do not mind. But as you can see, I am stuck up here." She swept her hands over her legs and gave a wry expression. "However, my niece's legs are not broken; she can stand in front of the Eiffel if that is the image in your head. She is young, she can pose for hours until your work is perfect."

Melisande, surprised at what her aunt had said, folded her hands and remained still.

He threw her a questioning look. She said nothing but neither did she protest.

He went to Juliette to kiss her hand and say goodbye. "I would like my art to improve. My art feeds a part of myself that is vital, and which is unfortunately starved at the hospital. Mademoiselle and I had some bad starts but hopefully she has forgiven me?"

Melisande did not reply but inside she felt they were on good ground.

Juliette arranged herself against the pillows before she said, "Melisande, before the doctor leaves, can you get one of our silk scarves? They're downstairs in a box behind the counter. The Doctor's mother may like one." She was referring to the scarves that they gave away as gifts to special clients.

As Melisande was making her way downstairs, she overheard Juliette say, "I like you, Doctor Martine. You have been very kind to me. I will tell you something in confidence: Melisande could have been my daughter indeed. Her father was very handsome—ooh la la!—I was madly in love with him—" and here she laughed before continuing in her lilting pleasant voice, "But it did not end up well, at least not for me. As the saying goes, my heart was broken. And oh, Doctor, believe me hearts take longer to heal than bones. I will give her permission to sit for you, but remember that she is someone precious to me and I do not want her hurt."

"The god Zeus must have been afraid of you and him," the doctor said. "You know the story told by Plato, do you not?" He continued talking but Melisande was now in the supply room and could no longer make out his words.

The young woman selected a lovely pink scarf and wrapped it in a box. Now she understood why her Maman disliked her aunt and why Juliette had left Lyon for Paris. Melisande wondered if her father had loved her too. About Juliette's offer to the doctor for her to sit as his model, she wasn't sure what to make of it. It didn't seem a big matter to sit for him—he had been most helpful to her aunt after all, and he could be amiable. She supposed he would want to talk about art; on that matter, they were equals.

Melisande returned to the room and handed the box to her aunt who in turn gave it to the doctor. "For your mother, Doctor," Juliette said. He took the gift and thanked her, then he turned to Melisande. "Perhaps one Sunday, if you are free, you can sit for me? But I will try to learn all I can beforehand, so I don't waste your time—" He stopped and shook his head, "No, I'm not being honest—it's so your comments may be less scathing. But I value what you have to say and you must feel free to tell me the truth." He took Melisande's hand and kissed it, his breath passing over it like a summer breeze.

Melisande caught her aunt hide her smile.

Before the doctor left, he told Juliette she could now put fifty percent weight on the leg, but that she had to continue using crutches, and she had to avoid using the stairs.

***

And so one Sunday, after stopping by the patisserie to pick up some cakes, Melisande arrived at his flat. After his visit where he had caught her working on the floor, he had continued to stop by to "check her aunt's leg." He was always solicitous of Juliette but he also took time to discuss his progress in art with Melisande. He confessed that he had been reading art books and doing simple sketches of people to improve his drawing. He waited several weeks before he asked Melisande to sit, and there she was navigating four flights of stairs, narrow, winding and dark. Remembering how quickly her aunt had lost her balance when she broke her leg, she hung on to the bannisters and carefully negotiated the stairs. Each floor had two apartments, but she saw no one and she wondered where people had gone to this Sunday morning.

Up and up she climbed and when she reached the top, suddenly there was light that burst through the darkness. Looking up she searched for the source of all that brilliance and saw a huge skylight that glowed like the moon. The golden light gave her a feeling of lightness, of joy, and she savored the moment. Melisande was still spellbound when suddenly the door opened and there he stood, Doctor Samir Martine, holding a metal whisk, the kind used to beat eggs. Using the whisk, he pointed upward. "I had that put in," he said. "I had a difficult time finding the right person who could do it, but here it is. What do you think?"

"It's very nice," Melisande said, politely.

"Nice? Nice? It is fantastic. Come in. Watch how, aside from being one of the best surgeons in Paris, I am also one of the best cooks."

His kitchen and dining area occupied a huge space that opened out to a small balcony. It was painted yellow so that the brightness you experienced in the hallway, carried through in this room and on to the balcony outside. Melisande could see the Eiffel Tower in the distance, its gray latticed metal gleaming in the early morning sun. The trees and bushes of Paris were still in bloom. The paulownia trees surrounding the Eiffel were heavy with purple flowers. He pointed these out to her, and he showed Melisande where he wanted her to sit so he could catch the tower and the trees in the background. The chair and easel were in place. "But first, breakfast," he announced.

He bustled about in the kitchen, while she stood uncomfortably clutching her wrap against her chest. She remembered how poor she and her mother had been in Lyon, and how they never had the luxury of having Sunday breakfast together. Sunday was the day they went to the market to sell the linens she and her mother had done. It came to her then that her mother would have liked this doctor, just as her aunt did.

She hadn't realize how stiff and awkward she must have appeared until he left the kitchen, walked to her, removed her wrap, and said, "Come, let us put this down." He lay it on a side table with a pile of art books, then he handed her a knife and basket and pointed at the baguette. "You are in charge of the bread and cheese. I'm in charge of the important part of breakfast."

His manner was easy and the way he talked made her want to laugh. His ease as he cooked impressed her. How meticulous he was as he picked up each egg from the basket, held this up in the light before cracking it into a bowl. He beat the eggs and proceeded to cook his omelet, soft and fluffy and warm, and before they sat down to eat, he placed a pat of butter on top.

He also had warm bread, cheese, some raspberries, and

delicious strong coffee, which came from a Brazilian patient of his. "Broken wrist," he said, "but I also fixed it perfectly."

Afterwards, he opened a bottle of champagne, from another patient. "And what was wrong with this one?" she dared ask, as she sipped from the glass he offered her.

"Nothing broken. He started to have difficulties walking. I taught him some exercises, and I told him to stop eating aubergine which is bad for arthritis."

The champagne was getting to her head and she was surprised when she teased him. "You know everything, then."

"No, not everything. About doctoring, yes, but not about art. I thought a lot about what you said about feeling in art. I've spent a lot of time preparing for today. My technique has improved. So today we will see if I can draw you, the Eiffel, and have feeling in the work, all at the same time."

He looked out at the sky and said the light was perfect. He led her out to the balcony, sat her down, and directed her to turn here and there to catch the light as he wanted it. He had requested that Melisande wear her white peasant blouse—he had seen it during a visit—cotton, gathered with strings that tie in front, long sleeves, quite simple. She had no idea why he preferred this instead of something prettier. In any case there she sat while he cocked his head to the right and to the left. Suddenly, he placed his charcoal down. "I saw an oil painting of a woman with this type of blouse—it was a Dutch painting—but she was not so—how do I put it?—stiff. She looked relaxed and her shoulder was a bit exposed. It looked less studied and was very interesting. Do not misunderstand, but would it be all right, if you untie the strings in front and slide the neckline off your right shoulder?"

And since she did not do so to his satisfaction, he came near her, "May I?" And he adjusted the blouse off her shoulder, his fingers touching her—warm, fleeting, like the sudden brush of a feather. She must have reacted because he said, "Pardon," but he made nothing of it and resumed his post in front of the easel. His right hand clutched the charcoal and moved furiously while his eyes moved from Melisande to the paper then back to her.

The sun's rays soothed her and she felt herself surrendering to the morning on that balcony. She was mesmerized. She lifted her chin higher to meet the sunlight and her body relaxed.

He nodded when she did that but said nothing. He appeared lost in his work. Melisande knew the feeling of being totally absorbed in one's work; she could get that way too when she was engrossed in her projects, and she would feel as if she were far away in another planet. Trying not to disturb him, she moved her head and saw that he had a birdfeeder attached to the railing at the other end of the balcony. It amused her to think that he had time to feed wild birds. Two red breasted robins were pecking away at the seeds. She looked out beyond them, at Paris that was waking up, the streets not as busy this Sunday morning. She remembered the conversation he had with her aunt about the Eiffel Tower. She had to agree with him that the tower was charming—yes, made of hard metal but it had grace as it peaked up to the blue summer sky of Paris, like a finger pointing to eternity.

"No," he interrupted me, "don't look out there, turn towards me please. There must be communication between the subject and artist, otherwise, I might as well be drawing a vase."

Melisande did as she was told and she observed his face, the furrowed brow, his intense dark eyes. She had gotten used to seeing him smiling and tossing out his boastful funny comments; this studious expression was new. He looked as if he were in prayer. The way the sunlight struck his hair made it seem lighter and created the illusion of a halo around his head. Now and then he would say, "Don't move," or "Lift the chin higher." Otherwise, they said little to each other, and after a while, Melisande felt like an inanimate object and she wondered if he would end up with work that was a faithful rendering but lifeless. To amuse herself she imagined dress designs and accessories for the fall, but he called her attention back. "Please, look at me."

She did, and the longer she stared at him, the more she liked his serious face. There was something going on inside him, something deeper than his flippant remarks, or his doctoring, or his art, something else.

Just when she felt she could no longer hold her position, he said, "Come, take a look."

Her muscles had tightened and when she stood up, she twisted her body and extended her arms. He too moved his neck and shook his arms, and the familiarity of stretching together made them smile.

"Come." His voice had turned low with undertones. He beckoned her and she went to him. The balcony was narrow and they stood very close to each other.

Melisande knew that she was not a bad-looking woman, but she had never considered herself beautiful. There were many women more attractive, especially in Paris, but the woman in his drawing surprised her. This was the image: Melisande was twenty-three years old, wearing a long flowing skirt and the off-shoulder cotton blouse. Her long hair flowed around her, her face caught the sun's rays, and she had an expression that was lazy and happy, and her mouth was slightly open, and her eyes had the expression of longing.

Earlier that morning, while getting dressed, she had thought the billowy blouse had been modest, frumpy in fact, but his picture showed all the curves of her breasts. She stepped away in embarrassment and crossed her arms in front of her chest.

"You are not happy with it? I've been working hard to get better." He was frowning. He seemed unhappy with her reaction.

She could not find the right words to tell him that the picture showed a sensuous woman, far more sensuous than she considered herself to be, so she turned away from him, but he touched her arm, and asked, "What is wrong? Please tell me."

"The drawing is well done—"

"You said that about my drawing of the Eiffel," he said, "Does this one also lack feeling?"

"No, not that. It makes me feel many things. Pride, shame … no, not exactly shame, but something like it."

"Shame!" His voice rose. "Ashamed because you are beautiful. Such foolishness." He was clearly cross and he turned away to wipe his hands on a rag, but he suddenly stopped. "Melisande, come here," he said. He drew her close, and with his large hands he touched her face, every part of it, slowly as if he were a blind man committing to memory her face—his fingers molding her cheeks, her forehead, her eyebrows, her lips, his fingers sliding down to her neck, to her shoulders. He slid her blouse to one side, exposing more of her shoulder, and he bent down to kiss it, his warm breath lingering on her skin even after he straightened his back.

It was there in front of them, Desire, and her breath caught as she wondered what he would do next. In Lyon, when Melisande was eighteen, Etienne and she had made love in the barn—clumsy and hasty lest they be caught. That had been her first experience with a man. She didn't know much about making love, but she was certain that there was something that hovered in that balcony, this Desire for the other, and the feeling was so intense she thought surely something further would happen. But to her surprise, he continued gathering his things and brought them inside.

Not knowing what to do with herself, she proceeded to tie her blouse together but he returned and stopped her. "Leave it that way. Come in," he said. "It's almost noon. Shadows are harsh at this time now. Can you carry the easel?" His hands were full of the other art supplies.

She picked up the easel and followed him to a room where he organized his art materials in a long bookcase against one wall. The other walls were covered with his artwork and when he saw that she was interested, he pointed out recent portraits of the butcher and the fruit vendor.

He was leaving the room when she caught sight of a solitary portrait near an alcove and she strayed briefly to have a closer look. It was an oil painting of an Arabic woman. The painting was crudely done, but Melisande could see that the woman was attractive and exotic, in her flowing skirt, and heavily beaded top. A thin veil covered her mouth and chin, as if she came straight from the deserts of Arabia. Her back faced the painter, but her head was turned to the side so you could see three-quarters of her veiled face. The gossamer-thin veil revealed her face, mysterious and sensuous. And her figure cut a most charming shape, as if she were caught mid-stream in a belly dance. The sight of this incredible woman filled Melisande with pain and jealousy. Doctor Martine had been visiting her and her aunt regularly, which made her feel to some extent that they owed him. Now she realized he had ties with other people, with this woman for instance, for surely his careful rendering of this beautiful woman indicated that they had a relationship. Melisande was certain he loved her.

The brightness of the morning left her, and in its place was a painful somberness. She caught up with him and she primly declared that it was time for her to go home. Moving like a puppet, she searched for her wrap and bag. She was poised to leave when he touched her arm and in a soft voice said, "Please don't leave."

"It is almost noon. My aunt will be waiting for me." In her distress her voice quivered, and she had to struggle to hold back her tears. At that moment, she felt foolish thinking that an important surgeon like him could care for a dressmaker like her.

He looked perplexed. "Something happened, and I have no

idea what it is. Your aunt will be fine. I have some nice arugula and goat cheese, and sausage. We still have bread and the cakes you brought. Let us have lunch, and explain to me why you are now upset. I need to understand what happened. You know, do you not, that I would never hurt you?" Gently, he removed her wrap and folded it, and he took away her bag as well. Instead of returning her belongings to the side table, he entered his room and placed them on his brass bed.

Melisande did not protest. He mesmerized her. His presence was big and overpowering. She thought she had loved Etienne, but this feeling was greater than that. It frightened her; this power that he had over her.

After banishing her things to his bedroom, he was back, and sounding like a captain taking charge, he told her to sit at the dining table and watch him make the best salad in Paris. Like a magician, he proceeded to throw together another wonderful meal, and he opened a bottle of red wine, and he chit-chatted about the people whose portraits he had done and the good weather they had been having, and later he cajoled her, trying to get her to explain why her mood had changed.

"It is nothing," Melisande began, determined not to tell him the truth, but remembering the mysterious veiled woman made tears spring to her eyes.

His dining table was round, not very large, and he placed his fork down and reached across the table. He swept away some tendrils of hair from her face, and he wiped away her tears. This tenderness made her weep even more and she sat there quietly sobbing.

"We had a nice breakfast, you posed for me, and it's true I made you sit too long. Could you be unhappy about that?"

She shook my head.

He continued, "Perhaps you were offended that I … I … took some liberties?"

He was referring to his kissing her shoulder, and she said nothing. The truth was that she enjoyed his admiration and desire for her. It was the woman in the painting who had upset her, who made her feel he belonged to some other woman, that she could never have him. She wondered if he was simply playing with her emotions, and what kind of cruel man could do such a thing.

Then perhaps he reviewed what had transpired that morning,

and it came to him: "You saw her picture? The woman with the veil?" He smiled and said, "She is my mother. I found a daguerreotype of her and made a painting from it. She was from Oran, in Algiers. Her name is Yasmin. My father was a surgeon, like myself; or I should say I became a surgeon like my father. He was assigned there. They met and fell in love. My mother's family were descendants of Muhammad; they, in particular, were not happy about my father. It is a long story and one day I will tell you all about how they overcame all obstacles. But for now, I have some nice bonbons from a beautiful nurse …"

Melisande frowned.

"… Who is older than my mother, and she gave me these because she says she enjoys working with me most of all because I am the best surgeon in Paris."

His audacity made her laugh. "Do you always have such a high opinion of yourself," she asked.

"Of course. One must believe in one's self. You have to believe in yourself. In your beauty, in your strength, and courage, your intelligence. I see all these in you."

His words made her face flush, and she turned away. He had a way of making her feel self-conscious. "Don't stare at me so," she said.

"Why not? I enjoy looking at you," he said.

"It makes me feel … how do I put it … embarrassed?"

"No, you should not feel that way. I don't want to embarrass you. I want to talk to you and make you laugh. I want to make you happy," he said. They had finished eating, and he had gotten up to start clearing the table. She helped him, and together they washed the dishes and put them away, like an old couple, which made her smile. In the distance a clock chimed two o'clock, and quickly he said, "You're fine, you do not have to go home yet." He took away the dishtowel from her hands, and in a voice throaty with desire said, "Spend the afternoon with me. I want to give you pleasure."

He must have read that there was no protest there, no resistance because he bent down and kissed her forehead, her eyes, and then her lips. And with his hand around her waist, he led her to his bedroom with the brass bed, and he cleared away her things from the bed, and lifted her unto it.

That day, after they had made love, he told her that Plato said humans were originally created with four arms, four legs, and a head with two faces. But fearing their power, Zeus split them into two separate parts, condemning them to spend their lives in search of their other halves.

Samir said that he and Melisande were very fortunate to have found each other, because they were meant to be one. He said, when they part, it will hurt them very much, because the one-ness will be separated once again.

Melisande remembered the summer afternoon when Samir had first visited her aunt—(it was the same afternoon when Melisande had fallen in love with him). Her aunt had revealed to him her thwarted love affair with Melisande's father. How broken Juliette's heart had been; hearts take longer to heal than bones, Juliette had said. Melisande understood then that what she had taken as sibling rivalry between her mother and Juliette ran deeper than that. But now, after Samir's story of the four-armed, four-legged being with two faces, Melisande saw that Juliette had not only lost a man she loved, but her other half—a vital part of herself. All these years, since Juliette left Lyon, she had existed as half-a-person. The good looks, the charm, the giggling, the coquetry were part of the sham to hide the lonely incomplete human being.

Even as she rested in Samir's arms, Melisande shivered thinking of her aunt's sad fate and she welcomed her feeling of wholeness with Samir.

ACKNOWLEDGEMENTS

"1943: Tiya Octavia" first appeared in *Fast Food Fiction*, Anvil 2003. It is part of Brainard's short story collection, *Vigan and Other Stories* Anvil 2011.

"1973: Recruiting" is part of Brainard's short story collection, *Vigan and Other Stories* Anvil 2011.

"Acapulco at Sunset" appeared in *Mindscapes*, Fall 1992; and *Philippine Graphic*, January 14, 1994. It is part of Brainard's short story collection *Acapulco at Sunset and Other Stories*, Anvil 1995.

"Alba" was published in *Studia Mystica*, Summer, 1986; it was anthologized in Asian American Women's United book, *Making Waves*, Beacon Press 1989. It is part of Brainard's short story collection, *Woman with Horns and Other Stories* New Day Publishers 1987.

"Almost Forgotten" was translated into Finnish and is part of the Finnish anthology, *Tulikaparnen* edited by Riita Vartti, Kaantopuri 2001. It is part of Brainard's short story collection, *Acapulco at Sunset and Other Stories*, Anvil 1995.

"The Artist" is part of Brainard's short story collection, *Vigan and Other Stories* Anvil 2011.

"The Balete Tree" was published in *St. Andrews Review*, No. 29 1986; it won the 1985 Fortner Prize. It is part of Brainard's short story collection, *Woman with Horns and Other Stories* New Day Publishers 1987.

"The Black Man in the Forest" appeared in *Amerasia Journal*, Vol. 12, No. 1 (1985-86); it was anthologized in *Filipino Women in America: 1860-1986*. It is part of Brainard's short story collection, *Woman with Horns and Other Stories*, New Day Publishers 1987.

"The Blue-Green Chiffon Dress" was published in *Focus Philippines*, September 1984 and *Home to Stay*, The Greenfield Review Press 1990. It was published in *The Perimeter of Light,* New Rivers Press 1992. It is part of Brainard's short story collection, *Woman with Horns and Other Stories*, New Day Publishers 1987.

"Butterscotch Marble Ice Cream" appeared in *AA Literary Realm*, #4, 1991; it was also published in *dIS*Orient Journalzine*, March 1994; and it was also published in *New to North America*, Burning Bush Publications 1997. It is part of Brainard's short story collection, *Acapulco at Sunset and Other Stories*, Anvil 1995.

"Casa Bonita" was first published in *The Quill*, 1992. It is part of Brainard's short story collection, *Acapulco at Sunset and Other Stories*, Anvil 1995.

"The Che Guevara Night" is part of Brainard's short story collection, *Vigan and Other Stories* Anvil 2011.

"Christmas Eve" is part of Brainard's short story collection, *Vigan and Other Stories* Anvil 2011.

"The Circle of Life" is part of Brainard's short story collection, *Vigan and Other Stories* Anvil 2011.

"The Dead Boy" was first published as "The Altar Boy" in *Philippine Graphic*, March 23, 1992; it was also published in *Fern Garden*, National Commission of Culture and Arts, 1998. It is part of Brainard's short story collection, *Acapulco at Sunset and Other Stories*, Anvil 1995.

"The Dirty Kitchen" first appeared in *Fast Food Fiction,* Anvil 2003. It is part of Brainard's short story collection, *Vigan and Other Stories* Anvil 2011.

"Flip Gothic" first appeared in *Contemporary Fiction by Filipinos in America*, Anvil 1997. It is part of Brainard's short story collection, *Vigan and Other Stories* Anvil 2011.

"Flying a Kite" is part of Brainard's short story collection, *Vigan and Other Stories* Anvil 2011

"Friday Evening at the Seashore" is part of Brainard's *Woman With Horns and Other Stories.* New Day Publishers 1987

"Jorge in Sagada" is part of Brainard's short story collection, *Vigan and Other Stories* Anvil 2011.

"The Last Moon-Game of Summer" first appeared in *Growing Up Filipino: Stories for Young Adults*, PALH 2003; Anvil 2004.

"Manila Without Verna" first appeared in the *Philippine Graphic*, October 23, 1995; it was published in *Linking the World Through English*, DIWA Scholastic Press, Inc. 2005. It is part of Brainard's short story collection, *Acapulco at Sunset and Other Stories*, Anvil 1995.

"Melisande in Paris" is part of the book *Please, San Antonio! & Melisande in Paris: Two Novellas, Special International Edition,* PALH, 2018.

"Miracle at Santo Niño Church was published in *Focus Philippines*, September 1984. It is part of Brainard's short story collection, *Woman with Horns and Other Stories* New Day Publishers 1987.

"My Mother is Dying" is part of Brainard's short story collection, *Vigan and Other Stories* Anvil 2011.

"On the Way to Kalighat" is part of Brainard's short story collection, *Vigan and Other Stories* Anvil 2011.

"Remembering Che Guevara" is part of Brainard's short story collection, *Vigan and Other Stories* Anvil 2011.

"The Rice Field" is part of Brainard's short story collection, *Vigan and Other Stories* Anvil 2011.

"Romeo" was first published in *A La Carte Food & Fiction*, Ed Brainard, Anvil 2007. It is part of Brainard's short story collection, *Vigan and Other Stories* Anvil 2011. It appeared in *TEXTSCAPES: 21ST Century Literary Landscapes of the Philippines and of the World*, 2017.

"San Miguel Allende" is part of Brainard's short story collection, *Vigan and Other Stories* Anvil 2011.

"Sid Lansky's Vacation" is part of Brainard's short story collection, *Acapulco at Sunset and Other Stories*, Anvil 1995

"Trinidad's Brooch" was published in *Songs of Ourselves: Writings by Filipino Women in English* (Anvil 1994). It is part of Brainard's short story collection, *Woman with Horns and Other Stories*, New Day Publishers 1987.

"Vigan" first appeared in *Going Home to a Landscape: Writings by Filipinas* (Calyx Books 2003); it also appeared in *Growing Up Filipino II: More Stories for Young Adults* (PALH 2010). It is part of Brainard's short story collection, *Vigan and Other Stories* Anvil 2011. It appeared in TEXTSCAPES:

21ST Century Literary Landscapes of the Philippines and of the World, 2017.

"The Virgin's Last Night" first appeared in the *Philippine Graphic*, April 24, 1995; it was published in *Fern Garden*, National Commission on Culture and Arts Philippines 1998; it also appeared in the anthology *Sojourns*, Leo Mar Concepts 1997.

"Waiting for Papa's Return" was anthologized in *Making Waves*, Asian Women United 1989; it was also published in *Home to Stay*, The Greenfield Review Press 1990; the story was featured in the Fall 1990 Writers' Program Quarterly of UCLA Extension; and it also appeared in *Asian American Literature*, Glencoe McGraw-Hill 2001. It is part of Brainard's short story collection, *Woman with Horns and Other Stories*, New Day Publishers 1987.

"Welcome to America" first appeared in *Bamboo Ridge*, Summer 1990; it is part of New Day's 1992 anthology, Cebuano *Harvest I*; the story won the Honorable Mention Award of the 1989 PALM Council short story competition.

"Woman with Horns" was published in *Focus Philippines* (July 1984). It is part of Brainard's short story collection, *Woman with Horns and Other Stories*, New Day Publishers 1987.

"The Syrian Doctor in Paris" was published in *Philippines Graphic*, November 10, 2014; it won Honorable Mention in the 2015 Nick Joaquin Literary Awards 2014 and it won Honorable Mention in the 2015 Nick Joaquin Literary Awards.

"The Turkish Seamstress in Ubec" was published in *Philippine Speculative Fiction*, Vol. 8, 2013.

THE AUTHOR

Cecilia Manguerra Brainard grew up in the port city of Cebu, Philippines, a place that retains its Spanish colonial influences, inspiring Cecilia to create her mythical setting called "Ubec" which echoes the Santo Niño Church, triangular Spanish Fort San Pedro, and old buildings and streets of the real Cebu. Her three novels—*When the Rainbow Goddess Wept, Magdalena,* and *The Newspaper Widow,* are set (even partially) in Ubec. Ubec also appears in her three short story collections*: Woman With Horns and Other Stories, Acapulco at Sunset and Other Stories,* and *Vigan and Other Stories.*

Cecilia is the author and editor of seventeen other books including *Fundamentals of Creative Writing, Fiction by Filipinos in America, Contemporary Fiction by Filipinos in America, Growing Up Filipino: Stories for Young Adults* and the follow up book *Growing Up Filipino II.* Many of her writings are used by educators in their classrooms.

Her work has been translated into Finnish and Turkish; and her writings are widely anthologized. Cecilia has received awards such as the California Arts Council Fellowship in Fiction, a Brody Arts Fund Award, among many others. She has also been awarded by the Filipino and Filipino American communities including an Outstanding Individual Award from her birth city, Cebu, a Filipinas Magazine Award for Arts, and others. Her books have won the Gourmand

Award and the Gintong Aklat Award.

She has lectured and performed in worldwide literary arts organizations and universities, including UCLA, USC, University of Connecticut, University of the Philippines, PEN, Beyond Baroque, Shakespeare & Company in Paris, and many others.

She has served in the Boards of PEN, PAWWW (Pacific Asian Amercan Women Writers West, and the Arts & Letters at the Cal State University LA. She co-founded PAWWA (Philippine American Women Writers and Artists) a support group that received funding by the California Arts Council.

She is married to Lauren R. Brainard, a former Peace Corps volunteer to Leyte, Philippines; they have three sons.

Her official website is ceciliabrainard.com.

www.ingramcontent.com/pod-product-compliance
Lightning Source LLC
Chambersburg PA
CBHW022003010726
47494CB00003B/875

9781953716019